AS WE FALL

AS WE FALL

Book 1 of the As We Fall series

ANYA WILDT

Violet & Lavender PRESS

Copyright © Anya Wildt 2023

All rights reserved. No part of this book may be reproduced or used in any manner without written permission of the copyright owner, except for the use of brief quotations in a book review.

Contact publisher at anya.wildt@gmail.com

Paperback: 978-87-974333-0-0
Ebook: 978-87-974333-1-7
Audiobook: 978-87-974333-2-4

First paperback edition June 2023

Edited by Nick Hodgson and Emily Oracle
Cover art and design by Jackie V. W. (@jiki_jackie_snikisnaki)

Violet & Lavender PRESS

https://www.anyawildt.com

To Jackie, who exceeded my wildest expectations of what love could be like.

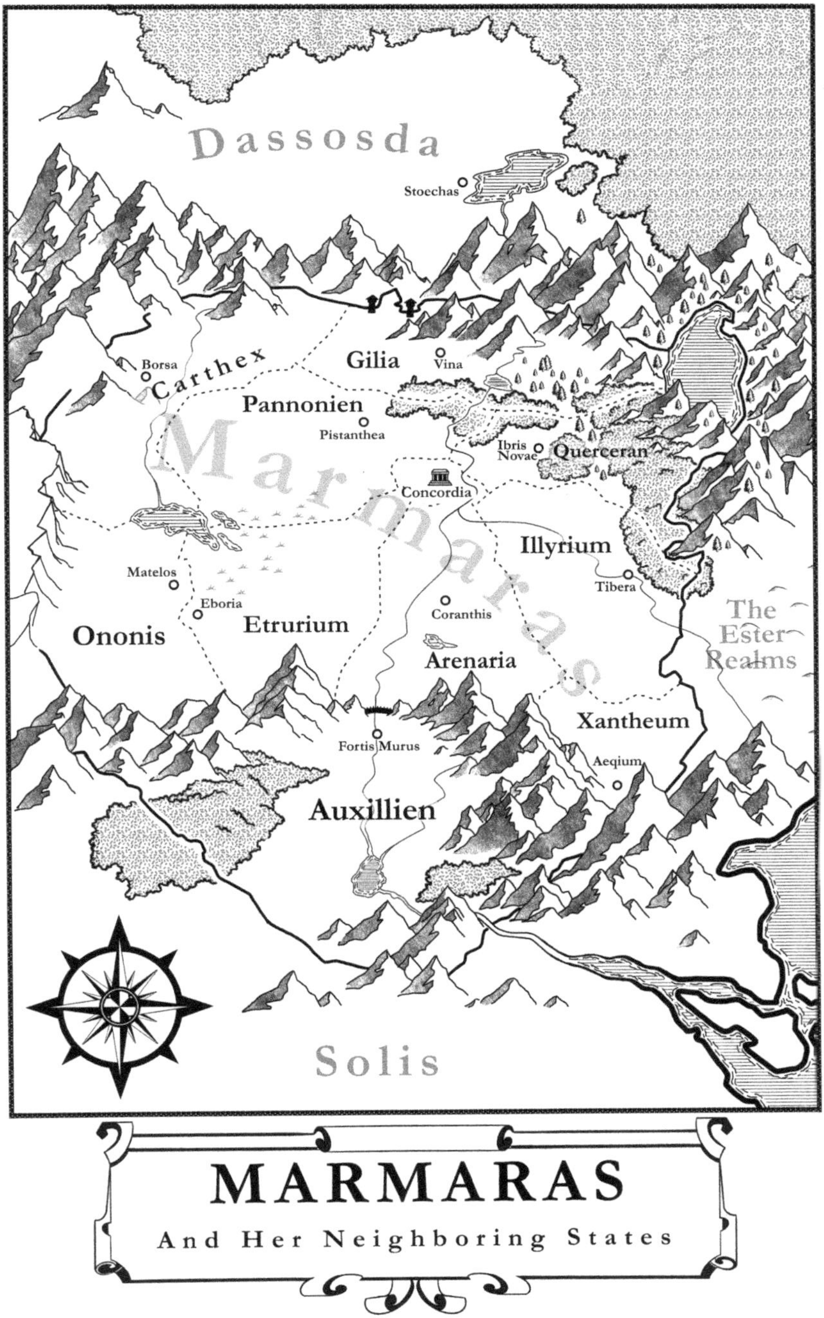

MARMARAS

And Her Neighboring States

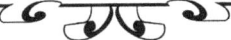

AS WE FALL

I

The glowing tail of a meteor stretched above the distant capital before fading among the stars.

"Meteors are a bad omen!" the guard closest to Domitris called, barely audible over the sound of galloping horses. Unease shot through Domitris' stomach. The last time he had seen one was on the night before the Overthrow.

"How so?"

The guard brought his horse closer, and the scent of warm sand billowed through the air as dust stung Domitris' eyes.

"They appear before moments of great change. And usually not the good kind."

Domitris shot him a look. "Very funny." He was in no mood for superstitious nonsense when he had an empire depending on him and the pit in his stomach was deep enough already.

"It's no laughing matter, Your Highness. Our fates are mapped out by the stars. It's wise to heed their warnings."

"The stars didn't win me the throne," he said and squeezed his legs into the sweaty flanks of his horse, urging it forward.

The capital lay dark as Domitris and his entourage galloped through the gates of Concordia. Their sole welcome was milky moonlight on the cramped houses of the lower city. When they left four months ago, the streets had been brimming with people, cheering as they sent them off for the provinces. There would have been people welcoming them home as well if they hadn't been a week late.

In the distance, the palace rose above the city in a jumble of columns, spires, and balconies. Its innermost parts had first been built as a simple keep, but over centuries of regents trying to leave their imprint on the world, it had grown into a grotesque amalgamation of architecture. Even under a new rule, the palace remained the powerful heart of the sluggish beast they called an empire.

It was a manifestation of luxury and decadence, yet whenever Domitris saw it from the outside, all he could think of was the palace stairs stained red with blood and nobles hanging by the neck from the marble walls. He shivered at the memories. The last time he had been away from the capital was before the Overthrow; two years ago, when he had led the rebellion south to rouse people from the provinces to stand up to the armies of the Supreme Emperor. Back then, he had returned with a militia. This time, he returned with a retinue.

The closer they got to the palace, the taller and more extravagant the surrounding buildings became. The torches that were lit every night to keep the paved road passable had long since burned out, but it was dimly illuminated by the light of the full moon. The soft cream color of sandstone houses was replaced with a cold sheen of marble loggias and archways that appeared as black vacancies in the darkness.

AS WE FALL

Domitris' sore ass and thighs objected when he coerced his tired horse up the first set of stairs to the upper city, but his aching muscles were the only thing keeping him awake.

A horse snorted behind him, and he looked back at the entourage. Some of them seemed to be sleeping upright in their saddles. No wonder—they had been riding for two days on end to make it back, pausing only when the horses needed rest.

He gritted his teeth and pushed his horse onward with a single thought in mind: home. Cobbled roads turned to broad, marble-paved streets as they continued through the city. The sound of hooves reverberated like thunder in the night, and sleep-deprived faces peeked out behind curtains to catch sight of the ruckus.

When they reached the shadows of the palace, and he handed off his horse to the stable hands, sweet relief washed over him. He was back in the capital at last, and just in time.

Instead of going through the main entrance, as he would have had they returned in daylight, he found one of the back doors to the west, closer to his quarters. Finally, he was on his own again. After four months in the constant company of guards and diplomats, a night alone would be glorious.

He skirted the barracks and the edge of the gardens before he found an entrance to a narrow servants' hallway, leading him through an undisturbed part of the palace. The small passage was pitch-black as he entered through a heavy wooden door, but he knew this path too well to need light. The door groaned on its cast-iron hinges when it shut behind him. He ran an outstretched hand along the rough stone walls to center himself in the darkness. Turning left and climbing the first series of stairs led him to one of the larger marble colonnades. The grooved pillars cast slanted shadows across the floor and the polished tiles glittered in the moonlight. As he walked the length of it, footsteps echoed against the arched ceilings. He stopped, but the steps continued.

With the dim light spilling in, he could make out nothing more than a dark shape appearing at the far end. No one should have been up at this hour. He stood, frozen, until a voice greeted him.

"The hero returns!" Ignotus said, his voice shattering the emptiness of the night. "Domitris, my friend, I thought you might come this way. So good to have you back."

Domitris gave a sigh of relief as Ignotus came to him, took his arm, and hugged him tight. Domitris returned the affection and smiled at his old friend. He hadn't seen Ignotus since he had left him in charge of Marmaras while Domitris toured the provinces to garner support for the new rule after the Overthrow. While neither of them had been trained in governance, Ignotus had always had a talent for it, and there hadn't been a doubt in his mind when Domitris had appointed him consul. Together, they had led the rebellion, and Ignotus remained his most dependable confidante.

"What are you doing up?"

"Your scouts returned in the evening and announced your arrival. I had to come and see you for myself."

"Well, how do I look?" Domitris asked. He stepped back, spreading his arms in show.

"Like you've been riding for a week. And you smell like it too." Ignotus nudged his shoulder.

Domitris laughed and squinted back at him, trying to see him properly in the darkness. Four months was a long time,

AS WE FALL

but he hadn't expected Ignotus to look so different.

"Well, you look like an old man. Since when do you have a beard? I remember when you could hardly grow fuzz." He patted Ignotus on a hairy cheek.

"You like it? I thought it made me look more authoritative." Ignotus put on a serious face that made him look very much the grown man he was.

"That is an important feature when taking care of an empire."

"It has been in good hands. I made sure to take care of everything, Your Highness," Ignotus replied sincerely.

They walked down the corridor, passing in and out of the shadows from the columns. It was remarkable how different the palace seemed at night. The white marble looked ghoulish instead of welcoming, the ornate stucco borders seemed to be full of faces, and the vaulted ceilings got lost in the darkness, making the open halls feel suffocating.

"How did it go in the provinces?" Ignotus asked.

Domitris sighed, exhaustion taking over his body once more. "There's a lot of chaos in the outer provinces. People are still angry, still scared, still skeptical about the new rule and making peace with Dassosda. Support for the capital is wavering. I fear the unrest will make Marmaras crumble from the inside if we don't manage to extend our support to the outer areas. Especially Auxillien—they will not back down from their claim of autonomy. They wouldn't even open their gates to let us in."

"That is a problem." Ignotus frowned.

"It is. There has been enough going wrong."

Ignotus patted him on the shoulder. "They elected you for

a reason. You have it all planned out."

Domitris let out a breath. "You're right. The festival will be the first step, and when peace with Dassosda is established, I think people will start seeing that we're on a better path."

Ignotus nodded. "Speaking of Dassosda, the delegation arrived three days ago."

Domitris knew they would have by now, but it was still a punch to the gut to hear it. He had tried so hard to make it back in time for their arrival.

"How did it go? Is she as fierce as they say?"

"She is. And as beautiful too." Ignotus grinned. "Too bad she is such a stone-cold—"

"Hey," Domitris said with a backhanded slap to Ignotus' arm, trying not to smile. "That's not funny. You know how important this alliance is. We need to be on her good side to ensure that there won't be an invasion."

"Calm down, Dom. I was joking. It will work out. You've done all the work, now get ready to reap what you've sown."

Domitris rubbed his tired eyes, his thoughts racing. "She's our best chance. Ultimately, her goal is the same as ours. If we fail to get the treaty signed, who knows how long before we face open war again? I can't see how Marmaras will scrape through another battle." The standing army under the crown was the smallest in decades after losing the legions of Auxillien. The previous century of war had left the empire with little money to take care of its people, let alone pay soldiers. Meanwhile, Dassosda was doing better than ever with a growing army and newer weapons.

Domitris looked up to meet Ignotus' dark eyes.

"You need some sleep," Ignotus said. "And maybe a good fuck. You've been on the road for too long."

Domitris huffed, and his shoulders relaxed. "How are you taking this so lightly?"

"Because we've got it under control. Listen, I've left every single record and protocol on your desk to have fun with. But please get some sleep first. And a bath," he added, the gleam back in his eyes.

Domitris smiled. "Thank you for your help, dear friend. As always."

They exchanged a firm clasp of arms and parted ways. Domitris dragged himself up the second set of stairs and through the deserted corridors to his rooms.

There were no guards at his doors. As he stepped inside, the sky lightened ever so slightly with the first signs of dawn on the horizon. He had never been away from the palace this long. Somehow, he had expected it to have changed, but everything was how he had left it, as if he had been gone no more than a day. He took a deep breath. After two years, it was finally beginning to feel like home. Passing through the entrance room, his hand glided over the polished table in the middle. No dust—Lyra had been cleaning. Inside his chambers, he drew the soft silk curtains to block out the oncoming morning and tumbled into bed. He barely managed to shrug out of his travel clothes and put the golden circlet from his brow onto the bedside table before he collapsed. His own smell hit him in the face against the fresh sheets. He really did need a bath.

He glanced at the closed door that led to the servant's room, but there were no signs of her. Having been away from Lyra for four months, he longed to see her now. Her lively chatter and mostly good-natured gossip would be music in his ears after the journey. He turned over in the bed and could hardly keep the thought present in his mind. Fatigue rushed over him and enveloped him in a hazy slumber.

II

"The bells! The bells are ringing! It's now! Move!" Domitris shouted amid the panic. Screams multiplied in the distance, rushing over every corner of the theater. The metallic smell of blood grew thick in his nostrils. His hands, clutching the hilt of a dagger, were wet and sticky. His heart pounded, ringing in his ears. He tried to drop the dagger, but it stuck to his hand. Screams and yells and gurgles blurred together all around him. Was it his own blood on his palms? No. The Supreme Emperor sat lifeless before him. The bells kept on ringing, the sound growing louder.

Domitris woke disoriented from a heavy sleep with a drumming in his chest. The bells were, in fact, ringing, which made his heart beat even faster. He was back at the palace. Also, he had overslept. Usually, Lyra woke him up at five, an hour before the first morning bell, so he could sit on his balcony with some work, alone, before commanding the council around for the rest of the day. Where was she? The pile of clothing he had discarded on the floor was gone and the curtains were already drawn. He dragged himself out of bed, the clammy fabric of his thin tunic clinging to his torso.

"Lyra?" he called, but there was no immediate answer. His throat was raw, and his back ached after the ride. A few hours of sleep weren't enough to make up for it. An entire week of sleep would hardly do it. Scanning the room, he found a fresh set of clothes laid out over the back of a chair. He glanced at the servant's door just as it swung open, and Lyra trotted in with a tray in her hands. The sight of her got to him more than he had expected. Unlike Ignotus, she looked just as she always did, with her brown curls pinned to the back of her head and her eyebrows high on her round, vigilant face. A high-pitched, incoherent sound escaped her, and she went for him, forgetting to put down the tray.

"Your Highness, welcome back!"

He smiled and bent down to embrace her over the tray and she returned the affection with her cheek. When he let go, she turned around and put the tray down. "Oh, how I've missed those big brown eyes of yours!" she said, reaching up and closing her hands around his face.

"And I have missed you," he said. They hadn't been apart for this long since he was a kid. She had joined his family's estate when Domitris was born and had practically raised him since. She was the one who had gotten him through the years after he was told his parents weren't coming back. And when he was elected emperor, he wasn't sure he'd have maintained his sanity if not for her. "Do you know that other company is very boring compared to you?"

She let go and wrinkled her nose over a smile at him. "Do you mean to tell me that scholars and guards and senators are dull company? I hardly believe it!"

He shook his head. "Are you well? You look well." For fifteen years her junior, he was sure he appeared more ragged and weary than she did, looking as beautiful and put-together as ever.

"I always am. We can talk more later. Now, eat your breakfast and go wash up. You stink like you've been living in the stables. I prepared the bath for you. You have a tight schedule today," she said, and was out the door again.

A warm comfort settled in him as he took the first bite of rosemary bread. His mouth watered and his stomach growled. The provinces had their merits, but no food was better than the capital's. Though they had eaten well at the nobles' residences, food on the road was mostly tough, dark bread that filled the stomach and kept for a long time, and he never wanted to see it again. Still chewing on a mouthful of bread, he went to the adjacent chamber, where a large basin of water sent curls of steam into the air, spreading the scent of lavender with it.

It was just warm enough to be unpleasant, but he sunk into it. Leisurely, he scrubbed away every trace of the journey and washed his hair thoroughly. It had gotten longer while he had been away, long enough to fall into his eyes, but he didn't mind it. He always thought the close-cropped military style was too severe on him anyway. He ran it backwards and wrung out the water.

When he was clean, he returned for more of the bread, only to find Lyra at his table, her gray eyes wide and her smile wider.

"Well?" she said. "Tell me everything!"

He joined her and leaned back in his chair, resting his ankle on his knee. "Four months is a lot to cover in a morning.

Why didn't you wake me earlier?"

She shot a look at him and pushed a filled cup closer. "You were sleeping like a sweet little piglet for once. You need all the sleep you can get. Marmaras is still reeling from the rebellion and now you have to convince the people that this treaty is a good idea. Have you practiced the speeches? I got word that you received them."

"I did."

The messenger had found the entourage a few weeks back. Domitris had read them every night before going to bed. "I'm ready."

She patted his hand. "Good."

There was silence while Domitris took a sip of honeyed water.

"The festival begins today," Lyra then said, stating the obvious. She looked like she was going to burst from all the things she wanted to say; she just needed the right prompt.

"Have you met them? The Dassosdans?" he asked. It gave him a deep sense of satisfaction to humor her when she was in this mood. She squirmed in her seat and an obnoxiously pleased look came over her face.

"I have!" She leaned her plump arms on the table. "This will be very interesting. Also, have you seen that the city is crowded with them? Dassosdans, I mean. They have been arriving for weeks, ever since the borders opened."

"That's the whole point," he said, putting the rest of the bread into his mouth.

"I know. But it's strange to see them here, after everything."

Domitris understood how she felt. It was how many felt about the allegiance. He tried not to feel it himself.

"It's a good thing," he said.

Lyra nodded and changed the subject. "There will be a large audience tonight."

"It will go well," Domitris said before she started to fret. "Now tell me my schedule for today."

"Council meeting at the next bell and then your private audience with the Dassosdan Minister after lunch." She looked up at him. "You want to be ready for that one. She's something."

"Have you met her?"

"Only briefly at their arrival. She might claim that Dassosda has no nobles, but her clothing and posture and nose in the air says otherwise. But have you heard the way they speak? It's like listening to my old matre back home!"

A smile tugged at the corner of Domitris' mouth. "No more of that now. What about the rest of the day?"

"Afterwards I'll prepare you for the show where you open the festival alongside the Minister. After that, the banquet at the palace will continue into the night."

Domitris pressed his fingers into his eyes, trying to get rid of the exhaustion. "I better get ready."

Lyra helped him dress. After being in riding gear for weeks and in traveling clothes for months, he wasn't dissatisfied being back in the palace standards. Over the obligatory floor-length white tunic, Lyra coiled a long piece of dark blue fabric with gold edges around his torso twice, then folded and fastened it at one shoulder. Purple had been the color of the Supreme Emperor for three hundred years, but it was chosen that the color of the Elected Emperor would be dark blue; the color of the people.

His gaze wandered out over the morning that settled in the palace gardens where the oncoming sun burned the dew off the grass in a calm haze. The serenity of it was such a contrast to the horrors committed inside the palace walls over the centuries.

"I can't believe it's already been two years," he said.

Lyra's hands worked on a difficult fold on the back of his shoulder but slowed down.

"You've done well in those two years," she said.

"I want to do better. I want this to go well. I want to bring an end to this war, for good."

"You're a good man." She finished the fold, then patted him on the shoulder. "And it will. In just five days, you will sign that treaty."

"If it all goes well."

"You said it yourself: it will." She took the circlet from the bedside table and placed it on his brow. They looked at each other and she squeezed his hand.

"I will leave you to it. Remember, you have to be in the council hall at eight when the second bell rings," Lyra said. "And, Your Highness?"

He looked up.

"You're as handsome as always."

He smiled at her, and then she was gone. An unidentifiable feeling of unease gnawed at him, but he didn't have time to nurture it. Instead, he turned his attention to the stack of protocols Ignotus had left for him in a tall, neat pile on his desk. He wanted to get a sense of what had happened in Concordia while he had been away. His head swam as he thumbed through the stack of papers. The rows upon rows of times, numbers, schedules, and lists blurred together and he couldn't focus. Skimming through records of travelers into the city from the day before, he gave up, put the stack down, and sat back in the chair with a sigh.

His mind was tired and cloudy, and he felt the impact of sleeping too little for too long. The thought of the audience with the Dassosdan Minister ran in circles in his head. He had yet to meet her himself—Dia, the head of the ambassadorial delegation Dassosda had sent for the festival. Marmarasi emissaries dispatched to Dassosda over the past two years to negotiate the terms had told upon every return of her astonishing wit, beauty, and intelligence, but also that she was fiercely determined and had little patience for the Marmarasi class system. Dassosda had denounced the monarchy and class system when they broke out of Marmaras to become a nation of their own almost a century ago. Dia was one of fourteen elected ministers leading the country, the one responsible for foreign affairs. He didn't look forward to tiptoeing around the innate Dassosdan resentment towards their common past. Or present, for that matter. He knew he had to try.

He got up and took a few aimless steps around the room, catching his reflection in the gilded mirror plate. He looked like an emperor. His fingers reached up to touch the circlet, and his dream of the Overthrow rushed into his memory. He hadn't had those dreams since leaving the palace. A hollowness coiled in his chest. He had let himself think that maybe they had finally disappeared for good. He rolled his neck from side to side, trying to relieve the tension.

It was a strange feeling that just hours ago he had sat around a fire next to soldiers and scholars, chatting about the constellations and eating soup. At first, everyone had been apprehensive about talking to him directly and the conversations often dimmed when he joined them at the fireside, but he had kept joining every night anyway. At the end of the tour, he knew the name of every single person in the entourage and even some of the names of their families, too. He knew who despised mutton and who could down a sack of wine in a single counting, as well as who always needed to be woken more than once and who was the best at playing dice without cheating. There hadn't been much camaraderie around him since his coronation. Not since his time in the army during the classical training, in fact. Back then, they had been sorted into units based on their age, not their house name or family status. Those had been some of the best years of his life, knowing the people around him and sneaking off with Ignotus to explore the city every time they had the chance. Sometimes he wondered if he should have stayed in the army, becoming a general like his sister. But then he thought of war and battles and the misery of soldiers and knew that the palace was the best place for him to be to have any sort of impact.

 The distant sound of activity from the city pulled him out of the memories. He still had a little time before the next bell, and he knew what he wanted to do. If he hurried, he could make it down to the marketplace and see the preparations for the festival with his own eyes.

 He shot a look around for Lyra, but luckily, she was nowhere to be seen. He pulled off the circlet and the overlay of blue fabric and placed them carefully on a chair. Then he stuck his feet into a pair of sandals and tied the strings around his ankles. Grabbing a sunscarf, he draped it haphazardly over his head and snuck out of his room.

 On the way to the main entrance his dream was still with

him, pressing images into his mind of how different the halls had looked on that night. He remembered where guards lay dead in the corridors, where servants were hiding to get out of the way, and how every piece of furniture was knocked over or set ablaze. He shook his head, as though he could make the images physically fly out of his mind.

Shielding his face from a group of courtiers, he hastened through the entrance hall before anyone could approach him. The sun had the marble steps burning beneath the thin leather soles of his sandals as he walked down the palace stairs. In the darkness of his return, the tent peaks of the marketplace in the distance hadn't been visible, but there they were, like treetops of a canvas forest. He wanted to see it for himself, even if just a glance. No one needed to know. He wanted to see the significance of it—Dassosdans here, in the heart of Marmaras, and not a single one in uniform. If he hurried, he could cut through the market and be back at the palace before the next bell. If not now, he wouldn't make it before the festival ended.

The smooth marble turned to cobblestone as he went south. There was a steady influx of people coming from the west gates, all headed the same way to set up camp and all on foot since commoners were not allowed to bring horses inside the city walls.

Their clothing told him many were Dassosdan. Where the Marmarasi still favored the elegant simplicity of tunics made from a single length of fabric, the Dassosdan garments consisted of multiple different layers and bold colors, many with patterns or embellishments using weaving techniques Domitris had never seen before. It did create a more disharmonious effect when looking out over a crowd, and Domitris was sure many nobles found it garish. The long sleeves and many layers didn't look comfortable in the Concordian heat, but he had to admit the eye-catching nature of it intrigued him.

Parents with children on shoulders or hips traveled with old men and women bent over walking sticks, tired from their journey. Young couples held on to each other or their carts, or both. Many stopped in the middle of the road, craning their necks to look up at the palace in wonder. Domitris turned his eyes the other way. The sound of tent pegs hammering into the ground clanged through the streets, and Domitris picked up his pace. The city looked so different in daylight than it had just hours earlier. The earthy smell of dirt and sweat from passersby tickled his nostrils. His heart beat faster as he made his way through the city, the exhilaration in the air getting to him, and his steps sped up. He hadn't been out on his own in what felt like forever.

He turned down a winding street, then followed the less crowded roads. When he was only a few turns from the marketplace, he passed an opening to a small plaza. He almost walked past it, but something caught his eye, and he went back.

A tall, robust woman with a sword at her hip was calling out to the people on the street. "Good sir! Good ma'am! Come closer to see the show! Hear the exciting tale of the poet and the muse and come sing along! There's always room for one more, you won't regret it!" She bowed comically low to a man passing by wearing a dirty wool garment and a toothless grin.

Then Domitris noticed the motley band of performers

behind her. An energetic boy who looked barely eighteen played the flute while a woman with long, blonde braids told a lively story in a clear and cheerful voice. In front of her, a young man in what could only be described as an outrageous outfit was dancing and acting to the story. His violet tunic was open on both sides down to his hips, where a gilded belt held it in place. The rest of the fabric flowed freely to his ankles, though any illusion of modesty was ruined by the slits up the sides, displaying more than was appropriate of his legs. The neckline plummeted down below his waist, leaving most of his chest bare as well as revealing a golden ornament dangling from his navel. And, as if the evocative ensemble weren't eye-catching enough, he waved around a silky shawl, golden bracelets jangling to the rhythm of his step.

Before them, a meager crowd of rowdy-looking people had gathered, breaking out in loud cheers and laughter every so often. Domitris was drawn towards the performance. There was something mesmerizing about them, the way they looked somewhat out of place in the streets of Concordia.

As he walked past, the tall woman bowed low to him as well. The performers looked foreign, but the play was in Marmarasi, so Domitris had no guess where they were from. It was definitely a kind of play they were putting on, and an offensive one at that. It was a parody of multiple different things. The flute music was from a common Marmarasi children's song, but the story being told was about how the muse 'inspired' the poet in tasteless, yet creative ways. Domitris failed to suppress a smile at a particularly lewd allegory. The dancer, with heavy golden paint on his lips and eyelids, was playing the muse. He danced around, swirling the shawl while enacting the scenes of the story and making flirty eyes and crude gestures with perfect timing, to the immense pleasure of the crowd.

As Domitris joined the gathering, a slim woman in pants turned over her feathered hat and started collecting money from the onlookers. Some threw in what little they had, though Domitris was sure that included pebbles and bottle stoppers. The music reached the chorus where the crowd could join in on the singing of the usual words of the song, all while the man continued in an excessively sensual dance. Domitris watched how his hips moved, making the slender chain at his waist sway. The precision and skill of his movements made it look effortless, though sweat glistened on his chest and arms.

At the edge of the audience, a man with a large gut and a scruffy beard reached his hand out as the dancer came closer and tried touching him, but the young man only made an elegant turn and smacked the hand away, wagging his finger in the air followed by the universal sign for money, which raised laughter all around. His light brown skin was accompanied by jet black hair and a slim face so captivating it could have belonged to a statue from the palace galleries.

When he looked up, he winked at Domitris, who realized he had been staring and had come to stand in the front row of the crowd. The woman with the hat suddenly appeared in front of him. She was pale with sharp brows, her dark eyes intense.

"Gonna make a contribution to the fine arts," she asked in a rough foreign accent, looking him up and down, then adding, "my good sir?"

Domitris fumbled with the folds of his clothes and found a

coin from his coin purse to put in the hat, and she moved on. Their act was probably not meant as entertainment for nobles and, despite his, admittedly lazy, disguise, he stood out. The material of his clothes was too fine, his sandals too clean, his hair too newly washed. Reluctantly, he made himself turn around. He pushed his way back out through the growing audience and got back on course. He had already stayed too long.

The marketplace was so near that he could smell the smoke and taste the spices in the air, but as he closed in, the mellow chime of the palace bells resounded through the city.

He was late for his meeting with the council.

III

The council meetings had never been his favorite part of ruling. There were always too many people with too many opinions just waiting to jump on the chance to get their own agenda through. Before the tour, he had tried to get out of them when possible, but there was no shirking his responsibilities now. Even though Lyra had scolded him relentlessly when he made it back with city dust up to his knees, she had helped him get dressed again as fast as she could. At least he looked the part. He squared his shoulders, held his head high, and conjured the needed air of assuredness it took to get people to listen. Then he headed in.

The droning of conversation stilled when he stepped through the arched doorway, all eyes turning to him. He kept his back straight and swallowed the surge of unease. He was the emperor—he was allowed to be late. He just had to make sure he didn't give them an excuse to think otherwise.

The morning sun gilded the pillars supporting the domed roof and the feeling of being back truly hit him. He went to the rostrum while the white-robed councilors shuffled to their seats in the tiered semicircle following the curve of the room. Nearly all fifty seats were filled for his return. The gold trim on their councilor robes glimmered amid the sea of ivory silk. Pausing, he looked around at the mostly familiar faces. Ignotus nodded at him from the front row. He was dressed in the cobalt blue consul robe, with the golden star of Marmaras shining from his right shoulder. The council secretary, Hephakles, saluted him from his desk to the side.

"It's good to be home," Domitris said, and gestured for everyone to sit down. After four months spent in the more informal halls of senator estates, it was surreal to be back in the stiff opulence of the palace. He pressed his palms into the familiar coolness of the marble rostrum while the councilors took their seats and Hephakles readied a scroll and stylus. Domitris steadied himself and found the appropriate voice.

"I'm glad to see all of you again, here, back at the palace. My thanks to Consul Ignotus for acting in my place while I was away and to those of you who hosted the entourage in the provinces." He made eye contact with a few and gave a nod. "Our scholars will be hard at work, processing all the information we gathered. The Supreme Emperor had lost touch with the state of the provinces and our job is to forge these allegiances anew. The good will of the senators has shown that the provinces will stand with Concordia and the crown under the new rule."

Councilor Gaius rose and Domitris made the mistake of halting, allowing him to speak.

"We are glad to hear it, Your Highness," he said, his deep voice ringing off the walls. That wasn't what he had stood up to say. "We look forward to meeting the new Auxillien senator.

When will they arrive?"

If there was one thing Domitris hadn't missed, it was Gaius' stupid, smug face. He had to tell himself not to take the bait.

"As you all know, the relations with Auxillien were strained during the Supreme Emperor's regime. They still refuse to name a senator and are therefore without official governance."

"What a surprise," Gaius said flatly with a quirk of his brow. Domitris noticed the young man beside him who was wrinkling his nose—a new face on the council. He recognized him as Gaius' nephew, Cassian.

"We cannot force them," another voice said, taking Domitris by surprise. It was Opiter, a senator from a border province who had always spoken in sharp opposition to the terms of the treaty with Dassosda, though Domitris generally knew him to be a reasonable man. "Auxillien's support needs to be voluntary. If we are to rush decisions and force compliance, we may as well have the Supreme Emperor still standing there," Opiter continued, and the annoyance in his voice suggested this wasn't the first disagreement between the two.

It managed to shut Gaius up, and he sat back down. Domitris looked from one to the other, then out over the council. "If there are no more disturbances, let us return to the matters at hand. My delay has caused urgency. So tell me, Hephakles, how are the preparations coming along for the festival?"

Hephakles scrambled among his notes while he got up.

"We're ready, Your Highness. The Dassosdan delegation has arrived, and we have planned the show for tonight with their arrangers. Tomorrow, Your Highness and the Minister will address the people together at the Panjusticia and announce the terms of the treaty. On the closing day of the festival, you will sign it at the theater."

At this, several of the council members shot up from their seats. Gaius was the first to speak.

"Your Highness," he said, this time with a sigh, his tone graver. "Are you sure this is what you want for our country? It will ruin us."

It was what he had expected from Gaius. This had been his attitude from the very beginning of their negotiations with Dassosda.

"You need to accept that the times have changed, Councilor! Marmaras as a warfaring nation is history."

Gaius was ready. "If we learned anything from the Supreme Emperor," he barked, "it is that anything can change! We never know what will happen, and this treaty will only make things more uncertain."

Domitris clenched his jaw. This sounded too much like the arguments they had already had months ago. He shot a look to Hephakles, who clapped metal against wood to quiet the room. Domitris took a breath while the steely echo settled.

"Before I left the capital four months ago, it was decided by me, as well as a majority of this council, to support and accept the treaty unconditionally. This was discussed thoroughly, then decided upon because there are no other viable options. Why is this debate still going on?"

No one was eager to talk now.

"Speak!" he said, looking at Gaius scowling back. Gaius rose.

"Your Highness, the treaty isn't signed. The military is what made our empire glorious; made it prosper. Giving in to their terms and diminishing the army will be a catastrophe."

When Gaius stopped talking, Domitris let him stew for a silent moment before addressing the issue.

"Have you spoken your mind? I've made my decision and made the plans for our country unambiguous. The council will not discuss the issue any further. Tomorrow, the terms of the treaty will be announced to the public, and that will be that. No one can hinder the progress we are making now. Am I making myself clear?"

"But Your Highness–" Gaius continued.

"I will hear no more of this! How much longer, Gaius, will you continue to test my patience?"

Domitris was boiling over, but Gaius plowed ahead.

"You must listen! You will undermine the authority of the palace and everything our nation stands for. The people will–"

"What do you care for the people? I, for one, will not march the children of Marmaras into an unwinnable war. I will not entertain this fantasy of domination any longer. It is not right. Face it! Generations of thoughtless military expansion has left us in this state. The only way forward is to break with that destructive tradition and embrace peace, open borders, and learn from our new allies for the benefit of all, not only the already too well off. Ensuring a good start to that collaboration is our biggest priority now."

Gaius' face turned vivid maroon, and he scoffed. "How can we model our nation after those commoner barbarians?"

Domitris pressed his palms against the marble to avoid balling them into fists. He shot a look to Ignotus, who also sat scowling at Gaius. He wondered how Ignotus had kept him in check.

"You can't be blind to the fact that Dassosda is doing

better than us in all regards and that they without a doubt would win if it came to war between us. The days of thinking that we have a claim on their resources in exchange for civilization must end. We have much to learn. Some more than others," Domitris said and looked stiffly at Gaius.

"Dassosda is the runt of the litter. Their country is barely a human lifetime old!"

Domitris' insides grew hot, and the shaking in his hands threatened to show if he didn't calm down.

"That runt outpaced us long ago. That runt is outdoing us in education, technology, philosophy, even productivity, if what our ambassadors have observed is correct. The emperors that came before us squandered our ability to claim any such achievements, and unless we are to take the reins and change our course, I fear Marmaras is truly doomed. Not to mention that their military forces are said to be stronger than ours."

"Not if we control the forces of Auxillien!"

"But we *don't*. And we will not risk civil war by staking that claim!" He heard his own thundering voice ring off the walls around the circular room. This was getting dangerous. Domitris was losing control.

Silence followed the echo of his words while Gaius looked as though steam might erupt from his ears, but he finally sat down.

Gaius was feeling too comfortable. Who else was supporting this madness? Domitris spread his hand on the white marble and let it cool him.

"I sincerely hope that this is the last I hear of the subject. You are my council. You are here to let me see all options and guide me, but the decision is mine to make and when I have spoken, you have no more say in the matter. Is that understood?"

There were mumbles here and there, but no one else was eager to make objections. Domitris gave the word to Hephakles, who turned the debate to more practical matters. Domitris observed the face of each councilor while Hephakles spoke. He needed them on his side for this to work.

When the midday bells finally rang, he was burning to get out of there. He pinched the bridge of his nose, trying to relieve the feeling that his head was going to burst.

He did his best to sneak away from the council hall unseen but got only halfway back to his rooms before a raspy voice halted him.

"Haven't you forgotten something?"

It was Hossia, his mother's mother. She was wearing her white gold-trimmed councilor robe, which made Domitris look twice because she usually refused to wear it, even for larger ceremonies. She had always taken pride in being a contrarian.

"Matre! I didn't see you at the council meeting."

She came towards him. To his relief, her small frame looked no less vigorous than the last time he had seen her.

"Good; I wasn't there." She cackled and reached her wrinkled hands up to embrace him. The strain in his chest melted away as the familiar scent of her spiced perfume enveloped him.

"How can you get back after so long and not come to greet your old matre?" she asked with a glint in her lively black eyes.

"Forgive me. It was a hectic morning and we only got back just before dawn. Why were you not at the meeting?"

She shot a look around them in the empty corridor. Behind her, the light fell through the open windows onto a mural on the wall depicting a century-old battle scene.

"I had some people I wanted to talk to. But don't worry, I've been keeping my eyes and ears open for you while you were away. I tell you, that council is a rowdy bunch of bastards. Only thinking about money, the lot of them. I still think you should get rid of them all."

"You know I can't do that even if I wanted to. The council was part of the election."

Hossia clicked her tongue and waved a hand at the air. She had always been quick to conspire and had very little trust for anyone but herself. Even though she liked to complain about the state of the palace, Domitris suspected she enjoyed being back surrounded by people and intrigue instead of tolerating the quiet life at their estate in the province of Arenaria.

"So where are you sneaking off to since you're not having lunch with the council?" she asked.

"I need a moment to myself before meeting the Minister. Or I fear my head will implode."

Hossia smiled, making her brown skin crinkle like a prune.

"Of course, my boy. Do that. But find time to sit with me one day." She pulled him closer by the arm and whispered, "We have things to discuss. I have some suspicions."

"When don't you?" he said with a smile, which only earned him a "Pfff" in return. She patted him on the hip and walked away with small steps, shooing him with her hand.

"See you, Matre."

In his room, Lyra poured him some water while he collapsed

onto the reclining couch with a groan.

"Was it that bad?" she asked, handing him the glass. He drank half of it and wiped his mouth.

"Do you know how hard it is to get anything done when half the council only pledged to me because they saw no other option? All they do is hold on to the way things used to be. They don't respect my decisions."

Lyra frowned. "So what? You don't need their respect. You're the emperor!"

Domitris sighed.

"I know what you need," Lyra said, disappearing from the room. She returned carrying a tiny silver platter with pistachio biscuits. "These always cheer you up."

Domitris' head fell back in amused annoyance. "It'll take more than a few biscuits to solve my problems."

"Come on," she said with a knowing grin. "It'll make you feel better."

He took one and stuffed it into his mouth. The fragrant delicacy crumbled as he sunk his teeth into it and made his mouth water. Before he realized it, he was reaching for another.

"Thank you," he muttered.

"Now, rest your head. You have to meet the Minister in an hour, and you don't want to be late for that."

"I'll get it together."

"Good," she said, and left him with his thoughts.

He stared up at the flowery frieze decorating the ceiling, as if there would be an answer written for him there. This constant uphill battle wasn't what he had expected when he took on the role of emperor. The council's bickering was already enough to bury him alive, and the treaty was only the first step. Afterwards, he would have his work cut out for him with reuniting the provinces and ensuring the very foundation of Marmaras wouldn't crack. The Supreme Emperor had left such a strain on the provinces with conscription and taxation to fund his wars that Domitris feared the relations were irreparable. The more he thought about it, the more insurmountable the task seemed.

With a sigh, he sat up and massaged the side of his jaw to loosen the tension. His solution for things he couldn't fix was simple—he refrained from dwelling on them. Instead, he had to focus on what he could do something about: making sure he charmed the Minister.

IV

"I've heard stories about you," the Minister said after they had exchanged the first pleasantries. She stood by the window, looking out over a courtyard, fiddling with the curtain. They were in one of the grander audience halls that was rarely in use these days. It was located in the oldest part of the palace, and the room was heavily decorated with polished furniture and thick curtains, the colors deep and dark.

Dia, with her pale blonde hair, stood out. She was still in riding clothes from her morning tour of the city, the ones people wore when actually riding a horse, not traveling in a carriage.

"Domitris, the First Elected Emperor of Marmaras. The most charming young man to walk the earth," she continued, a hint of scorn in her voice, "orphaned at barely sixteen, yet won the hearts and adoration of the masses and assumed the throne ten years later. A noble-born man of the people who single-handedly united commoners and nobles to topple the tyrannical reign of the Supreme Emperor and put an end to the war with Dassosda."

He liked how it sounded, hearing the story told like that, how it made him seem like some kind of hero from the old legends. It wasn't what had happened, of course. The commoners had already been preparing for years in secret, and the nobles had been easy to rouse in the end when the Supreme Emperor had started openly getting rid of anyone who disagreed with him.

She turned to look at him, as if she tried to see physical proof of the achievements. Domitris was a little taller than her and it seemed she tried to make up for it with her posture. "It's quite remarkable," she concluded.

Domitris took a few steps closer to the center of the room with his hands folded behind his back.

"It all sounds very impressive," he said, "but I think that exaggerates my role. I was more of an organizer and fighting instructor than anything. I didn't lead the uprising. The victory belongs to the people." He gestured for them to sit down in the high-backed chairs at each end of the low table that was the centerpiece of the room. She gave a quirk of her head and a tepid smile.

"And modest as well, I see," she said.

He couldn't tell whether she was sincere. It was fascinating to hear that they spoke the same language, but how seventy years of separation had made some words sound quite different and turned other words into something else entirely. Lyra had been right—the intonation and the drag of certain vowels reminded him of how his own old patre had spoken.

She walked over, her expression polite but unreadable.

"The story bears testament to your people's love for you nonetheless. Our own history is not often described so full of glory." She put a hand on the back of the chair instead of sitting down.

She looked younger than he had imagined, but the way she carried herself bore witness to her experience as an official. That she was beautiful was true. Her skin was pale like marble and her hair, short and wavy, fell down to just above her shoulders, surrounding her with a soft golden halo. He gestured for the chair once more and sat down himself. She did the same.

"I've heard rumors about you too," he said. "The ones about your beauty were not an overstatement. And your work as the head of foreign affairs is remarkable. To have accomplished so much in so little time... Being elected as the youngest minister in Dassosda is an impressive feat in itself, but negotiating treaties and establishing trade routes with the Far North... No wonder that such ruthless ambition made you the perfect candidate to deal with Marmaras."

She smiled back with the kind of rehearsed smile that revealed she was used to compliments.

"As you know, stories are usually better than the truth. If I have done well for my country, it is only because I have been able to build upon the work of those who came before me." She paused while she scooted forward in her chair to lean over and pour cold mint water into their glasses from the pitcher set out on the table between them. The servants had been dismissed from the room for their meeting. She continued.

"My impression is that it's not only the need to prove ourselves because of our young age that we have in common," she said, looking up, "but the wish to strive for progress as well."

Domitris picked up the glass she had filled for him and held it out in a small toast. The tone of her voice said that they were getting closer to dangerous territory.

Dia sipped at her drink before she went on. "We have to hope the public is ready to accept the terms of the treaty. Dassosda fears it might lead to unrest."

He had hoped they would stay clear of that topic, but apparently they were going to address it. He crossed his legs as she continued.

"The wall at the border is still standing. People are wary of the south." She met his eyes. The situation was delicate and dancing around the issues while trying not to speak out of place was an art form. Domitris knew that not everyone in Dassosda was happy with the peace treaty. Some had advocated for invasion, utilizing their chance at gaining control over Marmaras.

"People have just got their sons and daughters back from the front. I cannot imagine anyone will sacrifice that over this treaty," he said, putting his glass down a little too firmly.

She put down her own as well and wiped her fingers on her knees as she adjusted herself in her chair.

"I expect you are right, Your Highness. I do not believe your commoners would be troubled much by the peace." She paused. "Your nobles, I've heard, are more strongly bound to tradition than you are."

His ankle gave an involuntary jerk. He didn't like what she was insinuating. Maybe she was going to be more difficult than he had expected. He sat up straighter. He needed to convince her of how much things had changed since he had taken over.

"They are indeed," he offered, struggling to keep his voice

neutral. "But many of them do not hold the same power as they did with the old rule. We need to have faith in people's ability to change. I assure you, they are now actively committed to this rule. They have pledged their allegiance to me."

Dia clenched her jaw ever so slightly. "Do you mean to tell me the same people did not pledge to the Supreme Emperor?" she asked, the initial pleasant smile gone from her face and replaced by a stiff one.

Domitris furrowed his brows. Before he could come up with an appropriate answer, she continued, realizing her indiscretion.

"You must understand, considering Dassosda's own past, we are wary of a system where one person wields so much power. There are people who disagree with this treaty. People who think I'm a traitor just for being here. Some people do not believe it is possible to make an alliance with a country that still has division between nobles and commoners. They fear it will make Dassosda the same way again."

Domitris' heart hammered in his chest. His patience was wearing thin.

"Wielding power is sometimes no more than the art of compromise," he said with strained calmness.

There was a slight pause before Dia continued. "I've heard it said that there are those among your nobles who would rather cling to the ruins of what used to be than accept inevitable change."

A knot tightened in his stomach and his neck grew hot. Those rumors shouldn't have reached her. It was one thing to have treacherous gossip confined within the palace walls, but to have them spread all the way to the officials of Dassosda did not bode well. If she suspected there was unrest among the nobles, the peace could be in danger. Dassosda had demanded stability.

"I've heard the rumors as well, but I assure you, they are nothing more than that. Of course, there are people who disagree with me, but there is no hidden conspiracy. Evil tongues have blown common disagreement out of proportion."

She regarded him coolly but did not answer.

Domitris continued. "Without the resources and willing support of the nobles from every province, Marmaras would fall apart. Only by having the provinces work together can Marmaras hope to become more than the sum of its parts," he stated, feeling strong in his position.

"And would that truly be so bad? Look at how Dassosda blossomed after the separation from Marmaras," she said, without the tone to match the disrespect of her words.

It hit Domitris like a slap across the face. She had no idea what they had been through to get to where they were.

"I know Marmaras and Dassosda used to be the same country, but so much has changed during the separation. Marmaras needs this council and a strong leader. Something you wouldn't understand."

She huffed, and any pretense of civility between them was lost. "In Dassosda, we act on the voice of the people, not the whimsies of a council of the rich appointed by the rich," she said, and Domitris felt as though he might as well be explaining this to a flock of birds. She wasn't even trying to understand. He took a deep breath, regaining himself.

"And that is your right and your privilege. But people here are not ready to change that system. It's part of our culture."

"Is that what the commoners say as well?"

Domitris clenched his fist in his lap. "I spent half a year gathering the commoners, training them to fight, to resist the Supreme Emperor, establishing a bond between the commoners and the nobles. This is what they wanted."

"Oh, so you spent half a year in commoners' company and now you're the voice of the people. Tell me, during that time, did you spend your nights at the farmhouses of the commoners, or did you stay at your nobles' estates?"

This was a step over the line of keeping up diplomacy and they both knew it, the tension in the air palpable. The dark colors of the room seemed to close in around them. Domitris opened his mouth to counter, but the words did not come. Instead, Dia lowered her eyes and said, "This subject has gone on long enough. We're going in circles. Why don't we turn to the matters at hand?"

Despite it all, she sat relaxed in her chair, her brows only slightly raised. Irritation bit into him because he knew he didn't seem equally unaffected. He reached deep within himself to find the strength to end it sensibly.

"Certainly, Minister." Domitris reached for his cup while she waited for him to continue the conversation. Instead of drinking from it, he turned it around in his hands, the condensation wetting his palms. He tried to recall what they had been supposed to discuss. High-pitched chirping turned both their heads as a pair of sparrows landed on the windowsill to their left. Somehow, his anger seeped out of him, and he cleared his throat.

"I heard everything is ready for the show tonight," he finally said. He was grateful when she seamlessly accepted the change of subject.

"It is. And are you ready to address the people tomorrow?"

"Fortunately, yes. I received the speech weeks ago. And you?"

"It was a long journey from Dassosda. I had plenty of time to write it and practice on the way," she said.

Of course, she had no writer. Now that he had experienced the brunt of her opinions, it made him nervous.

"We need it to go well," he said without thinking.

"I'm aware," she replied sweetly.

Domitris let out a measured sigh.

V

Darkness curled its languid fingers around Concordia and torches lit up throughout the city, forming a winding map of light.

Needing to think over the meeting and the evening's coming events, Domitris had found his way to a third-story eastern balcony far above the kitchens. He should have handled it better, even though Dia was the one who had acted out of place to begin with. She came marching into his country, criticizing everything they had fought for without understanding how difficult it had been. She wasn't even born when Dassosda had detached itself from the empire. What would she know about having to fight for justice? He gritted his teeth, trying to push down the surge of aggravation rising in him. He couldn't let his anger get away from him; he needed to make her see how much Marmaras had changed, to convince her that she was not the only one serious about the peace. He had to smooth things over during the evening.

Trying to take his mind off it, his eyes wandered out over the city. This was one of the best views of the main street from the palace and the streams of people headed towards the theater crowded the roads like ants. It had been like that for hours, Lyra had informed him—masses of people coming from both outside and inside the city gates to see the show that would bring their peoples together. He wondered what kinds of acts Dassosda would bring to the stage tonight. He didn't know much about modern Dassosdan culture, but he had heard that Dassosdans valued beauty and elegance in their performances, in contrast to Marmaras' appreciation for displays of strength. What exactly that meant, he didn't know. Maybe there would be dancing?

His thoughts meandered to the dancer on the street. Intrigue stirred in him, and he contemplated trying to find the troupe again to see the performance in full.

The light spilling out from the windows behind him flickered as a shadow passed. Then Ignotus came out of the small door beside him.

"Hiding already?" Ignotus said and passed Domitris a cup of wine. The distraction was exactly what he needed. The tension in his shoulders lessened as he accepted the drink.

"I needed a moment," he said.

"How did things go with the Minister?" Ignotus asked with a knowing smile on his face.

"Questionably."

Ignotus leaned his shoulder against the wall. "I told you she wouldn't be easy." His grin fell. "How are you feeling?"

Domitris downed a large gulp of his wine. "It's strange, you know? That we did it. Everything we fought for is within arm's reach now."

Ignotus took a sip of his own drink. "It's a little early for that kind of talk, isn't it?" he said when he had swallowed.

"I just mean… is this what you had expected?"

Ignotus met his eyes. "Which part? You on the throne and the war over? I don't think any of us expected that. No offense," he added when Domitris put his head back against the stone of the wall behind him.

"Do you think accepting the terms of the treaty is a mistake?" Domitris asked.

"I told you what I thought before you left."

"And your mind hasn't changed after meeting them?"

Ignotus sighed. "I'm just not sure that it's the right way to do it. What they're asking… Marmaras will never be the same again."

"Wasn't that the whole point from the start?"

"Was it?" Ignotus countered, which made Domitris grit his teeth.

"Not this again. Not now. I need your support."

"When, then? When the treaty is already signed?" Ignotus crossed his arms.

Domitris turned to look at him. "I expect this kind of talk from the council, but not from you."

Ignotus let out a breath and uncrossed his arms. "Don't say that."

Both of them turned their eyes out over the city instead.

"Speaking of the council," Domitris said, "What is Gaius' brat doing there? What's his name—Cassian?"

Ignotus huffed. "While you were gone, Patolemus stepped down and there was an opening. You know what Gaius is like; he wouldn't take no for an answer. Cassian's stupid, but I figured he couldn't do much harm. Better him than one of the old elephants."

Domitris snorted. "I guess you're right."

There was a long silence while Domitris tried to think of everything at once. The sight of the torches in the streets tugged at a memory.

"Do you remember the first festival?" Domitris asked. The first festival had started on the night of the Overthrow, with a celebration at the theater once the blood rush had calmed down and the infatuation of victory had taken over. There had been spontaneous singing, dancing, and acting. The next year, they had made it a recurring event in honor of the new rule.

"Of course," Ignotus said. "That feeling... I'll never forget it."

"How is it only two years ago? It feels like a lifetime."

"It does, doesn't it?"

They stood, drinking beside each other quietly for a while.

"This almost feels like old times," Ignotus said with a reminiscing smile on his lips. "You know, when we first came to the palace."

Domitris smiled. "I miss those days. Back before we understood how terrible it all was."

"You mean back when I had to drag your ass out of the fire all the time?"

"It wasn't *all* the time."

Ignotus let out an indignant laugh. "Remember our first banquet? When you got so drunk you thought it was a good idea to crawl up into the east tower to impress Aelias?"

Domitris remembered all too well and put his hand over his eyes. "Stop reminding me!"

"Remember how he wasn't even at the banquet, and you

got scared when you reached the top and I missed the whole party because I had to spend the rest of the evening trying to rescue you?"

"You love that, don't you? Will you ever let me live it down?"

"We'll see. Maybe if you do something even more stupid one day."

Domitris shoved him with his shoulder and Ignotus responded in kind with a clap under his chin. Then they both finished their wine and Ignotus slapped him on the back.

"Well, good luck out there tonight. See you at the banquet," he said and headed back inside.

Domitris shot one last look out over the city, then headed to his rooms to prepare for the show.

Lyra was waiting for him in his bedchamber with the formal attire readied. She dressed him in a floor-length white tunic. Then came lengths of deep blue silk, which she draped around him with meticulous folds. It went over one shoulder, around him, then was fastened at the waist. She left a portion of the fabric to stretch out as a short train behind him that he would have to be careful not to step on every time he moved. She tied it all in at the waist with thin gilded ropes, weaving them into a pattern with complicated knots. It was tight and uncomfortable, but it highlighted the sculpting of his body. Examining his reflection, he was pleased with what he saw.

Over his garments, she fastened the dark blue emperor's cape at both shoulders with golden filigree medallion pins, the same way the Emperor of Marmaras had always worn it. The weight of it satisfied something deep inside him. Since the event was taking place outside the palace, he wore strapped leather sandals that were tied all the way up to his knees. Lastly, he was decorated with several jewelry pieces; large gem rings, a necklace with the star of Marmaras, and a trailing belt of polished gold.

He twirled the star between his fingers, feeling the points of its sixteen arms dig into his skin.

"Do you think it's grand enough?" he teased, as Lyra corrected knots at his torso.

"It's perfect. We can't let the Minister outshine you. I talked to her people and they're not holding back, so neither are we," Lyra said with a snicker.

Domitris tried not to smile too widely. It was good being back with her like this. So many things had changed around him since his coronation, but she hadn't.

"I messed up with her today at the audience."

Lyra looked up at him from her work. "I heard she can be difficult."

"It seems like no matter what I do, people think I'm not doing the right thing. Even Ignotus has his doubts."

"He's always skeptical; you know that. He means well. He's just worried about it all."

"Do you think I'm doing the right thing?"

"I think you were elected for a reason, and I believe that your heart knows what's right for Marmaras."

"That's a strangely diplomatic answer coming from you."

"I'm nothing if not agreeable," she said. Then she looked more seriously at him. "But I really do believe in you."

Domitris let out a breath. "Will you be there for the show tonight?" he asked.

"I've heard His Highness requires my presence, so I have no choice but to stand right behind him at the very best seats in the theater, I'm afraid."

Domitris laughed. "Good."

She tied the last knot, corrected some folds, and took a step back. "There!"

"How do I look?" he asked, holding his arms out and turned half a round to each side, admiring the folds.

Lyra looked him up and down, her eyes misty.

"You look like your father," she said, with a hand to her mouth. It stung. She put her hands on his arms and turned him to the bronze mirror so both of them could look at his reflection. She was right—he hadn't looked much like either of his parents as a child, but the older he became, the more it was his father's reflection staring back at him. The aquiline nose and the straight lines of his jaw were undeniably his father's, though he had gotten his mother's brown eyes and darker complexion.

"I wish they were here to see you. They would be so proud of you and what you have done." Her voice cracked. He hoped she was right. He wanted nothing more than to make them proud.

He put his arms around her, settling his chin on the top of her head. She sniffed into his garment, then swiftly pulled away and wiped her face.

"We don't have time to mess you up."

"I'm glad that you're here," he said, and she squeezed his hand.

"I always will be. Now, let's get you ready. No time for sentimentalities."

"You started it," he said, but she paid it no mind.

"You're missing something." She turned to the bedside

table and came back with the golden circlet. The old crown of the Supreme Emperor had been the same for centuries—elaborate and valuable, decorated with colored gemstones. The last time Domitris had seen it was when it had adorned the limp head of the Supreme Emperor, motionless in his throne, as blood stained his torso from where Ignotus had slit his throat. It had disappeared after that. Rumors said it had been stolen, melted down, and sold. The new crown made for the Elected Emperor was just the simple band of gold between her fingers. He slipped it on, and the familiar coldness of the thin metal rested against his forehead.

"Perfect," she said. "Now you're ready."

The council hall was brimming with people as the whole council as well as the twenty Dassosdan officials stood waiting for his arrival. It was a night of celebration and it showed. Every council member was wearing garments of pure white fabric with gold trim, equal in length to his own, each one more elaborately folded and tied than the next, making them resemble the marble statues of the galleries. Sun-kissed skin was covered up with white powder to make the vainest of the nobles appear more like statues. A few of them had incorporated an overlay of dark blue fabric as well. The Dassosdan delegation was a varied group in comparison, and none of them were inclined towards the fashion of their ancestors. There was no common theme, though russet, green, and blue seemed to be the most popular colors. Some wore long garments, some short, some had patterned overlays or veils fastened to their hairstyles, while others wore strange hats or jewelry.

Though the Dassosdans were generally fairer, they made no effort to disguise their natural skin, some even reddening their cheeks, making them look young and lively. Domitris couldn't help but think that, to the Dassosdans, the nobles must look antiquated.

His eyes caught on Dia, who stood in the midst of the crowd talking to some of the other Dassosdans. Lyra hadn't exaggerated. She was clad in a floor-length dress of gray silk, the neckline plummeting down the pale skin of her back. The light from the torches danced in the folds of the fabric. To complement the volume of the skirt, the ensemble was finished with an intricate silver hair ornament that fanned out from her head like feathers and glittered when she moved. The outfit didn't make her look garish, instead it highlighted the powerful air about her and Domitris wondered if it was wrong of him to think she exuded royalty.

Regardless of how their initial encounter had been, this was a victory. Marmarasi and Dassosdans alongside each other inside the palace. The magnitude of what they were working to achieve rushed over him as he watched them. This was it. This was the first step on the road to building a lasting peace between them, and the festival would be the catalyst. The spark of hope that had lived in him since the early days of planning the Overthrow dwindled away, only to be replaced by the more solid conviction of belief.

Ignotus caught him lingering in the doorway and came to greet him with open arms.

"There you are, Your Highness. Are you ready to make history?"

The hall fell silent, and all attention turned to him.

Domitris squared his shoulders and walked into the room to meet Ignotus halfway in a brotherly arm clasp. Ignotus was no exception to the hard-lived vanity that permeated the palace, and he had transformed as well. His beard was newly trimmed, his long hair woven through with gold threads and done up at the back of his head in elaborate curls.

"Tonight is the night we have been waiting for. Let's make this happen," Domitris answered, not to Ignotus but to the room. There was a cheer from both sides as people raised their cups in celebration. They watched him expectantly, waiting for him to lead the way.

The walk to the theater went through the underground passages connecting the palace to key locations all over the old city center. The first part of the passage, the part closest to the palace, was the best-kept, with the floor and ceiling still intact. Though torches were mounted on the walls for the occasion, a guard with a light led the forefront of the line of people, Domitris right behind him. As the people of the next highest rank, Ignotus and Dia walked side by side in his footsteps. Low chatter full of anticipation crowded the narrow passage.

"Are you excited for tonight, Your Highness?" Dia asked as they ducked under a wooden beam. Well into the tunnel, the floor and walls were nothing more than stomped soil and the edges were rounded and uneven. Domitris listened for a hidden meaning in what she said, but there was no edge to her words. Maybe she was also trying to lighten the mood between them after their meeting. He chose to follow her example of courtesy.

"I still find it hard to believe," he said, looking back over his shoulder, catching a glimpse of her glimmering in the low light.

"It has been a long while since there were Dassosdans on the stage of the theater in Marmaras," Ignotus said behind him and Domitris almost stumbled over a rock protruding from the floor. Domitris knew exactly when that had been, and he knew Ignotus knew it too.

"You're right," Dia said, her tone as calm as it had been when she asked the first question. "If memory serves, it was when your last Supreme Emperor publicly executed the most recent Dassosdan delegation, who were here to negotiate peace."

Domitris' heart quickened. Everyone in Marmaras remembered that event. It was the year they had begun planning the Overthrow.

"We were at war," Ignotus said flatly.

"A war instigated by Marmaras, no?" she asked, the high tone of her voice rendering the question bizarrely innocent. Domitris heard Ignotus take a deep breath, preparing for retort, and he decided to close down the subject.

"That's beyond dispute. And that's why we're here today, to make right of the past wrongdoings of our countries and sign the treaty that will make sure nothing like it ever happens again." Domitris' pace had picked up, causing the guard in front of him to walk comically fast. He didn't enjoy taking the Minister's side, but Ignotus was poking the fire.

"And what a treaty it is," Ignotus said, the excitement in his statement a little too grinding. "Tell me," he said to the Minister this time, "when you have disbanded our armies and confiscated our weapons, what do you intend to do with all that scrap metal?"

Domitris had to stop himself from spinning around and telling Ignotus off. He couldn't believe that Ignotus would bring it up at this critical time and in front of the Minister. He was about to apologize on Ignotus' behalf, but Dia was unfazed.

"We'll put it to good use, don't you worry. We might build something grand and useless. Any suggestions?"

Domitris' brows shot up in surprise, but he didn't look back. He hardly dared breathe, and it took Ignotus longer to come up with a reply than Domitris knew he would be happy with. At least their sense of humor seemed to align. When he finally spoke, it was to Domitris.

"I wish you luck, my friend. You have your work cut out for you."

Domitris let out an amused breath. He knew as much.

"Overthrowing a government and working with an unwilling council is no easy task either," he said, "but that has worked pretty well for me this far."

Ignotus didn't answer but clapped him on the shoulder instead. The Minister stayed silent. Domitris couldn't hide his relief when the torch in front of him finally illuminated the ascent at the end of the tunnel.

VI

As the row of people filed past him from the underground passage into the room behind the stage, Domitris took a moment to compose himself. He still couldn't see the audience, but their presence was undeniable; the low droning of thousands of people gathered in one place interfered with the rhythm of his heartbeat. The taste of oily smoke dried his mouth. He glanced to Dia beside him, her expression tight in concentration though laced with something else as well—not fear, but something like it. He recognized it in himself; anticipation more than anything, the kind that crowded your chest and made your heart beat in your throat. A roar from an animal somewhere turned Domitris' attention to the room. All around them, stagehands and performers scurried by, each trying to put the finishing touches to their acts in desperate attempts to achieve perfection.

The arrangers rushed around, trying to gain control of everything as they signaled for the nobles and the Dassosdan officials to make their entrance and find their seats. Domitris felt a strange prick of morbidity as he looked around at the joy and excitement that saturated the theater. It was both frightening and fascinating what two years could do to a place. But it wasn't just the passing of time—it was a revolution and countless sleepless nights of hard work.

As the nobles walked out, the roaring of applause and cheers from the crowd turned his stomach. His heart beat uncontrollably, the atmosphere reminding him too strongly of the Overthrow—when it had seemed most hopeless, and the rebellion was counting more wounded than not, the rebels had made it to these very rooms with a desperate push as the sun set. That event had marked the turning point when the rebels broke into the palace and the whole night turned in their favor. This moment was the future they had fought for.

When the next signal sounded, Domitris took a final steadying breath. He looked to Dia, who nodded, a slight smile frozen on her lips, and they took to the stage side by side.

The cheers were deafening as they walked in, and his vision blurred at the brightness of the fires burning in bronze bowls all along the stage.

As they walked over the sixteen-armed star sprawling across the floor, the cheering continued. Domitris threw up a hand, waving at the crowd, and squinted, trying to get the blotches of light to disappear from his sight. Rows upon rows of seats stretched out around him as far as he could see, reaching up into the starry night sky. The air was hot and humid and tinted with smoke.

The theater was built to hold the entire population of Concordia, but tonight it was overflowing. People sat both in and between the rows, everyone dressed for celebration, with intricate hairstyles and paint on their faces. Save for the occasional symbolic jewelry or traditional clothing, who was Marmarasi and who was Dassosdan was indistinguishable. In this moment, excitement united them all.

From their place in the middle of the star, Domitris lowered his hand as Dia did the same, waiting for the cheering to die down. When it didn't, he couldn't extinguish the smile burning on his face. Now he just needed to deliver his speech. The crowd quieted when he took a step forward, and he took a deep breath.

"People of Marmaras!" he managed, before the cheering rose again. He raised his voice to be heard, yelling at the top of his lungs.

"I see you out there. Every single one of you was here with me on this day two years ago, fighting for a better future—if not in body, then in spirit!"

The words lumped in his throat, and he halted while the next wave of exalted applause washed over the stage. He smiled, letting the noise flow through him, feeling it in his bones. "We are here today, entering a new era, because of you. Your bravery and strength made this possible. I will prove to you that your faith in me was not misplaced!" He looked around at the smiling faces beaming back at him while catching his breath before he continued. "You dared to dream of change, and I have brought it to you. Our neighbors are our enemies no more." He took another step toward the crowd, his heart thundering in his chest. "People of Dassosda, present on this day far from home, I salute you!" The applause changed in tone this time, coming from the Dassosdan minority in the audience. "On behalf of Marmaras and its people, I welcome you!" he shouted, throwing out his arms.

"That you are here sparks hope among us all. Let tonight be a joyous opportunity to learn from and about each other so we can kindle the flames of unity between us. Tomorrow we will deal with politics, but tonight we celebrate!" He took down his hands, his shallow breathing aching in his throat. The applause rumbled, sending shivers through the ground, and he couldn't get enough of it. He looked from one end of the audience to the other, then stepped back, reaching his hand out for Dia to step forward. The rest was up to her.

The cheers turned to mumbling and tension buzzed through the air like a swarm of flies. She waited until the murmurs quieted. For a second, Domitris wondered if she would be able to speak through the wall of voices surrounding them.

She stood, dignified, with her hands clasped in front of her, and took a deep breath.

"People of Marmaras!" Her voice carried as well as his own had. She did not wait for recognition from the crowd before she continued. "I know you look upon me as an intruder. It must be strange for you to see us here in your midst, with the shadows of war still looming over us." She paused, letting the whispers run rampant as a forest fire, fanning the flames with her words. When she continued, she raised her voice. "You may not trust me, you may not have any love left for my country or my people, but know this: I will endure your contempt!" Her hand went to rest over her heart. "What I do know is that you have love for your emperor. His Highness has worked fiercely and tirelessly for you, his people, even though this peace was not easily brokered. Your emperor does you honor and Dassosda wholeheartedly supports these efforts. I do not ask for your love. All I ask of you is that you do your emperor proud." Even the mumbling had quieted now, the crackling of the torches suddenly audible. Dia stepped forward and flung out her hand. "Our presence here is not an act of aggression but an appeal for reconciliation. All of us here tonight—we are the future of our countries, and *we* decide what to do with that position. We get to choose peace." Her crystalline voice resonated through every row of the theater and the silence that followed was deafening. Then the applause went wild.

The cheering was so loud it made Domitris' eardrums vibrate and he could hardly breathe. It didn't stop. It rolled over the stage in waves as Dia stepped back and they took their positions opposite each other, getting ready to bow to one another for the first time. They let the moment stretch, reveling in it. Domitris allowed himself to feel the relief that swelled inside him. Then they both bent down low, coming back up again to the sound of roaring applause. It continued as they crossed the stage to the raised marble stairs that split the audience in two. Guards in ceremonial uniforms stood all the way up along the steps, saluting them as they rose high above the stage. Ascending, Domitris kept his eyes on the crowd, waving to them with one hand while hoisting up the bottom of his garment with the other. People pushed and strained to get closer to the stairs, reaching to touch him, their fingers like soft grass against his legs.

The emperor's seat at the top of the stairs was canopied by dark blue velvet and flanked by delicate columns decorated with gold leaf flowers coiling from the base to the top. Domitris was still catching his breath when he stepped onto the platform. Aside from one too many guards, it was only the two of them there, making the emptiness of the seats surrounding the two marble thrones gratingly obvious. Lyra wasn't there yet. The absurd amount of food and drink set out for himself and Dia only highlighted the fact that this was a political ceremony; there would be no family or friends at their sides tonight. The sight stirred up a familiar hollowness in his stomach. No matter how hard he worked, no matter how well he did, his parents would never be there to see what he had achieved. Not even his sister had come to Concordia for the festival. She was still far down south in Auxillien, and he hadn't heard from her in years.

Dia tapped on the balustrade, and when he turned, she waved him over with a small flick of her hand. Everyone was waiting for their signal.

"What a view," she said as he stood beside her. And it was. The torches were like stars fanning out before them, mirroring the night sky.

"This is our doing," she then said with a complacent smile he hadn't seen on her before. The words sent a surge of pleasant heat through him.

"Let's drink to that tonight," Domitris said, and Dia's smile widened.

"Shall we?" She nodded towards the crowd. Tension and excitement were palpable in the warm air.

Domitris gave a nod back and took a deep breath. They both stepped forward as close to the balustrade as possible and declared,

"Let the festival begin!"

Once more, the crowd went wild, unrestrained cheering

enveloping them from both sides. Domitris took his seat in the marble throne beside Dia, and with a loud fanfare, a burst of opaque green smoke billowed up from the center of the stage with a crackling bang, setting the show in motion.

Domitris leaned forward in his seat to get a proper look at the two rows of performers entering through the smoke. Silhouettes of men and women spread out along the edge of the round stage and, as the smoke lifted, their vibrant clothing made it clear that they were Dassosdan. They all carried large hide drums held in place in front of them by thick straps. Domitris' attention was immediately caught by the bare skin of their torsos, where elaborate patterns were painted across their chests, starting at their nipples. He glanced over at Dia, who sat casually in her seat, looking unaffected. From how she presented, Domitris had expected Dassosdans to be more modest. On stage, the performers raised their arms simultaneously, mallets in hand, standing still as statues. Then, like the impact of a landslide, they slammed their mallets against the hides and the drumming pulsed through the theater. It was quick and rich and full of energy, and, for the duration of it, the whole theater took in the show as one. Domitris' pulse raced, his eyes glued to the performers. Their straining muscles glistened while the drumming painted stories in his head. Then the rhythm slowed down, changing in tone and intensity, resembling the beating of a heart. Dia turned her head slightly towards him and he scooted back from the edge of his seat, sitting up a little straighter.

"I'm impressed," he said with raised brows.

"Not what you had expected from a bunch of barbarians?"

"I don't th—"

"I know."

The steady beat of the drums continued as a new group of performers joined the drummers. They entered in a swirling motion, filling up the center, dancing to the drums that picked up speed again.

"Your speech," he said, and she looked up at him from the performance. "That was some change of tone from earlier today."

She picked up a cup from the table beside her. "Don't get me wrong, I stand by what I said. I don't believe in your class system. I think it will only cause you and your country more problems." She sipped her drink. "But I believe what's best for my country and my people is to never again be at war, and I will say anything it takes to get people to understand that."

"It was a smart move."

The drums droned low in the background as the dancers finished their act and roaring applause broke out again. Dia put down her glass and looked at him.

"I also meant what I said about you. I see how badly you want this, and I believe you can make it happen."

He scanned her pale eyes for intention. "I almost believe you mean that."

She returned her attention to the show. "You should."

Steps turned Domitris' head to the other end of the room, where Lyra came up from the back stairs. She looked the same as when he had left her, wearing the ivory, ankle-length tunic that most servants wore, except that her long brown curls were pinned more neatly at the back of her head and adorned with a cross-tied white ribbon.

"Your Highness," she said while she went to one knee, then added "Minister," as she made the set of hand gestures from her heart to her forehead as was appropriate from servants in public. He wanted to get up and hug her and hear her praise for his speech, but that would have to wait until they were in private again. Instead, he nodded at her with a smile. She got up and brought over a platter of fruit and the pitcher of wine to refill their cups, and the three of them watched the acts change in silence.

VII

"I would say that went rather well, Your Highness," Dia said on their way down the less glamorous back stairs. The last act had ended, and all performers had been on stage to receive their applause. By the end, the audience was unquestionably drunk and ready to continue the celebrations until dawn. Arms were slung around necks while toneless singing erupted here and there from groups getting up from their seats. The theater could no longer contain the underlying current of euphoria that spilled out into the night. People poured out through the exits, ready to take in every tavern, inn, and street throughout the capital.

"I daresay it did." He thought how Dassosdan and Marmarasi commoners would drink side by side tonight, how stories would be shared over spilled wine and how it would knit their countries together. He wanted to see it, to walk the streets and toast the men and women who would no longer be at war. He wouldn't, of course. The celebration at the palace would be something else entirely. Palace banquets were usually characterized by vanity and intrigues and political navigation among nobles who drank too much. When Domitris first came to the palace at fifteen, he had loved it and each banquet had been a highlight. But since his coronation, the banquets had only become another excuse for people to try to convince him to act in their favor.

The torches flickered as they walked by in the underground passage. Rolling his shoulders to loosen up only caused his clothes to tug and snare, the knots of the fabric digging into his sore muscles. Lyra, who had followed behind them quietly, came to his side.

"Your Highness, we should find you something else to wear for the banquet."

Domitris pulled at the knots straining around his stomach.

"Please do. I'm suffocating in this."

Dia rubbed her neck. "I should have thought of that. I'm stuck in this for the evening."

"You'll outshine every other person there. The nobles will be all over you," Lyra chimed in.

Dia gave a short, sweet laugh as they stepped out from the passage. "I hope that's a good thing."

"It is. As long as you know how to deal with them," Domitris said.

She smiled and raised her chin. "I can hold my own."

Domitris didn't doubt it.

They reached the stairs leading to the higher levels of the palace and came to a halt.

"Good luck with the wolves," Domitris said.

"We'll see if I need it." She continued up the stairs as Domitris and Lyra went west.

Going towards the west wing, they went against the

stream. Domitris had to greet several councilors on the way, some already with filled cups in hand or a glittering courtesan on their arm. The more time he spent out of the palace, the more the irony of it chafed at his mind. Nobles lived most of their life at the palace, the more time spent on bare feet the better, socializing only with other nobles. Yet he had still to meet anyone above inviting commoner courtesans into their bedrooms. Even if the nobles comprised quite a large number of people, it was also a limited number. It was far easier to keep loose relations to commoners than to risk the condemning gossip inside the palace if disagreement in bed arose. And it wasn't hard to find willing commoners. Gaining the favor of a noble had brought more than a few families out of poverty through the times, which ensured that beautiful young men and women were present at all big events at the palace, hoping to charm a noble patron.

He passed another couple, an aging councilor and a courtesan half her age, giggling too loudly at something she whispered in his ear. He had seen them so many times, waiting in line outside the palace to be deemed sufficiently attractive by the palace guards, hoping to be let in. It was a distasteful custom that cultivated the shallow worshiping of the young and the beautiful.

Lyra shook her head beside him. "Don't they know how silly they look? Dressed up like show horses to be paraded around, feigning interest and putting on love as an act." She huffed. "No self-respect. And I don't know who is dumber, the painted whores or the idiots who fall for them."

Domitris bit his lip, trying not to smile. "Aren't you being a little harsh?"

"Desperation is so ugly," she said.

When they reached his rooms, Lyra lit the lamps, humming a melody from the show.

Domitris sighed. "Please get me out of this so I can breathe."

She came over and started working at the knots.

"You looked very good on that stage. It went well," she said, holding a rope-end between her teeth.

He took off the crown and threw it onto the bed, massaging his temples. "It did," he said. "I'm glad."

"You should be. And you should look like it too," she added, looking up at him.

"I'm tired."

"Unfortunately, you are not a little child. You are a very important grown man who has a very important evening before him."

"You know, I could just stay here in my room all night and not go out for the symposium. I'm the emperor. Technically, I can do whatever I want."

The knots unraveled, slackening the fabric around him, and he took a deep breath.

"Technically, you could. But you could also go out there and strengthen political connections and, who knows, maybe you could even have a bit of fun for once?" Lyra gathered the rope in her hands and went to find new clothes. "You have been away for four months. There are new faces at the palace."

Domitris shrugged off the layers of fabric.

"Don't start. I don't have time for that. As you said, I have important political connections to strengthen."

She came in again carrying a floor-length white garment that would make him look like every other noble.

"It's about time you meet someone. You have to somehow, and it won't be by sitting in here." She threw it over his head, and he pulled at it to get it in place.

"That part of my life is none of your concern."

She fastened the ties at his shoulders and waist and took a step back. "Every part of your life is my concern."

"Well, it shouldn't be."

She ignored him while looking him over.

"The crown," she said and went to get it from the bed.

"No, I'll leave it here. If I have to go make connections, I want to talk to people as a person, not as the emperor."

She nodded. "Go have fun, then. I will use my servant's privilege and go to bed," she said with a smile. "I'll come check on you in the morning."

"Thank you, Lyra. And sleep well."

The heavy smell of spiced wine burned in his nostrils when he stepped into the overflowing banquet hall. Every noble who as much as half-cared what went on at the palace was present, even those from the furthest provinces. Few dared to miss whatever scandals or marvels the festival would bring. Looking around, he recognized the faces of some, knew the names and reputations of a few, but had spoken to only a handful.

A tune plucked its way through the air from the musicians positioned at a podium in the center of the room. Flutes played a well-known, cheerful melody accompanied by several small string instruments, allowing guests to join in with the lyrics, but the conversations were flowing too well for that at the moment. As he went through the party, he picked up bits of discussions about the show, the wine, and the current fashions as well as politics and philosophy, though the night was still a little young for that. Colorful courtesans were spread out around the room, already entertaining here and there. Some were dancing or telling stories, while others were stroking hands or whispering in ears.

He scanned the room for Ignotus, but there was no sign of him. In the far corner, a group of curly-haired lesser noble men in short robes crawled around on all fours, trying to outdo each other in re-enacting a Dassosdan act from the show with a tame lion. Their periodical roaring laughter was proof that they had long since drunk more than was good for them. Domitris bet a gold coin with himself that one of them would be puking into the ugly vase beside them before the night was over.

Off to the side, an older noble was groping a far younger courtesan, the two so closely wrapped up he couldn't see either of their faces.

As a servant glided past, Domitris accepted a cup of wine offered to him and sipped at it while he searched for a conversation to join. Cassian strode in beside him, wearing an embarrassing outfit—his upper body was bare, with nothing but a leopard skin draped across the shoulder, the flat cat-face hanging down over his chest. He strutted about, looking people up and down as he went. Domitris had to hold back a laugh as people looked back at him, astonished, which he seemed to interpret as awe. Part of Domitris wanted to get the whole thing over with and get some sleep, but another part—the one who had been drinking wine all evening—wanted to see what was going to happen.

The tune ended and was replaced by a stout woman

playing the lute while singing a nostalgic song of summer blossoms.

"Your Highness," someone behind him said, and he almost spilled his wine. Turning around, he was met by a councilor, Vinicia, a serious woman with round eyes that made her look like an owl. She stood with a glass in her hand but with a less than festive expression on her face. "May I have a word?"

The chance of it being good-natured small talk was minuscule, but he couldn't refuse. One night of fun was apparently too much to ask for.

"Yes, Councilor, of course. What is it?" He tried to look sufficiently interested.

"Welcome back. I wanted to have a word with you about the effects of the agricultural reforms. I know now is not the optimal time, but we've awaited your return all week and—"

Knowing that her money came from some of the largest rural areas west of Concordia, he knew already what her point would be and that they wouldn't agree. If he didn't stop her now, he would be listening to her for the better part of the evening.

"Can it not wait until after the festival?" he asked curtly.

She wasn't discouraged. Instead, her face fell into even more determined folds. "If it could, I would not bring it up. The harvest is late all over Pannonia because of the reforms and the drought has only accelerated the problems."

Before he could turn it over in his head and think of a way to delay the discussion for another time, he was called for again.

"Your Highness, there you are!" Another council member

came to join them. "I need to talk to you about the quarry in Carthex. There was a rock slide only last week collapsing the main entryway. We cannot get shipments in or out of the quarry. We need reinforcements."

"Last week? Why has this not already been dealt with?"

"Due to the cost, Your Highness, and the shortage of hands. It couldn't be approved without your presence. I sent a letter the same day, but it never reached you. Consul Ignotus has made a plan for it, but we need the emperor's approval of the suggestion."

"If the consul has found a solution, we act accordingly."

As if there weren't already enough to deal with, Captain Alba, head of the guard, closed in on them and, as she joined, they officially formed a circle. It was strange seeing her out of uniform. She wasn't quite old enough to be of his parents' generation, but the streaks of pure white in her hair made her look older than she was.

"Excuse me, Your Highness," she said, cutting in front of both councilors, and neither of them dared to object. "It's good to have you back where you belong. I need to have words with you before tomorrow. We're short on guards at the Panjusticia."

Domitris hadn't put her in such a position of power because he liked her, but because she had an ability to get things done. Her mere presence commanded respect, and she was always well prepared and well spoken.

Domitris gestured for the others to leave, pulling the captain off to the side. This shouldn't be a public conversation, but he knew her well enough to know that she wouldn't bring it up unless it was necessary. He lowered his voice as he said, "We can't be short on guards for the ceremony. Make sure the security is in order."

She leaned in with a frown between her white brows. "I will have to take them from the marketplace."

"If that is how it must be. Our primary concern is the ceremony."

The singer crescendoed into a shrill tone for the last line of the song and Domitris downed his glass, hoping to put an end to the conversation.

"Understood," she said flatly, and inclined her head.

Over her shoulder, Domitris found Dia across the room. She was talking to one of her countrymen and a couple of lesser nobles, but out of the corner of his eye, he saw councilor Opiter walking over to them, looking too resolute for Domitris' liking. He needed to get over there. Just as he put his glass down on a passing tray to get out of the discussions, two secretary scholars blocked his path. Before he could do anything about it, he was held up another ten minutes in arguments about how to standardize the size of wagon wheels and whether the taxation of livestock should be lowered before he managed to excuse himself again.

When he located them, Dia and Opiter were in deep discussion and the frown on Opiter's face made Domitris hurry. Just before he was within earshot, Opiter's frown turned into a wide grin Domitris hadn't seen on him many times before. As he approached, they moved so he could join their circle.

"Good evening, Your Highness," Opiter said. "Our northern guest was just telling me the most amusing story."

Domitris hardly believed his own ears. 'Northern guest'

was a welcome change from him. Before the tour, Opiter had refused to talk about them as anything but 'the Dassosdan intrusion'.

"I am glad to hear it," he said as a servant walked by, offering wine to those with empty glasses. "So, you get along, then?"

"Indeed," Dia said, smiling. "Councilor Opiter tells me about the state of the border provinces. Growing up in a small border region myself, it is very interesting to hear the Marmarasi side of things."

"You grew up so close to Marmaras?" Domitris asked.

She shook her head politely. "Your Highness forgets that Dassosda has several borders. I grew up in the north. It couldn't get farther from here."

The music changed again to bright flute tones and the surrounding conversations grew livelier.

"It was quite a show tonight, Minister," one of the lesser nobles said. "The Dassosdan set of skills is very impressive."

"Thank you. Many have been training for months, so it's good to know their efforts are appreciated. And I can only return the compliments, of course."

The marveling over the show went on for some time, and Domitris started to relax. Dia answered every remark elegantly. She was witty and skilled in her comments, both to the compliments and the veiled sharp remarks, and she had everyone laughing and talking and fawning over her as if she knew exactly what she was doing.

Eventually, the talk landed on the goings-on at the palace. One of the young nobles, who looked as though she hadn't been in the capital for long, interrupted as if she was going to burst from excitement.

"Have you heard?" she said, her eyes swimming. "It's going around that Aquilis, matre to Councilor Praxis, has been taking a commoner to the palace, intending to marry him!"

The other young nobles gasped, some because of the news, some because of the inappropriate topic in conversation with the Minister. Domitris glanced at Dia, but she only listened with a raised eyebrow, sipping from her drink.

"Is it really true?" a young man said. "If they do get married, Aquilis' life at the palace will be over."

"I don't think she cares," said the first woman.

Domitris closed his eyes briefly, hoping for the topic to die quickly.

The young man snorted. "She probably couldn't do any better. But still, to debase herself like that—"

Domitris cleared his throat, and the conversation stopped. The woman who had brought it up seemed to slowly realize her mistake and turned bright red.

Her friend tapped her on the shoulder. "Hey, why don't we go sing to the music?"

The woman nodded eagerly, and the two of them humbly excused themselves. A brief silence followed, but Opiter was quick to pick up the conversation.

"I'm very interested in your perspective, Minister. You'll have to come visit my estate in Gilia. It's especially beautiful in winter, though the roads are less passable, of course."

"I would like that," she said with a smile. "Let's arrange it as soon as possible."

Domitris could hardly believe it when they shook hands on it.

Later, after conversations had turned trivial, and the circle dissolved into minor, more private discussions, Domitris found himself alone with Dia, having retreated to the edge of the party by an open window. The stifling air inside was almost thick to inhale, making the warm breeze flowing in a welcome refreshment. It carried the scent of oil from the torches burning in the streets. Even this far above ground, the echoes of cheers and music from the city were still faintly audible.

"I'm impressed," Domitris said, looking out over the city. "If I didn't know better, I would have guessed you dealt with nobles for a living."

"Do you know what work I do in Dassosda?"

"You don't have nobles."

"True. But we have plenty of rich, entitled citizens who'll say anything to be heard."

"You handle them well."

"It can be beneficial to have the right kinds of connections."

She had turned to the darkness outside, the night accentuating her pale skin.

Domitris leaned against the windowsill. "Not everyone is finding the idea of a wholly independent Dassosda easy to swallow."

"These ancients will have to come around."

"They will. They only need to learn that their position won't be taken from them and that nothing will change but the formalities. Dassosda has been self-governing for the past century, after all."

Dia turned to the party again. After a short pause, she said, "It is either the very old or the very young who are too eager to resort to warfare."

AS WE FALL

When he looked at her quizzically, she tilted her head towards a loud group lounging behind a row of fuchsias. Domitris tried to pick up on the specific conversation over the noise.

"–And honestly, it's insulting," said a jarring voice, which could only belong to Cassian, "how he could consent to this truce. Now, if *I* were the emperor, I would never have agreed to their terms. Nor would I have accepted their surrender. What are they even doing here? For all I know, we're still at war and they shouldn't be here."

A muscle spasmed in the corner of Domitris' eye and he couldn't bear looking at Dia.

"Please excuse me for a moment," he said through gritted teeth, and Dia nodded, taking it much more gracefully than could be expected.

Cassian had been a pain ever since he came to the palace around three years ago and had only grown worse when he was adopted by Gaius after the Overthrow. As Domitris made his way over, Cassian was facing the other way, lying halfway down on a reclining couch being attended to by a courtesan who was massaging his feet. He didn't notice Domitris approaching, though all his friends went quiet.

"It'll never go well, I tell you. Someone ought to do something about it."

Domitris came up right behind him. "And if *you* were the emperor," he said, making Cassian flinch so hard he dropped the grape he had been twirling between his fingers, "how would you go about dealing with a bunch of unruly children discrediting you to the world behind your back?"

Cassian's face turned ashen, which was only highlighted by

his tawny hair, and he swallowed several times. At least Domitris now knew where the slander was coming from.

"What? Do you like it better when only you are talking?" Domitris asked.

A heavy palm landed on Domitris' shoulder and the smell of sweat hit him in the face.

"Now, now, Your Highness, I'm sure my boy was only joking," Gaius said and shot a look past Domitris.

"I'm sure he was. It is, after all, much past his bedtime, and he must be tired."

Cassian sat frozen in his seat, looking intensely to Gaius for assistance.

"You heard your emperor, didn't you? What are you waiting for? Go to bed."

Cassian was the first to rise, but every one of his friends did the same, their eyes glued to the floor. "Goodnight, uncle," he murmured as he passed them and hurried out of the room.

Domitris looked their way until they were out of sight. His hands balled into fists.

"It worries me where he learns such things," he said to Gaius, not meeting his eyes.

"That boy," Gaius said, shaking his head. "His parents were rotten apples, too."

Domitris crossed his arms. "You should keep a closer eye on him, then."

"The folly of youth." Gaius looked to the ceiling and threw out his hands. "What can be done?"

Domitris was about to argue, but as he drew in a breath, Gaius turned his attention to a greeting across the room.

"Oh, do excuse me, Your Highness. I have been looking

for this one all evening. Good night." And like that, he was gone, leaving Domitris with the boiling of his blood, the beginning of a headache, and an uneasy feeling in his chest. Dia was once again engaged in eager conversation, and he still couldn't locate Ignotus. The unmistakable sound of someone retching solicited gasps followed by a splatter as it hit the floor. When he looked over, one of the young nobles was clinging to the vase but had missed it by a hand, sending servants hurrying to clean up the purple mess. The smell of bile traveled through the room and Domitris finally decided that he had been present enough and gave himself permission to go to bed.

Worming his way through the people who were now dancing or singing or both, he was stopped halfway to the exit by commotion in the crowd.

"Give me back my money, you thieving whore!"

He got on his toes to see what was going on. It was a fight between the old noble, who he saw now was Patolemus, and the courtesan he had been buried in. Patolemus was sweating profusely and held the young man's hand high above his head.

"I told you I didn't take anything," the courtesan said quickly, trying to wrestle himself free. His bracelets clinked with the jerk of his arm.

That's when Domitris recognized him. Deep black hair, lips and eyelids painted gold—it was the dancer from the street. His face was hard to forget, with features so exquisite Domitris couldn't tear his eyes away. The full brows, high cheekbones, the sharp curve of his upper lip—he was a piece of art.

"Liar!" Patolemus sneered and tightened the grip on his arm, making the young man wince in pain.

They were drawing attention from the rest of the party and one of the palace guards headed their way, but in no apparent rush.

Domitris knew better than to intervene in a squabble like this, yet he felt himself moving towards them, getting there before the guard.

The young man looked up as Domitris approached, panting slightly. He had the most artful green eyes Domitris had ever seen.

"You're being a bit rough with him, aren't you, Patolemus? Is that really necessary?"

Patolemus yanked hard at the young man's wrist, so he lost his balance and stumbled to the floor, his golden hoop earrings swaying beneath his hair.

"This thief has stolen my coin purse," he spat.

"Hey, whoa," Domitris said, holding out his hands, trying to get him to calm down. "Why don't you let go of him for now? I'm sure we can resolve this."

Ignoring something so close to a direct order from his emperor would not go down well. Patolemus cast his arm aside and huffed in contempt.

The young man withdrew his hand and rubbed his wrist, readjusting his bracelets. "Listen, I didn't take anything, I promise!" he said, his eyes wide, his voice trembling just a little.

Domitris looked to Patolemus. "Is there any chance you misplaced it?"

Patolemus turned beet red and looked as though he was boiling under the surface. "Do you take me for an idiot? How dare you listen to a foreign whore instead of me?"

Patolemus had probably had too much to drink because that was overstepping a boundary. He was always quick to lose his temper, but he usually knew where the line was.

"I think we should give the man a chance and talk about this when everybody has sobered up," Domitris said, gesturing for the guard who had been keeping her distance while the scene unfolded.

Patolemus looked as though he were ready to punch someone, but started muttering swear words under his breath and staggered away before having to be escorted by the guard. With his attention split between the guard and the courtesan, Patolemus didn't see the servant with a full carafe of wine in his path, so when he tried to storm off, he collided with the poor man, whose carafe fell and bathed Patolemus in a fountain of deep red. Patolemus swore loudly at the servant and people stopped their conversations to turn and stare.

"What are you looking at!" Patolemus screamed at some young women whispering to each other, snickering at his misfortune. When the guard moved his way, Patolemus hurried out of the room, leaving a trail of wine.

Domitris turned to the young man, still sitting on the floor. He was doing a poor job holding back a smile, but Domitris could hardly blame him.

"Are you all right?" Domitris asked and held out a hand.

With Patolemus out of the room, the attention of the crowd turned to them. People whispered and ogled at the newcomer courtesan, and no wonder. Not only was his face extraordinarily captivating, he was also done up to catch attention. What he wore now was not the costume Domitris had seen him dance in earlier, but was almost as revealing. His torso was clad in cream gauze on the verge of see-through, and his waist was bound with a gold and turquoise sash holding up loose-fitting pants. Although his front and back were covered, the sides of his hips were conveniently bare, showing off his fine brown skin and leaving little to the imagination.

The young man took his hand, stood up and corrected his garment, the gold shimmering faintly on his face.

"Yeah, only my pride took a little hit there." His voice was crisp, like taking a bite of an apple, and he had a slight accent as if the words were a little too round in his mouth. It was, however, not the kind of southern accent Domitris had expected from his complexion. The man ran a hand through his hair and looked up at Domitris.

Murmurs crowded the room and Domitris felt the attention on them too strongly.

"Come with me," Domitris said.

VIII

Domitris led them out of the banquet hall, away from the party and onto a small balcony facing the city streets. This one was old and made of gray stone, weathered and rounded by age. There was a built-in long seat against the outer wall and velvety climbing ivy crept around the edges, enveloping the balcony. The stars glinted in the night sky and Domitris sat to better look up at them. He took a deep breath and the contrast of the fresh air to the heat inside made him feel the buzzing in his body from the many glasses he had drunk.

The young man went to the railing and took in the view, clearly fascinated.

"Is that the legendary Library of Marmaras?" he asked, pointing to the Panjusticia. Domitris couldn't help smiling. What a strange thing for a courtesan to ask. And the guess was painfully wrong. This many stories above ground, they could barely glimpse the light from the library and the academy grounds visible far in the distance.

"No, there, look." Domitris pointed to the glowing specks.

The young man's gaze followed the direction of Domitris' finger. "Wow," he whispered, his eyes fixed on the horizon.

The light from the torches along the streets illuminated his dark hair and the exquisite curves of his shoulders. Did he recognize Domitris from the street? Was that why he had come with him?

"I saw you dance earlier," Domitris said.

The young man didn't turn around from the view at first, but answered, "I know."

Then he let go of the railing and came to sit beside Domitris. The sound of a crash from inside and a group of people cheering broke the quiet for a moment. Then the stillness of the evening returned.

"What's your name?" Domitris asked.

The young man hesitated.

"Sinnan," he said. Then his manner changed. "Though I'd rather talk about you. What's yours?"

Now it was his turn to hesitate. Was he joking, or did he really not know? Domitris examined his face. There was no apparent recognition in his eyes, and Domitris had the impulse not to tell him. It would be refreshing to be with someone who didn't know him as the emperor. It could be fun. He wanted to see where it would lead if he didn't know. And then it just slipped out.

"Aelias," he said without thinking. He had no idea why the name of his former lover was the first that had come to mind.

"Aelias," Sinnan said to himself with a finger to his chin. "A strong name. I like it," he continued with a mischievous smile, stretching out his hand and letting his fingertips grace Domitris' collar bone. The gesture sent a jolt of heat through

Domitris' body, and he resisted the urge to shiver. He hadn't been this close to anyone for years. Sinnan was so near him now that Domitris could smell the strong scent of juniper on his breath. It was from alcohol, but not the kind served at the palace. Domitris swallowed.

He glanced down and a ragged X-shaped scar on the back of the caressing hand interrupted his thoughts. There was a matching one on his other hand. Domitris furrowed his brows and took the hand in his, running a thumb over the scar. When he looked to Sinnan for an explanation, Sinnan withdrew it and got back up. He turned around and leaned his arms on the railing.

"Concordia by night is a glorious vision," he said. "Though you must be used to it, of course." He looked halfway back at Domitris. "Are your quarters close to this view?"

Domitris let it go because Sinnan was already one step ahead, not missing a beat. The unspoken question of where this was going was in the air, and the thrill of the negotiations delighted Domitris. Everything was a move, and they were both playing the game. Domitris got up and stood beside Sinnan to see what he saw. The torches bathed the city streets in a magical hue.

"Not really. I live in a remote part of the palace," Domitris answered.

"Oh. What do you do here?" Sinnan asked, testing the waters.

Domitris thought about how to answer. How much could he say without giving the truth away? He settled on something sufficiently vague.

"Mostly administrative work."

"Hm, sounds important."

"It keeps me busy," Domitris said a little dryly.

"That must be a lot of responsibility," Sinnan said, leaning his head on his hand, looking up at Domitris. "I can hardly keep myself out of trouble," he said, and then, "Thank you for helping me out before." His tone was sweet and genuine.

"He shouldn't have been so rude to you. Patolemus tends to be…"

"A real asshole?" Sinnan suggested with a raised brow.

Domitris laughed without meaning to. The words were wrong in his mouth, like mud spatters on silk.

"What happened in there?"

Sinnan looked down, and a frown formed between his brows. He ran his finger in a circle on the balustrade as if uncertain how to answer. Eventually he said, "He crossed a line, and…" he hesitated. "When I told him no, he got angry and accused me of being a thief."

Domitris leaned his arms on the railing and folded his hands in front of him. "He should know better."

"At least I'm in much better company now." He looked down, then up, meeting Domitris' eyes.

Domitris had often had a hard time recognizing flirting in the past, but Sinnan didn't make it difficult. It was usual for courtesans to be flirtatious, but they tended to be demure and polite, trying to make sure they wouldn't lose favor with the patron they were pursuing. That also often made them very dull conversation partners, which, of course, was usually not how they made their money, so he couldn't blame them.

Sinnan fiddled with the golden hoop dangling from his ear,

his head tilted. His presence seemed to glow, and Domitris felt the warmth of his skin against himself. How long had it been since Aelias? Years. Years and years. Lyra was right; it was time to move on. For one evening he wanted to be only himself, to talk to someone without questioning what they would gain from ending up in his bed. If only he could take a break for one evening, from the council, from the palace, from being emperor.

"Is this how you usually entertain your guests?" Sinnan said, catching his eyes. "Hello?" He waved a hand at him.

Domitris' mind snapped back into place, and he exhaled. "It's been a long day." And this wasn't what he had expected for the night.

"If you're not interested I can—"

"No, it's not you—I mean... stay. Why don't we find another bottle and make this evening a good one?"

A playful smile graced Sinnan's lips. "I already have one." He walked over to the seat, reached down beside it, and pulled out a flask of wine.

Domitris gaped at the bottle in his hand. "Where did you get that?" he said, laughing, looking Sinnan up and down, trying to figure out where he had hidden it.

"On the way out," Sinnan said with a cant of his shoulder. "Anyway, I like your suggestion. Drink this with me and let us play a game of truth."

"A drinking game?"

Domitris grew more curious about the man in front of him by the minute. The gentle trill of crickets serenaded them in the evening hush and the jasmines from below coated the air with their sweet scent.

"Why not?" Sinnan asked as he plopped back down on the seat with the bottle in his lap. "Are you nervous?"

"Should I be?" Domitris couldn't deny the pleased tone of his own voice. Now it was Sinnan's turn to laugh, and Domitris sat down beside him.

"Maybe. I'm good at it." Sinnan propped one leg up beneath himself, turning towards him.

Domitris enjoyed the directness of his words and the ease of his movements.

"How does it go, then? The game."

"All right, so it's an assumption game. I make an assumption about you, and if I'm right, you have to drink and if I'm wrong, I have to drink and vice versa."

Domitris nodded. That sounded achievable, even in his current state of drunkenness.

"I'll go first." Sinnan thought for a while, looking around, then said, "You work at the palace."

Domitris smiled. "I just told you that. Isn't that cheating?"

Sinnan grinned. "If I'm right, I'm right. Take a sip!"

Domitris stared at him, then took the bottle and drank.

"Your turn." Sinnan pointed at him with a flat hand.

Domitris looked him up and down again while he thought about what to ask. What he wore, his hair, his face, all made Domitris want to guess at his profession, but after contemplating the options, he decided to try a safer road instead.

"You're in Marmaras because of the festival."

Sinnan raised a brow at him and gave a smile Domitris couldn't interpret. "Wrong. Though it feels like a good time to be here. You have to drink again."

Domitris drank and wiped his mouth. "Why did you come here, then?"

Sinnan shook his head. "That's not how the game works. You'll have to keep guessing. But it's my turn now. You are…" he began as he scrutinized Domitris' face, and then, as he settled on a subject, "the youngest child in your family."

"How…" Domitris said, and a triumphant gleam emerged in Sinnan's eyes.

"Well?" he said.

Domitris took another sip from the bottle while he tried to think of what to ask next.

"You can handle a few drinks," he guessed.

Sinnan grinned. "What gave me away?" he said, then reached for the bottle and took a long sip, the muscles in his throat moving as he drank.

"Right," he said when he had swallowed. "You've wielded a sword," he guessed, and pinched Domitris' upper arm.

He liked that question better. He took a swig. "You haven't."

Sinnan laughed and drank. "You got me there. I usually find persuasion more effective."

"Then you really haven't wielded a sword," Domitris said, and Sinnan laughed. Then Sinnan put a hand to his chin, finding the next question. Domitris' heart drummed with anticipation.

"You still live with your parents," Sinnan then guessed.

Domitris stopped mid-movement and his smile faded. "No," he said.

Sinnan's teasing smile diminished, and he reached for the bottle, trying to play it off.

"Well, I can't be right about all of it," he said, and took several long sips. "Your turn."

They played until the bottle was empty. By the end, Domitris still hadn't learned much about him. Only that he was older than twenty but hadn't yet turned twenty-five, that he was traveling, though he hadn't managed to get a single guess right about the reason, and that he knew how to ride a horse. Sinnan, on the other hand, guessed the month of his birth, that he was an early riser, the fact that he had a birthmark and where it was, and that he had a tendency to work too much.

Domitris hadn't drunk like this in a very long time. When they tumbled in over the threshold to the galleries to carry out Sinnan's latest idea—a tour of the palace—Domitris could hardly walk straight. He couldn't remember indulging so much at a banquet since his early years at the palace.

He swerved across the ancient carpet muffling his steps, unable to walk straight. Sinnan already stood further down the hall and laughed uncontrollably at Domitris' inability to keep his balance. The noise they produced was too loud for the dead silent halls of the galleries and Domitris' ears felt as if they were filled with cotton after all the sounds he had been bombarded with throughout the day. Sinnan staggered closer to him and now Domitris was the one laughing. He shushed Sinnan, trying to make the room quieter. Sinnan took hold of him, and they staggered together down the halls, pointing at the art, snickering like children at every little thing.

They entered a new room and Domitris stopped to stabilize himself while Sinnan lay down on the floor. After a moment, Sinnan pointed to the ceiling and whispered, "this is my favorite."

"What is?"

"The stars."

Domitris craned his neck to look up but decided it was too much effort and lay down beside him. He had never paid attention to this particular ceiling before, but Sinnan was right. It was beautiful. The room itself was small and square and only housed a series of paintings of pears from different angles. The ceiling looked as though it had been designed for a much grander room. It was parted into sixteen deeply set squares painted dusty midnight blue. Inside each square, the sixteen-armed star of Marmaras shimmered in silver paint that changed shade depending on the angle.

They lay like that in silence for a while until Sinnan suddenly got up.

"I've got an idea," he said. In a second, he was over, grabbing the frame of one of the larger paintings, portraying two slightly overripe pears leaning against each other.

As Domitris got up, the room swam around him. He steadied himself against the door frame and his stomach turned.

"What are you doing?" he asked Sinnan.

Sinnan waved him over. "Come help me with this."

"What for?"

Sinnan's eyes were wide, and he was beaming with excitement. "Let's take it."

"What? Why?"

"It'll be fun," Sinnan said and tried to lift it off the hook it was hanging on.

"Where are you going to put it?" Domitris asked, walking over to the painting. Sinnan let go of it and instead staggered over and grabbed the front of Domitris' clothes, then got on his toes, leaned in, and whispered, "How about your room?"

The hair at the back of Domitris' neck stood up, and a breath escaped him. He pulled his head back to look at Sinnan's slightly swimming eyes.

"Come on," Sinnan said at Domitris' silence. "I want you."

Somewhere beneath the layers of wine, he knew it was a bad idea, but how could he resist?

His rooms were dark when they tumbled in through the door. Only a single oil lamp burned by the bed, casting a dark golden sheen on the walls. Sinnan panted slightly as he put the painting down. Domitris shouldn't have brought him all the way here. He knew they shouldn't be doing this.

But he was too drunk to care.

Domitris stood by the foot end of the bed when Sinnan staggered over in the darkness. He lifted his hands up to each side of Domitris' neck and ran them down over his shoulders and arms, approvingly caressing his musculature. Then he lifted Domitris' hand and kissed his fingers, leaving a stain of golden paint. The paint was still luminous on his face, though it was smudged by now and crude this close. His dark lashes cast streaking shadows down his flushed cheeks. His touch, the proximity of his body, the look in his eyes made some sort of sense stir in the pit of Domitris' stomach.

"This isn't a good idea." He lowered his hand.

"Does it matter?" Sinnan asked, so close Domitris could smell the wine heavy on his breath.

Domitris' heart pounded against his ribs. The lavish, laid-back atmosphere they had cultivated all night was replaced with dangerous passion. There was no doubt about what Sinnan was asking, and temptation grew within him. Sinnan leaned in closer with a hand on Domitris' chest and whispered in his ear, "Please. Let me show you a good time."

Were all courtesans so brazen?

Domitris suppressed the voice in his head telling him to be cautious. He didn't want it to stop. He moved his hand up and stroked Sinnan's chin with his thumb, then bent down slightly and kissed him on the cheek. Sinnan didn't hesitate at the invitation. He reached both arms up and curled them around Domitris' neck. The metal of Sinnan's bracelets were cool against his skin. Their noses were so close that Sinnan's breath brushed against his face. Sinnan looked at him with huge eyes, then at his lips before bringing him in for a soft close-mouthed kiss that quickly turned into a wet, open-mouthed one. Sinnan tasted like the metallic aftertaste of the wine they had both been drinking all evening. He smelled like sweat and smoke and Domitris could feel himself go hard just at the kiss.

Hesitation crept back up on him and he pinched his eyes shut, trying to calm the storm raging in his mind. He didn't give into it.

It was only one night of weakness, nothing more.

Sinnan swallowed a moan from his lips and leaned into him greedily, nudging them both backwards. The back of Domitris' thighs hit the bed and their teeth clacked against each other. Sinnan groaned softly at the impact but didn't pull away. Instead, he lifted a knee to the bed beside Domitris while pushing down on his shoulders, forcing Domitris to sit down on the edge. Sinnan climbed onto his lap, a knee on each side of his hips.

Domitris' heartbeat was out of control, and he couldn't slow his panting. Sinnan pulled away from the kiss, only to nibble at Domitris' throat. Domitris stared up into the canopy of the bed without a coherent thought in his mind. It had been too long since he had been with someone. He wanted him closer. He wanted the sweet pleasure of friction. Reaching up, he grabbed hold of Sinnan's hip through the soft fabric. With the other hand, he tugged at the sash. Sinnan sat up, loosened a knot to the side, and let the sash fall to the floor. The fabric on his upper body opened all the way down the front, revealing pierced nipples and the delicate piece of jewelry dangling from his navel that jiggled with his movements.

Domitris slid the fabric all the way off. Sinnan's pants were still held in place by a smaller knotted band at his hips and Domitris took a minute to admire his torso with his hands, sliding them across his chest down to his navel, where he caressed the knob of metal holding the trinket in place. Sinnan sat still and let him do it. The sight of Sinnan on top of him made Domitris lose the last bit of restraint, and a hundred images of what they would be doing in five minutes rushed through his head. When Domitris' hands found their way inside the slits of the pants onto his ass, Sinnan spread his legs more, bucking his hips closer to Domitris', his weight pressing into his erection.

Sinnan looked at him, smiling at the discovery. Then he pulled away and slipped down between his legs to the floor, where his hands moved up Domitris' thighs, sliding up the fabric to expose him fully.

Domitris panted as he leaned back on his hands and watched him. Sinnan didn't look intimidated by the task in front of him and softly let a finger trace up the length before he grabbed hold with a warm, firm hand, delivering slow strokes. The sight was almost too much for Domitris to bear, and when Sinnan leaned in, his moist breath a precursor against him, his mind went blank.

"Will you let me?" Sinnan asked.

Domitris' cock twitched at the words and he let out a breath. His hand found the top of Sinnan's head before he closed his eyes.

"Please."

What followed was obviously not the work of an inexperienced man. Sinnan took him into his mouth, first just lapping at the head until Domitris was quivering, then he bowed down to take it all in, moving up and down while working his tongue as if he had done this a thousand times before. Even though Domitris wasn't exactly inexperienced himself, this eclipsed anything he'd ever had. The grip of Sinnan's strong, slender fingers around the base, the pressure of those exquisite lips, the slick warmth of his tongue, immediately had Domitris lightheaded and breathless.

The alcohol pumping through his body and the thrill of the night meant he lasted for only moments before he saw sun, moon, and stars as he hunched over and came hard into Sinnan's mouth with a muffled moan. Sinnan let it happen and swallowed efficiently before pulling away, wiping his lips.

When Domitris gained consciousness a short moment later, he couldn't believe he had let it happen. "I didn't mean to—"

Sinnan looked up at him, amused.

"Are you all right?" Domitris asked.

Sinnan sat up. "I think I'll manage," he said, and crawled onto the bed. "Though would you mind if I stayed for the night?"

Perplexed, Domitris gestured to the bed. "Of course!" He hadn't thought of asking him to leave.

Sinnan didn't hesitate. He shrugged off his pants and got under the thin covers.

Domitris turned to look at him. "You don't want me to… reciprocate?"

Sinnan propped his head up on his hand, and looked calmly at Domitris, smiling. "The opportunity to sleep in a bed like this is more than enough for me."

Domitris nodded and bent over to snuff out the lamp, then lay down on the bed, facing Sinnan. Sinnan was turned towards him, looking at him in the darkness. Release had made Domitris' intoxicated mind grow clearer, but he didn't want to examine the feeling turning in his stomach. He could deal with it in the morning. The room was spinning, warping the lines of the walls. He closed his eyes, but it only intensified the sensation. The sheets rustled as Sinnan turned over beside him. Domitris took a deep breath, and as he exhaled, his limbs grew heavy, and he was overcome with the exhaustion he had been pushing away all day. He couldn't wait for sleep to take him.

IX

Domitris' ears woke before his eyes to the sound of the morning bells ringing softly in the east tower and birds chirping outside his window. He had a throbbing ache in the back of his head, and it was only when he turned around and saw the sleeping Sinnan beside him that he remembered what had happened the night before. Then he saw the pear painting leaning against the wall opposite the bed and embarrassment flared in his chest. Sinnan's face was squashed against the pillow, his hair in disarray, and judging by the gold paint smeared all over his face, Domitris himself must look a mess. With his mouth open, he breathed heavily in Domitris' direction. His breath smelled terrible, but the taste in Domitris' own mouth was equally bad, and he smiled to himself at the situation.

He glanced around the quiet room. There was a while until any council activities began, so he decided to relax and enjoy the morning.

Just as he turned around to get a little more sleep, Lyra walked in and drew the curtains, her back turned to them.

"Good morning, Your Highness! I trust you slept well? We can't have you sleeping in all day, no matter the amount of wine you drank last night. It's an important day, remember? Wakey wakey!"

Light spilled into the room and fell onto the bed. Domitris sat up and Sinnan woke next to him.

When Lyra turned and saw he wasn't alone, she jerked, letting out a high-pitched shriek that made Sinnan startle and pull the sheets up to cover himself.

"I apologize for the intrusion," she said, immediately stopping what she was doing, and bowed down low, something they had agreed long ago she didn't have to do in private.

"Lyra, please, there's no need for that," he tried, but she had already left the room. Putting his hand to his warm face, Domitris started laughing. He felt like a schoolboy caught doing something he wasn't supposed to. Lyra had never before walked in on him having company in bed, since he didn't usually bring them back to his room.

Sinnan blinked and sat up slowly. Seeing Domitris snickering into his palm made Sinnan giggle and point at him. This only made it all funnier to Domitris. Soon he was laughing uncontrollably, the corners of his eyes stinging with tears.

"You look terrible," Sinnan finally said, sleep still stuck in his throat.

"You should see yourself," Domitris answered, wiping his eyes.

Sinnan touched a hand to his face and when it came back stained with gold, he wiped it off on his thigh. "Your servant seemed a little on edge."

"Believe it or not, but I don't usually do this kind of thing." Domitris turned to look more directly at Sinnan in the sunlight. "But I had a good time."

"I heard the morals of the palace were rather casual in that regard," Sinnan said.

"They are, I suppose. Among the nobles."

"But what, you're just a purist who is never tempted?"

"No, that's not it."

"What, then? Too important to bring anyone into your bedroom?" he teased with a smile and propped his head up to rest in his hands.

"I would hate to think so."

"You're not some sort of monk, are you?" he asked, brows furrowed.

"A what?"

Before the conversation went any further, Lyra entered the room again, this time with formal servant etiquette. She bowed down low and kept her right hand to her heart as she spoke, which was strange to see from her in his own room.

"I forgot to ask if His Highness and his guest would like breakfast served now or later?"

"You can set it out when it's ready, thank you, Lyra."

She bowed down again and backed out of the room.

Sinnan slowly sat all the way up, rubbed his eyes again, and blinked against the sun from the windows. He sighed, running a hand through his hair. Then he froze and his head whipped around so quickly a lock fell out of order onto his forehead.

"You're the emperor," he said, his green eyes wide, staring at him in astonishment. Domitris shrugged with a smile, but before he managed to say anything, Sinnan swept away the sheets, cursed in another language, and hurried out of the bed. His foot caught on the linen on his way out and he almost fell face first onto the marble tiles. He got up and scuffled, confused, around the room looking for his clothes.

Domitris regarded him over the edge of the bed, watching the panic unfold.

"What's going on?" he asked, getting out of the bed.

Sinnan gave up on finding his clothes, smacking a hand to his eyes. "I didn't know."

"Calm down, I didn't mean to mislead you," Domitris said.

Sinnan lowered his hand and scanned the room again for his clothes. Domitris discovered he was standing on Sinnan's pants. He picked them up and tossed them to him.

"It just happened," Domitris continued as Sinnan put them on. "I thought you maybe knew who I was and was playing along," he lied.

"Well. I didn't."

There was a small silence. Domitris took a step towards him. "Does it matter?"

Sinnan looked at him in disbelief. "I have to get going."

He headed for the door, still half naked.

Domitris sidestepped into his way and Sinnan stopped before he could grab onto him. Domitris put his hands up, making it clear he wouldn't touch him.

"Please, just wait. How about we find you something to wear first and you join me for breakfast?"

Sinnan hesitated at the suggestion, looking directly at him. Then he looked around the room, seemingly considering his options. Domitris could see his mind racing behind his eyes, his jaw muscles clenching.

Domitris didn't know what was going on, but he didn't want him to go. Not yet.

"It's just breakfast," he said, soothing his voice.

Sinnan tapped his foot a few times before visibly giving in, his body relaxing, letting down his guard.

"I guess that can't hurt," he finally said with a sigh. Then he sat back down on the bed.

"So, if what I know about the emperor of Marmaras is right, your name isn't Aelias."

"No," Domitris said. "Domitris is fine."

"Not 'Your Highness'? Are we so intimate already?" he said with a smile and an arched brow.

Domitris leaned against one of the posters of the bed. Sinnan's upper half was still bare and Domitris smiled at the reminder of the events of the evening.

"Considering last night, I'd say—" He didn't finish the sentence because the door opened, and Lyra stepped in with a large tray of food and set it on the table. She looked stiffly down on the tray, trying not to stare at whatever was playing out between them. It was amusing to see such self-restraint from the nosiest woman on earth. Domitris stood up, trying to make eye contact with her.

"Sorry, Lyra, but could you find something casual for my guest to wear? And for me as well."

She side-eyed Sinnan. "Certainly, Your Highness."

There was mostly silence while they both cleaned themselves up. Domitris couldn't help stealing looks Sinnan's way. In the mornings, Domitris would usually get ready by himself or with Lyra. It was strange having someone he didn't know there with him. He also couldn't believe he had ended up with a stranger in his bedroom at all. He probably shouldn't have asked him to stay, but he felt the need to make up for his deception. He knew he would be hearing Lyra's opinion about it later, but he didn't really care. Even though Sinnan was ridiculously beautiful, that wasn't why this had happened. He had been fun to be around. Casual. Something almost unheard of at the palace.

Domitris got out of the clothes he had slept in and stepped in front of the long, gilded mirror plate on the wall to wash his face. He almost gasped when he saw himself: gold paint was smeared all over his mouth and, when he looked down his body, the gold glittered vividly from somewhere else as well. He wrung the cloth and scrubbed his face and then his body until he was clean. In the mirror, he caught a glimpse of Sinnan grinning behind him.

When he was done, he sat down at the table and poured two cups of water, and Sinnan joined him a short while later. Lyra had collected Sinnan's clothes from the day before in a small pouch for him that he hung on the back of the chair. He was now completely without paint, wearing a simple calf-length tunic fastened at both shoulders and with a single tie-in around the waist. It was such a contrast to how he had looked the night before. The ensemble was almost too simple for his features, yet he was no less exquisite for it.

Catching his attention, Sinnan pointed around the room and said, "I have to take a piss. Where's the…?"

Domitris dared to assume the meaning.

"Through that door." He pointed to the opening in the corner leading through to the washroom.

Domitris used the opportunity to go out on the balcony to get some fresh morning air. He took a deep breath and leaned against the balustrade, looking out over the gardens. In the distance, there was already activity from servants maintaining trees and bushes.

Despite the aching in his head, and still not having had a full night's worth of sleep, he was surprisingly well-rested. Sinnan's company had been a kind of fun he hadn't had in a long time. With nothing but work for the past two years, he deserved to unwind for a little bit. Besides, it was just breakfast. It was not like he would be seeing him again.

Domitris' eyes drifted to the training grounds in front of the military buildings, which were uncommonly quiet because of the festival. The trainees were usually woken up at dawn to start their morning training. He remembered all too well being young and getting chased out of bed to run laps around the palace before breakfast.

Sinnan cleared his throat behind him and came out onto the balcony. His black hair moved in the wind, and, for the first time, there was something almost timid about him.

"Sorry I panicked. I... I didn't expect to end up... here," he said, gesturing towards the inside.

Domitris scratched his neck. "Do you regret it?"

Sinnan didn't answer immediately, which made Domitris look up at him. He was met by an expression he couldn't read.

"I–" Sinnan started as if he was going to explain something, but then he stopped and slumped back against the wall next to the door, his arms folded in front of him. "No."

Domitris' heart beat a little faster.

"Well, me neither," he said, taking a small step towards

Sinnan, but then his stomach growled loudly as a reminder that he hadn't eaten last evening and had only consumed large amounts of wine since then. Sinnan raised his brows.

"I haven't eaten anything since before the show yesterday."

"Me neither. Or well, I ate *something*," Sinnan said, "but I'm still pretty hungry," he added, his steady face creeping into a smirk.

Domitris was dumbfounded for a short second, then started to laugh. "You're terrible!"

"That wasn't the impression I got from you last night," he responded and laughed too.

They left the balcony behind and went inside to the table where the platter Lyra had prepared waited for them. Cured meats were artfully displayed on silver plates next to triangles of hard cheese and bowls of nuts and grapes. Small tubs of olive oil and golden honey glistened in the morning sun, and they would be fighting the flies for it for the rest of the meal. Domitris sat and broke off a corner of bread, the flakes of salt clinging to his fingers, then passed it to Sinnan.

For the first time since interrupting the scene with Patolemus the night before, the conversation halted between them and Domitris found himself wishing the pitcher had been wine instead of water. He knew Sinnan's name, but what more did he know? That he was great company in bed, certainly, but that hardly qualified as a topic of conversation over breakfast. Why had Sinnan reacted so strangely to finding out he was with the emperor? Domitris watched Sinnan dip his bread into honey with one hand while taking three slices of cheese with the other. Mid-way through the first bite of bread, while drops of honey fell onto the table, he stopped chewing.

"What?"

Domitris figured he had been staring, so he turned his concentration to putting meat on a small plate for himself.

"Yesterday was your first night at the palace, wasn't it?"

"Was it that obvious?" Sinnan continued chewing, breaking off a small cluster of grapes and grabbing a handful of nuts to add to his plate.

"No, I mean—I feel that I would have heard about you if you had been here before."

Sinnan picked up his glass and swirled it around a bit, licking his lips.

"You're also not from Marmaras, am I right?" Domitris asked.

"Very observant of you,"

"Where *are* you from?"

"Do you want to take a wild guess?" he said, his face once again full of playfulness.

Domitris paused, looking properly at Sinnan. The black hair and the brown skin suggested somewhere to the south like Solis, but the unmistakable Solisian accent was not the one rounding his words.

"Have you seen the ocean?" Domitris asked to at least have a chance.

Sinnan smiled, then downed the rest of his water. "I certainly have."

"The east, then?"

Sinnan shook his head and nibbled at the cheese. "Not even close. Want another try?"

Domitris hesitated with the guess, but he tried it anyway. "You don't sound it, but Solis?"

He raised his brows a little. "No," was all he said this time.

"I guess I'll have to give up then," Domitris said, and took a big bite of bread.

"Háfren," Sinnan said. "In the Heathlands. Or 'the Far North', as you like to call it here."

Domitris looked him over once more. Northerners were known for being tall and rough and pale. He had never seen anyone he imagined looking less like a Háfrenian.

"I've never met someone from the Heathlands before."

"Well, now you have," Sinnan said.

"What are you doing so far south?"

"You ask a lot of questions."

"You don't answer many of them."

"Where are *you* from?" Sinnan asked, his eyes pinched.

"Here. Arenaria. The province just south of Concordia."

"So, how did you get elected emperor?"

Sinnan was giving him a taste of the same scrutiny and Domitris decided to humor him, giving thought to the question. It wasn't one he had answered before, except to himself.

"People were fed up with how things used to be. They wanted change."

Sinnan leaned his head against his fist. "And are you going to give them that?"

His face was earnest. There was no malice behind his words. It was the sort of objective question that only someone looking in from the outside could ask.

"I like to think that I will."

Sinnan only nodded in return, soaking his next bite of bread in the oil. Making jokes, talking back, asking about politics—that he wasn't a trained palace courtesan was clear, but then again, few were. Most were merely aware of what advantages birth had given them and came to the palace seeking easy fortune. He expected Sinnan was no different. Domitris was then hit with the realization that he was supposed to pay him somehow. A pang of guilt shot through him because he hadn't thought about it earlier. He looked around the room, then got up.

"Wait here," he told Sinnan, who was still happily eating. In the dresser, he found a spare coin pouch. It seemed wrong to start taking coins out even though the pouch was heavy, so he made a quick decision to give it as it was. He had, after all, had a good time. Then he went back over to the table and placed it gently in front of Sinnan and sat down in his chair.

"I don't know your rate," Domitris said, concentrating on a new piece of bread.

Sinnan picked it up, loosened the ties and peered down into it before putting it away in the folds of his clothes without commenting on it.

"So… When do you have to be somewhere?" Sinnan asked, not meeting his eyes. A warm breeze carrying the perfumed scent of jasmine blew in through the window. A bit of residual honey glistened on Sinnan's bottom lip.

"The treaty announcement is today at noon," Domitris said, and nothing more. He didn't strictly need to be present for the council activities of the morning. He could get Lyra to send word to Ignotus to stand in for him.

"Right," Sinnan said before stuffing a cheese-crusted slice of bread into his mouth.

"How about you?"

Sinnan gestured to his mouth and chewed faster. When he had swallowed, he said, "I'm going down to the marketplace today. My friends and I are setting up a booth for the festival."

"A booth? I thought you…" Domitris trailed off and could see by the look on Sinnan's face that he shouldn't finish the sentence.

He cleared his throat instead and said, "Is it with the same act as yesterday?"

"No. No, that act has its crowd, and the marketplace won't be it."

"What will you be doing, then?" Domitris was getting curious.

Sinnan smiled. "Come find us when you're there and you can see for yourself."

That did sound tempting. "I can't. I'm not going."

"What? Why?"

"The festival is for the people. If I went, they would have to make a whole official ceremony out of it and it wouldn't be the same."

"You're joking, right? Couldn't you just go anyway? I mean, unofficially? I bet not many commoners know what you look like. I passed a whole row of statues of the emperor getting here and I sure didn't."

Domitris hadn't thought about that option. From his pause, Sinnan picked up that he was considering it.

"Come on, you really should. Go with me. My friends won't be needing me much today, anyway."

"You won't be dancing?"

"Do you want me to?" Sinnan said with a smile and sucked a bit of oil off his finger.

Domitris huffed a small breath of laughter and looked off to the side. Sinnan knew how to work his clients.

"What do you say?" Sinnan asked.

Domitris shouldn't have even considered it. He should have been spending the morning getting ready for the announcement of the treaty at noon and getting to the work that had piled up. Going out only meant letting the work wait for him like a fire burning on his desk and he couldn't risk showing up for the ceremony unprepared. He looked over at Sinnan again, who sat there with nothing but the promise of his company. Domitris knew, of course, what the right answer would be, but instead he said,

"I haven't been to the marketplace in ages."

X

Booths spilled down alleys and streets the closer they got to the marketplace. They had left the main road to go south and now their path sloped downward, bringing the myriad of people and stalls into view. Stands were clustered everywhere, forming broad and narrow paths webbing out over the square in a chaotic mix of tents of various shapes, sizes, and colors. Seeing the usually vacant space around the forum transformed and thronging with people was astonishing. They passed the arch straddling the road, signifying the entrance, and the crowd grew denser by the step, the stalls and booths squeezed more tightly in between each other.

Sinnan shot him a look. "Are you ready?"

Domitris adjusted his sunscarf and looked out over the market. He was finally there and was going to see it all. Not just from afar on official business, but up close. He shoved the thought of the work he had abandoned at the palace out of his mind. "I can't wait."

He tried to keep his eyes on the road, but he was

captivated by the sights around him. The stands seemed an equal mix of Dassosdan and Marmarasi, though there were booths and people sprinkled in from the shores of the Ester Realms and the Far North as well. Everywhere, people tending the booths were shouting in a cacophony of accents, many attempting to mimic the general Marmarasi dialect to sell their wares.

As they were jostled along the packed rows, Domitris noticed the activity in the camps behind the booths as well. Thick smoke rose from simmering food and the smell wafted through the air. Men and women went about their business while the laughs and screams of children chasing each other joined the rest of the noise. The marketplace had never been this full in Domitris' memory. When the Supreme Emperor closed the gates to Concordia years ago, the influx of traders had decreased drastically from one day to the next. The only part of the marketplace that had been used for years was the large, roofed forum in the center of the plaza. It was almost unbelievable that this was happening right in front of his eyes, and all because of the Overthrow.

"Sinnan!" a clear voice shouted behind them and they both stopped.

"Oh, that's Jenine." Sinnan got on his toes to scout above the crowd.

"Who?"

Before Sinnan could answer, a stout woman in a linen shirt and skirt poked her way past a man selling seashell jewelry. Just as she closed in, a cat dashed between her feet and she stumbled, letting out a squeal while she tried to save the contents of her basket from flying out. She crashed into

Sinnan and he groaned as he caught her, almost tumbling backwards himself. When he lifted her back on her feet, she brushed blonde strands of hair away from her freckled face and checked the basket. Domitris recognized her as the one who had been telling the story at their performance the day before.

"I'm so happy I found you," she said. "We've been really worried, you know. When you didn't– What are you wearing?"

Sinnan grabbed her shoulders and turned her to Domitris.

"Hey, Jenine, meet my new friend," he said and smiled at Domitris. "I met him at the palace last night."

She looked up at him with raised brows and big green eyes that almost rivaled Sinnan's, although hers held nothing of the mystery or mischief that tinted Sinnan's.

"Is this…" she halted, looking to Sinnan again.

"This is… Aelias," he said with a knowing quirk of his eyebrow. "Aelias, this is my friend Jenine. She's part of my troupe—my family."

"Right. It's good to meet you," Domitris said, and from habit made the most used commoner greeting of putting his hand to his heart and then his stomach, even though she clearly wasn't Marmarasi. She was pale and pink and looked exactly like what Domitris imagined someone from the north would look like. Even so, she returned the greeting and added the gesture to her forehead, signaling respect.

"And you as well," she said, and added "good sir," hesitantly, as if unsure how to address him.

"No need to be formal," he said, trying to put her at ease.

"Aelias wanted to see the market, so I brought him. We were just headed to the camp so I could tell you that everything's fine," Sinnan said, and they all began walking again.

"You better," Jenine reprimanded. "Amelia is tearing everyone's head off since…" she trailed off. "Anyway, I went to stock up on a few things before we open up shop today."

Domitris glanced into the basket, where a head of cabbage lay beside some fennel, garlic, wood shavings, at least three sets of crows' feet, and a few other items he couldn't discern. He had no idea what they would be used for, but he hoped it wasn't cooking.

"I better hurry up and talk to her. Are you and Ennio managing the stand today?"

Domitris lost track of their conversation as they approached the center of the market. They passed rows of stalls selling wares of no coherent theme; dyed brocade fabric, cheeses, carved lanterns, and all sorts of animals in cages. Domitris wanted to halt every two steps to look at it all, but he was trying to keep up with Sinnan and Jenine, who moved smoothly through the crowd. They turned several corners and walked through an area where booths offered games and activities that tested skill and luck for a single coin, and shining prizes hung from the canvas canopies. When the crowd got so dense that it closed in around them, Domitris almost lost his companions from sight, but then Sinnan's hand reached back and found his own, taking hold while leading him along the paths with Jenine in front of them. Sinnan's grip was warm and firm and Domitris felt a little out of breath from the pace. He knew it was unreasonable, but he had hoped for more time alone with Sinnan.

"Where exactly is your camp?" Domitris asked, yelling to

Sinnan, who was snaking his way through the throng of people.

"Out on the edge of the market to the southeast," Sinnan said, glancing back. "We're almost there."

Everywhere Domitris looked, there was at least one place selling food and all the different smells made his mouth water, even though he had just eaten. Sinnan dragged him past an area of entertainment with nooks where people in costumes told stories and played instruments, and low stages where painted people barely dressed danced for patrons at round bronze tables. Was that how Sinnan had been getting by as well? The crowd cleared and soon the three of them could walk side by side again.

"More people have been coming every day." Jenine looked around, her plump face beaming at all the activity. "I think business will be good."

"How long have you been here?" Domitris asked.

Jenine looked at her hands while counting on her fingers.

"I suppose we've been in Concordia about a month now, wouldn't you say?" she asked Sinnan.

"A month and three days," Sinnan said, with his attention somewhere else.

"If you say so. Anyway, the marketplace is much nicer than where we were staying in Tenebris when we'd just arrived."

Tenebris? Domitris looked them both over. Tenebris was the part of Concordia where no nobles found themselves. It was the only part of the city still without sewers, and it was full of rats and thieves and people without traveling passes who couldn't get a permit to stay anywhere else in the city.

Sinnan elbowed her and cut in. "We weren't there for long.

We were just waiting to get our permit for setting up at the market."

"Right," she said, biting her lip.

"Great, we're here!" Sinnan said as they came to a halt in front of a round booth stocked with wicker baskets in varying sizes, some so small Domitris could fit them in his hand, others so big that he could hide inside them.

"Could you... wait here for a moment?" Sinnan asked.

Jenine kept her eyes on the wares in her basket, but Sinnan met his gaze, looking calm.

Domitris threw out his hands. "Sure."

"I'll be right back," he said, backing away with Jenine, and then the two of them darted off to the side. Domitris looked around, tucking his scarf a bit more around his face, hoping not to get noticed. It was hot in the early sun, but people smiled and laughed all around him, seeming to have eyes only for the entertainment. Further down the path, Sinnan and Jenine disappeared into a slim, mustard-yellow tent with a starry banner on top hanging limply in the morning heat. Domitris kept his eyes on the tent. He shouldn't have been as intrigued as he was, and he knew he shouldn't have allowed Sinnan to talk him into going with him. That he was hiding something was obvious, but Domitris couldn't help wanting to figure out what it was. He leaned forward to get a better look at the tent and noticed the sign above the entrance. A folded, wooden sign with signs of wear and scratches hung a little crooked and declared in hand-painted letters:

Alleviation, cures, amulets, and dispelling of ill omens

A smaller sign hung on the entrance:

Your fortune awaits you another time
Come back later

Domitris hardly managed to wonder before raised voices from the tent interrupted his thoughts. His curiosity got the better of him, and he moved closer.

"You *what?*" a voice shouted, and an argument broke out, though Domitris couldn't hear the words. A brown-haired head with eyes like thunder popped out for a quick second before disappearing again. She was the pale woman who had seen right through his disguise when asking for money. Domitris walked closer.

"You brought him *here?*"

The sound of Sinnan shushing and whatever he said afterwards was muffled. Domitris closed in. He was standing right next to the tent but as he leaned closer to the canvas, Sinnan came rushing out with an unreadable smile on his face.

"Not fond of waiting, I see."

"I was just…" Domitris said but didn't come up with even a half-decent excuse. The look Sinnan gave him stopped him from trying. "If your friends don't want me here, I can go."

"No. No, no, no, don't mind that. It's not every day that someone down here gets a visit from the palace," he said, looking over both shoulders. "They were just surprised."

Domitris hesitated. How much had he told them?

Sinnan put on a theatrical voice, bowed down low and said, "Welcome to our humble stand! I brought you here to show you what we do." He got up and pointed to the sign.

"Let's go find you some good fortune," he said with a wide smile.

Domitris looked from Sinnan to the sign and then back to Sinnan.

"What?"

"Good fortune. You know... you'll have more luck in your endeavors and such."

"I know what it means, but isn't that... just nonsense?"

Sinnan grinned at him. "Of course it's nonsense, but it's so much fun. Come on!"

Domitris shot Sinnan a skeptical look, but Sinnan pulled aside the goat pelt serving as a door and beckoned him inside.

As he entered, the scent of a dozen different herbs and spices overtook his senses and he did everything he could to suppress a sneeze. The tent was stuffy, and no wonder because there were four other people in there, obviously in the middle of a discussion he had interrupted. When they all stared back at him, stunned, Sinnan was quick to take over.

"Good morning, troupe. Nice to see you too. This is my friend Aelias, from the palace," he said. "Aelias, this is our stand, and these people here are my family."

From left to right, he introduced them. Jenine, who he had already met, stood at the back and took out the items from her basket and placed them on shelves. She gave a quick smile and a bow when he gestured to her. Contrasting Jenine's sweet demeanor, Amelia was the storm cloud who sat next to her on a stool at a low, round table. She had her arms crossed and didn't greet him. Domitris was pretty sure that if she'd had the ability to burn holes in him with her eyes, she would have. The young man sitting next to her, who had played the flute at their performance, was named Ennio and looked intrigued more than anything. He was twirling the end of his dark braid and had an air of self-assuredness about him that made Domitris think that he would have fit right in with the young nobles at the palace, had his circumstances of birth been different. The last person in the tent, Bardeia, was the woman with the booming voice that had been the reason he had noticed their play at all. She was the only one of them who got up from her seat after the introduction.

"Welcome, good sir," she said, moving her hand from her heart to her forehead, signifying his higher status. Standing, she was a hand taller than himself, her body built for combat, the scars on her face showing she had taken her fair share of battle. She was smiling now though, her eyes soft and welcoming. The skin pulled taut around scars on the left side of her face, making her look more intimidating than her voice led on.

"Thank you–" he said, but was interrupted by Amelia, who stood up from her stool and stormed past him out of the tent. Domitris raised a brow at Sinnan, but he only rolled his eyes.

"Jenine…" Sinnan said.

She fidgeted with a clove of garlic before putting it down. "I'll talk to her. It was nice meeting you." With a wave of her hand, she disappeared out of the tent.

"What was that about?" Domitris asked.

Sinnan took a seat on one of the stools.

"Honestly, that's just Amelia. Forget about her. We're here to have fun."

"I have to leave you as well," Bardeia said. "The camp down the road needs help setting up, and I promised to lend a hand after they secured this spot for us. But Ennio, when you're done here, if Sinnan leaves, get Amelia to come back and be here with you until I return."

"Not when she's like that," Ennio said, which solicited a very tired look from Bardeia. Domitris noticed he had a northern Marmarasi accent unlike any of the others.

Ennio crossed his arms. "Fine!"

Bardeia turned to leave but stopped in the opening and looked back over her shoulder.

"And Sinnan–" She cast an accidental look at Domitris, hesitating, as if changing her mind about what to say. "Come find us later, all right?"

Sinnan dismissed her with a wave of his hand. "I will."

She nodded, and then she was gone as well.

"Then it's just the three of us," Sinnan said, rubbing his hands together. "Ennio is all we need, anyway. Jenine's sachets are the best at regulating people's emotions, but Ennio's charms are unrivaled."

Ennio leaned his hands between his legs on the stool, looking for a moment like a lost puppy. Domitris ran a hand over his jaw, not sure what he had gotten himself into.

"It's fine, I don't need a charm," he said, but Ennio's eyes lit up and he gave a triumphant laugh.

"That's where you're wrong, good sir. Everyone needs a charm!"

Domitris looked to Sinnan, who nodded. "It's true."

Ennio got up and pointed for Domitris to sit down on the small chair on the opposite side of the table.

"We just need to figure out what kind will be most beneficial to you," he said, rubbing his chin and looking

Domitris up and down. "You don't strike me as the type who needs luck. Nor help with persuasion. How about a love potion? Oh! Maybe you have trouble in bed?" he said, sitting back down, crossing his legs.

Domitris' face went warm. "That's not–"

"No, you're right. If that were the case, Sinnan wouldn't have brought you here. No…" Ennio said, leaning forward. He squinted, looking Domitris in the eyes. "There's something else troubling you." He sat back up and crossed his arms. "You have trouble with nightmares."

How could he possibly have known that? Domitris had hardly said two full sentences.

"Everyone has trouble with nightmares," he said. "That's just a lucky guess."

"Even so, I think you will find this useful," Ennio said, getting up. He turned his back to them and rummaged through boxes and jars on the shelves, stuffing things into a tiny embroidered pouch. Then he plucked the heads off a few dried flowers, crushing the petals and adding the bits to the blend. When the pouch was full, he twisted the top to close it. With a glance back at Domitris, he ran a finger over an assortment of colored strings hanging from the side of the shelves.

"Now, which one should we choose?" he said, tapping his chin. "Blue, I think. For reflection." He turned around and fastened the indigo string around the pouch. "I sense there are memories you want to forget, and yet, you cling to them for a reason. That must mean you still have something to learn from them."

It was purposefully vague and still, everything Domitris

had ever wanted to forget started running through his head. The loss of his parents, Aelias, the night of the Overthrow… He tried not to let it get to him.

"That would be true for anyone," he said again.

Ennio didn't answer. He reached out his hand, the small pouch hanging from it by the string. "Put this under your pillow and you'll see it will work wonders."

Domitris looked from the pouch to Ennio, then back to the pouch, trying to keep the feelings aching in his chest at bay. "How much?" he asked, still skeptical.

Ennio shook his head. "Consider it a gift."

"Are you sure?" He glanced at Sinnan. It felt wrong to accept anything from them, no matter how small.

"Of course! Any friend of Sinnan's is a friend of ours," Ennio beamed, before adding, "Just remember to tell everyone where you got it."

Domitris took it and ran his thumb reverently over the embroidered stars decorating the coarse linen. "Thank you," he said, meeting Ennio's shining brown eyes. Ennio responded with a bow while Sinnan got up, his stool scraping against the ground.

"Oh well, I just wanted you to see what we do and check on the troupe before we delved in to all the fun." He turned to Ennio. "You won't miss me too much if I show Aelias here around the market, will you?"

It stung inside Domitris every time he heard that name. He really wished he had thought of another.

Ennio made an indifferent gesture. "Would you change your plans if I told you to stay?"

"I love you too. See you later. Tell the others I'll be back before noon."

"Didn't think so," Ennio said, waving his goodbye.

"Thanks for…" Domitris said, holding up the small pouch before tucking it into the folds of his clothes. The motion released the comforting aroma of chamomile, lavender, and fenugreek, as well as a few other spices he couldn't identify.

Ennio smiled a little half-smile. "Any time."

Sinnan left the tent, flipping the "Come back later" sign to "Come inside" on the way, and Domitris followed. Together, they made their way down one of the less crowded streets towards the entertainment.

XI

"Was everything all right with your friends? They seemed a little... rattled," Domitris asked.

Sinnan had been quiet since they left the troupe behind. They walked side by side along the small paths on the outer edges of the market. The tent had been stifling, and it was a relief to be out in the open again, despite the many people and the burning sun.

"Don't mind them," Sinnan said, with no concern in his voice. "They're not fond of outsiders. And Amelia and I got into an argument yesterday."

"Should I bother asking why?"

"Only if you want to hear years' worth of intrigue." Sinnan spun around and walked backwards. "Come on, forget about all that. Let's have some real fun."

Real fun. Domitris liked the sound of that. Sinnan turned his attention to the market.

"What should we do first?"

He was so easy to be around. Maybe he wasn't completely honest, but he was straightforward, and Domitris hadn't had a boring second in his company. Domitris held out a hand towards him. Sinnan looked a little perplexed but took it, coming closer.

"Afraid I'll disappear?" Sinnan smiled, and his earrings glimmered in the sunlight.

"Not really. I'm just having a good time."

"Well, that was the whole purpose of going," Sinnan said. "So, what do you want to do?"

Domitris ran over the options in his head and remembered the games they had passed earlier. It could be fun getting to show off a little.

"Want to try besting me in a game?" he asked and let go of Sinnan's hand.

Sinnan laughed heartily. "You realize you don't stand a chance, right?"

Domitris raised a brow. "Prove it."

"Come," Sinnan said with a wave of his hand and set off towards the other end of the market. Turning down the small paths closer to the forum, they passed rows of people standing in line in the downtrodden grass with bottles and wooden buckets, waiting for their turn at the drinking posts. Sinnan stopped at a small intersection.

"Before we get there, let's go down this way; there's something you need to try."

Knowing what little he did of Sinnan, that could mean almost anything. Still, Domitris followed, and they squeezed their way into an area where several stands displayed the amber banners of Auxillien. Domitris caught himself scanning the people there for any resemblance to his sister. He knew, of course, that she wouldn't be here. No officials from Auxillien would, but apparently that didn't stop something in him from hoping.

Sinnan halted in front of a round booth selling an array of sweets, varying in shape and color, presented neatly in glazed clay bowls. Tending it were two vendors, a man and a woman, both at least a decade older than Domitris, and Auxillien-looking with dark hair and skin. The woman was filling a paper cone with dried fruits for the customer next to them.

Sinnan leaned in over the counter to look at all the sweets and glanced back at Domitris. "You have to try these. They're so good."

The other vendor had been standing with his back to them, but at Sinnan's words, he turned around and greeted them with a bright smile and put his hands on the counter. "What can I do for you beautiful people on this fine day?"

His garment was folded down from both shoulders to his waist, leaving his upper body bare, pearls of sweat glistening on his skin. Domitris couldn't remember ever seeing Auxilliens in Concordia before and he was excited to see what wares they had to offer. Domitris looked over the selection.

"Get the pink ones," Sinnan whispered to him, not quite low enough to be discreet, and pointed to a bowl filled with pale pink squares.

Domitris smiled at the vendor and inclined his head towards Sinnan. "What he said."

The vendor bowed and reached for a pair of delicate wooden tongs. "Your man has good taste," he said. "An Auxillien delicacy! You can't get anything like it here in the north."

"I haven't been lucky enough to visit yet," Domitris said,

remembering the defeat when he and the entourage had arrived at the walls of Auxillien, and they had refused to let them in.

"Yes, we don't have much interaction with the north these days," the vendor said. "It's a shame, but we have to take care of our own."

Domitris knew well the inward-looking mentality of Auxilliens that had only become stronger over the past decades.

"It's good to see Auxillien's presence here after all," Domitris said while the man gently picked up the yielding squares with the tongs, placing them in a small cone one by one.

"I know we're not really supposed to since our leader is staying put, but you know, business is business," the man said, wiping his forehead with the back of his hand. "I couldn't pass up an opportunity like this."

The old customer beside them paid and left and was immediately replaced by a mother with her child. The girl started screaming and crying when she was told she couldn't grab for the sweets. Domitris smiled at the other vendor, who did a trick with a coin to amuse the little girl.

"If all goes well, something will be figured out, so Auxillien will be a proper part of Marmaras again," he said.

Sinnan got to his knees to do his own trick for the child while the mother made their order.

"Well, I think it's right what our leader is doing. Auxillien needs autonomy," the man said.

Domitris had to blink an extra time. It was strange hearing that said to his face without the usual layers of diplomacy. Was he really standing in the middle of a festival celebrating the new alliance and advocating separation?

"But isn't unity more important? Marmaras will be much better off if all the provinces work together."

"Oh, you're one of those, huh?" he said with a wide smile. "If you ask me, Concordia needs to stay out of our business. The only reason Auxillien is finally thriving is because we managed to isolate ourselves after the Supreme Emperor executed our last senator."

The woman beside Domitris picked up the girl and let her hand their coin to the woman behind the counter. After they'd said their goodbyes and left, the woman at the stand put away a few things and picked up a basket.

"I'll go get more flour," she said and kissed the man on the cheek.

Domitris couldn't let what the vendor had said pass. "But it's not the Supreme Emperor who's reigning anymore. The Elected Emperor is actually trying to–" He was cut off by the vendor who called after the woman.

"Remember to get more eggs as well, my dove!" Then he rolled up the top of the cone and put it on a scale. "Where were we? Right, I'm sure he has the best of intentions, but we're managing just fine, better even, on our own. Why would we ruin that by making a deal with that new milksop they call the emperor now? No, it's good he was turned away on his little tour. There's no way we should trust a bedwetter like that just because he talks fancy and looks good."

Domitris was dumbfounded. He shot a look to Sinnan, who raised an eyebrow and looked as though he were holding back a laugh.

"Don't you think he's on to something, though?" Domitris tried. "You can't just dismiss his ideas because you don't like him."

"You're Concordian; of course you think that," the man said with a deep laugh before he continued. "It's not about him. Concordia has pissed all over us for decades. Just because the new boy wears a different hat, he's still a noble from the palace who can do whatever he fancies. He will never understand the situation like us down here living normal lives."

A knot of anger turned in Domitris' stomach. "I think it seems like he wants what's best for all of the provinces," he said, scorned.

"That's a nice thought, isn't it? But it's more complicated than that. Don't feel bad about it. Most people can't keep track of it, anyway."

Domitris didn't know how to answer that, so he found himself nodding a little, getting out his coin for the sweets. When the man handed the cone over the counter, he said, "Who knows, maybe I'm wrong about it all. I only saw the new emperor in action yesterday and, between you and me, that Dassosdan Minister stole the show. It will be interesting to hear what he's selling out to secure this peace deal."

Domitris knew he should keep his mouth shut at this point, but he couldn't help himself. "You disagree with the peace?" he asked, taking the sweets with one hand while paying with the other.

The man shrugged. "If I'm being honest, I don't really care much about that whole deal. Either way, I don't think it will impact Auxillien that much."

"Even if war broke out again?"

"That would be a fight between Concordia, the provinces, and Dassosda. Auxillien's walls and legions will protect us."

The man must have seen the apprehension across Domitris' face because he adjusted the waist of his robes and laughed. "Oh well, we're not here to talk politics all day long! Don't look so serious. It's a nice day and you seem to be in good company. Go enjoy that instead of standing here, getting all worked up. Here, I'll hand the two of you a sample of coated almonds as a thank you for the talk. Have a nice day." The man scooped a spoonful of almonds into another cone and handed it to Sinnan.

"And the same to you," Sinnan said, and pulled at Domitris' arm when he didn't move.

"Right, have a nice day," he finally mumbled, and the two of them left the stand behind.

"I imagine that hurt a bit," Sinnan said. "He was not gentle with his opinions, huh?"

Domitris bit at the inside of his lip. It wasn't exactly what he had hoped to hear. The man had thought Domitris to be a commoner like himself and he had heard his thoughts as one. It was good to hear things like that unfiltered for once, but it didn't change the fact that it was painful to receive a critique of everything he stood for right to his face.

They stopped in the shade of a crooked oak tree.

"Hey, forget about him," Sinnan said. "Remember how a minute ago you were bragging about how you never lost a game and said you were having fun?"

Domitris couldn't help laughing. Right. He could worry about that later. He didn't have much time left with Sinnan, and he wanted to make the most of it. He forced the vendor's words out of his head. "I don't think that's exactly how that conversation went," he said, lifting a brow at Sinnan.

"Whatever. Now, *please* open the cone of sweets. When you taste them, you'll forget anything bad ever happened."

"There's no way they're that good." Domitris unrolled the top of the paper and held it out towards Sinnan. He took two pieces and shoved them in his mouth. Domitris reached into the cone and when he grabbed a square, it was molded by his fingers in the heat. Biting into it, it was soft, overly sweet, and the fragrant taste of roses spread through his mouth. It was like standing in the rose gardens of the palace on a late summer evening.

Sinnan made a slightly exaggerated moan of satisfaction as he chewed. "Aren't these the best thing you ever tried?"

Domitris licked off the powdered sugar that stuck to the tip of his fingers.

"They're good," he acknowledged.

Sinnan looked at him. "That's it? That's your reaction to the actual taste of love?"

Domitris laughed. "Is that what love tastes like?"

"I imagine it comes pretty close," Sinnan said, his head tilted.

The air was warm and saturated with the smell of food and people and animals. This was good. A kind of good he hadn't felt since… He didn't want to finish the thought. He shouldn't be feeling that way about someone like Sinnan, but right then, he just wanted the moment to last as long as possible.

"So…" Sinnan said. "Are you ready for the games?"

Domitris took a deep breath and closed his eyes to savor

everything he was feeling. Then he looked at Sinnan.

"Let's go."

There were a couple of classic ones he knew—like one where the goal was to hit an apple with an arrow from a distance and another where metal rings were thrown around a pole two people tall—but there were also some he had never seen before. One was a silly guessing game where you bet money on the weight of a pregnant goat; another was a complicated one with a lot of hoops and rules he couldn't figure out, even though he saw three different people playing it.

"Where do you want to start?" he asked Sinnan.

Sinnan looked around.

"Let's start at the beginning and work our way through."

Time became meaningless in Sinnan's company and hours passed without Domitris realizing. Sinnan had been shockingly accurate in guessing the number of beans in a large jar, Domitris had hit the apple with an arrow, both of them had managed to drink a large holder of milk in short enough time to win a prize, but neither of them had guessed the weight of the pregnant goat.

"The best one is the next one," Sinnan said. "As I see it, so far, we're even, so the next one will settle the score and we can finally declare that I'm the master of games."

"If you win," Domitris said.

"Oh, I will."

Sinnan half-ran all the way to a faded blue tent where colorful balls lay in piles on the counter and a solid board was propped up as the back wall. A small distance from the back, four tables were placed each with a milk jug on top. At first glance, the booth was empty, but at their presence, a woman only slightly younger than himself popped up behind the counter. The motion threw her into a coughing fit, and she held up a hand and gestured 'just a second'. When she was finished, she broke into a wide grin.

"So sorry about that! Welcome to the stand, Sinnan. Good to see you," she said, and they clasped their hands in greeting. She was no doubt Marmarasi, but he couldn't place her accent, and her booth bore no provincial banners.

"Hey, Eleria, are you hiding from your customers?"

"Just taking a break before the real crowding starts after lunch when people have had enough to drink for honest competition. I expect it to pick up after the ceremony," she said, and turned her eyes to Domitris. "And you brought a new friend today?"

"I did. We are here to play," Sinnan said with a smile, leaning in over the counter.

"That'll be two coins," she said, unaffected, sticking her tongue out at him. "For each of you."

Domitris fiddled with his coin pouch and paid what she asked. Eleria put out two stacks of balls in front of them.

"What do I have to do?" Domitris asked, looking from the milk jugs to Sinnan.

"See that blue circle on the back wall? You have to throw a ball aiming for that circle, then the ball has to bounce off the back wall and into the jug. If you get three of six balls into the jug, you get a prize," Sinnan explained.

Domitris looked from him to the balls to the blue circle. "That's impossible."

"Are you giving up before you've even tried?" Sinnan

teased.

"No way."

Domitris picked up the balls and got ready to throw. He focused on the circle and threw hard. Too hard—the ball bounced off the wall and came flying back, almost hitting him in the face. Sinnan and Eleria laughed so much it sent Eleria into another coughing fit. Domitris was determined to do better on the next throw, but this was much too soft and hardly reached the back wall, which only resulted in their laughing starting all over again. He threw the last four balls the best he could, but none of them ended up near the milk jug.

"I told you it was impossible."

Sinnan and Eleria shot each other a quick look.

"Well, then it's my turn. Move over." Sinnan nudged Domitris to the side with his shoulder. He took a deep breath and shook his hands. He got ready for his throw, and the first ball bounced beautifully off the back wall and right into the jug. So did the second, and the third. The fourth missed by a hand, but the last two went in as well as the first three. Domitris gaped at him, mouth open, as Eleria winked at Sinnan, handing him his prize. "Congratulations, sir! You have done the impossible and won yourself a lucky token!"

Domitris was irrationally annoyed that Sinnan had done so much better. Sinnan took the prize and laughed as he thanked her.

"See you later, Eleria. Good luck with the customers."

He took Domitris by the arm and led him away. When they were out of earshot, Domitris asked, "How on earth did you do that?"

"Is it so hard to believe I'm just better than you?" Sinnan

said with triumph saturating his words.

Domitris crossed his arms, gritting his teeth.

"Fine," Sinnan said, "I'll let you in on a little secret: don't aim for the blue circle, it's much too high for the balls to bounce back the right way." He laughed at the outrage on Domitris' face. Of course, it had been a trick.

"Isn't that misleading people?"

"Only when people are stupid enough to fall for it," he said, elbowing Domitris in the side.

Time was running out as they sat on an old ruin of a wall, eating the lamb skewers Domitris had bought for them on Sinnan's recommendation. Sinnan licked away the sauce running down his fingers while Domitris let out a comfortable sigh. The chatter from the crowd around them was refreshing in an overwhelming way and he let himself listen in on bits and pieces of conversations.

"Did you enjoy it?" Sinnan asked, still chewing. There was something so immediate and easy about him that made Domitris yearn to stay.

"I did. I wish I could come here every day of the festival."

"Can't you?"

Domitris dared to imagine it. "We'll see. Maybe if the next days go well, there will be time for me to sneak out."

"Sounds like a plan," Sinnan said, fiddling with the bracelets on his arm. Then his smile vanished.

"Oh, shit—" Panicked, he looked around himself, patting the folds of his clothes, forgetting the grease on his fingers.

"Did you lose something?"

"Shit! It's not here! My bracelet..."

Domitris looked at the three he was still wearing, all

twisted gold of different makings. Sinnan buried his face in his hands and groaned.

"Hey, I'll check at the palace. It must have fallen off in my room."

"It could be anywhere," Sinnan said, staring into the distance.

"If it's there, I'll find it."

Sinnan shook his head, composing himself. "Thank you."

The ten o'clock palace bells chimed above the noise, reminding Domitris that he had the most important speech of his life to give in just two hours. The celebrations the day before had brought people together, but now the time had come to see if the treaty would tear them apart when the terms were finally announced to the public.

"I have to get going." He took a last large bite from the skewer and got up. "I have to be at the Panjusticia for the ceremony before the midday bell."

Sinnan rose as well. It had been fascinating to get a taste of his life. To know that he had a group of people he was so close to—Domitris could only dream of that. He got out the small pouch he'd gotten at their stand and felt the embroidery again. He would put it under his pillow when he went back to change.

"Thank you for today," he said, then hesitated. "What do I owe you for your time?"

Sinnan came closer. "How about I come see you again tonight and we'll figure that out?"

Domitris raised an eyebrow and looked towards the palace. He shouldn't accept the offer. He'd had his fun, and it wouldn't look good for him to be seen with a regular courtesan at the palace. The nobles were gossips and conspirators, and people might distrust where his priorities lay if they saw him spend time with a courtesan instead of doing administrative work from sunrise to sundown. This was not the time to give them anything to fuel their slander. He looked again to Sinnan, who was carelessly spinning one of the gold bands at his wrist. There was nothing inside him that wanted to say no.

"That sounds fun," he said.

Sinnan smiled a quick one-sided smile and wiped his hands on his garment.

"Tonight, then."

XII

When the noon bell of the palace was echoed by the bell towers of the Panjusticia, Domitris stood ready in the empty main hall. His helpers hovered around him like wasps around wine, but there were no sounds other than their mumblings, making the place feel even emptier. Usually, the Panjusticia was crowded with people in rows throughout the hall, sometimes far out into the streets, who came to have their grievances heard.

He knew Dia and her entourage were somewhere in the building as well. Domitris brushed a hand down the folds of his garment and shot a look at the closed gates. The murmur of the crowd beyond set him on edge, and he stretched his neck from side to side to loosen up.

"Stand still," Lyra grumbled and went in a circle around him to make sure the folds were straight. She tucked in a stray rope-ending that had come loose from the ties around his torso.

From the moment he came back, she had reprimanded him about sneaking off again, lecturing him about how irresponsible it had been to return so late, and when he admitted that he had been with Sinnan all morning, she outright scolded him as if he were a little boy again. Domitris only managed to appease her by reminding her that they were late and had to hurry to get ready, so now she was using her pent-up anger to make sure he was impeccably—though hard-handedly—dressed.

Back in the day, before the Overthrow, the Supreme Emperor or Empress of Marmaras would have been dressed up with a gilded breastplate and armor as well as a sword and a cape for a large interstate event like this, no matter whether they had ever commanded an army. With the new alliance, Domitris had advocated for the importance of toning down the outward image of Marmaras as a warfaring nation.

Unlike the splendor from the night before, what he wore now was classical and simple in the conservative Marmarasi style. The whole garment was deep, dark blue with several under-tunics and two long pieces of fabric that were draped over his shoulders and fastened invisibly at his waist.

He liked how powerful it made him look, but the damp heat was suffocating, and he wanted to tear off at least three layers.

Lyra took a step back, biting the inside of her lip as though she wasn't quite satisfied. She snatched the circlet from his head, polished it in a fold of her own garment and put it back. He had to bend down for her to reach the top of his head properly and she took the opportunity to fix the parting of his hair while she was at it. When she looked sufficiently pleased, Hephakles dared to approach. Lyra had sent him running once already, threatening to step on his bare feet if he

AS WE FALL

didn't give her space to finish dressing Domitris.

"Your Highness, the speech?" Hephakles reached out a hand.

Domitris had been clutching the paper in one hand, running the words over in his head, though he hadn't needed to look at it again. He had forgotten he was still holding it, and when he handed it back to Hephakles it was creased and wrinkled where his hand had been.

"Now remember," Hephakles said, putting the speech away into the folds of his clothes, "look up at all times, stand tall and speak as loudly and clearly as you possibly can."

"Yes, as always, I know," he snapped without meaning to.

Hephakles nodded, trying to calm his idle hands. He looked more nervous than Domitris felt, but then again, Hephakles always did. He was just doing his job, and Domitris knew he should be more patient with him. Leaning forward, he gave Hephakles a pat on the shoulder.

"It'll be fine. We finally get to act after all the talking. It's actually happening—everything we've worked for."

With a relieved sigh, Hephakles' eyebrows traveled upwards.

"You're right. It's still unfathomable, Your Highness."

As if from thin air, Captain Alba appeared behind Hephakles. She stood more than a head taller than him, and when Domitris' eyes went to her, Hephakles turned and gulped at her presence.

"Your Highness." She folded her hands behind her back as she waited for Domitris' attention. She was in full military regalia, the bright crimson of her uniform stark against her white hair.

"Thank you," Domitris said to Hephakles to let him go.

With a polite nod to both of them, Hephakles darted away as fast as he could without looking disrespectful.

"Yes?"

"Everything is ready. The perimeter is secure, and all guards are at their posts." She looked as unamused as she always did, her eyes narrow and cool, like a falcon waiting to strike.

"Good, well done."

She nodded, then turned on her heel, the red cape billowing behind her as she went out the door.

"We're ready now, Your Highness," Hephakles said, reappearing behind him. "Get in position."

Considering he was the emperor, he was surprisingly often given orders. He shot a look at Hephakles but did as he was told and walked over to stand behind the gates. Someone behind him blew a sharp signal horn, which resulted in a resounding fanfare blaring beyond the gates. With it, the doors parted.

He was ready.

Stepping into the harsh sunshine, the light blinded him, and the cheers and noise of thousands of people hit him like a storm. People filled the seats of the two-storied, columned archways that flanked the courtyard as far as the eye could see, and they were all cheering uncontrollably at his appearance. Here and there in the top rows, they were hanging out over the railings, waving bright scarves. In the ground rows, children squeezed their way through the legs of the guards to get a closer look while old people huddled around in the shadows to avoid the heat. He held up his hand in a waving salute and greeted the people with a smile.

These were his people. This was what he had fought for. It was nothing like it had been on the tour where, in some provinces, his arrival had been welcomed with lukewarm enthusiasm at best. It had always been said that the emperor belonged in Concordia, and right now, he felt it. With the cheering in this moment and the success of the show the night before, for once, everything was going exactly as he had hoped it would. The years of planning and hard work would pay off, and it was only a matter of days.

He kept waving to the crowd while he walked the distance from the hall to the raised marble podium in the courtyard, stretching out in front of him. Historically, this was the place the emperor had addressed the army in times of war, meaning it was big enough to hold all the legions of the once great empire.

Since it hadn't been used for militaristic purposes for decades, Domitris had turned it into the Panjusticia, where commoners could go to get their complaints heard.

He reached the carved steps of the podium and ascended. The last time it had been used for a gathering this large was exactly two years ago, when the new rule had been declared and again a month later for the election. That month had been one of the most hectic in his life; organizing a campaign alongside Ignotus and the handful of other candidates all while dealing with the chaos inside the palace. Every day, he had made speeches in Concordia while his group of supporters, led by Hossia, had campaigned for him in the provinces. After four long weeks, people could vote in every province, and in the capital endless rows of people had waited in line to cast their votes into the massive urns erected on the podium. The next week, he had stood where he stood now, to be crowned in front of all of Marmaras. That day, people had not been standing in the columned rows to the sides but had filled the courtyard.

Presently, the grounds had been cleared and there were guards everywhere to keep people in line. From the podium to the end of the courtyard, re-callers were instated to repeat the words to carry the message, since it was impossible for one person's voice to reach across the entire area.

Domitris raised his arms, signaling for the crowd to quiet down. A surge of pleasure went through him as people followed his command. His pulse spiked from all the faces looking back at him. At moments like this, he felt in his heart that he was born to lead a people.

When the noise eventually subsided, the next fanfare blared, and the gates opened again.

Dia walked out with a confidence he hadn't seen rivaled many times in his life. Coming towards him, she looked like a star personified, with her pale golden hair and all dark clothes. She was wearing the Dassosdan version of ceremonial clothing; it was like nothing Domitris had seen before. She wore a plain dark, almost black, tunic, but not like the ones in Marmaras; this had slits up to her waist in both sides and was fastened with a broad metal belt over her stomach. When she walked, a pair of loose pants tucked into closed boots coming all the way up to her knees were visible beneath. Dassosda had no king or queen, so she wore no crown, but on her shoulders gleamed a pair of sharp epaulets over a long-sleeved shirt that clearly signified *her* rank as the leader. It looked strong and official, but it was also painfully Dassosdan in the way that it was designed for a somewhat cooler climate and not the baking midday sun of Marmaras.

Coming forth, she looked neither intimidated nor uncomfortable with the crowd as she waved at them. On one hand, he didn't care for being outshone, but on the other, he was as intrigued as everybody else to see her in action. She had proven her ability to handle an audience the day before, the way her words demanded attention and respect. Today, the crowd cheered every bit as loudly for her as they had for him.

She climbed the stairs and stepped onto the podium, facing him. The cheers raged on, and they stood, relishing them, smiling to each other. Despite their initial meeting, he thought of her as an ally. When the moment had lasted long enough, the crowd was hushed to silence and Domitris turned to the people, breathed deeply, and got ready to speak.

"Dear friends from the north. On behalf of the Marmarasi people, I bid you a most sincere welcome."

As he spoke, the re-callers repeated everything he said word for word like a great echo.

"We have all worked hard for this day to come true and we are honored, humbled, and grateful for the peace to finally become a reality. We will no longer have to send our sons and daughters to the front lines. The century of war is coming to an end."

He paused, adding space for the message to carry, and looked around at the countless faces turned to him. It was a victory just saying those words. Delivering the next part, clearly and with no hesitation, was crucial.

"Peace," he started, "rarely comes without compromise, and this one is no exception. Marmaras is entering a new era and, for us to prosper anew, we have to leave old methods behind." He looked around. There was no change in the faces yet. "That is why it has been decided that Marmaras will accept all of Dassosda's terms for the treaty unconditionally. And with it, the war," he said, pausing for the last words to have the necessary impact, "will officially be over." The silence broke as mumbling rushed through the crowd. He couldn't let it catch. He raised his voice.

"We are here to announce these terms before we sign the treaty on the last day of the festival. From tomorrow, if you have questions or concerns about what this will mean for you and your family, you can come to the Panjusticia and you will be heard."

The mumbling settled and was replaced by reluctant anticipation. Now was the time to get it out there.

"The first of these terms has already come into force and is why we stand here today: the complete opening of the borders, as well as retrieval of all guards from the border outposts. This functions both ways. Previous trade routes will be re-established and wealth to the realm will no longer be acquired by conquests and blood, but by trading with the north."

He took a step forward.

"The second term is that Marmaras will diminish its armed forces under the crown to half the size of the current army. This goes for all provinces pledged to the crown as well. Dismissed soldiers will be compensated and aided in finding gainful employment."

Many started clapping and cheering loudly, most likely parents who had lost children to war. But now there were also a fair number of people who were looking to one another and frowning. Domitris cast a glance towards the closest row where the council sat. The ones he had expected nodded, while others let their passive scowls speak for them, Gaius among them. He turned back to the masses and braced himself. When he announced the next part, it could not be taken back.

"The third," he continued, "is that Dassosda from here on will be regarded as a nation of its own and any former claim to the land by Marmaras will be forfeited."

This conjured gasps and the precursors for shouting. Domitris tried not to let it affect him. He forced himself to keep his eyes ahead and not look over at Dia. How could anyone think that the peace could be settled while they still claimed Dassosda as part of the empire? Guards along the flanks stepped up to regain order. Domitris took another deep breath. There was no going back now.

"With this follows the inevitable fourth term. When the treaty is signed, Marmaras no longer has any other territories than those within our borders and will therefore no longer hold its status as an empire but will become a kingdom instead. The Elected Emperor will become the Elected King."

This term had been hard for even Domitris to swallow, but he understood the necessity of it. As long as Marmaras considered itself an empire, war would never end. The need to conquer would persist. It had been the most contested term within the palace walls, and it would have been naive to think the public would find it any easier. The thought of Marmaras as the center of an empire was part of their culture. It was in their blood. He had expected the shouting and the angry thumping of feet, but he had only hoped for the cheers that also billowed up from all around the courtyard. As expected, it was a mixed reception, and the cheering barely overpowered the shouting. It nagged him. The public sentiment could turn and become dangerous if it weren't managed. He had experienced up close how the many could overpower the few.

He looked from one side of the courtyard to the other, his heart pounding against his ribs. A hand graced his shoulder and Dia came forward to take the center of the podium. She seemed too calm; the realization that they could be in danger if she didn't manage her part of the speech clawed at his nerves.

"People of Marmaras, my brothers and sisters from Dassosda," she said, her voice sharp, and the crowd quieted again. The Dassosdan edge to her words was harsher when she shouted. "Today we make history!"

The silence stretched while she looked at the audience all the way around. "I promise you," she said with emphasis on each word, "this day will be remembered. It will not be easy, but it will be worth it in the end. This treaty will make our countries prosper and flourish and not because we are fighting, but because we are cooperating."

Domitris took in the sight of her as she spoke. Her success the day before hadn't been because of luck, it had been because of carefully cultivated skill. She didn't react to the emotions that fluttered through the crowd—she formed them.

"There has been so much animosity between our peoples for so long because of decisions made by our ancestors, but we will let it divide us no longer. Standing united will always make us stronger. Every fiber of my being believes that, and looking at you side by side today makes me trust that feeling. Together, we are doing now what no one has managed for almost a century—not because they couldn't, but because they wouldn't!"

The disapproving muttering died down. It was as if everyone present held their breath, turning over her words in their head.

"The will to move forward," Dia continued, "is always the first step on a longer journey towards reconciliation." She paused again, then added more softly, "I am proud of all of you. Together, we *will* succeed."

For a second, time stood still. The shouts of anger had been drowned out by her words, and all attention returned to the podium. Then clapping broke loose, the sound like a herd of animals stampeding toward them.

Relief rushed through Domitris, and something fell into place within him. The years of written correspondence hadn't prepared him for how valuable an asset she would be. She smiled at him with raised eyebrows as if to say, *'That wasn't half bad.'*

They stepped towards each other and the gap between them became no more than a pace. When the fanfare sounded once again, they reached out their hands and met in a firm handshake that cemented the alliance. They let the gesture linger while the clapping turned into cheering again. Dia looked as calm and in control as ever, but this close, he could see the sun getting to her too, the tips of her bangs wet against her forehead. As the call from the horn ended, they let go. Within the second it took for them to move apart, an arrow materialized out of thin air and bit into the flesh of Dia's shoulder.

The world ground to a halt for part of a second before anyone realized what had happened. Then Dia cried out a shriek that made Domitris' skin crawl. It took a moment, but then the people in the closest rows started screaming and shouting and the noise rippled through the crowd like a stone thrown into still water. No one had apparently seen where the arrow had come from, because every guard just stood and looked around in bewilderment. Turmoil broke out in the rows between the columns, where people shoved and jostled to get away from the cage the seats would become if they were under attack. Children howled while guards pushed and shouted to get people into lines. Domitris searched the rooftops. Just as he caught a glimpse of a hooded figure disappearing behind an edge, he was grabbed by the shoulders and yanked off the podium by Alba.

"Get him! He was on the roof!" he shouted, pointing for the spot as she dragged him away.

"My guards are on it," she hissed. "We have to get you to safety."

He struggled in her grip as he craned his neck to look for Dia. She was kneeling on the polished stone surface of the podium while two scholars in green medical robes attended her, busy pulling the cut-off arrow out through her arm. Dia was clenching her jaw, wincing in pain, but she didn't make a sound. They had cut off most of her long sleeve to get to the wound. When they pushed through the last bit of the shaft, she groaned in relief, but then the blood started flowing freely, running down her arm.

"Do something!" Domitris shouted to Alba in the noise, and she pushed him forward, hard.

"I am. Now, move."

All around them, people knocked each other over in the rows and Domitris kept stopping, trying to turn around, wanting to stop the chaos.

"Get the crowd under control before someone is trampled to death!" he shouted at her.

"Your Highness, we are on it!" she shouted right back at him, tightening her grip, her fingers digging painfully into his shoulder. "Now get inside before they get you too, and this gets even worse."

"The Minister—" he protested.

"—Is right behind us! You need to calm down and get to safety," she growled. Before he could make any more protests, they were inside the silence of the main hall of the Panjusticia once more. Alba handed him over to three palace guards before she rushed out the door again and disappeared from his vision. He took three helpless steps to one side, then to the other, before turning around, headed for the gates again. In the same moment, they swung open, and Dia was carried inside.

"We have to move her directly to the palace," one of the scholars said as they walked past him.

He hurried to her side, keeping up with their pace. "Did you see anything?"

Her eyes were stern, her skin pale and clammy. "No more than you did."

Domitris nodded. "We'll find them," he said in desperation. She made no answer, only closed her eyes. He stopped following and they disappeared with her down the steps to the corridor leading to the palace. The gates opened up again and a new guard came rushing in with a grim look on his face.

"Have you caught the archer?"

There was a strange pause.

"Well?" Domitris hissed, taking a step forward, wanting to wring the words out of him.

The guard flinched, then stuttered out, "Your Highness, you'd better come see this."

"Tell me what's going on here," he demanded from a guard on the edge of the chaos.

"She's dead, Your Highness, the perpetrator. Seems like she was shot by an arrow herself while climbing down the building."

"Shot? By whom?"

The guard shook his head.

"We don't know. It wasn't any of our men."

Domitris shook with frustration as he pushed through the onlookers gathered in a big circle outside the courtyard. In the center, a short woman lay dead on the ground, her legs at an odd angle and an arrow in her chest, her eyes still open. It was clear she was a Dassosdan insurgent, wearing a gray robe over a russet tunic and loose-fitting pants that tied at the ankles. No one in Marmaras would wear clothing like that.

A medical scholar stood with Alba, who was kneeling beside the archer. Domitris gritted his teeth. He couldn't make sense of it.

"Why was a Dassosdan shooting at the Minister?"

Alba and the scholar exchanged a glance that made Domitris' blood boil.

"What?"

Alba looked up at him. "We don't think the arrow was meant for the Minister, Your Highness. It was meant for you."

XIII

Domitris barged into the guardroom with Ignotus in tow, interrupting the heated argument Alba was having with two Dassosdan officials.

"How could this happen?" Domitris yelled.

Alba stood at the end of a dark wooden table, her ears bright red, her shoulders tensed up around her neck, her hands balled into fists. "As I've been explaining for the past half hour, we don't know." She sounded as agitated as Domitris. "We had guards posted on the rooftops, but they didn't see the shooter until it was too late."

"That excuse isn't good enough," Domitris sneered, and Alba completely lost her temper.

"It wasn't an excuse, it was an explanation!"

He had never seen her like this. Personally, Domitris didn't know her very well, but it was common knowledge that she couldn't stand being in the wrong. He tried softening his tone, knowing she wouldn't like the next question. "Is every guard accounted for?"

There had been problems with guards taking bribes in the

past, letting people who were willing to pay stick their nose into any kind of palace business, but Alba was one of the reasons they had got that under control. Still, he had to ask. The personal offense was vibrant on her face.

"Every single one," she said, enunciating each word clearly.

"This shouldn't have happened," Ignotus said briskly, stepping up beside Domitris.

Alba took an unrestrained step forward, boiling. "How dare you whelps come in here and tell me how to do this job? None of you could have hindered this. Not even you." She pointed a finger to Domitris' chest. "I told you we were short on guards, didn't I?"

"And I told you to get it under control!"

"How am I supposed to do that when you keep sending guards out of Concordia to the provinces? This is your fault!" Alba roared.

How dared she? Providing guards to help in the provinces had been essential to strengthen the provinces' allegiance to the crown.

Ignotus stepped in front of Domitris. "I think we should try continuing this calmly," he said, with emphasis on the last word.

Alba took half a step back and took on a more dignified posture. Domitris exhaled. He needed to settle down to get anything constructive out of the conversation.

"Do you have any theories about who might have been behind this?"

Alba glanced sideways at the Dassosdans. "You saw her. You saw what she was wearing. To me, that's your answer right there. The Dassosdans were never here to make peace, only to incite chaos while they still have the advantage."

"So, you believe this is a Dassosdan conspiracy?"

"I have no reason to suspect otherwise. The fact that they are shit marksmen and nearly took out their own leader instead almost makes it amusing."

"This is outrageous!" one of the Dassosdans roared. "How can you stand there and let her and say that? You cannot let accusations like that fly before the situation has been investigated."

Alba huffed. "Come on, they'll say anything to cover it up! How can you be so blind?"

"That's enough!" Domitris slammed his fist on the table, and the three of them quieted.

"I want this squabble over immediately." He turned to the Dassosdans. "I apologize. I will discuss this with the Minister when I'm done here. Please excuse us."

They looked from Domitris to each other, contempt plain on their faces. As they marched out, one of them said, "This insult will not be taken lightly."

Domitris turned, glaring at Alba, who stood quietly, grinding her teeth. Rage churned inside him, tearing through his body. If her words affected the tenuous peace he had painstakingly built between the two nations, everything he had worked for would come crumbling down.

He had to cool the blaze of anger in his chest, or it would affect his voice. As calmly as he could muster, he said, "We will have a serious discussion about your position here when the festival is over. Until then, I'm stripping you of your title. I want you out of my *sight*."

Alba scoffed, her fists clenching at her sides. "You will

AS WE FALL

regret that," she said, vicious anger coating her words. "You know that no one can do it as well as I can."

"Get out," he said, facing her head on. He didn't want to hear another word from her. He just wanted her gone.

She glowered at him, then picked up her helmet and stormed out, the crimson cape flapping behind her.

With a trembling hand, he slammed the door shut. He and Ignotus looked at each other in the sudden silence.

"You make rash decisions when you get angry," Ignotus said.

Domitris didn't need a reprimand just now. "I need you to take over management of the guard."

Ignotus raised his brows. "Me?"

"Yes. You know you were second choice, anyway. It just made sense to give it to Alba to keep your schedule more open. I know it's a lot to take on, but just until the end of the week, then we will find someone else."

Ignotus nodded slowly. "Of course, Your Highness." He placed a hand on Domitris' shoulder. "You can count on me."

When he knew he couldn't wait any longer, Domitris walked down the corridors towards the north wing of the palace to find Dia's room. He had drawn it out, trying to think of some way this wouldn't end badly, but it had resulted in nothing but the shadows growing longer. The guards now posted in every doorway stepped aside when he walked by. Reaching her door, he paused again, looking around the corridor for something, anything, to aid him, but there was nothing there except low reclining couches strewn with red velvet pillows.

He knocked. Dia's voice, sounding surprisingly gentle,

welcomed him in.

She sat at her desk, her back turned to him, scribbling on a piece of parchment. She was wearing a new shirt, still long-sleeved. If he hadn't known better, he would have attributed the stiffness of her back to her general manner of carrying herself and not the fact that she'd just had an arrow sticking out of it. She put down the stylus and turned to look at him but didn't get up. Her face was even paler than usual. Domitris did his best to relax his shoulders.

"Forgive me for intruding, Minister," he said. "Are you... all right?"

"Thank you, but let us skip the formalities for now. We have more important matters to consider than etiquette," she said with the inkling of a smile. "You can call me Dia."

He nodded, then walked in and stood behind one of the chairs by a small table. She kept an eye on him and gestured for him to sit.

"Have you already contacted Dassosda?" he asked as he sat. Dia didn't look nearly as tired as Domitris thought she should.

"You know I had no choice. They will hear about it in the morning from every Dassosdan present. I wrote them as soon as I returned in the hopes that my account of the events will reach the government first. I'm advocating that this isn't a break of the ceasefire because of the–" she paused, glancing out the window, "circumstances. We can't yet say who opened fire on whom."

Domitris relaxed back in his chair, letting out a sigh. "That will buy us some time."

She gave a brief nod and looked back at him. Even with a

wounded shoulder, her posture put Domitris' to shame, but he couldn't be bothered to put on airs. Exhausted from anger and fear and chaos, his shoulders slouched, and his hands lay limply in his lap.

"I don't know what to say. I don't understand how this could happen."

"No, but it did. Now we have to find a way to deal with it." She winced when she leaned back against the chair. It was the first sign she had shown of the injury.

"How's your arm?"

She raised her brows slightly and looked down on her shoulder. "It's still there. Trust me, I can feel it," she said and flashed a smile. "You know, your scholars said that I'll never wield a sword again with this arm," she added and looked up at him with an expression he couldn't read at first, but then it dawned on him.

"You've never wielded a sword."

She brushed a strand of hair out of her face. "No. And I hope I'll never have to. Not a single Dassosdan politician is from the army, did you know that?"

Domitris let the comment hang unanswered in the air.

Dia sighed and shifted in her seat. "May I speak plainly?" she asked.

"I hoped you would."

"I'm not sure what to think. I heard about the archer and how it's said that she was Dassosdan and that you were the real target. But I'm not convinced. I have my own thoughts about what happened, of course, but it does seem very muddled. I think there's more behind this than it seems."

She paused and looked at him. She was right. Domitris had

been searching for a straightforward answer, but like her, he was reaching the conclusion that there probably wasn't one.

"I agree," he said, turning his hands up. "The question is, what do we do? What happened today is a bad sign. I'm not sure it went to plan, which means we could still be facing danger."

She stroked her chin. "Indeed."

Silence fell while each of them got lost in contemplation. Domitris knew what he had to ask, but he searched for the right words. Until now, she had been nothing but an asset, so he decided to trust her with his thoughts.

"What do you think is the right thing to do? Do we need to cancel the festival to keep the people out of danger? Do we postpone the signing of the treaty until the perpetrator has been caught and brought to justice? Whatever message we send could turn the tides of the sentiment of the public. We need to act carefully."

A furrow formed on Dia's forehead as she thought. "I think that is out of the question. The festival is meant to bring people together through interaction and celebration, and that is what we need to back up the treaty. If we cancel, we only show that our combined nations are not stronger than one single arrow."

He weighed her words. It was the answer he had hoped for. It would have been good to have had an adviser half as sharp as her around.

After a small pause, she continued. "To cancel is to show weakness to the culprits, whichever side they are from. The treaty must be signed at all costs. You know as well as I that this is the one chance we get. Not much has to go wrong before we stand on the verge of open war yet again." She looked out of the window, her eyes darting with thoughts. "Dassosda fears invasion so much that they will strike first if they feel the risk arising. The embers of the last battle are still smoldering, just waiting to be rekindled."

Domitris exhaled. "We can't have that."

"No, we can't," she answered in a soft voice.

Domitris tapped his finger against his knee. "There are enough on both sides who would choose that option. We need to be the counterweight."

"I agree," she said. "We continue as planned."

Domitris rose from his chair. "I guess that's it, then. Unless you think there's more we need to discuss?"

Dia rose as well. "If you don't mind, Your Highness, why don't you join me for a drink before you go? I think we should celebrate that both of us are leaving this day alive. And there are still many things to discuss about the future of our joined nations."

He raised a brow at her. She still stood tall, even though the afternoon was bleeding into the early hours of the evening. His own body ached from the tension of the day. He couldn't imagine how she was feeling.

"I wouldn't mind a drink, but let us save the important political decisions for another time."

She smiled and relaxed her stance. "Very well." She gestured to a couch on the opposite wall. He sat while she went to the back door and called to her servant for refreshments.

"Now," he said when she joined him, "tell me what I have still to learn about Dassosda."

As he left Dia's room after the last bell had rung, he had a feeling in his stomach that everything would look brighter by morning. What had happened today would not stop them or the future they had in store. He yawned, only then realizing how tired he was. It was well into the night and his shadow from the torchlight was his only company as he walked down the corridor. He couldn't wait to collapse onto his bed and sleep all night, hopefully without the gore of the day turning into a new nightmare. When he finally reached his chamber doors, he was happy to close the polished wood on the world behind him. Stumbling for his bed, something flickered in the corner of his eye.

    He wasn't alone.

XIV

The single oil lamp by his bed lit only the corner of the room, leaving the rest in shadow. But framed by moonlight was a dark shape, sitting quietly by the window, looking at him. For a moment, Domitris couldn't breathe past the tension in his body.

"I heard what happened," Sinnan said. "The whole city is talking about it."

In the turmoil, Domitris had forgotten everything about the engagement they had made earlier. He sighed, letting his body relax. Despite the initial shock, he wasn't wholly angry about the distraction.

"How did you get in?"

Sinnan sat relaxed in the chair as if he had been there for a while. By the empty platter and half-empty cup of mint water, it was obvious Lyra had been by.

"It was surprisingly easy. I just walked in through one of the doors close to your quarters and told the guards that the emperor had requested me in his rooms," he said, pretending to inspect his fingernails. "They all seemed to believe me, and someone even gave me directions. Maybe you should consider getting the security around here reinforced." His eyes were bright and playful in the low light.

Domitris stopped, his pulse quickening. How could the guards be so reckless after what had just happened?

Sinnan saw the expression on his face and quickly jumped to admission.

"Hey, no, I was just joking. Lyra let me in. The guards were actually holding me up and getting quite pissy. If she hadn't come, I could have spent the rest of my days in the palace dungeons."

Domitris sighed, rubbing his neck. "The palace doesn't have any dungeons."

Sinnan held up his cup. "You should hold on to her, you know. Lyra. She makes excellent drinks," he said and took a sip.

Domitris huffed a breath of amusement. Sinnan's laid-back charm was so much easier to deal with than everything else that was going on.

"I don't know what I would do without her. She's been there for me my whole life." He sat down on the edge of the bed, facing Sinnan, who regarded him carefully.

After a small silence, Sinnan said, "There's chaos out there tonight. People are on edge."

"I know," sighed Domitris.

"Is she all right? The Dassosdan leader?"

"Well… her wounds will heal, but now we face much bigger problems."

Sinnan propped a foot up on his chair and rested his arm on his knee. "I'm glad she survived. It sounded awful."

Sounded? All of Concordia had been there.

"You weren't in the crowd?"

Sinnan looked down. "No. We had matters to deal with."

Domitris remembered the glimpse of tension between Sinnan and his troupe that morning. A thought crept up on him. Could they be involved?

"Is everything all right between you and your friends?"

Sinnan smiled a little and ran a hand through his hair. "Don't worry about them. Our problems aren't exactly huge political issues."

Sinnan had been cryptic from the start. Did he know more than he was letting on?

"It was an unskilled marksman," Domitris said, keeping a close eye on Sinnan's reaction. "They say the arrow was meant for me."

Sinnan looked up at him, and the tone in his voice changed. "Why?"

The surprise was genuine. Or he was an exceptional liar. Domitris had to push it a bit further.

"No one knows yet. No one agrees on anything. Some say it's a Dassosdan conspiracy, some say it's Marmarasi rebels dissatisfied with the treaty. Others say it's rogues trying to monger war," he added, keeping eye contact.

There was no reaction in Sinnan's eyes other than mild surprise.

Domitris sighed. "Only one thing is for certain—they've managed to create division between every faction."

Sinnan adjusted his position. "I'll say."

They sat quietly in the darkness, the lamplight flickering, casting unruly shadows around the room. Domitris looked

Sinnan over again and felt stupid for even considering it.

He ground his palms into his eyes. "I have to get to the bottom of this. I can't believe I have worked so hard for this for years, only to see it crumble between my fingers in less than a day."

Sinnan rose, unhurried, and came to him. He wasn't wearing the white palace garments he had borrowed earlier that morning. Instead he wore an ankle-length burgundy tunic with slits up to his hips, ensuring glimpses of his legs with each step. His golden earrings and bracelets complemented the fabric perfectly. He brushed down Domitris' arm, taking his hand. Something about the air in the room changed and his own moans from the night before echoed in his mind. His heartbeat picked up pace as Sinnan placed one knee on the bed beside Domitris' lap and placed his hand on the back of Domitris' head.

"How about I make you forget all of that for a little while?"

The smell of bonfire smoke clung to his clothes. A frustrated breath escaped Domitris and, despite exhaustion to his core, he felt himself wanting it. He closed his eyes and let Sinnan move closer, lifting his other knee to the bed to sit astride him. Sinnan ran a hand through Domitris' hair before he put his mouth on his and kissed him briefly, staying close.

Yes. This.

Domitris wanted to hold on to him and not let go. To stay like this and never have to worry about the world again. Domitris' hand moved to the back of Sinnan's waist. He squeezed him closer, kissing him back. He let the kisses travel down Sinnan's neck and soon, moist breath brushed his ear.

Sinnan took hold of the shorter hair on the back of his head and led their mouths together again, this time more eagerly. The kiss deepened and Sinnan's hot, wet tongue slithered into his mouth. Domitris couldn't help a muffled moan mix with the kiss, and he pushed their torsos closer together. Sinnan pushed him down onto the mattress and positioned himself properly on top of him. Sinnan leaned down on one elbow and kissed him again, hard, and messily.

Something was off.

He was turned on just the same, but today, he wasn't drunk on sweet wine and hadn't been influenced by the loose atmosphere of the party all evening. Sinnan was enchanting, but the man on top of him wasn't the passionate, energetic person he had spent the day with. He felt more... determined than lustful. Had it been like that yesterday as well? Domitris couldn't tell. Sinnan's hand was stroking his chest and traveled downward slowly.

He grabbed Sinnan's hand, stopping him. Sinnan looked confused as Domitris searched his eyes for any trace of want. He couldn't find it.

Letting go of his hand, he sat up halfway, Sinnan tilting off him.

"What's wrong?"

The room suddenly seemed too small and constricting, the air too warm around him.

"I–I need air." Domitris shuffled off the bed and headed for the balcony, leaving Sinnan behind. Outside, he leaned against the balcony railing, letting the evening breeze fill his lungs. He turned his eyes to the gardens and tried to steady his breathing. The night spun, and his heart continued to hammer against his ribs. Thoughts clouded his mind, twisting and turning like eels in a bucket.

With soft steps, Sinnan came out and joined him. He leaned back against the railing, nonchalantly placing his elbows on it. He regarded Domitris in calm silence.

Domitris rubbed his face before meeting Sinnan's gaze.

"I'm sorry about that."

"Don't be." Sinnan looked away, his cheeks flushed. "I was just… surprised. People don't usually tell me no."

Domitris nudged him lightly. "Well, one time had to be the first."

Sinnan didn't laugh. "What are you going to do?"

Domitris sighed deeply. "I don't know. I don't know how to handle it. I have to find out what is going on and save the treaty. Everything depends on how I handle this situation." His hands balled into fists again, the agitation growing with each heartbeat. "If I let this get out of control, we could be facing war. Do you even know what that means?"

Sinnan met him with a cool gaze but didn't answer. Instead, he turned around and looked out over the gardens as well. The torches hadn't yet burned out.

"I haven't seen gardens like these in a long time."

"Me neither," Domitris answered, the anger draining out of his muscles. Sinnan shot him a quizzical look.

"I mean, I used to come here all the time, but I haven't seen them in months. I chose these rooms because of their view of the gardens." He thought it had been smart—that he'd have many more opportunities to go out for a stroll if he was closer by. In reality, he'd had few moments to himself since the election.

Sinnan looked back to the windows and then out over the vista. The moonlight shimmered in the still surfaces of the water gardens to the east, the columns of the major aqueduct leading into the palace visible from the balcony.

"I did wonder about the reason for the... modest location. But I see it now; it is quite a view. I bet this is the quietest place in the entire palace."

"Do you want to take a closer look? There won't be anyone else in the gardens at this hour."

Sinnan's face lit up and there was no doubt that was a 'yes'.

Passing Lyra's room, they snuck down the corridor, down the servants' stairs and out into the small, secluded garden. It lay beyond the themed gardens and the hedges were thick and unbroken, obscuring the view to the rest of the palace grounds. This meant that it wasn't an obvious place to entertain guests, though it definitely had been some kind of ceremonial garden, once. Now it was a mostly forgotten refuge where the fig tree leaning against the wall wasn't trimmed down as often as it should be, and the withered grass stood tall along the tiled pathways. In the middle, there was a rectangular pond encircled by rows of midnight blue tiles, and on one end stood a simple marble bench. Over the pond towered a wisteria arbor in full bloom. When experienced from the balcony, it was a sweet, perfumed scent lining the air, but standing under them, the air was so thick with the smell of the vanilla-scented flowers it was almost dizzying. Sinnan inhaled deeply and took in the impressions around him. He strolled around quietly for a while, then placed himself on the bench by the pond. Domitris went to the fig tree crowding the passage by the door and picked a couple of indigo fruits hanging from a low branch.

They had both left the room barefooted and Sinnan stretched out his legs and placed his feet in the water, creating disturbance in the surface for the silvery moonlight to dance in. Domitris joined him on the bench and handed him one of the figs. They sat like that for a while, eating the sticky fruits. Domitris looked down on the painted tiles at the bottom of the pond, the ripples of the water making the delicate flower patterns move.

"This is nice," Sinnan said into the quiet of the night.

XV

*T**he walls closed in around him, and the hallway grew longer as he walked for the gilded door.* He kept walking towards it, stretching out his hand to turn the handle, but with each step, he was further from it. Raised voices argued somewhere in front of him, behind him. One of them was his own. He swallowed and looked over his shoulder. The voices grew louder, shouting words he couldn't make out. He turned, wanting to get away from there, and the whole hallway rotated. The door was once again in front of him. The handle turned on its own, the door opening up. He tried walking the other way, away from it, but he was pulled in. He ran but only came closer to the room. It was dim inside in the waning light. A figure sat on the throne with something in his hand. Something grim.

A severed head.

Domitris backed up, nausea raging in his stomach, but his steps led him closer and closer. The last light of the sunrise fell in through the barred windows, casting shadows over the head. It turned in the figure's hand, staring back at him with still eyes. The face was his own.

A familiar voice spoke his name.

"Domitris."

The bells were ringing.

"Domitris, wake up."

He blinked his eyes open, his body shuddering. Where was he? Ignotus crouched beside him, but he was in his own room, in bed. Bells were ringing somewhere, but it wasn't the morning bell; it was the high-pitched ringing of the alarm bells. It had to be the early hours of the morning, judging by the light.

His dream faded, along with the memory of the quiet evening he had spent with Sinnan.

Ignotus' face was gray, his teeth gritted.

Domitris' stomach sank, and he sat up. "What is it?" he said and had to clear his throat.

Ignotus' breathing was shallow. When the words came, they were ragged and painful. "The city is burning," he said.

A gasp came from the back door and Domitris noticed Lyra was up, still in her night robe, hair down, clasping her hands to her mouth. Sinnan stirred awake at his side.

"What? What happened?" Domitris sat upright, barely covered by the sheets.

Ignotus shot a look past Domitris at the tousled mess beside him that was Sinnan. "You better come to the council hall at once. We shouldn't discuss this in front of the—" he paused then found Domitris' eyes again, "entertainment. Hurry, I've roused the council."

He turned to leave, but Domitris grabbed hold of his wrist. "Tell me."

Ignotus turned his eyes away. "It's bad, Dom." Time stood still between them for a heartbeat. "The Panjusticia is burning to the ground as we speak."

AS WE FALL

All the breath left Domitris' lungs. This could not be happening. He couldn't comprehend. A pain shot through his chest as he tried to breathe, each thought shattering in his mind.

Ignotus gently tugged his hand off his wrist. "Come, quickly. You need to deal with this. Now." He gave him a lingering look before he turned and left without waiting for him to form an answer.

Lyra stood, unmoving, both her and Sinnan seemingly not daring to breathe. It was too much. Everything was slipping out of his control. All he could do was stand at a distance while it all crumbled around him. Lyra came to him, reaching out her hand. He took it and she squeezed his own tightly.

"Your Highness." Her voice quivered. "We need to get you ready."

Right. Ready. He had to do something. "Just find me anything. I need to hurry."

"No." She let go. "We have to do this properly. It has never been more important for you to look strong in front of the council."

He nodded absently, and she left for the back room.

Sinnan gazed at him while Domitris struggled to wrap his mind around the news.

Their evening in the garden seemed so far away, as if it had happened in another life. As if Sinnan hadn't lain beside him only hours ago in the darkness, casually holding his hand and telling him badly translated jokes. The image of him was too much. It was unbearable how he sat in the bed, carelessly half-naked, mirroring neither the fear nor the anger raging within himself. Simply present and so close.

Lyra came in, carrying everything he needed. It could have been bedlinen, the armful of white fabric, but it wasn't. It was lengths of pure white silk, the kind that was impractical for anything other than standing and that stained if you as much as looked at it.

"You have to do what they expect of their emperor. Show them exactly how strong you are. Show them that this won't discourage you and that it won't break what you have been fighting for. You have allies who support you; remember that. And most importantly, you have the power of the people. They're counting on you," she said, dumping the clothes in his lap, taking the golden circlet from beside the bed and placing it carefully on his brow. "You were meant for this." She took his face in her hands. "You always were. And you will succeed."

His chest lightened, and he closed his eyes, taking a deep breath. "I will do everything I can to prove you right."

Sinnan had gotten out of the bed and shrugged into his own garments. Lyra cast him a glance, then said, "I'll leave you to it. Call me if you need anything."

He nodded, and then she was gone. Domitris got up and looked at Sinnan while he flung his robes around himself.

"I have to go see the troupe and make sure they're all right," Sinnan said, fastening his waist ties.

"Of course." Domitris fumbled with the second overlay meant to function as a cape, and as it caught on the pin at his shoulder, he crumpled it up and tossed it to the floor. The pin had sprung open, and he couldn't get it to fasten again, causing a fold of silk to drip down over his chest. He almost flung the pin across the room. Sinnan stepped closer, preventing his childish impulse, and took over. He managed the fabric calmly and secured the pin.

They regarded each other for a short while before Domitris asked, "Will I see you again?"

Sinnan's green eyes didn't falter. "Let's count on it," he said, the emotion in his voice hard to read. "Now, go rule."

Domitris took a last deep breath before he headed out the door, leaving Sinnan behind.

He walked into the council hall, then stopped in his tracks. A cone of smoke rose in the distance, marring the oncoming morning. The sight of the bright orange glow that licked up where the Panjusticia's towers had been was like a punch in the gut. Until that moment, he had thought he could still prevent it somehow, that it hadn't been true. The realization that it couldn't be stopped turned his stomach.

The room gradually materialized around him and the voices that had been muffled in his ears were now insects, buzzing too loudly.

Not only had the council been sent for, but the Dassosdans as well. All fifty council seats were occupied and the room was overflowing. Arguments raged between people from one end of the hall to the other. Dia and Ignotus talked calmly by the rostrum, Ignotus with a hand to his face at the chaos in the rows in front of them. There seemed to be as many different discussions as there were people, and no one listened to one another. Domitris wanted to turn around and walk the other way, to leave it behind and let someone else deal with it. But he carried Lyra's words in his heart.

He knew what he had to do. He walked to the center, taking his position in front of the rostrum, and filled his lungs.

"The meeting has started. Take your seats."

It broke up some of the arguing, but most people paid him little attention.

"SILENCE!" Ignotus yelled and came to stand at his side. "Your emperor is here," he stated, then walked over and sat down in the front row, followed by Dia.

People reluctantly found their seats, and the silence settled. Domitris then addressed Hephakles, who sat ready at his secretary's desk, looking pale.

"What is being done?" Domitris asked and shot a look out the window.

People squirmed where they sat, some too eager to talk, and buzzing broke out again.

"Quiet!" he shouted at them with as much authority as he could muster. When it was possible to hear above the noise, Hephakles stood up. He looked on edge, like everybody else, but readied himself, clearing his throat.

"Your Highness, the main structure of the Panjusticia has already fallen. A few buildings to the west have caught as well, but the guards are trying to get it under control. All available palace guards have been sent there to handle the fire."

"Yes, good. We need all hands on it. Putting it out before the whole city burns is our first priority."

People nodded, but tension sizzled in the air. He knew his next question would be a stick to a wasps' nest, but he had to ask it.

"Now tell me," he said to Hephakles, "who did it?"

He had hardly put out the question before accusations started flying.

Hephakles did his best to clear his throat again and get his voice through the noise. "We don't know." Someone in the rows scoffed, but Hephakles tried not to be distracted by it. "We have no information about the culprits. We will search for witnesses as soon as the fire is manageable."

Cassian stood up with a pat on the shoulder from Gaius. "These are obviously attacks conducted by enemies of the empire." His eyes narrowed. "And who else could that be but the Dassosdans?"

Several Dassosdan officials and council members shot up to let accusations and defenses fly across the room. Cassian simply sat down with a stupid smirk on his face, crossing his arms. Heat shot through Domitris' veins. He wanted to grab Cassian by his robes and throw him out of the council hall himself. He looked over at Ignotus, who seemingly had the same thought. Ignotus had said Cassian couldn't do much harm, but Domitris was starting to question that.

Dia stood up, the fingertips of her good hand resting on the panel in front of her. The other arm hung limply down her side.

"Your Highness. Honored council members." She didn't need to shout to be heard. "Petty arguments will result in nothing but animosity. The attempt on my life and the attack on the city were obviously orchestrated by more than a few common criminals. These are people with the resources and determination to pose a real threat. The ones who did this knew where to strike for it to hurt the most. And clearly, it has worked." She took the time to look around the hall, lingering on those who had been most vocal in their arguments. She looked at Domitris. "What we need to do now is take action."

The atmosphere was strained, as if it would snap any

minute. Her words weren't a challenge. She was getting them back on track, helping him take control. It was their opportunity to show a united front in finding a solution.

Domitris leaned forward on his palms. "And what do you suggest, Minister?"

"That we create a specific plan for how security around the city can be increased and–"

Gaius rose, his hands folded over his stomach, and cut her off. "I think the Minister is talking some sense in this instance. But we all know that it won't be possible, don't we, Your Highness? We don't have the resources in the city. Which has been pointed out on countless occasions."

Spiteful satisfaction glowed on his face. It was obvious where Cassian had gotten his insolence from, though Gaius had had more years to perfect it. Domitris' pulse raced, his heartbeat pounding in his ears. He had to swallow to keep his composure. Gaius threw out his hands and continued, facing the council instead of Domitris.

"We have to acknowledge that this situation is too dire for our young emperor to manage. Elected by commoners does not mean fit to rule."

Each word spiked anger into the pit of Domitris' stomach and his muscles started to shake. He had to contain it. He couldn't lose control of himself. Not now. Gaius turned back to face him. "Maybe we should learn from Dassosda, since you're so eager to model yourself after them, and delegate some of the responsibility to get this under control?"

"Hear, hear!" someone called out and Gaius spread out his arms.

Pinpricks ran down Domitris' spine as anger swelled inside

him. He had to get Gaius back in line. Every moment Gaius was allowed to parade his disrespect around, Domitris' influence on the council diminished.

"You have waited for this moment, haven't you, Gaius?" Domitris' voice trembled as he ground out the words. "All you want is to see me fail to gain more power for yourself. You have no interest in what's best for this country!"

Gaius scoffed. "My concern has always been for the empire. That's why I have to speak up! An emperor who's more concerned about going on trips to the provinces and rolling around with whores than taking care of the capital isn't what's best. We need someone who will take action. Someone strong!"

Rage flooded Domitris, taking over every sensation in his body. How *dared* Gaius insult him like that in front of the council? In front of the Dassosdans? Gaius was turning everyone against him. Domitris refused to let Gaius be his downfall. If authority was what they wanted, they would get it.

"Spreading lies and discrediting me as ever, Gaius? This is what you choose to do? Fine! Let it be known that while the council bickers, the emperor acts. If I can't trust this council to support me or be helpful when I need it, I will get it under control myself!"

Murmurs spread as Domitris turned to Hephakles. "Close the city gates! No one will leave or enter without proper documentation."

The whispers became objections. Domitris raised his voice. "We will search through every crevice of the city for the culprits. If they're still here, we'll find them. If they aren't, they won't get back in."

Hephakles stood frozen as if he waited for Domitris to change his mind.

"Do it!" Domitris yelled and slammed his hand down on the rostrum. Dia shook her head slightly, but he ignored her. He would show them he could manage whatever was thrown at him. *He* had been chosen to rule. Eventually, Hephakles followed orders and scribbled on a piece of parchment that he handed to a guard. Domitris looked around the hall at the stunned faces.

"The meeting is over," he snarled. "Get to work." Then he spun on his heel and stormed out.

The pit in his stomach grew with each step, but he couldn't let it consume him. There was no way around it: a firmer hand was needed, and he would make them all see that he had earned his title. Before he was halfway down the corridor, Hossia was beside him.

"Walk with me, Domitris." She took his arm and slowed their pace. He didn't want to face her now.

"Do you think I made the wrong decision too, Matre?"

"I think you do what you have to," she said, not looking at him but on the hall ahead. "But he's agitating you on purpose, Gaius. And you're falling for it."

"What do you want me to do? I can't risk everything falling apart because I don't dare make decisions. I need to show that I'm in charge."

She patted his hand and led him to one of the outside corridors. The heat of the morning was turning harsh, but in the shadow of the awning above, the tiles were cool against his feet. At the other end of the corridor, a servant was cutting the stray edges of a hedge. Hossia lowered her voice.

"It is not an easy time for you to come back, and you knew that when you left. Leaving the palace is always a precarious business for an emperor. History has taught us that it tends not to go well."

A wasp buzzed past too close to his ear and he swatted at the air with an idle hand. "Are you saying this is organized within the palace walls?"

"I'm not sure what I think yet. But there are murmurs spreading lies about you and stirring up anger."

"What do they say?"

She shook her head. "The nobles are a bunch of turncoats and buffoons who would rather listen to gossip than think two coherent thoughts."

"Don't make me beg to hear slander. I'm better off with your honesty than your protection."

She looked over one shoulder and pulled them further into the shadow. "You heard him in there. He's busy repeating the same nonsense. That an emperor elected by the people cannot be a true leader. That leadership should be bestowed upon you by an emperor and not by a people. But you know this; it's what they have always said. Now there are more than whispers that say that you're not strong enough. That your concern for this treaty has made you weak and that you grovel for Dassosda. And the newest gem is that you lie with foreign whores who cloud your mind."

It was incredible how nothing was beneath them. What did that have to do with any of this? He gritted his teeth. "That's—"

She held up a hand and shushed him. "The rumors make

the Dassosdans wary. Some are afraid of signing the treaty, speculating that it will make a new invasion easier if the tides turn. They are not comfortable with the division and animosity of the Marmarasi nobles. The Minister, of course, is very civil, but the rest of her delegation seems to be sowing doubts."

That didn't bode well. They couldn't afford for the alliance to go awry just days before they signed the treaty. He combed his fingers through his hair and let out a sigh. How was he supposed to get this under control when everyone was turning against him?

"None of this was supposed to happen."

"No, it wasn't, but it did and now we have to deal with it." She stopped, looking up at him. "Dear boy, no one is destined to make the world a better place. The people who succeed in creating change for the better are the people who cannot sleep at night if they don't. Those are the people who change the world." He said the last sentence with her.

The words stung. His mother used to say that to him as a child. It was ingrained in him. It was those words that had brought him here.

"I miss her," he said.

"I know. I miss her too."

"I wish I could ask her and Father for advice. I can't trust the council in these times. It feels like I'm all alone with this."

"I can't help you either, but I know you're not alone. You were chosen by the people. The first Elected Emperor in Marmaras' history. You're bound to face challenges, but I know you will find a way to handle it. Maybe the advice you seek is not possible to find within the walls of the palace?"

When he looked back at her in confusion, her eyes

warmed and she nudged him gently with her wrinkled fist.

"I've heard you've had company for a few days, and I've also gathered that your company might be impartial. Why don't you ask someone who knows the word in the city instead of asking all these soft-footed donkeys who have not been outside the palace doors for years?"

Was she suggesting asking Sinnan for help?

"I don't think he's..." The right person to ask? Capable of helping? Willing to? Domitris wasn't sure what he was going to say.

Hossia's eyes narrowed. "I didn't last this long at the palace by only keeping to the doves within the walls. Often, the pigeons in the gutters know where to find the tastier seeds."

He mulled it over. Maybe she had a point. He had no other contacts on the outside, and Sinnan did say his troupe had been there for a while. They seemed like the kind of people who knew how to stay informed. Though, there was no way of knowing if they could be persuaded to help.

"The rumors will flourish if anyone finds out."

"Then don't let anyone see you."

"May you live forever, dear Matre. I don't know what I would do without your guidance."

"Then I have one more piece of advice for you," she said, taking his hand. "You are a good man, but get that temper of yours under control. It won't serve you in the long run."

Memories of his parents filled his head as he parted from Hossia and went to his rooms. It had been a long time since he had let himself wallow in those feelings. Most of the time, it was too painful. When they died, he spent years trying to think of them as little as possible. It was more than a decade ago that he was told they wouldn't be coming back. Even after all this time, the bitterness of that day still devoured him. He dug his fingernails into his palms and forced away the ache that was building in his stomach. He didn't have time to dwell on it. He wanted to get out of the palace as soon as possible.

When he stepped into his room, Lyra came to him.

"They are closing the gates," she said, the lines around her eyes heavier when she wasn't smiling.

"I'm aware. Can you help me find something unremarkable to wear?"

She let her hands fall down her sides. "You're not going out, are you? You have meetings all afternoon!"

"I'll make it quick. Get Ignotus to cover for me until I'm back."

He looked away as she stepped closer.

"I think it's unsafe for you to go sneaking around the city alone and unprotected."

"I won't be alone."

She stopped and looked directly at him. "You're surely not leaving the palace at a time like this to go find the courtesan, are you?"

"His name is Sinnan, and yes, I am. I think he might be able to help me."

Her eyes darkened under her neatly shaped brows. "Help you? With what? Relieving tension? Shouldn't you–"

"Don't–" he interrupted her. "I hate to argue with you." He couldn't deal with her now. For once, he wished she would keep her opinions to herself.

She looked away. Then she took a few shallow breaths and

sat down in one of the chairs. "I don't trust him."

Domitris sat down opposite her. "You don't have to."

Her shoulders slumped, and she drummed her fingers a single time on the table. "It's just... don't get too attached."

Where was this coming from? Did she have no concept of how serious the situation was?

"You realize there are more important matters at hand, don't you? I'm only going to see if he can help me gather information."

She wrinkled her nose. "It's good you're opening up again, but you don't want it to be with someone like that."

"What is that supposed to mean?"

"You need to find someone... suitable."

"You mean someone from the palace. Someone noble."

She crossed her plump arms. "And I'm right to think so. You are the emperor, after all."

"That's enough. I told you—it's information I'm after. I need to get out of here and do something. There's no one here I can trust."

"You wouldn't have said that before the tour."

The fury he'd been holding down boiled over. "I don't know if you've noticed but the city is *burning*!" he yelled at her. He regretted it as soon as it had left his mouth, but she couldn't have chosen a worse time to agitate him.

She raised her brows and got up from the chair, ending their argument.

He kept his eyes on the floor as she walked past him.

"If anyone comes looking for me, tell them I'm out."

There was silence for a second before she turned around.

"Your word is my command, Your Highness," she said sourly and closed the door behind her.

XVI

Finding Sinnan was the first step. The late morning was sweltering hot once again, and navigating through the marketplace without Sinnan was harder than finding pearls on land. It was close to impossible not to bump into people while making his way through the tent rows. Outside the forum, he had to dodge a man swinging a duck by the neck to kill it and stumbled over an overturned basket behind him. In the middle of the hectic crowds, he could almost forget what had happened during the night, the atmosphere was so full of life. Avoiding a woman rolling a large barrel across the path, Domitris adjusted his sunscarf to make sure his face was hidden. That he was here at all was reckless. First the assassination attempt, then the fire—to think he wasn't a target would be foolish. Still, he needed to do something. The thought of staying inside the palace while waiting for the guards to stumble upon evidence was unbearable. He wanted to find whoever did it himself, if only to wipe the smile off Gaius' face. It wouldn't be long. He would make it back before anyone noticed he was gone.

The sour smell of body odor and animal droppings burned in his nostrils as he passed the corner of the marketplace selling livestock. Drops of sweat trickled down his temple, and he wiped off his forehead with the side of his hood. Finally—a stand he recognized. He knew where to go now. Rounding the next two corners, the yellow tent entered his vision. As he approached, his hopes diminished. On the front of the entrance hung the sign that said:

Your fortune awaits you another time
Come back later

Were they out? For some reason, he had expected them all to be where he had left them. The lunacy of what he was about to do came sneaking up on him. If they weren't here, he had put himself at risk for no reason. He didn't even know if they'd be able to help him. But something in his stomach told him he had to try. They would have a camp somewhere behind the rows of booths. A few steps to the left, Domitris slid in between the coarse canvas of the tents and out through a line of newly washed laundry. The camps behind were huddled in small clusters even less organized than the booths. He halted in the shade of the nearest camp and searched the small sites for familiar faces.

There. Not far over, Bardeia sat in a loose tunic by a gentle fire, stirring a stew. Her brows were furrowed, and she kept turning her head to talk to Ennio by the tent behind her. No sign of Sinnan. Or Jenine. Or the angry woman—Amelia. Domitris hoped nothing had happened to them during the night. The fire hadn't been close to the marketplace, but with fire often came panic. He exhaled. Should he just go over there? Looking at the camp, he hesitated. He had met them only briefly, but he had the feeling they would be apprehensive about welcoming him if he came without Sinnan.

He crouched down in the shadows of the surrounding tents, staying out of sight. Trying to combat the heat, he dislodged the stopper from his drinking skin and took a long draught. Out of the corner of his eye, he scanned the nearby area. What he saw made him inhale the water instead of swallowing it. As he attempted to suppress the oncoming coughing fit, the water burned up through his nose and stung in his throat. Not far from the camp, Amelia and Jenine stood pressed up against the trunk of one of the large pine trees flanking the area. Jenine's cheeks were flushed bright pink while Amelia had her face buried in her neck. Amelia's hand was stuffed down the front of Jenine's skirt and she definitely wasn't helping her with the lacing of her undergarments. Closeness between couples was nothing unusual at the palace, but stumbling over intimate relations outside in broad daylight was something else. A memory of himself and Aelias years ago in the palace gardens, sneaking around, trying to find a secluded spot, popped up in his mind. They had probably looked much the same. While he tried to cough up the water from his lungs as subtly as possible, a voice from behind interrupted him.

"What are *you* doing here?" Sinnan asked, looming over him in his sitting position. "I thought you had important matters to attend to."

Domitris flinched out of reflex, as though he had been caught doing something he was not supposed to, and tried clearing his throat. Sinnan looked different from when they had parted this morning. His outfit bordered on decent with the neckline reaching only half-way down his chest. The bottom part had no slits this time, though the hem did end rather immodestly above his knees. Getting up, Domitris wiped his mouth and brushed his hand off down the front of his clothes.

"I came to see you, actually, but I didn't want to... disturb," he said, nodding towards the couple.

Sinnan shot a casual look in their direction. "If I had to wait not to disturb the two of them in their lovemaking, I would get nothing done," Sinnan said dryly and waved at them, making a silly face, but they paid no attention to the world around them. Sinnan could have been turning somersaults, but it seemed like nothing could tear their attention from each other. Sinnan turned back to him.

"Do you want to tell me what you're doing here instead of finding out who's destroying your city?"

Heat crawled up Domitris' neck; he was suddenly too aware that he had come without a solid plan. He had to try something. "I came for your help."

Sinnan raised a brow at him. "Me? What can I do about it? I thought you had a full council of nobles to deal with situations like this."

Domitris couldn't help the annoyed huff that escaped him. "They're useless. All they do is squabble. The only thing they can agree on is how incapable I am. I have to sort this out myself."

"Then what are you doing here?"

Domitris crossed his arms and looked Sinnan over. "I

thought I might try my luck with someone who knows the word around town and knows where to look for information. You said you'd been here for a while."

"We don't know anything."

"I'm not trying to–" Domitris sighed. "I need to find someone who'll be able to ask around for information. I can't do it myself."

"Have your guards do it." Sinnan took a step back.

"I'll make it worth your while."

Sinnan didn't answer. Instead, he looked over at his friends.

"I'm glad they're safe," Domitris said, following his gaze.

"So am I," Sinnan said absently. Then he looked back at Domitris. "Rumor says you've closed the gates."

How information spread so quickly never ceased to baffle Domitris. It had barely been an hour.

"Until the perpetrators are found, I can't take any chances. Which is why I'm here, asking for your help."

After a short pause, Sinnan said, "We might be able to help you. We'll need to talk to the others first." He quickly followed it up with, "I can't promise anything."

They stepped out from their position behind the tents and approached the campfire. Amelia and Jenine had apparently finished what they were doing because they sat by the fire with the others. Jenine was smiling and fixing her braids while Amelia held a hand around her waist.

"Look who we have here, the master of disguises," Amelia said when she noticed them, which made Bardeia and Ennio turn around. "Or I suppose we should be bowing to His Highness?"

Of course, Sinnan had told them who he was. Jenine elbowed her and shushed, then kissed her on the cheek.

Sinnan turned to him. "Don't listen to her; her humor is an acquired taste."

Amelia didn't answer the critique. Instead, she kept a wary eye on Domitris.

Bardeia was the first to rise, leaving the large wooden spoon in the pot. She nodded towards Domitris. "Welcome back, Your Highness. Or I guess I should ask how we should address you since you don't seem to be here on official business."

He hadn't noticed the first time they had met, but he now realized that Bardeia was Marmarasi. Not only that, but her dialect was hauntingly familiar, reminding him of Arenaria, where he was born. Her hair was lighter than what was common in Marmaras, except for the mountain provinces to the north, but as he stood close to her, it looked as though it could have been lightened on purpose. Her clothes weren't traditionally Marmarasi either. It occurred to him that she looked like someone who didn't want to be recognized.

"You can call me Domitris. I'm here to ask for your help, so I don't expect you to grovel."

"We'll see if we can remember the orders," Amelia said.

"Enough. Stop it now, love," Jenine whispered at her. "He's *the emperor*," she added with wide eyes, and seemed to think he wouldn't hear it.

Amelia huffed in contempt, then got up and strode for the yellow tent behind them. Jenine didn't follow her but shook her head. Domitris looked to Sinnan for an explanation, but none came.

"Ignore her. Come, sit down. We have things to discuss," Sinnan said to both Domitris and the others.

Domitris took a seat beside Sinnan on a tree stump as one of five spots around the fire.

"Did you eat?" Bardeia lifted a stack of wooden bowls from the ground beside the pot. "We were just getting ready for lunch."

That he had intruded on their privacy was obvious, but dismissing their kindness seemed worse.

"I did not, thank you," he said, and Bardeia proceeded to fill bowls with stew for everyone around the fire.

Before an awkward silence set in, Sinnan took charge. "As he said, Domitris is here for our help. He needs us to find someone who'll talk. Someone who knows what happened during the night. I suppose," he added, and looked at Domitris. Domitris nodded.

"We don't know anything," came a prompt answer, this time from Ennio.

"He said he'll make it worth our while." Sinnan looked to the three of them.

"Why do you think we'll be able to help you?" Bardeia asked.

He looked around at them as they regarded him with suspicion. "To be honest, I don't know what else to try."

They shot each other disbelieving looks.

"Look, I know this must seem strange, but I'm in trouble. My city and my country are in danger. I have to do something, and I don't know where to start."

Again, the troupe fell silent. None of them seemed eager to talk, and they all looked to Sinnan. Sinnan gestured silently for them to say something, trying not to let Domitris see it. Ennio shook his head and Bardeia only looked stoically back at him. They seemed to be having a completely silent argument. In the end, Sinnan sighed, then turned to Domitris and put a hand on his arm.

"Could you give us a minute? We need to discuss a couple of things. Don't get up, we'll go find Amelia," he added when Domitris was about to rise. Domitris nodded and the four of them abandoned their food and went into the tent where he had first met them. Left behind with the crackling fire as his only company, he picked up his stew. It was surprisingly good, though the ingredients were more than a little rustic. Nothing he wasn't used to after four months spent mainly on the road, though there were spices in it he had never tasted before. A bird trilled in a tree to his right, and he took a deep breath of the sultry summer air. He closed his eyes and stretched his neck. As he put the next spoonful of stew into his mouth, a familiar voice chafed at his ears.

"That would be perfect, wouldn't it? I don't see how he'll make it through this."

Out on the path along the booths, Cassian was surrounded by three of his noble peers being led by a stocky commoner through the marketplace. The four of them were strutting about like little peacocks. Too sparkling, too pretty for the brown dust that rose from the ground when the wind swept through the small paths. What was he doing out here? Domitris was convinced Cassian hadn't set his soft feet outside the palace walls since his arrival in Concordia. He didn't believe for a second that they were just out to have fun. Leaving his stew behind, he jogged over close enough to follow without being seen. It was the first time Domitris had ever been grateful that Cassian's voice was jarring and loud enough to rival a squealing pig.

"Maybe we can finally get someone decent on the throne."

A knot tightened in Domitris' chest. Was Cassian involved in this?

One of Cassian's companions replied something Domitris couldn't hear as he snuck past a booth reeking of smoked fish. When they were back in sight, Cassian scoffed and continued.

"No, but I'm glad they did. It puts his incompetence on display. Shows him what he gets for making deals with commoners."

The man in front of them shot a look back at Cassian, who pretended not to notice, his nose in the air.

Maybe not then. But maybe he knew something. Domitris kept following.

"You think it's the Dassosdans?" a girl said, barely audible.

"Who else?" Cassian drawled. "They're unreliable rats who're just waiting to invade to get back at Marmaras and take our resources because they're stuck with inferior land. I don't trust them for a second."

It was like hearing a parrot regurgitating Gaius' warmongering. They weren't all equally enamored by his drivel, because another young man in the group shushed Cassian while trying not to make a big deal out of it.

"What? Afraid someone will hear me? What will they do about it?" He spat at the ground in front of a small cheese stand. "Nothing."

Domitris gritted his teeth as he tried not to let Cassian's petty malice get to him. The man in front mumbled something and pointed ahead. When Domitris looked around for the best route to get closer, his attention caught at something a few booths over. A ruckus had broken out at a food stand where a girl with a long blonde braid was yelling her lungs out at a burly man behind the counter. The clatter of pottery smashing against the ground made people turn and stare as the man stepped out from the stand. Domitris couldn't get wrapped up in it. He tried to get his attention back on his mission of following Cassian. Domitris stepped around the next booth to where they had just been, hoping he hadn't gone too far ahead.

Where were they?

He turned his head and searched the roads to all sides, but there was no trace of Cassian or his friends. How could he have lost them? They were just there! He tried following the direction the man had pointed in, but only got to a busy intersection where clusters of stands were mingled with tents in all directions and vendors were shouting at the top of their lungs. Domitris had to fight the urge to bang his head against the nearest hard surface. He stood still for a few seconds, searching the crowd, trying to listen for Cassian's voice, until an old crone smacked the back of his knees with her cane to get him out of her way. That solidified his decision of dropping the matter and getting back. It probably wouldn't be long before the troupe would be waiting for him.

As he made his way back, the crowd grew denser at the stall where the ruckus was turning into a fight. The girl's creative profanities became louder as Domitris wormed his way through the mass of people. Her dialect was strange in his ears until he realized she was Dassosdan. He turned to the argument again just as the girl spat in the man's face, making him bolt forward. The girl tried to run, but he grabbed her hair and screamed at her, his face brought all the way down to hers. Domitris stood frozen. He couldn't intervene—there was too much attention directed their way and he couldn't risk being recognized. Why wasn't anyone doing anything? He scanned the area for guards. To his confusion, two city guards, unmistakable in their red uniforms with the star of Marmaras emblazoned across the chest, were idling not far from the scene. They stood, leaned up against a wall, keeping an eye on the pair while sniggering to each other. The girl scratched at the man's arm, which made him let go of her hair, but only for a second before lifting his other hand up to strike her. Domitris took a step forward and his stomach clenched as the man backhanded her across the face. Blood trickled down the space between her nose and her mouth and she let out a horrible croaking sound. More people around the marketplace stopped what they were doing to stare. The man fumed and was going to punch her again. Domitris looked frantically around for someone to intervene. Then a gasp sounded through the onlookers, and someone cheered. When Domitris turned back to the fight, Bardeia towered over the man, bracing the raised arm, and Sinnan stood as a barrier between them as well, though his frame was smaller. Bardeia didn't look friendly or soft in any way now and her voice was intimidating as she spoke.

"That's enough."

The man swallowed and backed up but it didn't stop him from spitting in the direction of the girl.

"Filthy intruders," he mumbled before finally retreating to his stall. Only now did the guards get up and take fast steps towards Bardeia. She held a hand out towards them and backed away.

"We don't want any trouble."

The guards looked at each other and shrugged, then trailed off, going back to their spot in the shadow, brushing off the dust from their ankles.

In the meantime, Sinnan had disappeared with the girl. It took Domitris a few turns to locate them, but eventually he found them sitting by some stairs close by. Sinnan talked calmly to her, providing a piece of fabric for her nose. She sobbed into it while he sat down in front of her. Sinnan then said something that conjured a shaky laugh, and she nodded. He wiped the tears from her face with a gentle hand and produced a copper coin from behind her ear with the other. Sniffling, she accepted it. She got up and kissed him on the cheek before darting off with a wave of her hand. Sinnan had his eyes on her until she disappeared down the street.

Sinnan acknowledged his approach by looking his way, but he said nothing.

"What are you doing here?" Domitris asked.

"When you weren't in the camp, we went to look for you to make sure you hadn't gotten yourself into trouble. Where were you?"

"I thought I saw someone I knew and got caught up in the... Was she all right?"

Sinnan hesitated. "Not really. I mean, it seemed like her nose wasn't broken or anything, but she was pretty shaken."

"She was Dassosdan, wasn't she?"

Sinnan crossed his arms and looked him in the eyes. "So?"

"What happened?"

They both stepped aside to let a man pushing a cart pass by.

"She said she had picked up one of his wares to get a closer look and he accused her of trying to steal it. Called her a thief."

Domitris grimaced. That didn't bode well. He had hoped people had moved beyond such sentiments by now.

"Why are your nations still fighting anyway?"

Domitris sighed. "History. With Dassosda gaining autonomy, Marmaras only reigns over the original eleven provinces and won't be an empire any longer."

"Why do people care about that?"

"It's hard to explain." Domitris looked around. "You know the star of Marmaras? Its sixteen arms represent the sixteen provinces that used to make up the empire. Being an empire is in our blood, it's deeply ingrained in our culture. People feel like Dassosda is taking that from us. And I think witnessing Dassosda thriving makes it worse. That kind of bitterness causes prejudice to flourish. I had just hoped feelings like that would vanish the more people interacted."

Sinnan searched his face. "Uniting two nations that have been separated for almost a century is bound to stir up trouble. And having guards that just point and laugh at any squabble isn't doing much good."

Domitris' stomach turned. The behavior of the guards had been unacceptable. "I'll find out who those two are and have them turned away."

Sinnan huffed. "You don't get out of the palace much, do you?"

"What do you mean?"

"We have only been in the city for a month, but if I understand correctly, it's more than you have been here lately."

"And?"

"The guards are like that all the time. They don't stop conflict when it arises; they just hang around and take food from people and threaten anyone who has a problem with it."

Domitris tried to process what he was hearing. Alba was a rigid ass, but she had known how to control the guard. Or so it had seemed. It slowly dawned on him that the state of the city might be worse than he had thought. Chaos had risen while he had been away. All the work with the treaty had lulled him into thinking that signing it would be the end of all the disorder, but he was coming to realize that it was only the beginning of all the work they had to do to bring peace.

"I'll have a talk with the one in charge."

Sinnan shot him a look. "They bear your symbol, don't they? I think they're your guards. Or at least your responsibility."

"I can't be everywhere at once. I have to delegate responsibilities. That's what good leaders do."

"Good leaders trust in the right people."

Domitris was going to say something, but he closed his mouth. Sinnan's heart was in the right place, but it wasn't that simple. He did admire his ability to stand up to anyone at any time, though. Not many people dared to discuss disagreements so openly. Domitris found himself thinking that if there had been more people with Sinnan's character at the palace, everything might have gone a little easier.

Sinnan didn't push it further. Instead, he said, "Let's get back. The others are waiting for us. And my stew is getting cold."

When all of them were gathered around the campfire again, Sinnan and Bardeia filled the others in on what had happened. Then, after everyone had finished their food, Bardeia cleared her throat. "Let's get to the point."

They all nodded, exchanging glances. Jenine said, "Sorry about earlier. We usually try to keep our business our own and stay out of trouble." Her hands fiddled in her lap. "But we'll help you."

Domitris looked at them—properly looked at each of them this time. There was something off about them. The five of them were an unlikely band of people, and the urge to flow over with questions to understand who they were and what they were doing here whirled in his mind. Jenine and Amelia were foreigners as well. Northerners. And not from the Heathlands like Sinnan. The group seemed to wish to be taken for traders, but their skills with performing said that there was more to it than that. And what were they doing this far south? It didn't really add up. But it wasn't the time to ask questions if he wanted their help. They were obviously guarding their privacy, and he didn't want to risk driving them away. He drew a shallow breath.

"I was–" Domitris began, but was cut off by Amelia.

"First, tell us what you know." Her dark hair fell about her shoulders as she leaned forward, elbows on knees. She seemed to have taken personal offense at him from the moment they met, but he had no idea what he had done to deserve it.

"You know about the fire. I imagine Sinnan has told you…" he trailed off as they nodded. Of course, Sinnan had told them everything he had heard that morning. He made a mental note that he needed to be more careful. He tried to stay on track—this was where his gut feeling had led him. "I went to get an explanation from the council, but there was no consensus about what had happened. They say that the fire started sometime during the night, but there is no evidence to lead us to the arsonists. Some nobles think Dassosdans did it. The Dassosdans are angry at the accusations and say that it was Marmarasi who did it and no one is the wiser."

"Who do you think did it?" Amelia asked.

Domitris turned it over in his mind. As Dia had said, it was someone who knew where to strike for it to hurt the most. Someone who was taking advantage of the unfolding chaos to stir up unease and undermine him and his rule. There was no lack of people standing to gain from everlasting unrest. Tenebris was still teeming with thugs related to criminal circles within and outside Concordia, he knew that. It was a blemish on the city, and his next undertaking would be weeding out every single one of them. He didn't want to admit any of this. And he assessed that he didn't have to.

"I don't know what to think. I don't want to believe that it is either, but that brings me nowhere."

The answer must have been sufficient, because Amelia sat with a hand to her mouth, frowning at the information.

"As we said," Jenine began softly, "none of us saw the fire ourselves. We were only awoken by the chaos during the night and saw the flames." She looked away, and Sinnan nodded for her to continue. "But there have been rumors floating around all day and we've heard people talking. We've agreed that we can ask around and try to get more information."

He let out a sigh. "It's all I hope for. Thank you."

Jenine rubbed her palms on her thighs and hesitated

before she said, "Though it could prove dangerous. It's a big risk for us to go snooping around. We might attract attention."

Domitris raised a brow at her.

"We won't do it for free. We want something in return," Amelia stated.

He folded his hands. "I expected as much."

The troupe looked at each other.

"No questions asked," Amelia added.

Domitris nodded.

Amelia sucked in a short breath before continuing. "We want merchants' passes."

Domitris shot Sinnan a look, but his eyes were fixed on the ground. Merchants' passes were the documents that let traders travel through walled cities unhindered. The passes usually weren't difficult to obtain in any major city if the person requesting could prove honest business. Even the troupe's small stand should have been able to qualify. That could mean one of two things: either they hadn't been able to convince a merchant guild clerk of the legitimacy of their trade, or their passes had been taken away, which usually only happened if the holder was deemed lawless. And they would have little use for them when they were already in Concordia, which could only mean…

"Are you planning to leave?"

"Eventually," Bardeia said. "Since the gates are closed, we'll have to stay put, for now. But it would help us when we move on."

"Why don't you–"

"No more questions," Amelia said with the kind of anger that easily replaced fear.

AS WE FALL

Silence hung in the air between them, straining the atmosphere. Domitris backtracked. He had to be careful.

"And in return for the passes, you'll do your best to get me information?"

Amelia and Bardeia nodded.

Domitris looked around at the troupe. Even if they couldn't help him or didn't follow through on their part, he had nothing to lose. "I accept your terms."

Domitris heard a collective exhale from Jenine and Sinnan, as if they had been holding their breaths.

"Good," Amelia said. "We'll see what we can do. Meet us back here tonight. We'll tell you what we've learned, and you'll bring the passes."

Domitris nodded.

When he had said his goodbyes and headed back, Sinnan came running after him. His chest was visible at the front of his low-cut tunic, and the gold at his wrists jangled as he caught up. Domitris' heart quickened. It had been good to see him again, even like this. Sinnan stopped to catch his breath, and before he could think the words escaped Domitris.

"I had hoped for more time with you this morning."

It was a stupid thing to say in the middle of everything that was going on. But Sinnan's eyes briefly widened, and his lips curled into a smile. Then he reached out a hand and Domitris took it gently.

"Maybe we can do it again sometime?"

"Yeah?" Domitris tugged him closer. He smelled sweet, of rosewater and sweat, and Domitris was overwhelmed by the urge to be closer to him. Leaning slightly forward, Domitris tugged a lock of hair back behind Sinnan's ear and Sinnan took the bait. He leaned in and their lips met. It was soft and brief and lovely and Domitris didn't want it to end. "I'll look forward to that."

Sinnan took a step back and fiddled with an earring. "So will I." He let go of Domitris and looked as though he was deciding to head back. "One more thing. Don't tell anyone you were here with us. We don't want to get involved in any of this."

"Of course. I promise."

XVII

Back at the palace grounds, the column of smoke rising from the Panjusticia was visible in the distance to the west. His heart sank. At least now he'd done *something*, even if that something was asking five commoners for help. He hoped it would pay off.

He snuck past the stables, not wanting to be seen. He needed to think over everything. It wasn't supposed to have happened like this. He had expected some trouble, some dissatisfaction, but Dia shot and the city burning down? He could never have been prepared for that. Maybe he had been too naive, thinking their nations could get along. So much blood had been spilled between them, so much animosity still existed. What if the treaty was only going to cause more damage? Instead of improving relations, it could rip them apart and destroy both countries in the process.

He made it to his rooms. He hoped Lyra wouldn't be there so he could get a moment to himself to figure out what his next step should be. But when he entered, there she was, changing the sheets.

"Oh good, you're back already," she said, not looking up. So, she was still angry with him. He put his flask and cape away and stood in the open doorway to the bedroom.

"Is there news about the fire?"

She tugged at one end of the sheet. "They say it's under control. But have you seen the smoke? You can see it all the way from here."

"I noticed. Is there progress in finding who's responsible?"

"I don't know. You'll have to ask someone else." She straightened, hands on her hips.

They stood like that for a moment as silence fell between them.

"Lyra, I'm sorry."

She sighed and raised her brows. "It's a mess, isn't it?"

"I'm trying to figure it out."

"I know." She continued folding the sheets in on themselves. "Ignotus came by looking for you; you just missed him. He was going to the arena to blow off some steam, I guess, but he wanted to talk to you."

"Thank you. I'll find him."

"He seemed worried about you. And he's not the only one."

"I'm the least of our concerns right now."

"I want you to be careful. It isn't safe out there."

"I'm going out again tonight."

She let out a sigh and looked at him with tired eyes.

Frustration boiled inside him again. "I can't just sit in here and *wait*."

She shook her head and disregarded his words. "I'm telling you, I don't know what the two of you did, but I'm still scrubbing golden paint off from everywhere in here."

Domitris' cheeks went hot. "That wasn't—I didn't..."

"All sense is out of your head with that one, isn't it?"

Why wouldn't she let it go? He thought he had made it clear.

"I don't want to discuss it with you."

She pursed her lips, her round face turning rounder, and picked up the pile of linen. "I'll take these downstairs."

Domitris looked at the bed, then remembered.

"Wait, did you find a bracelet while cleaning? Sinnan thinks he lost it here that night."

"A bracelet? No. But I can keep an eye out for it if you want."

"You're a lamb."

She headed for the back door.

"Lyra?" he said after her, and she halted. "I'm glad you're here."

She turned around to give him a little smile, and then she was out the door.

Finally, a moment to himself. He went out onto the balcony and filled his lungs with warm air. The midday sun baked the stones underneath his feet and waves in the air made the palace ripple in the distance. Drops of sweat formed at the back of his neck and he wiped them off with a brush of his hand. What now? How did he move on from here? He put his elbows on the balustrade and pressed his palms into his eyes. Racking his brains, he tried to think of whom to ask for help, but nothing came to him. It seemed his group of allies grew smaller each day. He didn't know what to make of it all. Hossia had told him to trust Sinnan; Lyra had told him not to. He wasn't sure it mattered. Not if they were able to help. He looked out over the gardens and the rough, cream-colored cliffs that ended the palace grounds. In the end, he decided to leave it behind and find Ignotus.

The training barracks lay behind the palace, and strong youths trained in the blinding sun. It was past midday, which meant only those who had finished their classical education were on the grounds. The men and women, a decade younger than himself, were the ones who had excelled in military techniques and were at the end of their education, ready to be funneled out to the legions of the provinces. They had chiseled arms and legs formed by hard, daily fighting, the physique that was quickly lost once you left the military. Domitris had been good about maintaining a soldier's lifestyle even after becoming a politician, especially as it had been necessary in the Overthrow when both he and Ignotus had taught commoners to fight. During the past four months away, he had been immersed in the role of a true politician, his days spent talking and sitting at a desk more than anything else. The honor guards had indulged him in the occasional sparring match, but it was not enough to keep up that sort of training. When in the military, Ignotus and himself had always tried to outdo each other. It was the kind of competitive behavior that belonged to the recklessness of youth. Some days, they had been running rounds all morning, fighting two-on-two matches before lunch, trained endurance all day and riding in the afternoon, and still the two of them would meet for a private match in the arena in the evening to test who was the strongest that day. Usually it was sword-fighting, but some days, when it had been a particularly rough day, or if they were angry with each other, it developed into plain old fist fighting. He had broken Ignotus' nose that way once or twice and lost a tooth himself, but they always made up after that. There was something about letting go of the frustration and anger, letting it become physical impact instead, that soothed the mind.

The larger arena was located with the armory in a round building behind the barracks. The arena itself was surrounded by a low wall and gravel coated the floor. Inside, he found Ignotus at the far end, practicing blows with a wooden sword on a wooden opponent. Ignotus hadn't heard him enter, so Domitris stood back and watched him. His blows were strong and precise, his tanned body dripping with sweat. He was wearing the short red fighting garments resembling army uniforms that allowed for optimal movement of the arms and legs. They also had the tendency of riding up, exposing more of the thighs than was appropriate outside of battle. He was panting hard and looked like he had been at it for a while. His form showed that he had not been neglecting his daily training since becoming a politician. The muscles of his arms and back tensed and swelled with his movements. Domitris walked over to a stand holding identical wooden swords and lifted one up. The blisters on his own hands were from the reins of his horse, not from a weapon. Nonetheless, his body was longing for a round in the arena. He swung his legs over the low wall and tapped a pillar with the sword, making Ignotus spin around. Ignotus forced a smile through the panting and relaxed his shoulders, loosening the grip on his sword.

"I hardly remember the last time we stood here together," Domitris said, stepping forward.

"I do. I made you bite the dust." Ignotus' smile was genuine this time.

It was true. They had always been fairly equal, but after assuming the throne, paperwork had taken up more of his time, making him skimp on physical training. This meant that even though Domitris was good with a sword, Ignotus had been better for a while. Domitris also knew he couldn't beat Ignotus now, but he liked a challenge.

"How about a rematch? That seems only fair."

"In that case, I think we need real swords, don't we?"

"Right."

They reached backwards behind the low wall and each found a shiny metal blade fastened to the side. These were unadorned, made for practical reasons alone and full of cuts, their edges rough from years of use. They stepped closer and positioned themselves in front of each other. It felt good to be wielding a weapon again. The weeks after the Overthrow, he had insisted on going to the barracks to keep up his daily routine. They had always been taught not to let their last association with fighting be blood. Otherwise, they might never be able to pick up a sword again. Even now, flashes of what he had done on the night of the Overthrow burned in the back of his mind. Every day, he hoped to forget it. Yet he knew how important it was not to let the guilt take over and become afraid of combat. Those skills had served him well that night. And it was impossible to know if he might need them again someday. He refused to become another soft-footed politician who was nothing but words and ideas. He wanted to—needed to—also be one of action, who could stand beside people in the hour of need, and not a helpless strategist who had never known battle. The Supreme Emperor had always had a talent for the strategics of warfare, or knew how to cultivate the generals that did, but as far as anyone knew, he had never set foot in a battle himself. Not that that was any different for most nobles who were not of the military, but Domitris felt it important to know what fighting for life and death meant if you were in charge of other people's fates, sending them to war.

Ignotus stepped forward, dragging the tip of his sword along the floor before raising it quickly, making the gravel fly. Domitris turned his sword over in his hands. The worn leather at the hilt was sticky in his grip. He slid his sandalled foot backwards in the gravel for a better stance.

They struck at the same time, clashing blade against blade. Ignotus' grip was firm, and the metal strained where their blades met. Ignotus was the first to give in, lowering the sword swiftly. A steely echo rang out between them, and he let the next strike fall at once, only avoided by Domitris by a hand.

Domitris' heart was racing already, his blood pounding in his veins. A slight tingling traveled up through the back of his hand, where he clutched the sword. Ignotus wasn't holding back.

"No warmup today?" Domitris asked.

"I had my warmup before you came. Do you yield already?"

"Not a chance. Give it all you've got."

A curve tugged at the side of Ignotus' mouth, and he landed the next blow head on, which Domitris parried with ease. They were so close now that the sweat on Ignotus that had dried and broken out again several times made Domitris' nose curl. He broke the parry, took a sidestep back, and readied his sword. Then he swung, taking the offensive, testing Ignotus' defenses with each blow.

Ignotus hadn't been idle, because he countered the thrusts as they came, and his footwork did not betray him. He was still standing in the center, though they had switched sides and Domitris had won no ground. Strands of hair had come loose from where it had been fastened in a braid at the back of Ignotus' head and he blew them to the side with a sharp exhale. His dark eyes gleamed beneath his brows and a drop of sweat trickled from his temple to the sharp angle of his jaw. Domitris' sword slid into his left hand, and he shook his right, clasping and unclasping his fingers before settling the sword again in his right.

"Not bad," Ignotus said as they circled each other for a few steps. Then he came forward, quickly. He dealt a series of hard strikes head on that made Domitris stagger backwards while parrying. The raw strength of Ignotus made the strikes difficult to block, and Domitris' whole body stung with each hit.

Then, Ignotus swung his sword forward in an exaggerated motion and Domitris widened his stance to block.

But the hit never landed.

Instead, Ignotus kicked his foot out hard, slamming it into Domitris' shin, knocking him off balance. Domitris tumbled to the ground, landing in the gravel on his elbow, earning him a large scrape down the arm. His sword flew out of his hand. When he looked up, Ignotus had the tip of his sword against his chest, smirking insolently. In that moment they were both fifteen again, rolling around in the dust together. Except this time, Domitris was the only one on the ground.

He couldn't believe he had let himself fall for such a cheap trick. He panted hard and sat up to wipe off the gravel stuck in his skin. "I forgot what a cheater you are."

"I don't remember us establishing any rules." Ignotus lowered his sword and reached out a helping hand instead. "Besides, I would have won anyway. I just didn't want to draw out the humiliation."

"You are an ass, and you know it."

"If it wins me the fight, I'll be an ass any day."

They put back their weapons and went outside, observing the recruits perform their drills.

"Is there any news about the fire?" Domitris asked.

"Nothing yet."

"Then what is it? Lyra said you came to see me."

"I did. I wanted to discuss matters privately with you." Ignotus looked over both shoulders and pulled him closer. "People say you're not handling the situation well. There are rumors you went frolicking with your whore instead of dealing with the issues at hand."

Domitris stopped walking. Sometimes, he got the feeling that Ignotus enjoyed being blunt. "Who could you possibly have heard that from?"

"You know how news travels at the palace."

"I would have thought you knew better than to buy into rumors. I did go to see him, but it was to get information." He side-eyed Ignotus. "I don't trust the council on this matter."

"Could he give you any, then?"

"We'll see."

Ignotus didn't seem satisfied with the reply. "You must see how it looks."

Domitris sighed. Should he say it? If he voiced his suspicions, he wouldn't be able to take it back. And what if Ignotus couldn't keep his mouth shut?

Ignotus interrupted his thoughts with a hand on his shoulder and a hard squeeze. "There's something you're not telling me. Come on, Dom. I want to help."

Domitris stood for a moment more in the burning sun, consumed by doubts. Then he gave in. He had always appreciated Ignotus' advice, even when he didn't like what he had to say.

"Could the fire and the assassination attempt have been orchestrated by people from the palace?" He hated how paranoid it made him sound.

Ignotus let go of his shoulder. "What makes you say that?"

"What if there's someone who wants to get rid of me?"

"Come on… Gaius has always been like that."

"I know, but could he be taking it too far? Or what if he has influenced someone else? I saw Cassian at the market earlier and he was saying all these things and… acted suspicious."

Ignotus stroked his chin. "Cassian? He's little more than a child."

"We were around his age when we planned the Overthrow."

"Maybe, but come on. He doesn't even know his own ass from his face. How could he be planning to take down an empire?"

Domitris' shoulders relaxed, and they started walking again.

"You're probably right. As always. With everything that's happened... I can't keep my thoughts straight."

"No wonder. We're in too deep as it is. But I'll keep an eye on him, just in case."

There was silence between them while they made their way back to the palace.

"So, are you meeting him again?"

"Who?"

Ignotus gave him a look that said he knew who he was talking about. Domitris decided there was no need to tell him the details.

"I hope so."

"That must be one glorious ass he's got to have you running after him like a drooling puppy."

"Do you ever think about anything else?"

"Tits, sometimes." Ignotus grinned. "Did you see the little redhead who came to my room after the banquet?"

"No. I didn't see you at all that night, actually."

"No, that's true; your eyes were probably buried between the ass cheeks of your new friend."

"If I didn't know better, I would think you were jealous."

Ignotus shook his head and laughed. "That's rich."

They went on, leaving the training grounds behind. Insects buzzed lazily past them, headed for the gardens to the east, and the air carried the scent of jasmine wilting in the heat. When they reached the shadows of the spires, Ignotus shot him a serious look. "So, do you have a plan?"

Domitris remembered the last words Sinnan had said to him before he left. *Don't tell anyone.*

"I'm going out tonight to look for clues."

Ignotus' smile vanished. "Tell me you're not serious. You can't go running off, I need you here. Let the guards handle the city. You need to mind your appearances now. We need a strong leader to unify the council."

"And what am I supposed to do? Attend court dinner tonight and make small talk?"

Ignotus threw out his hands in exasperation. "Yes! That's exactly what you're supposed to do! It's what the council wants right now. Your presence."

"So everyone can keep saying I'm weak and can't handle the job? I won't stand for it. I'd rather do everything I can to unravel who did it and prove them wrong."

There was a short pause.

"Then I'll go with you,"

"No. I'll be safer alone."

Ignotus looked calmly at him. "Mhm," he said, and Domitris got a feeling that he wasn't convinced by his lie. "Well then, be careful."

XVIII

"We found what you were looking for, but I don't think you're going to like it," Sinnan said. Domitris stood with Amelia and Jenine next to the cold campfire. Dust particles from the roads danced in the light of the setting sun and the market still bustled with life.

"Why not?"

Sinnan kept his voice low. "The informant is a little shaky. We found someone who seemed like they knew more than they were willing to tell me, but they told us they knew someone who could be convinced to talk under the right circumstances."

"What does that mean?"

"Money, I suppose, as always. We have to meet them at a tavern in Tenebris tonight."

Of course. Where else than the dark, sweaty armpit of the city?

"Already?"

"Isn't that a good thing?"

"Right. I was just surprised. You are very efficient."

"Speaking of," Amelia finally cut in. "Did you bring us your end of the deal?"

The documents. Domitris reached into the folds of his clothes, got out the papers and held them out to her. Gingerly, she took them and counted that there were five.

"I'm going to hold on to these." She stuffed them down into her satchel.

"It doesn't sound like there are very high chances of success, though," Domitris added.

"Told you that you wouldn't like it." Sinnan grinned. "If you have anything planned with better odds, by all means, let us know."

Sinnan was right. Domitris had no better ideas. At his silence, Sinnan added, "Ennio and Bardeia went on to the Panjusticia to see if they could find anyone who was there when the fire happened. Amelia and Jenine will ask around the other camps tonight."

Domitris gave an appreciative nod. "Thank you."

"Thank you for the passes," Jenine said, smiling. Amelia gave a curt nod back.

"Well, we better get going," Sinnan said. "They wouldn't specify a time or the name of our informant, so we'll just need to be there until we find them."

"Remember to be careful," Jenine said, and hugged Sinnan tight. She released him, then hesitated when she looked at Domitris, but leaned in and gave him a hug as well. She was soft and short and smelled like flowers. It was a small gesture, but it was surprisingly touching to Domitris.

"You know I always am," Sinnan said with an expression that probably meant he wasn't.

Jenine grabbed his wrist and looked him sternly in the eyes. "Promise me."

"We'll be careful, I promise!"

Then she smiled and let go.

Amelia leaned in close to Sinnan and whispered something Domitris couldn't hear, but it made Sinnan grin and slap her on the arm. She ran her fingers through his hair and said goodbye before placing her hand around Jenine's waist.

Domitris and Sinnan left the marketplace behind them and headed northwest for Tenebris.

This wasn't what he had expected, but Domitris couldn't deny the immense satisfaction at the prospect of spending the whole evening in Sinnan's company. And finding the informant, of course.

They walked in silence for the first little while until Domitris' curiosity got the better of him. "What did Amelia say to you?"

Sinnan laughed. "You don't want to know."

He decided to trust Sinnan's judgment on that one. "Fair enough."

At first glance, the city seemed to be sleeping when they made their way down the winding paths towards Tenebris, but when they lingered in the dark corners, Domitris noticed other figures doing the same. The closer they got, the more the city crumbled around them. All the houses were only one or two stories high, and the streets were full of holes. They moved forward through narrow paths, and since it hadn't rained for weeks, Domitris didn't want to think about what had turned the dusty ground into mud. It was hard to tell whether the few establishments here and there were still in business, with their crooked signs and drawn shutters. In several places, roofs had been mended with scrap wood instead of tiles. The few people they passed looked sick or drunk or both with distrusting eyes that seemed to assess whether mugging them was worth it or not. Chills ran down Domitris' spine and he had to fight the urge to turn around. He didn't particularly want to get into a fight over the contents of his coin purse before they had even met their contact.

They followed an alley leading to the side of a tattered building, which turned out to be the tavern. At the entrance, a drunk was making a ruckus, arguing with the hired muscle at the door who was telling him to go home. Sinnan reached a hand out, halting Domitris from going any further. The two of them stayed hidden in the shadows while they watched the argument turn into a fight, if that was the right word for what transpired.

The drunk threw a punch at the large woman at the door without hitting anywhere near her. Instead, his fist flew through the air, and he spun around with it. This seemed to be the last straw for the woman, because she clenched her fist and punched him in the gut so hard, he slumped to the ground. He groaned, face half-buried in mud, and didn't get up.

The woman wiped her hands on her already filthy tunic, spat at the man, and went back inside. Sinnan looked up at Domitris from his bent-over position, a sly grin on his face.

"I haven't had one of these nights in ages. Are you ready for some fun?"

Domitris wasn't sure he found the prospect of their night as amusing as Sinnan did. Domitris was used to being around commoners, but the ones he had met were all respectable people working hard to better their lives. The people in front of them were hoodlums. Not that there was never fighting at the palace, but wrapped in silk and perfume, scandals tended to seem less uncivil. Before he could second-guess their plan, Sinnan moved forward, stepping over the drunk man, who was seemingly still breathing, and went straight for the door. Before he pushed the handle, he turned around, looking Domitris up and down. "Try not to look too rich, will you?"

Domitris furrowed his brows. "Not sure that's possible in these." He tugged at a fraying hem of his newest attempt at a disguise. Sinnan looked back at him as if he were trying not to roll his eyes. Just as he pulled the knob, the door flew open by itself, and a band of loud people tumbled past them onto the street. Domitris stepped aside to get out of the way while Sinnan looked as though he hardly noticed the group, pushing through them to go inside. Domitris followed when the path was clear, entering the tavern's main room. It was barely the size of his own quarters. The air was stuffy, and the ceiling was so low that Domitris was convinced he could slam his head against it if he straightened his back properly. The noise of rowdy conversation and cups clanging together made hearing each other difficult. No one batted an eye at them entering, so their attempt to fit in seemed to work.

Sinnan didn't even need to look around to act as though he knew the place and headed for the bar. The man behind the counter was wiping a suspicious-looking yellow liquid off the countertop with a soaked brown towel fastened to his belt. Sinnan elbowed Domitris in the side and he realized he had been staring and probably making a face. Sinnan leaned in over the counter and flashed his most charming smile.

Domitris hadn't been sure, but Sinnan didn't seem to know the bartender; instead of greeting him, he said, "We would like two cups of your cheapest alcohol!"

Domitris shot him a look, definitely not wanting to try the cheapest drink this place had to offer. The bartender looked back at them indifferently, then bent down and took two mugs from a shelf, which he thumped down in front of them with a grunt. Domitris paid the man while Sinnan took the mugs enthusiastically.

There were a few vacant tables at the back of the room and Sinnan headed straight for them. He placed the mugs on a table and slid onto one of the benches. Domitris was about to sit down on the opposite side, but Sinnan kicked him under the table and patted the seat next to him. Confused, Domitris sat down beside him instead. Sinnan scooted closer, leaned his arm on Domitris' shoulder and put his mouth to his ear. "This way we can keep watch better," he whispered. "There's no reason for you to be staring into the wall and no one will suspect two lovers out for a night on the town."

Lovers out for a night. Domitris liked the sound of that. Maybe when all of this was over, he could truly take Sinnan out. Somewhere nice. He turned to Sinnan to air his thoughts, but when he looked at him, Sinnan put his hand on Domitris' and laughed heartily as if Domitris had said something funny. Then he leaned in again and whispered, "Stop that! Stop looking so confused and out of place; someone will notice eventually. And don't sit up so straight, you look like you have a bottle up your ass."

Or maybe not. Sinnan was fun, but he didn't exactly fit in

at the palace. Domitris tried to relax in his seat, taking on more unfamiliar gruff mannerisms. Sinnan looked at him, shaking his head, but instead of arguing more, he handed Domitris the mug of opaque liquid.

"What is it?" Domitris asked, swirling the fluid around to get an impression of the viscosity.

Sinnan hesitated, then put his nose to the cup and smelled it, immediately pulling his face away with a wince.

"Yup, just as I thought." He coughed. "It's posca."

Domitris smelled it himself. The pungent smell of vinegar brought tears to his eyes. "Have you had it before?"

Sinnan let out a huff. "We practically lived off the stuff back when…" He trailed off. Domitris raised an eyebrow at him. Sinnan apparently still didn't want Domitris to know anything about him. What was he so afraid of?

"Back when…?" Domitris tried.

"You know, it tastes better than it smells," Sinnan said and brought the cup to his lips.

He knew it was no use pushing Sinnan to talk since it would probably make him more careful with his words, but Domitris became more curious every time they met. "I really hope it does."

Sinnan laughed. "How is it, in Concordia, people say 'to your fortune,' right? Well, on the road, we say 'to the night.'" He held out the mug to clunk it against Domitris'.

Domitris smiled a little skeptically. "To the night!" he said, and Sinnan's cup met his, the liquid sloshing dangerously up the edges.

They both took big swigs of the beverage and Sinnan downed more than half before slamming the mug back on the table. It wasn't very strong, and it really wasn't as terrible as Domitris had expected. He couldn't imagine favoring it over the sweet fruit wine served at the palace, but he didn't hate it.

"Now what?" Domitris asked, wiping his mouth with the back of his hand.

"Now, we wait," Sinnan said. "The contact wouldn't suggest a time. He just said we had to be here and then he would find us."

Domitris nodded and looked around the room. In the far corner, a group of hunched-over, scruffy-bearded men growled at one another and sent glances over their shoulders. Domitris looked away to avoid eye contact. A nudge from Sinnan made him return his attention to his drink. Sinnan moved his mug from side to side along the grain of the table, then looked up at him.

"We can't just sit here and do nothing. It'll look suspicious. We better find a way to pass the time."

That was true. If they kept on like this, Domitris would have had staring contests with every person there within minutes. No one looked suspicious of them yet, but they were being noticed.

"Any ideas?"

Sinnan speculated a little, but then he leaned over the table and rested his head against his fist, looking back at Domitris. "Tell me something about yourself."

That wasn't what he had expected from Sinnan and, for someone that secretive, it was a dangerous game to play. But Domitris wasn't above it. Maybe it could help pry Sinnan open. Though, as he tried to think of an answer, it was as if everything interesting Domitris had ever experienced vanished from his memory. His mind was blank and, as the seconds passed, he was more and more aware of how long it was taking him to come up with something to say. Finally, he chose the only thing he could think of.

"I didn't always want to be a politician."

"Is that so? What other glorious careers did you consider? General? Ooh, medical scholar? No, wait: lion tamer."

Domitris scratched the back of his neck. "When I was a child, there was a season when I really wanted to be a farmer."

Sinnan raised his eyebrows and burst into laughter.

"Hey, don't laugh. Farming is an honorable profession."

"Mhm?"

"It was after my first year at the academy when I went back to my parents' estate in Arenaria over the fall—"

"How old were you then?"

"Around seven, I think. Anyway, I discovered that the nearby farm had five kids, some of them my age, and I ran around all harvest season playing with them and the animals and they showed me how to feed them and everything."

Sinnan smiled at him in disbelief.

"Back then, I had no idea that my family actually owned their land, and that I wasn't like them at all."

"That's kind of sad," Sinnan said with a crinkle of his nose.

"Which part?"

"All of it. I can't imagine baby Domitris feeding the pigs and goats, thinking it a viable career option, then going home to his marble mansion to bathe in mint water and sleep on silk."

Domitris snorted. "Maybe someday I will be. When I retire

from the palace, I'll show you I can be the best goat farmer in all of Marmaras."

"Yeah, sure, and then *I'll* be the emperor."

Domitris tilted his head. A flash of Sinnan with the crown over his dark hair popped into his mind. It was exquisite. The contrast to reality, to Sinnan's badly dyed garment that he had changed into for their outing, brought a smile to Domitris' lips. The tunic fastened sloppily at his waist and the beet-colored fabric was fraying at the seams. The only flourishes were ribbons fastening the sleeves and it was strange to see him in something so simple. It didn't suit him.

When Sinnan finally stopped grinning, he wiped his eyes and sat back up to finish the rest of his drink before getting up from his seat.

"I'm going to need something stronger for this."

He shuffled over to the bar and Domitris kept his eyes on him as he came back with another pair of large wooden mugs, this time filled with dark ale.

"This should do it," he said with a smile, and sat back down.

Domitris picked up his posca to finish it before moving on to the next drink. As he emptied it, Sinnan was halfway through his own ale already.

"It's your turn now," Domitris noted, nodding to Sinnan.

Sinnan put a finger to his chin to imitate, thinking hard about the question.

"When *I* was a child, I was almost eaten by a whale."

A whale. Domitris had seen their bones on markets and heard about them in legends but had never met someone who had actually seen one.

"Is that really true?"

"Fine; maybe not exactly," he admitted with a grin. "But I saw it all the way up close, and it almost knocked over our boat! I fell into the icy water with it and was sick for weeks afterward." He gave a small whistle. "My parents were so angry with me."

"Why?"

"Well, I wasn't supposed to have been there," he said with a reminiscing grimace. "My oldest brother had talked all winter about these caves he had discovered by the cliffs facing the sea and how, when early spring came, he was going out in his boat to explore them. I was probably about nine at the time, and I would not let it go. I begged him for weeks to go and was a real pestilence, but our parents had already forbidden it. Then, when the day came that he prepared the boat, I snuck on board and didn't come out before we were well out on the water."

Domitris nodded for him to continue. He enjoyed sitting back and listening to Sinnan talk.

"Of course, my brother got angry when he saw me and immediately started an argument, and while he was yelling, this huge spray of water shot up just off to the side of the boat." Sinnan sat up and mimicked the motion with his hands.

Domitris laughed. "You're joking."

"No, I swear, we saw its back and tail come through the surface and disappear again and then, out of nowhere, it jumped up out of the water right next to us! I don't remember this part so clearly, but apparently, I got so scared I backed out over the side of the boat and fell into the water."

Domitris turned in his seat to see him better. "Did it attack you? The whale."

"No, but it did circle back around, and it might as well have opened its mouth and swallowed me whole."

"What happened then?"

"I'm not sure how, but my brother pulled me onto the boat again and we sailed straight back. When we finally got home, we had been gone for hours and my parents were so angry that I had disappeared and got even angrier when they saw I was all wet and shaking. My mom gave me a slap across the face so hard I'll never forget." Sinnan placed his chin in his hand.

Domitris looked at Sinnan again, as if he would be able to see it on him. "I can't imagine my parents doing something like that to me."

"You must have had a very different childhood than mine, then." Sinnan's smile faded.

Domitris felt like he had trespassed. Crossed some line Sinnan had never set up. He wanted to remedy it. "So… What was growing up in the Heathlands like?"

Sinnan wagged a finger in the air. "It's your turn now. Can you top the whale story?"

He thought about his own parents and if they had ever been that angry with him. "There was this one time when I was even younger, before I went to the academy, where I almost got into a lot of trouble with my parents."

"Ooh, do tell," Sinnan said, interest piqued.

"Well, I don't know how much you know about Marmarasi history, but the country Marmaras, before it became an empire, was founded centuries ago by a collaboration between five families. Those families have all been significant down through the centuries and hold a lot of power, even today. One of those families was the Supreme Emperor's, as you might know. His lineage was the first and only one of the five to end because he refused to name a successor after the death of his only daughter."

"I didn't know that," Sinnan said.

"No, I didn't expect you to. Also, it isn't actually important to my story." He lowered his voice. "It's just, my family is one of the five from back then, which carries a lot of weight in Marmaras. One of the proofs we had of our lineage was this very delicate, very valuable vase with portraits and monograms on it."

"Oh, no." Sinnan grinned.

"Oh, yes." Domitris took a deep breath. "So, when I was about four or maybe five years old, I thought an important vase like that needed something in it, so I thought I would make my parents happy and took the vase outside and filled it with soil and put a pretty flower in it. On my way inside, I tripped up the stairs and, of course, I dropped the vase, so it smashed into pieces. I was devastated. I knew I would get in trouble, so I tried to hide it by burying it in the garden."

Sinnan's eyes glistened. "What a brilliant plan."

"Apparently I thought so. But my sister, Oedica, found me while I was doing it and she *panicked*. She let me have it, but she didn't tell my parents. Eventually they discovered the vase was missing and tried to get us to say if we knew anything about it. I was so scared I didn't dare to admit it, and when our parents threatened us with exile if we didn't tell—as a joke, of course!" he added when he saw Sinnan's expression, "Oedica said she had done it and took the blame for me."

Sinnan looked at him with raised brows. "Your sister sounds kind. None of my siblings would have covered for me like that to protect me. Even when threatened with exile." Sinnan looked at him. "You two must be close."

Domitris shrugged. "We used to be. She didn't handle it well when our parents died. She's eight years older than me and I think it hit her differently. She became really closed off after that and could barely stand to look at me, let alone talk to me. She was always in the arena, focused only on her training. Then eventually, when she was appointed general in Auxillien, she left Concordia and never looked back. I haven't seen her in years."

Sinnan's gaze faltered for the first time, as if it struck something within him. Domitris didn't ask. Beneath the shiny surface, Sinnan seemed to be so full of pain. When he never found an answer, Domitris changed the topic. "So, you have a lot of siblings?"

"Is that really what you want to know about me?" The crooked smile was back on his face.

"I want to know whatever you want to tell me." Domitris looked him in the eyes as though that would reveal any of the mysteries inside him. Too bold, apparently. Instead of answering, Sinnan looked around.

"Wait a minute; I've got a better idea." And then he was off again at the bar, saying something to the bartender Domitris couldn't hear. The bartender shook his head, then Sinnan said something more, to which the bartender responded by pointing to some shelves at the back wall. Sinnan went to get something and returned to their table with a hide cup and a whole handful of dice.

"Let's play," he said, smiling at Domitris. "Do you know how to play Chances?"

Sinnan was slippery as an oiled snake and seemingly determined to keep Domitris at a distance. "Another drinking game?"

"There's no better way to pass time."

If that was how it needed to be, Domitris would play along. "You'll have to teach me."

Sinnan lit up. "Fine. Listen carefully."

Domitris listened to him explain the rules while he started on his ale. It wasn't overly complicated, but it also wasn't simple.

"So, you take the dice and jumble them in the cup. You start with just one and you have to do a certain action based on the number of eyes, and then the number of dice increases each turn. You have to do all the actions in the correct order when you read the dice from left to right. The first to fail to remember the actions has lost the game."

Domitris nodded. So far, so good.

"Now comes the hard part. If the die shows an uneven number, you have to pat your left shoulder with your right hand and take a sip of your drink. If it shows a four, you pat your right shoulder with your left hand, if it shows a two, you touch your nose, and if it's a six, you have to yell 'Chances'. Also, if there are two or more fives in the roll, you start the round by clapping your hands, and if all the dice show the same number, you have to go bottoms up on your drink."

Domitris squinted at the dice, trying to remember it all. "That's a very arbitrary set of rules, isn't it?"

Sinnan shrugged. "That's the beauty of it. Let's start and

see if you are able to keep up." He picked up the cup, shook it, and put it on the table. When he raised the container, it revealed a six.

"Chances! Your turn."

Domitris shook a single die, and it clattered against the tabletop as it landed. A four. He stared at it for a second, then touched his nose. Sinnan laughed and held up a finger.

"Nope, sorry! Right shoulder, left hand. We can call that round a trial, but from now on, we're keeping score," he said cheekily. "Now, we start over."

They played the game for a while, and Domitris got better at remembering the right actions. They got as far as playing with six dice, but three ales and eleven rounds later, Sinnan had won eleven times. Domitris felt the warm buzzing of the alcohol and he could see it in Sinnan's flushed cheeks, too. His spirits were high, and it was obvious he liked the endless winning.

A fuzzy feeling spread through Domitris' limbs. The sizzling atmosphere, the lightness in his chest, Sinnan's carefree laughter—it seemed as though, no matter what was in store, this night would be one to remember.

XIX

The noise in the tavern didn't subside as the hours went by. Neither did the thickness of the air or the stench of the people huddled around every table. Someone had thrown up on the floor at the other end of the room and a man behind them kept letting out rolling farts.

Sinnan began stacking the dice on the table and made a tall, wobbly tower that fell over between his fingers. The cross-like scars on the back of his hands were luminous in the candlelight. *Why do you have those scars?* Domitris knew he couldn't ask that question. It was obvious now that he saw them like this that they were no accident. It looked like the wounds had hurt. He couldn't tell if they were from a knife or maybe from a branding tool. Sinnan huffed and smiled at Domitris. His eyes were glossy, and he looked a little mussed. No wonder—it was getting late, and they hadn't gotten much rest last night. Sinnan looked back at him indifferently, as if he were thinking about something else far away. He had a black line of dirt on his collarbone. Domitris reached out and wiped it away with his thumb. Something changed in Sinnan's expression, and he suddenly seemed very present, if not entirely sober. His eyelids were half closed, and he leaned in, breath heavy against Domitris' skin. Sinnan lifted his hand up and brushed it against Domitris' face, his eyes traveling down, landing on his mouth. His touch burned on Domitris' cheek. What was going through his mind? Domitris didn't move, didn't do anything, while long seconds went by. Eventually, Sinnan put his head on Domitris' shoulder. Domitris breathed calmly, but his heartbeat quickened. He wanted to reach out and touch him, to pull him closer and hold him, but he feared that if he did, the moment would be over. Sinnan was like smoke. If he tried to grasp onto him, to claim him, he would slip through his fingers.

"It's been nice having you here–"

"Shhh!" Sinnan interrupted him and sat up.

"I just wanted to–"

"Yes, that's fine!" Sinnan hissed. "Look, by the door—I think our contact is finally here."

Sinnan nodded towards a figure entering the room. He was covered by a hooded cloak made from a fine fabric. His posture and cloak alone said he was a noble, and his neatly shaped beard revealed him to be a scholar from the library. It was jarring to Domitris how obvious it was. Did he look like that? Was that why people were staring? The man stood a little aimlessly and scouted the tables until his gaze fell on them. He stopped in his movements, trying to check them out while not being too obvious. Sinnan made eye contact with him, and the man came over.

"Good to see you, brother," Sinnan said.

"That phrase—it is you, then," the man said and looked

over both his shoulders, then at them. He froze as he searched Domitris' face, his eyes widening.

"I know who you are," he said hoarsely. The words sent chills down Domitris' spine. He got the feeling that someone was watching them and couldn't help looking around. Sinnan leaned in over the table and shushed the man.

"Keep it down, or we will all be in trouble. Now get to it. My contact said you wanted to meet us here."

The man sat down and pulled his hood back enough for them to see his face properly. His cheeks were sunken and dark circles hung heavy under his eyes.

"I did. I do…"

A roar of laughter from a nearby table made the man shake.

"Keep talking," Sinnan said, not paying attention to the room. He nudged Domitris with his elbow and gestured for him to hand over the money. Domitris got out the coin purse and put it as discreetly as possible on the table next to the dice cup. The man put both his hands flat on the table, then stared from the pouch to Domitris, a deep furrow forming between his brows. Slowly, as if still contemplating, he reached out and took it, tucking it away in the folds of his clothes.

"I–I thought what they were doing was for the better, but I was wrong. I don't want to be a part of it anymore."

"Part of what? Do you know who started the fire?" Domitris asked as quietly as possible.

The man's gaze flickered between Domitris and the table.

"Your Highness–"

Sinnan shushed him again. The man got his shaking under control and took a shallow breath. "They'll kill me and then my family if they find out I told you."

"You came here because you were prepared to talk. You got the money, so get to the point," Sinnan said in a surprisingly harsh voice Domitris hadn't heard from him before.

The man exhaled and closed his eyes. "There is," he mumbled, "there is... dissatisfaction."

"Among the nobles?"

The man nodded. Domitris knew as much, but his palms turned sweaty. For some reason, he hadn't expected his suspicions to be confirmed. Or maybe he had just hoped for it to be untrue. "Are there plans to dethrone me?"

The man's face was pale as a corpse and beads of sweat studded his forehead.

"Tell me their names. Is it Gaius?" Domitris asked, before his eyes caught on the group at the end of the room. Two men had stood and were walking towards them. The man flicked a glance over his shoulder and fear rippled across his face.

"I can't. Not here, it's too dangerous. Too many ears. I thought this would be safe—but no." He got up.

"Wait," Domitris hissed. They were so close.

The men that had been coming their way went past them to another table, only looking at them to gawp at Sinnan.

"No. No, it's not safe. Come to my office at the library tomorrow. Ask for Taxon. I promise I'll tell you everything then. Where it's safe," he whispered. "This was a mistake."

Before any of them managed another word, the man swung around and practically ran for the door. Domitris considered chasing after him, but causing a scene would get him nowhere.

And then the man was gone. Domitris fell back into his seat. The feeling of being so close but gaining nothing tired him to his bones. *A conspiracy.* He should have seen it coming, should have paid attention to the rumors. Gaius had been warmongering for months. His mind was fuzzy, his thoughts ringing in his ears. *Focus.* He shouldn't have drunk as much as he had. Leaning over the table, he rubbed his face with his palms.

All the pieces were falling into place. Now he needed to do something about it. He still needed the names. He had to tread carefully from now on if he wanted to find out how deep it went—how many had been turned against him. He would have to go to the academy in the morning. If he could get the information he needed, he could have Gaius exiled by the end of the week. Oh, how infinitely satisfying it would be to get rid of him.

He looked over at Sinnan, expecting to see his exhaustion mirrored, but Sinnan didn't look tired anymore. His eyes were fixed on the empty chair in front of them. Domitris could tell he was listening for something, and he tried doing the same. Several people had entered during the past hour, and pretty much everyone was drunk by now. There were so many conversations going on at once, mixed with laughter and belches and swearing, that he didn't know what to listen for in the impenetrable noise. He tapped Sinnan with a knuckle and Sinnan's consciousness returned to their table.

"Listen," he whispered. "The group by the door. I think the new guy knows something."

An especially shabby-looking man had joined the table and was boasting about something, holding his mug high in the air.

"...those marble-lickers will pay anything to get other people to take care of their mess!"

Sinnan turned to Domitris with a crooked brow. "We might not have to leave empty-handed after all. We have to get closer. Follow my lead," Sinnan whispered and left the table before Domitris had any say in the plan. Domitris could have slapped him. He scurried out from his seat and took long strides to keep up with Sinnan. In seconds, they were over at the table, and everyone looked up at Sinnan as approached, their conversation dying down.

"Good evening! We couldn't help overhearing what you were saying, and we want in," he said.

The boasting man crossed his arms and exchanged a glance with the rest of the group. "Is that so? What makes you think we'll tell you anything?"

"Just a hunch," Sinnan said, leaning his palms on the table, cocking his hip.

Domitris gritted his teeth. What was Sinnan *doing?*

A man with a face like a rat and a mop of tangled hair turned beet red as he leaned back in his seat. It was obvious that these guys weren't used to that kind of attention from someone like Sinnan. It was astonishing, Sinnan's ability to make people twist and turn at the bat of his eye and a few well-chosen words.

Sinnan proceeded to fling his arms around Domitris' neck and ran his finger up and down his chest. "We're eloping lovers, you see, and we could really use a quick and easy job to get the money to get out of here. The guards don't open the gates for anyone, as you know, so it helps to have something to convince them." He locked eyes with the man who had been talking. In the lack of anything better to do, Domitris tried to look as intimidating as possible at the rough faces glancing up at him.

The man snorted. "Easy? I said nothing about easy! I bet you could earn more money on your hands and knees anyway," he said with contempt and the surrounding crowd sniggered and hollered.

A beast of a man with a neck like a bull's said, "Yeah, I'll pay you a copper coin right now if you come suck me off in the alley!" which conjured outright laughter.

Sinnan's expression hardened, but his voice was still soft as a spring day. "As tempting as that offer sounds, it would be a shame to interrupt your celebration, and my lover here gets terribly jealous." Sinnan's hand flattened against Domitris' chest. "You better take good care of me tonight," he moaned, obviously to distract them. It worked beautifully.

The bragging man's grin turned into a scowl.

"It's nothing for someone like you. My cousin got paid a week's worth of silver and a horse to do business for some idiot at the palace with the only condition that he used the horse to leave the city afterwards."

"What was the job?" Domitris asked.

"He talks! Well, fuck if I know. All I know is that he rode from here a happy man."

"What are you so excited about, then?" Sinnan asked.

The man's eyes were gliding all over Sinnan's body and he seemed to be oiling him up in his mind. He spread his legs further, and Domitris wanted to gag. "Before he left, my cousin told me that someone needed hands, so I went to a place where I was given a bag of coins to…" he trailed off, seemingly deciding he was giving away too much.

Sinnan held his gaze and didn't give up. "As I said, we want in," Sinnan said without a trace of the cheerful loudmouth he was portraying seconds ago. "How do we get in touch with them?"

"No, sorry, sweet cheeks. If you want some of mine, I want some of yours," he said, looking Sinnan up and down, smiling with his rotten teeth.

"Let's go," Domitris whispered to Sinnan, but he ignored him.

"We'll see if that can be arranged," Sinnan said instead.

The man licked his lips.

Domitris froze, hardly believing what was going on while the crowd laughed, and an especially greasy man bumped Domitris' shoulder with his fist.

"What a catch! Don't you keep him satisfied, big guy?" he taunted, but Sinnan was unfazed.

Domitris leaned in again and said, "Forget it. Let's get out of here."

Sinnan turned to him and Domitris couldn't make out the meaning of the annoyance on his face. He didn't have time to figure it out because someone pushed Domitris so hard he smashed into the table next to them.

"Didn't you hear? He wants to stay with us. Now piss off."

The rat-faced man grabbed Sinnan's arm and didn't let go when he tried to wrestle it free.

And then it escalated.

Sinnan landed a punch in his face so hard that blood came spraying out of his nose. He let go to grab at it, hopelessly trying to contain the downpour. This prompted another of the men to fly up and throw a punch that hit Sinnan square in the jaw and sent him to the ground. Domitris threw himself between them and stopped the man's arm mid-air before the next punch landed.

The man with the rotten teeth caught Domitris' eye as he slid away in the turmoil, and in that same moment, someone slammed their foot into the back of Domitris' knees. He toppled over and pain shot up through his body as his kneecaps and wrists impacted with the rough stones. Beside him, Sinnan had regained his composure and yanked Domitris' assailant's leg violently backwards, making him fall over, face first. A crowd formed around them and cheers from the onlookers mixed with the shouts of their attackers. Domitris saw only a glimpse of a wooden chair before it was smashed into his upper back, taking his breath from him. He collided with the floor, only semi-averted by his forearm.

Domitris groaned in pain and his whole body cramped as he tried to scramble to his feet. Sinnan had gotten up in the meantime. He caught the chair-thrower, flung him to the ground, placed his arm between his legs and rammed it backwards over his thigh. The man screamed as his arm bent out of shape and gasps escaped from the crowd. The rat-faced man with the bloody pulp for a nose was up again, and he looked angry. Something slim and silver glistened in the light from the oil lamps. Domitris had only just gotten up. He hurt all over and couldn't get his legs to move fast enough.

"He's got a knife!" he yelled out, trying to get it through the noise.

Luckily, Sinnan heard him. He managed to duck down as the man with the knife charged, and instead of colliding with

Sinnan, he crashed into a table, sending mugs and platters flying.

The giant appeared from behind and flung himself at Sinnan, grabbing hold under his arms. Incapacitated, Sinnan struggled, spouting foreign profanities as he tried to kick him in the shins.

Since Domitris' attention was on getting to Sinnan, he didn't notice the attacker in front of him before a fist was planted firmly in his gut. He went down again, doubling over as he gasped for air, nausea turning in his throat. The man shoved him to the ground, straddling him, ready to punch him in the face.

Sizzling with embarrassment from the fall, Rat-face got up and turned his beady eyes on Sinnan. He slithered close, squashing Sinnan's cheeks with one hand while bringing the knife to his face with the other.

"We'll see how pretty you are after I'm done with you."

Domitris braced his arm against the punch and prepared himself for the sound of Sinnan's scream. He couldn't let it happen. Instinct took over and his free hand frantically searched the floor around him for a weapon. His fingers looped around the handle of a mug, and he used all the strength he could muster to bash it into the temple of his assailant. The man above him crumbled, clutching his head, and Domitris shoved him aside. He flew up and lunged at the man with the knife, yanking him away from Sinnan and planting his fist in his already broken nose. The man yowled, and the knife dropped to the floor. In a fluid motion, Domitris twisted his arm, and he contorted in pain as a swift kick to the back of the knees brought him down.

AS WE FALL

When Domitris turned around, the giant had forced Sinnan's arms behind his back and was dragging him away. He was almost a head taller than Domitris with arms to match—Domitris had no chance with his fists. He had to think of something else. He grabbed an ale from the closest table.

"Duck!"

Sinnan threw down his head and Domitris flung the contents of the cup into the man's face. Drenched, he stumbled backwards, losing hold of Sinnan as he fell over a chair.

"You two better fucking run!" one of the onlookers yelled.

Sinnan's eyes met Domitris' and they both bolted for the door. Stumbling out into the darkness, Domitris grabbed Sinnan's arm to make sure they ran in the same direction, back the way they came. Distant shouting and hasty footsteps warned them that some of the men had given chase. Domitris didn't dare glance back. They kept running through the darkness, down narrow alleyways and across ragged streets, until Sinnan grabbed hold of him, forcing them down a cobbled backstreet where he found a nook. He pushed Domitris in tight against the wall and pressed against him.

The pursuers would run by them any minute and it was hard to control their panting. Sinnan buried his face in the fabric of Domitris' clothes to cancel out the noise. The moist heat bled through the linen and clung to Domitris' chest. He tried to hold his own breath, but the beating of his heart in his throat was unbearable. Heavy footsteps came closer and closer. They were right next to them now, and Domitris held his mouth and nose shut with his hand.

Then the footsteps went past them.

And became distant.

They stood completely still to make sure the pursuer was gone, then ran back towards the tavern, ensuring they wouldn't walk into an ambush further down the road.

Eventually, they found a safe path, taking them south. Neither of them said much on the way; they just focused on getting as quietly and quickly back to safety as possible. They made their way through the narrow streets and out on the torch-lit main road, which they crossed to continue south to the marketplace and the camp.

Finally feeling as if they had escaped the danger, and the thrill of the fight leaving his body, aching spread across Domitris' back. He shot a look at Sinnan. Even in the low light, the big red mark appearing on his left cheek was painfully visible. When Sinnan caught him looking, he moved his jaw around, massaging it with his hand. He winced at the touch, letting out a groan.

Domitris laughed, but it came out as more of a rasp.

"I'm sorry. About tonight," Sinnan said quietly.

Domitris nodded. The atmosphere changed. "What was your plan? Were you really going to go with him?"

"No. I mean… I don't know," Sinnan said, and looked annoyed. "I guess I counted on talking my way out of it. That I could get him to tell me before anything happened. Men like that need the promise of reward to do anything."

Domitris looked back at him in stunned silence. That was his plan? Had he been so drunk he actually thought that was a good idea, or was he a worse planner than Domitris had thought?

"Not my best plan, all right? I'm sorry about what happened. I really didn't mean to get you dragged into a fight like that."

"I know. It wasn't your fault. Those guys were scum," Domitris said calmly, realizing that the knot in his chest wasn't anger—it was fear. It had been way too close. They could have been properly hurt. Sinnan could have been sliced open or... worse. At least he seemed to know how to defend himself. "Did you really break that guy's arm?"

Sinnan looked down at his feet. "It's a mean trick I've had to pick up along the way."

Domitris tried not to imagine exactly what that meant.

As they walked back to the campsite, Domitris had no idea how late it was. Judging by the almost pitch darkness, it wasn't close to sunrise, yet the lack of activity around the camps said it was past midnight. Only a few torches here and there were still lit, a few night owls up talking around fires.

The troupe's camp was completely dark. Amelia and Jenine were nowhere to be seen, and it didn't look like Bardeia or Ennio had made it back, either.

"Do you think the others are safe?" Domitris asked.

"Hm?" Sinnan looked around in the darkness. "Oh, it looks like Amelia and Jenine made it back a while ago."

Domitris looked around the empty campsite. "How do you see that?"

Sinnan pointed to their tent. "Do you see the ribbon on the front?"

Domitris nodded.

"We have a code. When we go to bed in our tents and all is well, we tie a white ribbon at the entrance, so we all know that we're back and that we're fine."

Domitris noted that the three other tents were lacking the ribbons. "Bardeia and Ennio are not back yet," he stated.

"No, it looks that way. Well, I guess that means we're the lucky ones who get to sleep." Sinnan flashed a teasing smile and headed for his tent, where he bound the ribbon. Domitris sat down on one of the logs beside the cold fire while Sinnan readied his pallet inside his tent.

"Aren't you worried?"

Sinnan sighed, left the mattress, and came over to sit beside him.

"Living on the streets is dangerous. Earning money by running around the scary parts of big cities at night is a risky business, but we usually have no choice."

Domitris hadn't really seen it before, or maybe he hadn't wanted to see it. He had been blinded by their smiles and laughter and brightly colored clothes and tents and jewelry, and it only now dawned on him that the troupe were little more than beggars.

"Of course, I'm worried. I'm always worried. These people are my family. Every time I don't know where they are or whether they're safe, I'm worried. The only way not to be consumed by it is by sticking to our codes and not thinking too much about the rest. 'Anything that happens can be dealt with in the morning,' is what we usually say to keep from lying awake all night."

He looked at Domitris to see if he understood.

"It sounds like a tough life."

"It is a tough life," Sinnan said as he got up and headed for his tent, leaving Domitris alone in the darkness.

"Are you coming?" Sinnan stuck his head back out of the tent opening.

Domitris looked around. "Coming where?"

Sinnan rolled his eyes and let the flap fall down again. "Suit yourself if you want to sleep upright on a log all night, I won't stop you, but if you change your mind, there's room in my tent."

The silence stretched while Domitris contemplated the suggestion. Somehow, it felt much more intimate to be sharing a tent than a bed. Or was it because they were on Sinnan's territory now, and not his own? He was trespassing. He shouldn't be here. He considered if he should go back to the palace, but nothing in him wanted to. *A conspiracy.* If someone was out to get him, he wanted to keep as far away as possible until he figured it out. And he didn't want to leave Sinnan. He finally got up and walked over to the low, beige tent, got on his knees in front of the entrance, and pulled the flap aside. It looked low and cramped from the outside, but inside it was surprisingly spacious.

"Do you want a tour of the residence, or do you want to come in?" Sinnan pulled off his tunic and got under the threadbare covers. Domitris scooted inside and got down beside him. The pallet was big enough for both of them if they lay close enough.

Sinnan let out a sigh and closed his eyes. The warmth of him burned where their skin touched.

"Turn me over if I start to snore," Sinnan mumbled into Domitris' shoulder, and like that, he was out, already breathing heavily. Domitris lay flat on his back, steadying his breathing, trying to calm the spinning in his muscles. He couldn't tell whether it was from the alcohol or the fight. His whole body ached. The tent had the earthy smell of moisture despite the unrelenting heat. It was the kind of scent a tent gained from years of usage in all kinds of weather and having to pack up before the morning dew had dried. He couldn't sleep with the events of the night churning through his mind, playing and replaying the fight in his head. It mixed with thoughts of Sinnan and the troupe scrambling to get by, of how Sinnan had learned to break a man's arm without blinking, of Sinnan who was ready to throw himself to the wolves to get what he wanted. An insect buzzed somewhere, trapped underneath the outer tent. As the fight played over in his head for the fourth time, he faded into a hazy sleep.

XX

When the birds tattled of sunrise and the first activity of the marketplace began, Domitris opened his eyes to the beige inside of the tent. The sound of cart wheels grinding over sandy roads mixed with croaky mutters of morning voices penetrated the thin canvas. He sat up. The air inside was hot and stuffy as they had been two people sleeping in a space meant for one. He found he had slept surprisingly well, considering the arrangements. He also found himself alone.

His garments were crumpled up in the foot-end of the mattress and he put them on, hitting the top and sides of the canvas with his arms as he tried to maneuver into them. Once dressed, he crawled out through the opening, leaving the flap open for air. The tent cover was wet with morning dew that shimmered in the sunrise and his hands left dark prints where he touched it. He went to the fire, where everybody stared at him as he approached. Jenine stirred the pot while Amelia braided her hair down her back.

"Look who's decided to join us. Did you sleep well, Your Highness? I hope the ground was not too hard on your delicate backside."

Apparently, Amelia was a morning person. Bardeia shoved her playfully, grinning at the comment.

Domitris didn't answer. He wasn't in the mood for her brand of humor. Instead, he sat down by the fire with the others. "Is there any news?"

"It seems we had the most interesting night yesterday, can you believe it?" Sinnan said.

He could. He was certainly hoping no one had been in more trouble than them. The mark on Sinnan's jaw had turned an interesting shade of plum overnight, almost matching the beetroot tunic he was still wearing.

"It sounded like you put up quite a fight," Bardeia said and patted him on the back, right where he was hit by the chair, and he grimaced in pain. They all laughed. From the sound of it, Sinnan had already entertained them with the story. He felt his back with his hand, not quite able to touch the soreness, but the bruising was obvious just from moving his shoulder blades around.

Not wanting to relive it once more, he changed the topic. "Did any of you learn anything?"

The smiles settled, and Jenine distributed breakfast.

"Probably not what you were hoping to hear," Ennio said.

A small bowl of what looked like gruel was offered to him, and he took it before returning his attention to Ennio.

"What?"

Ennio looked to Bardeia, and she took over.

"Well, I suppose the point is that we didn't learn much. We tracked down some eyewitnesses who were there when it happened."

While she talked, Domitris cooled a spoonful with his breath and took a bite. It was sweet and sticky in his mouth. He wasn't sure he really enjoyed it, but it tasted nutritious.

"And?"

"They all said that it was a group of rowdy drunks coming to the Panjusticia and that they were acting strangely."

Distracted, he burned his tongue on the next bite. He forced the scorching lump down to get the question out.

"Strange how?"

Ennio chimed in again. "Something didn't add up. Several people said that the arsonists acted really aggressive at first and then very obviously lit torches and drenched the building in oil before setting it on fire. A few people interfered, but they started fights with anyone who tried to stop them."

Domitris' heart sank with each piece of information. "It adds up perfectly." He thought of what the man with the rotten teeth had said. It had to be connected. Nobles giving money to lowlifes to ruin the city—it was suddenly so clear. Someone was trying to sabotage him while his attention was on the dealings with Dassosda.

"Were they Dassosdan or Marmarasi?"

Domitris could guess the answer from the small silence that followed the question.

"The arsonists were all Marmarasi," Bardeia answered. "Multiple people said that."

He sighed and mulled it over. "Why the Panjusticia though?" he asked. "Why not target me directly?"

Amelia leaned forward, elbows on her knees. "It seems like someone is trying to make you look bad."

He looked up at her pale face, and she met his eyes with a

pointed gaze.

"It makes sense, doesn't it? If they can undermine you and everything you stand for, it'll be much easier getting rid of you. A direct assassination attempt can be covered up or justified, or even make a martyr of you, but to see you fail, to have the city crumble under *your* rule, especially in light of how torn people are over that treaty, seems like a perfect way to crush whatever support you have."

A strained silence fell over them all. Domitris put his head in his hands. She was right, of course, but to hear it like that was almost unbearable.

"I don't understand," he said, mostly to himself. He had worked so hard to do the right things.

Amelia continued. "Why do you find that so hard to fathom? You people have lived with that blood purist you called an emperor for more than half a century who did nothing but start wars and cater to the nobles sucking his ass all day. How did you expect this peace to go?"

Subtlety was not her weapon of choice.

"If given the option, I believe people would always want peace."

Amelia scoffed.

"Hey," Sinnan said, interrupting whatever she was going to say next. She clenched her jaw.

Everyone took a spoonful of their breakfast, and the noise from the market took over while wooden spoons fiddled in bowls.

Sinnan swallowed and pointed his spoon towards Amelia and Jenine.

"So… Did you guys see anything here at the market?"

Jenine tapped the butt of the spoon against her chin. "Yesterday we didn't think much of it, but now..." She looked over at Amelia, who was stuffing her face with porridge. "There was this man who came not long after you left. He looked like he was from the palace. Fancy hair, purple robes, things like that. He was very young, though."

That had to be Cassian. Who else would prance around the market like that for everyone to see?

"Blondish, mid-length hair, not that tall?" he asked.

Jenine nodded. "Yeah! Something like that. You know him?"

"I wish I didn't. Did he do anything?"

"He was visiting someone, it seemed. He was drinking with a group a few camps from here."

Amelia swallowed her food. "He didn't really do much. Just acted friendly with that lot. We haven't seen that many nobles at the market since we got here, so we found it odd. And now it seems downright suspicious. But like Jenine said, he was so young—didn't really seem like the scheming type."

"Where's the camp he joined?"

"They've packed up. They're not here anymore."

Domitris ran a hand over his chin. It seemed like he wasn't making any progress at all. He was still no closer to a name, and he only felt more unsafe. His only hope now was Taxon. It would be a risk going that far away, but under the circumstances, it was a risk staying at the palace, too.

"I have to get going to make it to the academy before the noon bell. Thank you for all your help. And for the food."

Sinnan shot up from the log he had been sitting on so fast it tipped over. "Take me with you."

"What?"

"Take me. To the library."

"You have fulfilled your part of the agreement. I can't expect anything more from you."

"It's not that. It's just... this will be my only opportunity to see the Library of Marmaras. I've dreamed of that my whole life." He said it as he brought the log back up and placed himself on it.

Domitris looked at him again. It sounded like a lie. How would Sinnan know about—

"He means it," Amelia said. "No, seriously. He's been talking about that library ever since we made our way towards Marmaras."

"Are you sure?" he asked Sinnan. "With the ride, it'll take the whole day."

Sinnan cast a glance around at the others. Bardeia nodded.

"I'm sure. Please?"

The look on Sinnan's face was unambiguous. He really wanted to go.

"Of course. I'll be happy to have the company. I'm going back to the palace to get a horse and get cleaned up. I'll meet you back here when I can."

Going home from the marketplace, he passed by the Panjusticia to see the state of it himself. It was a gloomy sight. He stood in front of the charred skeleton of what had been a magnificent building the day before. He had stood here, right here, what felt like hours ago. This was a direct affront to him, the treaty, and everything he stood for. He had dared to hope for success. He had believed, for a brief second, that everything would fall into place. His insides felt like the crumbling structure in front of him. Standing there, he struggled with the thought that his own nobles had done this. To him. To their own city. Were they truly so full of hatred?

Smoke still oozed from embers among the rubble, though the fire had been put out several hours ago. The smell was wretched and the whole scene was miserable, even in the rouge light from the sunrise. He didn't want to linger; there was nothing he could do about it now. Except make sure that something like it never happened again.

He went on to the theater to make a shortcut through the passage to the palace. He ended up in the council hall, which he expected to be empty, but instead he found Ignotus. He stood hunched over, scribbling away at a scroll. He was in disarray, his long, dark hair messy and wearing clothes from the day before. But then again, so was Domitris.

"Wh–" started Domitris but was cut off when Ignotus looked up at him, his eyes wide and furious.

"Where have you *been?*" Ignotus hissed. "I've been looking for you all morning."

"You know I was out."

"Yes, but I didn't think that meant all night and all morning. It's not safe out there!" Ignotus sounded uncharacteristically desperate.

"I *know* that. That's what I'm trying to do something about!" Domitris' own irritation grew. "What's going on with you? You look like you haven't slept all night."

That made Ignotus stand down. He took a deep breath and relaxed his shoulders. "I haven't. I've been up working, trying to fix this mess. Do you know the amount of silver and how many people it'll take to rebuild the Panjusticia? More than the crown has, currently." His dark eyes met Domitris' pointedly.

"Are you blaming me?"

Ignotus raised his brows. "That's not—no." He sighed. "I'm just concerned. From the reports, it seems barely half the guard is loyal to the crown, crime in Tenebris is on the rise, and there's growing unease among the Dassosdans."

Domitris knew he should have been on top of those things as well, but his focus had been elsewhere.

"I'm doing my best here. We're in more trouble than I thought."

Ignotus moved closer, lowering his voice. "Did you discover anything?"

Domitris wasn't sure how to phrase it. "Remember what I said to you yesterday about it coming from inside the palace? Well, it seems I was right."

Ignotus' eyes widened. "What? Now you really do sound paranoid."

"You know better than I do how Gaius has been criticizing me while I've been away."

"And you think he's trying to take your place and burn down the city at the same time?"

"Him, and Cassian. And probably others as well. I'm not sure. I'm riding to the academy to meet with an informant."

There was a slight shift in Ignotus' stance, and he crossed his arms. "An informant? A scholar?"

"Yes. But I don't know how much he knows yet. I'm going there to find out."

Ignotus nodded and his eyes searched Domitris' face.

"You look terrible. What happened last night?"

Domitris stretched his aching back. "It's a long story. I'll fill you in later."

Ignotus relaxed his shoulders and uncrossed his arms. "Fine."

Domitris patted him on the arm. "Will you handle the council today? I won't be back before evening. Keep Gaius and Cassian under observation, and watch who they interact with."

"Of course."

Domitris clapped a hand to the side of Ignotus' neck and walked past him to change as the first bell of the morning rang in the distance.

In his room, he found Lyra, polishing the bronze mirror plate with more force than necessary, warping the reflection.

"We've talked about taking your frustrations out on the furniture," he said, startling her.

She jerked around and the concerned line on her forehead transformed into an angry frown in the space of a second.

"I've been so worried! You didn't come home all night! I almost sent the guards out looking for you," she said with the shrill tone she only used when she was genuinely upset with him.

"I told you I was out. I didn't mean to worry you," he said, trying to sound remorseful.

She slapped him with the polishing cloth. "You can't keep doing this."

"I know. I won't. I have to go to the academy today but after that, I promise to slow down."

"The academy? Today? What on earth are you going there

for? What about your meetings?"

"Ignotus is taking care of the meetings. I've found someone who might know who was behind the attack and the fire."

Lyra's jaw clenched and her lips tightened.

"I'm being careful!" he protested.

She took a deep breath and visibly decided not to argue with him. Her posture softened and she nodded towards the table. "I made you breakfast."

The sight of the untouched tray waiting for him made his insides writhe in guilt. He picked up a piece of bread and the nostalgic scent of thyme only made the feeling worse. He didn't have time to eat it and even if he did, he was still full. "Can I bring it with me for the journey?"

"That's up to you," she said. "By the way, do you know where the silver pitcher is? I can only find this ugly carafe." She picked up the brown glass carafe and poured him a cup of mint water.

"I haven't seen it."

"I must have misplaced it in the kitchens," she mumbled to herself. "Make sure to drink something. I'll go find you some waxed cloth for the food."

"Thank you."

When Lyra scurried out of the room, Domitris downed the cup of water and plopped down on the bed with a sigh.

The aroma of lavender and spices hit his nostrils and he was confused for a second until he remembered the charm he had tucked away under his pillow. As he got it out, the scent spread through the room. It stirred up emotions in his heart he couldn't define. The troupe had so little, and yet, they had offered him a gift. It was a small thing but somehow it felt more valuable than any of the finery he had been gifted by senators on the tour. He couldn't say his nightmares were gone, but he appreciated the gesture nonetheless.

Preoccupied with his thoughts, Lyra startled him when she came back up the stairs and he shoved the charm back under the pillow so he wouldn't have to explain it to her.

"Here you go," she said and started packing up the food.

He got off the bed and wrapped his arms around her small shoulders. A surprised squeak escaped her, but she returned the hug and patted his arm.

"What was that for?" she asked when he let go.

"I don't know where I would be without you."

She laughed and continued securing the little bundle.

"Nonsense. Now, you better get going if you want to make it to the academy and back before dinner. I expect you to be home early. You haven't had enough rest since you came back and it's beginning to show."

He couldn't help smiling. Her honesty was always a breath of fresh air. "Don't worry, I will."

The road to the academy was long, even on horseback, but with Sinnan nestled against his chest, telling tall tales from the troupe's travels, time seemed to fly by. Drops of sweat trickled down the back of Domitris' neck in the heat from the sun shining down from an uninterrupted sky. Moist friction formed where Sinnan's shoulders pressed against his skin. He didn't mind it—the heat. They had more than enough water in the drinking skins dangling back and forth in time with the horse's steps, and he was in good company.

Sinnan had changed into a new outfit by the time Domitris picked him up and though it was nowhere near as scandalous as what he had seen him in so far, it did make him wonder whether Sinnan owned any respectable clothing at all. His jade-green tunic hit his ankles when he stood, though it had to be hitched up above his knees to sit astride the horse. Any modesty was lost by the low cut of the neckline and nonsensical sleeves that had slits all the way from his shoulders to where they fastened at his elbows, leaving his upper arms bare. He clearly wasn't bothered by the heat either, because instead of wearing his embroidered sunscarf over his hair, he had tied it around his waist.

Sinnan stretched his hands out in front of him while they trotted on along the broad gravel road, his bracelets glinting in the sun.

"I can't believe how much I've tanned while we've been here."

Domitris wasn't fair-skinned himself, but Sinnan was all golden brown. Domitris stroked the skin of his shoulder through the open sleeves.

"Has it changed?"

"Yeah. I was much paler back in Háfren. You know, when the sun sets not many hours after noon most of the year, it drains the color from you pretty efficiently."

"Does the time of the sunset change a lot?"

Sinnan turned his head to look at him. "Well, yes. In winter, the morning starts halfway to noon, and the evening ends not long after lunch."

"That sounds dreadful. Like the underworld."

Sinnan laughed. "I used to like it. There was snow and the

lakes froze over. And sometimes the sea did too. Newly fallen snow shimmering like stars in the winter sun is a hard sight to beat."

Domitris tried to imagine it, but he had never seen snow. The northern Marmarasi mountain provinces had snow in the winter, but that wasn't a place where nobles found themselves if they could help it. The closest he could get was thinking about the endless piles of salt outside the salt mines in the south.

"The best part is the summer nights, though," Sinnan went on. "The sun hardly sets, and the nights are long and light and warm. I'll never get used to the summer evenings being dark here."

"It sounds as though you liked the Heathlands."

"I did. Especially the weather. And the seasons. I miss it."

"Why did you leave?"

Sinnan absentmindedly ran a thumb over the back of his hand. It hadn't been voluntary. "We just do sometimes, don't we?"

Another sore spot. No wonder. Every time Domitris got too close, he shirked away. What would it take for Sinnan to say a single, genuine thing? Domitris pushed back the urge to wring the answers out of him. Before he had found out how to phrase the next question, it was too late. Sinnan shot up from where he had been leaning on him.

"Look, we're almost there!"

The academy came into view and towered up in front of them with every step. Sinnan's breath went shallow as he observed it.

The grounds around the academy were plains as far as the

eye could see, though Domitris knew there was a steep drop somewhere in the distance, ending the plateau. In addition to the school, the academy included the Library of Marmaras and the national archives. Where the palace was architectural chaos formed through half a millennium of shifting trends and influences, the academy was planned and measured and perfect.

The whole complex was a village of its own and though it was still within Concordia's walls, it was solely because the city wall had been torn down and rebuilt around it centuries ago when the academy was erected.

The front gate to the academy was located at the end of a long set of flat stairs where they closed in. The top of the gate was decorated with a massive marble arch, which was mirrored at the foot of the stairs. Along the arch, large, stiff letters of the old writing system declared:

YOU NOW TREAD THE ACADEMIC PATH

The stone pillars supporting the arch featured large, unblinking faces—the same man, all of them—carved out from the stone, looking in every direction.

They had taken it all in silently, but now he nudged Sinnan. "Do you see the creepy stone faces?"

Sinnan had been looking above it, up on the Scholar's Cone, stretching into the sky, but turned his face to the marble arch instead.

"Those are terrifying. Who is it?"

"That's almost the most terrifying part. They were supposed to be Galana, the empress who ordered the academy built, but that face is Phelan's, the emperor who ruled when the construction finished. He ordered the design changed to feature himself instead."

"If that isn't the way of the world, I don't know what is."

When they reached the stairs, Domitris hopped off the horse and helped Sinnan down. Then he tied their drinking skins to his belt and stuffed the small pack of provisions into the folds of his clothes. They left the horse behind at the small stable building that stood strangely in the middle of nowhere, but there was an eager attendant and several well-groomed horses munching happily on a sheaf of barley.

Sinnan was already at the foot of the stairs and as they climbed it, the three main buildings slowly appeared. The most noticeable of them was the Scholar's Cone to the south that had been visible even at a distance. It was the living quarters of the guardians and scholars and had gotten its name because of the large, spiraling shape that expanded upwards. To the north was the Marble Hall, which was where most learning activities took place and where the classrooms were found. Between them there was a square building that was the entrance to the library. Domitris hadn't been here since his graduation more than a decade ago. A dizzying, sweeping feeling came over him and he couldn't help smiling. It had been his home for most of his childhood years and he had taken mainly good memories with him.

"This is amazing," Sinnan whispered.

They reached the top and went through the gate where an enclosed plaza formed the entrance to the village. Grape vines twirled around grooved columns that formed an arbor above a set of curving stone benches. A few kids out of class lounged around on the benches, reading or talking. The gentle splashing from the fountain in the middle added a touch of serenity.

They passed a young couple of a laughing girl lying in the lap of a boy with blond curls while he fed her grapes and played with her hair. Sinnan's eyes were everywhere, hungry, as if he would miss something if he didn't look around fast enough.

Passing through, they entered the village properly and the myriad of smaller buildings that hosted mainly students and visitors became visible. Domitris craned his neck to get a glimpse of the building where his old room had been. They passed several groups of people on the way towards the library. The scholars were easily recognizable figures with their gold-trimmed black robes and floppy pointed caps, which Domitris had always thought looked like fat little cornucopias. Some of them carried scrolls from one place to another while others were in heated debate and still others were accompanying classes of young scholars, all dressed in gentle pink, their long braids coming down their backs under pink caps. The sight of them made Domitris remember exactly how it had felt back when he had been one of them. Every experience had been new and exciting.

The classes were larger now that he had opened up the schooling for commoners last year, but in their robes and long hair, who was commoner and who was noble was indistinguishable. One group sat in a lecture pit around a scholar who pointed furiously at a scribble on an easel with a long wooden stick. The kids in the front were frowning but attentive, while most of the kids further in the back had blank looks in their eyes. Two kids were holding hands, one of them whispering to the other before they giggled. The atmosphere was busy but tranquil, and the air was thick with ideas and thoughts.

"There are so many kids here," Sinnan said, observing the pink groups around them.

"Of course. It's the academy."

"Do they come all the way from the city every day?" Sinnan asked.

Domitris wondered how that would work. "No, they live here. From when they are five until they graduate. Then some go to the palace, some go back to their estates, some stay to become scholars…. It depends."

Sinnan frowned, as if ten new questions formed in his head. "So, they live away from their families all of their childhood?"

"They go home during the fall months and a few times during the year."

"I knew the Marmarasi system was strange, but that doesn't make any sense. You're barely around your family until you're, what, fifteen?"

"Well, the kids are busy with their studies and finding their place in the world. There's no real need."

"No need? For family? You just leave children on their own like that?"

Domitris slowed his pace. "It means that young people get to experience independence. I don't see what's so bad about that."

Sinnan was going to say something more, but just then, they passed a road so familiar to Domitris that he had to change their course.

"Hey, come this way. I want to show you something."

He led them down a narrow path to the right, took a turn, then another, and then–

"Here," Domitris said as they walked through an opening in an unkempt hedge. It was a cramped, cobbled yard with a faded statue in the middle and a fountain so small it could have been a drinking post. "I haven't seen this place in a decade. I used to come here all the time as a kid. Ignotus and I found it one day when we were ditching class and figured it was the perfect hideout."

"You, skulking?" Sinnan grinned.

"What? I was a wild child." Domitris walked over to the statue. Most of its features were lost with time and lack of maintenance. The outstretched pointer finger was broken off and still hadn't been fixed. His lips quirked as he remembered the panic when his and Ignotus' fooling around had snapped it off, how they had scrambled to return to the plaza and pretend that nothing had happened. Sinnan came up beside him, his shoulder brushing against Domitris' arm, pulling him back to the present.

"For some reason, I find that hard to believe," Sinnan said, his voice breathy. He blew a damp lock of hair away from his forehead, his expression easy and amused. The other days he had spent with Sinnan, there always seemed to be something else going on underneath, but right now, in this moment, he was just there.

Sinnan placed a hand on Domitris' chest, the sweet proximity overwhelming.

"Is that so?" Domitris said, getting lost in Sinnan's green eyes. It was as if the small garden existed outside time and place. Like this was the whole world and there was nothing else he had to think about. *Irresistible.*

He leaned forward, slowly, and stroked the unbruised side of Sinnan's jaw. Sinnan fluttered his eyes shut and didn't move. He looked like a different person, standing like that, waiting to be kissed. Domitris wanted the moment to last forever. He put his forehead against Sinnan's and buried his hand in the soft hair at the back of Sinnan's head. Then he let the kiss land lightly on his lips. He lingered for a little while, and then Sinnan kissed him back. Sinnan's hand slid from Domitris' chest to around his neck and he pulled him closer. It set everything ablaze in Domitris, as if the heat would consume him entirely. The taste of Sinnan's mouth like this—sober, present, accommodating—was enough to undo him. Sinnan pulled back slightly to look up at him, his dark lashes heavy, his lips wet. Domitris swallowed and let out a shuddering breath in the space between them.

"Don't you have somewhere to be?" Sinnan said so softly it was almost a whisper. Domitris' breath hitched.

"Don't remind me," he said, but he let go of Sinnan and pulled back. Running his hand over his face, he sat down on the overgrown seat opposite the fountain. "I'll just need a second."

Sinnan sat down beside him with an endearingly satisfied smile. Then he sprang up again and went to the statue, narrowing his eyes.

"No way." He pointed to the copper plaque beneath it. "It is! It's a statue of Giladenes!"

Domitris didn't have to look to check. He knew it was.

"How on earth do you know that?"

Sinnan was inspecting the chiseled sword and the folds in her garment. "Carantacula's Journey was my favorite story as a child. I used to pretend to be Giladenes and go on adventures in the forest by my home all the time."

Domitris raised a brow. "Weird choice for a kid. We just played marauders and soldiers or something like that."

Sinnan turned to him, a playful smile teasing his lips. "How very uneducated of you. Your professors must weep."

"Wait a second. I didn't know that play was performed so far north."

"It wasn't," Sinnan said, running his fingers over the stone. "I read it."

Domitris looked him up and down. *"You* read it?"

"What, you didn't think I could read?"

Domitris opened his mouth to say something, but then it occurred to him it was probably exactly what he had thought, and heat rose along his neck. It was, after all, only nobles who were taught to read and write in Marmaras up until just a few years ago.

"No. I just meant… *I* didn't even read all of it."

Sinnan had crossed his arms and didn't look entirely pleased. "Seriously," he said flatly, but then the sound of the noon bell vibrated through the air and broke off whatever conversation would have followed.

It was a strange sound, so very familiar that it instantly brought back a thousand memories, some tangible, others not. It was nothing like the clear sound of the palace bells he was used to hearing every day now.

"We better get going," Domitris said. Sinnan gracefully let it go and followed him back to the main road. It nagged at the back of Domitris' mind though, that he still knew very little about Sinnan as a person and every effort he made to try to get to know him was carefully evaded. He looked at Sinnan again while they walked. Reading old, foreign plays as a child didn't go very well with whatever he had imagined about Sinnan. But then again, what had he thought? There was nothing about the fine build of his limbs that suggested farmer's boy or sailor or baker or anything like that, but there wasn't anything noble about him either. Did everyone learn to read in the Heathlands? He had never heard of that, but he didn't know much about the Far North. The black hair, the green eyes, and the brown skin were atypical for Heathlanders, who were mostly very pale with fairer hair. The way he talked about the Heathlands was so genuine—*that* part couldn't be a lie. He wanted to know. He wanted Sinnan to tell him everything about himself, and he didn't care what it would reveal. He wanted to stop time right that second and ask him all the questions that were burning in his mind, to crack him open and let all the secrets spill out. But they had gotten to the main road, and there was the library, resting atop the next set of stairs.

The rectangular sandstone building in front of them was flanked by pillars of green marble that held up the roof. Above the pillars, the roof was bordered by a frieze in reds and blues and gold. The last time he had been there, the paint was faded and peeling off in places, but now, the colors stood out crisp and newly restored. The roof tiles were the old kind that had a ridge along the center and had gone out of production long ago. All along the path to the entrance hung deep black banners with the academy symbol—a stylized, white aster. The building was deceptively small. The whole thing was hardly bigger than the palace stables.

"Is that the library?" Sinnan asked as they ascended the stairs, a hint of disappointment to his words.

"It is," Domitris only said, because he knew that the building in front of them was just the glazed cherry spilling out of the cornucopia. What was visible above ground was nothing more than the cover and the entrance to the actual library, which was located inside, plunging down countless stories into the underground where books, scrolls, and documents were better protected from temperature fluctuations. But he didn't want to spoil it for Sinnan. He needed to see it for himself.

"It looks... smaller than I had expected," Sinnan said.

Domitris didn't answer, just kept an eye on him as he looked around. They walked in through the doors of the cool stone building and echoes from hushed whispers bounced off the walls in the hall. The building was empty except for an enormous, circular hole in the ground with a railing around it, and stairs leading down to the lower levels at the side. At this point, Sinnan seemed truly confused and kept looking to Domitris for an explanation.

"You'll see," was all he said.

Their footsteps echoed as they walked across the checkered green and white tiles. As they closed in on the railing, light and noises billowed up from the circular hole and Sinnan practically threw himself over the balustrade to peer down as they got there. Down it went, so deep into the ground that the lowest stories were swallowed by darkness, making it look like a bottomless pit from this far up. A string of soft echoes—footsteps, people turning pages, hushed talking—drifted up toward them like vapor. A crate hoist with a load full of boxes and scrolls on the opposite side of the railing whirred as someone on a lower level yanked on a lever.

"*Woooow,*" Sinnan whispered.

Domitris smiled at the awe on his face, and he glanced down again. It was truly awe-inspiring looking down, down, down on the many stories stacked on top of each other, coiling endlessly. The railings spiraled downward with each story, resembling the pattern of an enormous seashell.

It was mesmerizing to behold.

"Shall we go down?"

Sinnan looked up at him, eyes wide as platters. "I've never been more ready for anything in my life."

Together, they headed for the stairs.

XXI

As they passed the edge and went beneath floor-level, the temperature dropped from sweltering to pleasant and the air grew so dry that Domitris' eyes started to feel like raisins. The air blew in through the latticed ventilation shafts that lined the walls to keep the temperature stable and the air parched.

"How far down are we going?" Sinnan asked.

"Not sure. We're asking here at the first level."

Sinnan paused to look around when they reached the first floor and Domitris passed him to go to the curved counters of the reception. Asking the guardians was the way to gain information about anything in the library. Slowly, Sinnan followed behind him.

"Can I help you, good sir?" a young man in all black guardian apprentice robes asked from the other side of the counter. He looked like it hadn't been many summers since he'd finished the classical education. Domitris could tell, not only from the lack of "Your Highness" but also because he hardly shot him a look before ogling Sinnan, that the young man had no idea who he was.

"I'm looking for someone. A scholar; Taxon, to be specific."

"Just a moment, please." He disappeared shortly before coming back with an older, meaner-looking woman in full guardian attire with the star of Marmaras embroidered on the front and back of her black cloak.

"You're looking for Taxon?" she asked. "You need to go to the fifth level where the archivists sit. Section seven to find the department of provincial records. His office will be there. Anything else?"

"No, thank you, that will be all," Domitris said with a smile, but the woman didn't return it. The apprentice hiding behind her, however, was winking discreetly at Sinnan, but Sinnan just smiled indifferently back at him. They turned and walked away from the counter.

"You really are very popular. Be careful you're not tempted," Domitris said teasingly.

"Who, the runt? That one hardly has hair between his ass cheeks yet. He needs a pat on the head and a nap before thinking about getting fucked by some random stranger. What is it you teach kids here?"

Domitris laughed too loudly, which resulted in three different guardians shushing him. That made Sinnan struggle to choke back a laugh of his own and they hurried on from the reception.

Going for the stairs, they passed a series of faded maps, and Sinnan stopped to inspect them. The most prominent drawings were clearly the newest. There were duplicates showing the same overview, but with varying details. Some were so old they were yellowed and crumpled.

"Is this the library?" he asked, hovering a finger over the first map.

"Yes." The circular nothing in the middle and the lines splayed out in every direction, detailing shelves and offices said it was. "That one is where we are now."

There was a separate map of every floor, and Sinnan walked along the display to inspect them. On all the lower levels, the word 'archive' was plastered over the whole floor-map. The library of Marmaras had become one of the wonders of the world due to the sheer amount of information stored in its depths. It had grown to its enormous size because it was required by law that any new information brought into the capital by travelers had to be copied and stored before it was returned. Over the centuries, the library had grown deeper and deeper into the ground to make room for it all. Even though the lowest levels were the newest, they were the most rough and cavernous since less money had been allocated to prioritize it over the years. If it kept growing like this, they would have to expand upwards, eventually.

Domitris looked impatiently towards the stairs, but Sinnan was too caught up to notice. At the end, Sinnan had crouched down to look at one of the old ones.

"What about this?" he said, pointing to the very last map in the row. Domitris walked over. That one wasn't the library. It was a myriad of intertwined and connected paths and halls on a long, rectangular paper, double the size of the others with no descriptions. It looked like a spider's web, if the spider had spent all night drinking wine.

"The chalk mines," he said. "There is a huge network of mines under the academy grounds, but they haven't been active in centuries. They say the chalk for mortar for the palace came from those mines before they started using concrete. I'm not sure it's possible to go down there anymore. I know it was at some point, but that must have been before my time."

"Hm." Sinnan shuddered at the cool breeze running past them.

Domitris looked to the stairs again.

"I should get going and find Taxon. Do you want to stay here and look around? I'll find you afterwards."

Sinnan looked up at him from his crouching position.

"Would that be all right?"

"Of course. There are probably more interesting things to look at up here, anyway."

Sinnan's eyes sparkled as he stood to look around. "See you later, then. Good luck."

"Thanks." Domitris looked back at him in amusement. "I hope it's everything you've ever dreamed of."

"Oh, you have no idea," Sinnan said, and Domitris continued down, alone.

On the fifth level, light became sparse, and the amount of activity dwindled drastically. Endless rows of shelves filled the halls in front of the offices located deep within and the dusty smell of old paper hung heavy in the air. Searching for section seven, he greeted a pair of scholars headed for the stairs, pale as ghosts against their black robes. He fumbled around in the cramped, maze-like corridors for ages before he found it.

Light spilled through a crack of the door, illuminating the nameplate next to the tenth office he checked: *SCH. TAXON*. Even though the door was ajar, he knocked, making the hinges squeak. When no answer came, he nudged it open and peaked inside.

"Master Taxon?"

There were no signs of him, but several oil lamps burned in the small office and heaps of papers cluttered the solid desk at the back of the room. He couldn't be far away. The floor creaked as Domitris moved forward, and he spun around per reflex.

"Master Taxon?" he called again, louder, but the only sound was his own breathing and the occasional crackling of lamp wicks.

Papers lay scattered on the desk, as if someone had been searching for a specific piece of information. He slid a few papers aside, scanning the text, but the writing was so crooked it was indecipherable.

Behind the desk, a curtain covered a narrow doorway. Could he be in the back? Domitris pulled aside the curtain and found a small hallway with three closed doors. He knocked on the first one before opening it. It was an unlit storage room no larger than a closet.

He opened the next door, and it led to a proper room. From the dim light spilling in, Domitris could make out the frame of a simple bed. He narrowed his eyes and his heart jumped to his throat—there was someone in it. Domitris' mind screamed at him.

Sleeping. Surely, he was sleeping.

A lump formed in his throat. He knocked on the open door, but the figure didn't move. His mind reeled, not wanting to draw the conclusion that a man lay dead in front of him.

Taking a steadying breath, he backed out into the hallway

where he found a burning candle. He had to confirm it before he went running for help.

He mustered the courage and returned with hesitant steps. The flickering candlelight revealed that the figure lay with his back to the room.

Domitris reached forward, slowly, to shake his arm. The second he was close enough to touch him, his foot landed in something sticky. When he lowered the light, he almost dropped the candle as the flicker caught the sheen of a black puddle. The unmistakable, sickly sweet smell of blood hit his nostrils. He gagged, lurching upright, trying to steady his shaking hands.

"Master Taxon?" he tried and moved a reluctant step closer to see his face. His eyes stared unblinkingly into the wall, but there was no doubt it was the man they had met in the tavern. The necklace of gaping flesh where his throat had been slit shook Domitris so deeply he dropped the candle into the pool of blood, snuffing it out.

A door slammed in the front room, and his heart almost leaped out through his mouth. He swung around and stumbled into the hallway. His head swam, and he had to fight to keep the contents of his stomach down.

Screams mixed with the sounds of fighting erupted somewhere far above him. He stopped moving, supporting himself against the wall as he tried to listen, but the rush of blood in his ears and his own ragged breathing drowned out the faint noises. Then a deep rumbling and a crash so loud he felt it in his bones tore through the building.

He staggered to the office where the lights were still burning. Thick smoke poured in through the vents, overtaking the room. He bolted for the door, but it was closed and he knew before he grabbed the handle that it wouldn't open. His breaths were shallow, panicked huffs and the room started spinning.

The smoke grew denser by the second, stinging in his eyes, penetrating his throat and nostrils. He lifted his head to breathe above it, but it had already filled his lungs. He coughed, heaving for air, trying to waft away the smoke, but it only made it dance in uncontrollable swirls.

He slammed on the door as hard as he could, trying to shout for help, but only gargled, raspy noises came out. He banged harder, throwing his body against it, hoping for anyone to hear him. His vision swam, his head spun. He slumped down against the door, still trying to pound on it for help.

The room was pitch black and he couldn't tell if it was because his eyes had failed or because the lights had gone out. He sank to the floor, trying to find air. Was this his demise? Had it come for him already, like this? Thoughts of the underworld sent desperate trembles through his body.

Then someone banged on the other side.

He couldn't make out the words, but it was unmistakably Sinnan's voice. He kept yelling the same thing. Finally, Domitris heard it: "Hang on!"

There was a crash from the other side. And another, and the door was torn open to a wall of whirling smoke. Water welled up in Domitris' eyes, blurring his vision. He wiped at it with his knuckles.

A hand grabbed his wrist. Sinnan hoisted him up and flung Domitris' arm over his shoulder, supporting his weight while hauling him out of the room.

"This way," Sinnan said, dragging him the best he could into the open. Domitris tripped over the shelf that had been knocked down in front of the door. The smoky air was scorching and smelled of oil and charred paper. Flames rose from the bottom of the pit, the ventilation breathing life into the roaring flames that licked their way up the woodwork. Sinnan dragged them towards the hole as another spine-chilling crash shook the ground. Splintered wood swished through the room and an intense pain cut through Domitris' shin. At the same time, Sinnan cried out what could be nothing but a swear word in another language and half-dropped Domitris.

"They've crashed the top of the stairs!" Sinnan yelled in despair. "Can you stand?"

Domitris nodded and leveled himself, succeeding despite his wobbly balance. Sinnan ran towards the middle, and Domitris only now noticed he had wrapped a scarf around his mouth. His silhouette disappeared in the smoke for a short while, then he came running back and propped Domitris up against him again.

"You have to follow me," Sinnan said, desperation growing in his voice. As they closed in on the center, the heat grew more and more intense. Sinnan got them to the stairs and dragged them down the steps. Domitris dug in his heels, wresting himself free.

"What are you doing?" Domitris managed. "We can't go down, the fire is coming from the lower levels!"

Sinnan grabbed onto him again and forced them onward. "We have to get to the crate hoist!"

The hoist. Sinnan was a genius. With the only stairs going

up destroyed, they had no way of getting to the top, but the hoist might still be working. It was operated from a couple of levels below them, so they had to continue towards the flaming inferno. Domitris leaned against the railing and steadied himself to let Sinnan move with more ease.

They found the right level, and the stench of oil engulfed them. Barely visible through the smoke, the spiral staircase suspended in the air between the upper floors loomed far above them.

Sinnan let go of Domitris and searched frantically for the hoist along the railing.

"Here it is!"

Domitris limped over to him. The hoist was a huge cog-like wheel operated by a lever controlling the ballast that could be lowered or raised, depending on whether the raft should go up or down. Sinnan yanked the lever. With each pull, the raft came closer. Luckily, it hung in the air only a few levels above, and it was soon at the railing beside them.

"Get on!" Sinnan commanded, as he hopped onto it himself. Domitris struggled to get his body to cooperate, and Sinnan had to pull him over. Sinnan then rocked the lever from side to side, trying to figure out how to get them up.

"How does this *shit* work?" he yelled in exasperation. With a desperate tug, he finally switched the mechanism, so each yank made them go up, but only a little with each turn.

"NO!" Sinnan got more and more panicked. He let go and looked helplessly around for something else to save them. They were dangling in mid-air, far above the bottom, and there were no exits, no other ways up, nowhere to go. His arms fell limply at his sides, and he looked like he was giving up. But only for a second. Then he looked to Domitris, an idea bright on his face. "Listen, you have to widen your stance, and hold my weight. Got it?"

Confused, Domitris did as he was told. He spread his feet and bent his knees. Sinnan turned, put his back against Domitris, and kicked the lever with all his strength. He rammed into Domitris' chest as he kicked, and Domitris did his best to weather the force. The wheel came apart quickly, and after the third kick, the lever broke. The cog whirled on its own, the raft flying upward. For a hopeful second, it seemed to work. They came closer and closer to the railing at the top until the raft suddenly lost speed. Then it halted, and started free falling instead, right for the blazing flames below.

Their yells mixed, blending together, making it impossible to tell who was louder. Domitris' stomach felt like it had grown wings and was exiting his body. The raft spun through the air, and it was little more than a second before it hit a railing on the way down and they were both thrown to the floor.

Sinnan got to his knees while Domitris rolled on to his back, groaning. The smoke was impenetrable around them. They couldn't stay there. The outline of Sinnan turned to him.

"What do we do?"

Domitris sat up and couldn't tell whether the pain in his back was new or from the night before. He pinched the bridge of his nose. *Think*. This wasn't his demise, not yet. Sinnan had come for him, and they were going to get out of there.

"The mines." He shuffled over to Sinnan. "If we can find the entrance, we can go through the mines!"

"Are you sure? Didn't you say they haven't been used in centuries?"

He got up and offered a helping hand to Sinnan. "I don't know what else to try. I really thought your idea was going to work."

"So did I." Sinnan took his hand and got up. "Fine, we continue down. Where are we?"

Domitris looked around in the nearly pitch blackness. "Almost at the bottom, I think. The stairs are over there."

The smoke billowed up through the staircase leading further into the ground. Maneuvering down them seemed like suicide, but they had to try.

He grabbed Sinnan's hand to lead on. He tried not to breathe, but the smoke got in everywhere. Hurrying as much as he could, he slipped on a step, and a wave of intense pain shot through his shin as he scraped his calves against the stairs the rest of the way down.

He stumbled onto the floor of the very bottom of the library, much too close to the roaring fire that worked its way up through the hole. They scrambled to get as far away from it as possible, the smoke so dense it threatened to choke them. Domitris swallowed, his throat parched and ashy.

"Look for a door," he rasped. "It's probably small and somewhere along the edge."

They split up, and Domitris rummaged around in the darkness with his hands outstretched. Desperation grew as he fumbled through the smoke and found nothing. Like a hammer to the face, it hit him that the entrance might have been sealed up. This dark hole would be their grave after all and they would perish together with the greatest wonder in Marmarasi history.

"I found something!" Sinnan yelled across the room.

"There's a hatch! I found a hatch!"

Domitris got up and stumbled through the darkness in the direction of his voice. He almost fell over Sinnan, where he was crouched down, trying to yank open a wooden hatch that wouldn't budge.

"It's locked. What do we do?"

Domitris could tell Sinnan was running out of steam. By instinct, he took over and yanked the handle. It gave, and then it opened. Sinnan gaped at him.

"It was just stuck."

"I don't care," Sinnan shouted at him. "GO!"

XXII

It was a long climb down the ladder, Domitris waiting every step for the wood to give out under their weight. Eventually they reached the bottom, fortunately without the help of gravity.

He collapsed to the floor and so did Sinnan, when he caught up. The complete silence was the most striking thing after escaping the roar of fire. The noise still howled in his ears. He let his head sink backwards and rest against the stone. They were both panting heavily in the absolute darkness around them. Domitris couldn't see his own hands, even when he held them right up in front of his face. They sat there in silence, panting, until Sinnan started to shiver.

It was cold this deep underground, and the floor was wet. Distant sounds of drops falling into pools of water echoed intermittently against the walls.

Domitris steadied his breathing and his thoughts, trying to fight the dread creeping up on him. Panicking wouldn't help him. The longer they sat there, the smaller their chances of ever getting out. He gently lay a hand on Sinnan. "We should get going."

Sinnan didn't answer for so long that Domitris thought maybe he hadn't heard him.

"How big did you say these mines were?" Sinnan finally asked, his voice quivering.

"You saw the map." The answer was 'uncomfortably big'. It would take hours to walk from one end to the other if you had a map and light, and they had neither.

"The library seemed to be over the center," Sinnan said. "And it looked like there is an entrance to the east and to the north. Or has been, at least."

"We better start walking, then."

"How do we know which direction to go in?"

There was dead silence while Domitris thought. "We take a lucky guess."

Sinnan shifted in the dark.

"Or do you have a better idea?" Domitris asked.

"No, you're right. We better get going."

As Domitris got up, a sharp pain shot through his leg, and he groaned.

"What is it?" Sinnan came closer in the darkness.

"My leg. Something isn't right."

Sinnan grabbed his arm. "Sit down; I'll check."

Domitris slumped back down, and Sinnan knelt beside him. His hand grabbed softly up and down Domitris' leg until another burst of pain exploded in his shin. Domitris yelped and slapped away Sinnan's hand on reflex.

"There's something stuck," Sinnan said, tapping a foreign object sticking out of the side of his shin. Domitris reached down and felt a thin, ragged stick about a hand long poking out of the side of his leg. Nausea swirled in his stomach.

"It feels pretty superficial. Hold on, I'll pull it out," Sinnan said.

Domitris braced himself and held on to Sinnan's shoulder.

"Here we go." Sinnan grabbed hold of the stick.

Searing pain shot through his leg and Domitris swore loudly. Thankfully, it was over surprisingly fast, and the pain turned to dull throbbing.

"Did you get it?"

"Yes, here." Sinnan handed him the shard of wood. It felt much smaller in his hand than it had in his leg.

"Can you walk on it, you think?"

"Only one way to find out." He rubbed his leg and flexed his foot a few times. It didn't seem as bad now that it was out.

Domitris struggled to get up, but Sinnan was there beside him, supporting him.

Side by side, they dragged their heavy feet through the darkness, a hand to the clammy wall for support. Since the library above them faced north, they chose the direction they both agreed was most likely to be east. That way, they would get out inside the city walls and hopefully not too far from the horse. Domitris had lost a shoe somewhere in the process, so he took off the other one and walked barefoot in the cold water.

It took time getting used to moving forward when he couldn't see anything. Every step was like disappearing into a void and he could hear Sinnan fumbling his way forward just as much as himself. After a while, though, it became apparent that the tunnel was going straight forward without much variance. The floor and walls were sleek, and eventually the desire to move quickly overshadowed the fear of falling or walking into something.

It was impossible to tell time or distance in there. As they went further into the darkness, Domitris' feet told him they had been walking for an hour, but he couldn't tell if it had truly been more than ten minutes. The only thing that gave some sort of certainty that they were actually moving forward was the variation in the size of the tunnels, judging by the echo of their steps and the amount of water at their feet. They walked so close that their arms occasionally brushed against each other. It was a gentle comfort in the middle of the hopelessness.

After a while, the tunnel grew wider, and they drifted apart as they both held a hand to the wall.

When he spoke, Sinnan's voice was surprisingly far away.

"I'm coming over to you, so we don't end up going different ways."

Domitris held out his arm in Sinnan's direction. "Here, take my hand."

Instead of getting a hold of it, Sinnan walked into his fingers and Domitris' palm graced his abs.

"Please tell me that was your hand."

Domitris laughed. "It was! Here." He ran his knuckles down Sinnan's arm and grabbed his hand. Sinnan accepted it, intertwining their fingers.

For a brief second, Domitris caught himself thinking that being stuck down here maybe wasn't so bad after all. Then his mind recoiled at the stupidity of it. He refused to acknowledge any of the oncoming thoughts that fought for his attention and instead squeezed Sinnan's hand tighter.

They continued onward for yet another undefinable amount of time.

When his own feet ached and his back hurt, Domitris said, "Let me know if you get tired and need to rest."

Sinnan huffed and said theatrically, "Did Giladenes get tired when she walked through the underworld for three days?"

"What?"

"From Carantacula's journey, remember?"

"I don't think I ever got to that part."

"It's the second story of the book," Sinnan said dryly. "You know, when Giladenes travels through the underworld to fight her inner demons and bring the sun back to the surface because it was stolen by darkness?"

"As I said, I didn't read all of it."

Sinnan gasped loudly, as if he took personal offense. "Or any of it, apparently. The Elected Emperor of Marmaras, the first of his kind, the Hero of the People, is an uncultured swine," he said, his voice full of mock disdain.

Domitris laughed. "Well, does she make it?" he asked.

"I won't tell you," Sinnan said. "You really should finish it yourself. It's worth it."

"If we ever get out of here, I will."

"Oh, it's one of my favorites. A tale of bravery and hope and love! Could it get any better? That story taught me never to give up, even when things get dark. You have to keep hoping. The alternative is worse."

It never ceased to amaze Domitris how Sinnan was able to remain optimistic under the direst of circumstances. He was right, of course. Speculating about whether they would survive wouldn't get them anywhere. Either they would get out, or they wouldn't. Worrying wouldn't change the outcome, only add misery to the journey.

Sinnan trailed off, and they stopped talking because the ground beneath them sloped steeply upwards and Domitris had a creeping suspicion they had found a dead end.

They kept walking and had to crawl upwards until they could reach the carved-out ceiling.

"The road is blocked," Domitris said, and he could hear the hint of panic in his own voice.

"We can't go back," Sinnan said. "We've been walking this way forever."

Domitris slumped down. It had been so hard to tell which turns to take. They had tried walking in the straightest direction possible and had avoided any side tunnels. Maybe they should have examined the spot where they had drifted apart; maybe there had been several ways forward. But that had been ages ago.

Sinnan continued worming his way forward, and loose rubble slid down beneath his footsteps.

"It isn't blocked!" Sinnan said. "There's a way through! But the passage isn't very big. Hold on."

While Domitris got to his feet and crawled up towards Sinnan, he could hear Sinnan's labored breath and the sound of hands scraping against rubble. Chalky dust filled Domitris' nostrils as he got closer.

"Help me with this," Sinnan said, and Domitris got down on his stomach, stretching out his hands. Sure enough, there was a long opening between the ceiling and the floor, but it was so narrow that Domitris was only just able to put his arm through it. He felt Sinnan digging and pushing the rubble away beside him, and he started doing the same.

It got bigger and bigger and after a while, Domitris could stick his head through it.

"I'm going through," he said.

Sinnan gave his arm a squeeze. "Be careful. There are some sharp rocks coming out of the ceiling."

The way to the hole was too steep to go through with his feet, so he had to dive in head-first. He stuck his head through it again, then his arms and shoulders, and grabbed the ground on the other side. It went as steeply downward, judging by the slope beneath his hands.

"Here I go."

He pulled his torso through and pushed with his feet. The second he was free of the hole, he tumbled sideways down the slope, which went down much steeper and farther than he had anticipated. He spun uncontrollably down the rubble, the ground scraping against his skin. He tried his best to weather the fall without hitting his head. Eventually, he lost speed and was able to slide carefully down the rest of the slope, where he landed on what felt like a small plateau. The way down had felt longer than the way up, which meant that he was now below the level they had been walking on. It was impossible to tell whether that was a good thing or not.

"Are you hurt?" Sinnan's voice echoed from above.

"I don't think so!" he called back. "But wait a second before you come down."

"Why?"

The echo was louder than he thought it should be and

something was off, but he couldn't tell what in the complete darkness. He crouched down and inched forward with his arms in front of him. He had hoped not to be right, but there, not far ahead, was a ledge. If he hadn't gained foothold, he could have tumbled right over the edge, and it was impossible to see how far down it went.

"It's not good," he said.

"What?"

"There's a drop. Listen."

Domitris picked up a rock and dropped it over the edge. It was a free fall because there was no sound for a short while and then the unmistakable plop of an object falling into water.

"That didn't sound very promising," Sinnan said, his voice bouncing off the walls. "Now I wish I had gone first. Having to go down now that I know I'm headed right for an abyss is a little disturbing."

"Just go down really slowly. If you can, try getting your legs through first."

Sinnan was smaller than him, so he might be able to do it.

Sinnan laughed nervously. "Great then, here I go."

Domitris couldn't see him but listened closely, his heart still pounding in his chest after his own fall.

"My legs are through, I'm letting go," Sinnan said and the next thing Domitris heard was a loud cry of pain and then the sound of Sinnan sliding down the slope.

"Help! Help! I can't stop!" Sinnan shouted in panic, which at least made it easy to hear where he was. Domitris braced himself and went into the line of Sinnan's yelling, and in the next moment, Sinnan's body slammed into his. Domitris fell over, smacking his head into the ground, his teeth slamming hard against each other. They both held on tightly, not daring to move. Domitris' jaw and neck buzzed with pain as blood rushed through his veins. He noticed Sinnan was shaking uncontrollably, and he sat up to rest Sinnan against him.

"What happened?"

"I–I think I bashed my face against the ceiling going through and I completely lost my balance."

"Are you hurt?"

"I'm not sure. Nothing is broken, I think. Though I scraped my palms all the way down." He lifted his hands up from where they had been resting against Domitris and brushed them off gently. Domitris sucked in a little air between his teeth. "How about you?" Sinnan asked.

"I'm fine. A little beat up, but overall fine, I think."

Sinnan didn't answer, but Domitris thought he could feel him nodding. They both sat up alongside each other. After a short moment of silence, Domitris said, "We have to keep going."

"I know," Sinnan said, "but how?"

Another silence.

Sinnan said what Domitris didn't dare.

"Do we… jump?"

"Did you hear how far down it was? I don't think we'll make it. We have no idea if the water is deep enough to land in."

"You're right. Before we consider jumping to our deaths any further, let's get up and check if there are any paths leading on from here."

"Don't fall," Domitris said.

"Hold on to me while we look."

They got up and, clinging to each other's hands, they edged to the side. Nothing but wall. They walked slowly to the other side, careful they didn't get too close to the edge. Domitris' free hand patted the wall in front of him and suddenly felt a corner.

"I think this might be a path," he said, pulling Sinnan closer to it so he could feel it too. "Do we go in?"

"I don't see another option," Sinnan said, weariness heavy in his words.

"We can still jump," Domitris said dryly, which solicited a small laugh from Sinnan.

"Let's never talk about that again. Come on, let's go," he said, taking the first few steps into the tunnel. Going ahead, the echo disappeared and Domitris felt almost relieved that the walls were closing in.

They kept walking forward in the darkness, and little by little, Domitris managed to put away the fear that they would walk out over an edge any minute. His muscles ached, and the walking became tiresome instead of uplifting again.

"Can we rest for a while?" Domitris asked. He wanted to get off his feet, if only for a short time.

"Of course."

They sat down against the curving wall, their shoulders touching. Domitris' mind was a black hole and the ringing in his ears persisted with every beat of his heart. While they both sat in introspective silence, they drained the last water from the waterskins and shared the provisions. The thyme bread had been squashed a little and tasted faintly of smoke, but it filled their growling stomachs. When it was all gone, Domitris tried to push away the realization that this was the last meal they would have, if they didn't get out of there. His chest ached, thinking of Lyra having prepared it for him that morning, and that was the first time the thought of never getting out truly scared him.

Sinnan was the one to hesitantly break the silence between them. "Domitris?"

The tone of his voice was soft with a cautiousness he hadn't heard from Sinnan before.

"Hm?"

"What happened to your parents? You said they died, but… there was something else to it, wasn't there?"

No one had asked him that before because everyone at the palace knew exactly what had happened. Everyone mostly ignored it, pretending they had died of natural causes.

"They were killed. The Supreme Emperor made sure of that."

He had never talked openly about their deaths but saying it down here in the darkness was somehow less difficult.

"Did he have them murdered?"

"Yes. But not in the quick, easy way where their throats were slit in the night. They were sent to Carthex."

He hesitated, not sure how to explain it, and Sinnan gave him time.

"Around a decade ago, during the front-line war in the last battle against Dassosda, there was a bad outbreak of the plague in several villages in Carthex on the western border."

"The plague? Do you still have that here?"

"No. It was a shock to everybody back then. There hadn't been outbreaks for more than a century. The villagers were suffering, with no food, no clean water, and no help, so the ones who didn't die from the illness died of hunger and neglect."

The warmth of Sinnan's skin against his own made it easier to get the words out.

"And the Supreme Emperor sent your parents there?"

"They had been speaking out against him and the expanding war efforts for years and protested the decision to seal off the plague villages to let the people all die before it spread. He didn't tolerate disloyalty. In the end, he said that if my parents felt the villagers needed help so badly, they would be the ones to do something about it. It was the same as a death sentence."

"Why didn't they flee? Or hide?"

"I don't know. They didn't tell me. I always imagined that they couldn't turn their backs on those people. No one else, among the nobles anyway, wanted to help, so maybe they did what they thought was necessary, even though they knew it would kill them. After a few months, a letter arrived, stating that their bodies had been found."

Sinnan's hand found his knee. "I'm so sorry."

"So am I. I miss them."

Sinnan stroked his knee, and for a while, that was all that happened. Knowing he was there gave Domitris the strength to eventually get up, and he helped Sinnan to his feet as well.

For a long while, neither of them said much, and the only sound was the steady tapping of their footsteps. It was Sinnan who eventually broke the silence, and when he spoke, there was a strange gravity to his words.

"Did you ever wonder," he said, "if anybody would care if you just disappeared one day?"

"You mean if anybody would mourn my death?"

"No, I mean—if a new day dawned, and you weren't there—not dead, just gone, poof, vanished—would anyone truly care?"

Domitris gave thought to the question. Would they? As emperor, he was replaceable, and it was not like his close social circle was endless, but even so, that question had never crossed his mind. When his parents died, when Oedica left him behind, when he had felt the most alone, there had always been someone there for him. Lyra, Ignotus, Hossia. They had always cared, so much.

"I think they would," he said. "Why?"

Sinnan continued talking in the same matter-of-fact tone he had asked the question. "It's just… there was a point in my life where I thought about it a lot. And at that time, the answer was no. I had no one in my life who would have cared if I was gone."

Domitris looked to where Sinnan's voice came from but couldn't see him. His footsteps continued forward at the same steady pace.

When Domitris didn't answer, he continued. "Do you know what that made me realize?"

Domitris could only speculate about the despair that would follow such dark thoughts.

"It made me realize that I needed to find people who would."

The hairs stood up on the back of Domitris' neck.

"It wasn't long after that I found Amelia and Jenine. Then Bardeia and eventually Ennio. Since then, I haven't been alone."

He looked again at Sinnan and could just about see his silhouette. Was his mind playing tricks on him?

"Sinnan—"

"I see it!" Sinnan said. "Look, there's light coming from ahead."

They kept walking, their pace increasing. The light was an eerie, cold one, and the tunnel narrowed in around them as they got nearer. They had to duck to walk the rest of the way through the narrow opening, and it soon became clear that it wasn't the exit. Instead, they found themselves in the largest hall they had been in thus far. It was vast and square, with a vaulted ceiling, visible in the cold light. The floor was covered in water and the source of the light was the moon shining in through a hole in the ceiling so high above them that the hopelessness grew in his stomach. They were not out yet. And there was no way they could climb to the top and get out that way, either.

Neither of them spoke. Domitris took careful steps through the water, the movement echoing softly around the room. He halted in the beam of smoky light coming down. The disturbance in the water made swirly reflections dance on the walls and ceiling. He wanted to scream. He wanted to tear his hair out and scream at the top of his lungs.

But he was so tired. Maybe what he wanted was to lay down and sleep and never get up. He stared into the light and let it blind him. If he thought about it hard enough, maybe he could soar up through the hole.

There was a splash of something landing in the water behind him and he turned to it, his vision stained with a white circle. He blinked a couple of times, and Sinnan's figure came into sight, slumped against the wall.

"We're never getting out of here, are we?" Sinnan said. "I didn't think this would be how I died. I always imagined it to be some kind of fight for the greater good."

If even Sinnan was losing hope, they were surely doomed.

They couldn't both lose hope now. He had to do something.

"Would Giladenes give up if she lost her way in the underworld?"

Sinnan didn't answer.

"Would she sit and wait for death to take her, or would she fight until she had nothing left to give?"

"You don't even know the story," Sinnan said, his voice meek.

"Maybe not, but you do. Now, what would Giladenes do? Her story would not have been the same if she hadn't faced any obstacles, right? That much I know."

Sinnan's head still hung between his shoulders.

"You need a rest under any circumstances," Domitris said. "Sit for a while and be sure to drink some water and refill your waterskin. I'll take another look around." When no answer came, he decided to leave Sinnan be.

He went to inspect the other side of the room. Water dripped from the ceiling into pools on the ground and a small stream flowed somewhere, but he couldn't tell where it was. His eyes were still getting used to the darkness again. Soon, he found a pitch black archway. He took a few steps inside to make sure it was a tunnel and not just a hole. It was a tunnel, though staring into the complete darkness again after having seen light was more than a little discouraging. Domitris' stomach sank when, a few paces beside it, he discovered another tunnel. Immediately, he looked onward and found yet another and walking to the far corner of the room, there was one more. Four different tunnels were leading on from the big hall. Domitris felt like a herd angry of horses were running rampant in his chest. Now he wanted to slump down and wait for death to come if it meant not walking a single step further inside the dank mines.

"What's wrong?" Sinnan asked.

"There's more than one path to take."

"How many?"

"Four. As far as I can tell, at least. What do we do?" He felt stupid for trying to evoke hope in Sinnan. He was right. There was no way they would get out. Domitris heard him get up and walk over.

"Do you see them?" Domitris asked.

"I see them," Sinnan said thoughtfully. He paced along the wall, inspecting each tunnel.

"What are you doing?"

"Wait a second. Could you move a little further away? Try to stand as still as possible. And don't say anything."

Despite wanting to argue, Domitris took a few steps back and kept quiet. When the sound of his movement in the water died down, he tried to figure out what Sinnan was listening for. Domitris didn't hear anything but the mellow sounds of the cave; dripping, the occasional animal moving in the water, small squeaks of rats communicating. Sinnan stood in front of one of the tunnels, his feet firmly planted on the ground, doing something with his hands that Domitris couldn't make out. After a while, he moved on and did the same in front of each tunnel, and then he went back and forth a couple of times. When he had been to the second one from the right twice, he finally turned around.

"I think it's this way."

"How can you possibly know that?"

"Come." Sinnan waved him over. "Sitting at the other end of the room before, I felt a draft." He dipped his hand in the water, wiped it off, and held it up in front of the tunnel. "It seems like the draft is coming from here," he said.

Domitris bent down and put his hand into the cold water, wiped it off on his clothes, and held it up. Sinnan was right. His hand instantly got colder, and a breeze caressed his fingers.

"I feel it," Domitris said, trying not to get his hopes up.

"I think this is the way," Sinnan said again.

They ventured into the tunnel. Blackness enveloped them once again and Domitris felt like he was in a nightmare, floating through nothingness with only Sinnan's breathing beside him to keep him sane.

Telling time in the darkness became impossible again. Domitris' feet had been sore for a long time, but now they were outright painful. An acrid smell got more pungent as they walked forward. The tunnel had become wide and lofty and the air above them grew thick with the flapping of wings.

"Do you hear them?" Domitris whispered.

"The bats? Yeah, there must be hundreds of them. Smells like it too."

"Do you think that's a good or a bad sign?"

"Assuming they leave the cave sometimes, I would guess it's a good sign."

"I hope you're right."

They continued and, just to do something, Domitris tried to count his steps. He lost count somewhere after 600 and started over. When the tunnel curved sharply, Sinnan stopped.

"Can you smell that?"

He stopped and smelled. The air was fresher.

"We must be close."

They picked up their pace and the further they went, the lighter it got. Suddenly, he could see the outline of Sinnan beside him again. Sinnan laughed, heartily and freely. A small spot of light became visible in the distance and they both ran for it. Water splashed around their feet as they rushed forward. There it was, the exit, right in front of them, and the light shining brightly in through the cave opening was the full moon hanging low on the horizon. Sinnan ran out ahead of him and breathed in the cool night breeze. He jumped up and punched his fists into the air.

"Woohooooooooo!"

He held his hands to the sky, his slender frame silhouetted by the stars. Domitris had stopped near the exit of the cave, exhausted. He looked around, trying to figure out their location.

It didn't look how he had expected it to. They had walked north instead of east. They were outside the city gates and nowhere near their horse. He knew because the burning library was visible far, far away above the mine, the light from the fire painting the sky above it a dreadful shade of red. The good thing was that they were much closer to the city than he had expected, and it would only take a few hours to go back on foot. The relief of getting out alive was already replaced by the crushing realization of the circumstances.

"So, he was right," Domitris said. "Taxon. The tavern wasn't safe at all. Someone heard us."

"So it would seem."

"He was dead, you know. I found him down there."

Sinnan looked back at him with raised brows. "That's awful."

Domitris sighed. "I need to get back to the palace."

"True. But first, we need a rest. Sit down."

Sinnan found some dry shrubs and twigs and stacked them up into a small fire. From of a pocket on the inside of his clothes, he got out a piece of flint and a curved piece of steel. He clacked them against each other until sparks went flying and the twigs caught. They were lucky everything was so dry.

They sat down and stared into the gentle flames.

"How did you know you would need those?"

"I didn't. I bring them with me everywhere I go. You don't go to bed hungry or cold that many times because you couldn't light a fire before you learn that you'll need it when you least expect it."

Sinnan was finally visible in the warm glow. Domitris gasped. He had a long, sharp cut across the cheek below his right eye, blood streaming down his face. Or rather, it had been. It looked mostly dried by now except for the ragged cut. Sinnan's eyes widened in surprise, and he touched a hand to his cheek, his fingers coming back reddened.

"Oh shit, I completely forgot."

Domitris winced. "How are your hands?"

"I think I'll get to keep them."

"Let me see."

Sinnan hesitated but stuck out both his hands for inspection.

AS WE FALL

Domitris took them and gently folded out his fingers. They were covered in small scrapes and cuts. He traced a finger over his right palm, then bent down and kissed it.

Sinnan almost pulled back his hands in surprise, but then he gave himself over to it. They sat like that for a short while before Domitris let go.

"You came back for me."

Sinnan looked away. "How could I live with myself if I didn't?"

"You owed me nothing."

"I know."

"I've never seen anyone work as quickly or be so determined."

"I panicked," he said, meeting Domitris' eyes. Domitris had expected him to look frightened and small, but he didn't. Most of all, he looked tired, but nothing in him mirrored the dread that raged inside himself.

They sat in silence while the crackling of the fire kept them company. The night was still and warm and tragically beautiful.

"How will this ever end well?" Domitris asked.

Sinnan stared into the night. After a beat of calm silence he said, "Stars are not the only thing on the horizon."

Domitris looked at him for an explanation.

Sinnan pointed out over the plains stretching in front of them. The first signs of sunrise appeared as a slim orange brim in the distance.

"Look," he said. "There's hope too."

XXIII

The journey back to the palace on foot was tedious. They had been walking for hours through the mines already and their feet were tired and sore. When they finally reached the west gate, swallows were chasing insects in the sunrise and the morning dew evaporated from the wilted grass in misty swirls.

A small encampment had sprouted up on each side of the road leading to the gate. There had been more traffic into the city than ever during the past months because of the festival, but the unlucky ones who had just arrived were now stranded outside the wall. Most would have traveled too far to turn back and had instead set up camp, waiting for the gates to open up again.

"How do we get in? You've sealed off the city," Sinnan said from their position in the shadow of the wall. Domitris wasn't blind to the irony of the situation. He looked up to assess their options. Two guards were stationed at the top of the wall in small open towers on each side of the gate.

"Can't you just tell them you're the emperor and to let you

through?"

"Those are city guards. They will never have seen me, and I doubt anyone would believe it if I came in looking like this."

Sinnan smiled as though he were trying not to laugh.

"I see your point. But then what do we do?"

Domitris looked around for a solution. The walls were tall. Too tall to jump over, too smooth to climb, and guard towers were positioned at regular intervals.

"We need to get in now. Should we try asking around the camp if anybody knows of a way?"

Sinnan lit up. "I like your way of thinking, but I have a better idea. Wait here."

He bolted off towards the tents before Domitris could say a thing. In the meantime, he kept an eye out for guards or other potential problems, but it was a calm morning and there was not much activity. The low tents were colored mauve in the early light and only a few families had started their day. Even the watchdogs still lay sleeping here and there outside the tents.

He didn't see Sinnan again until he was right beside him with a grin on his face.

"Look what I found." He held up a coil of solid rope.

"I'm pretty sure you stole that."

"You can go over and try trading for it with your dirty clothes if that's what you want, but I thought you wanted to get inside."

Domitris clenched his jaw. He knew he was right.

"What's your plan?"

"I noticed Marmaras is not above building battlements with crenelations. It wouldn't be the first time I've climbed a wall with a rope, and merlons almost make it too easy."

"You can't throw a rope up that far."

"Oh, but I can. I'm starting to feel like you're not paying attention," Sinnan said and tied a complicated knot, creating a loop at the end.

"Come, let's go past the gate and continue north. I have a feeling that landing in Tenebris on the other side is our best shot at making it through."

Domitris nodded. "That's also closer to the palace."

Sinnan stopped and grabbed hold of him. "I can't. I need to go see the troupe and tell them I'm safe."

"But we need–"

"No, *you* need to get back to the palace. *I* need to go back to my friends and tell them I'm still alive."

Domitris stopped him. "I get that. What I wanted to say was that we need medical attention. Both of us. You're hurt, Sinnan. Please go back with me and let my physicians patch you up. We can go and see the troupe first, of course. I'll go with you."

Sinnan looked back at him, confused. Domitris started walking again. "But we need to hurry."

Sinnan didn't object and caught up with quick steps.

They reached the far end of the wall where it merged into the cliffs and found a spot between two guard towers. The towers were far enough apart that they could slip by unnoticed.

"They'll see us," Domitris said when Sinnan got ready to throw the rope.

"No, they won't."

"You know they're armed with crossbows, right?"

Sinnan looked at him in horror. "You people are savages,

do you know that?"

A flicker of doubt passed Sinnan's eyes as he searched the wall for another spot, but then he shook his head.

"This is our best chance," he confirmed, and readied the rope.

Domitris held his breath as he threw. The rope soared up into the sky, hit the side of the merlon, and fell limply down in front of them.

Domitris shot him a concerned look.

"Shut up; I didn't say I would hit it the first time. Be patient."

He threw again and once again the rope landed like a dead snake at their feet. And again. Domitris bit his tongue, not knowing how to react. But the fourth time Sinnan threw, the rope tightened and was strung against the wall.

Domitris smiled at him, impressed.

"I told you I could do it," Sinnan said. "Now comes the hard part. Do you want to go first or should I?"

Climbing wasn't in the repertoire of Domitris' usual activities. Getting a demonstration from Sinnan before attempting it himself seemed like the wiser decision.

"You go."

Sinnan nodded and took hold of the rope with both hands. Then he positioned his feet against the wall and, with long steps, he climbed up, the rope-end dangling beneath him. After barely a minute, he disappeared over the parapet and stayed down. His head popped up a moment later between the merlons and he signaled for Domitris to come. Domitris grabbed the rope like Sinnan had done and braced one foot against the wall and pulled himself upwards. It was much harder than Sinnan had made it look and holding on to the rope hurt his palms. He only made it three steps up the wall before the rope slipped between his fingers and he crashed back onto the ground. His tail bone collided with the rubble and pain sent tears to his eyes. He fell over, biting into his hand, trying not to make a sound while he waited out the aching throbs. Sooner than he would have liked, he stumbled to his legs and took a few deep breaths. He rubbed his hands and gathered strength before he tried again.

Now he knew what it took, at least. This time he moved much more steadily up the wall. His stomach turned when he sensed the ground far beneath him. Sinnan's head turned to keep an eye out for guards, but no one had seen them. Domitris was panting as he closed in, his arms and hands getting tired. He needed to go just four more steps. Exhaustion and hunger were wearing on him and he had to focus all of his energy on holding on. When he was almost there, Sinnan leaned out and offered his hand. Domitris reached to take it, but his feet slipped on the bricks and he slammed his knees into the wall. He would have fallen all the way back down if it hadn't been for Sinnan, flinging his upper body over the wall to catch him. Sinnan helped him regain his footing and pulled him upward.

"You're too heavy!" Sinnan shouted in panic. They both groaned with effort until Domitris managed to struggle over the edge and they collapsed onto the wall path with far too much noise. The guards from both towers came out to investigate. Sinnan turned to him.

"RUN!"

Before Domitris could ask where, Sinnan jumped out over

the wall to the other side and landed on a rooftop. Domitris didn't have time to think about it because the guards were loading their crossbows and taking aim. He heaved himself to the top of the ledge. As the first bolt whistled past him, he forced himself to leap out over the edge as far as he could, aiming for the rooftop ahead. Wind rushed in his ears and his stomach swirled as he soared through the air. He landed hard on the uneven tiles and caught a chunk of the inside of his cheek between his teeth at the impact. His jaw twisted at the pain and the taste of metal spread in his mouth. He stopped to tongue at it, but Sinnan was crouching down further ahead, waiting for him. One of the guards blew a horn and Sinnan bolted onward. Domitris picked himself up and followed him.

Going for the next leap, Sinnan stepped on a roof tile that slid underneath his foot. He grabbed at Domitris for balance, making them both glide off the roof, right into a dunghill beside a set of dingy pig stables. Sinnan was the first of them to get up. He took a couple of limping steps, clutching his side, then ducked into the nearest stable. Domitris followed him. They crouched down under the window just inside the door. Sinnan rested his head against the wall and sat there, panting. Domitris got down beside him, spat out a warm mouthful of blood, and welcomed the opportunity to catch his breath. The guards wouldn't find them there. When they had waited for an uncomfortable amount of time in deafening silence, and they were sure the guards wouldn't follow them, they crawled out and hurried southward.

The rest of the way to the marketplace, they went mostly in silence, walking as fast as their aching feet would let them.

When they closed in on the camp, emerging from behind the yellow tent with the morning light at their backs, Amelia elbowed Bardeia and Ennio beside her and they tensed up.

"We told you already, it's just us here!" Amelia called.

"What are you talking about? It's me," Sinnan said.

Amelia and Bardeia startled at the sound of Sinnan's voice and Jenine shot up behind them. He ran to them, and Jenine threw herself at him, bursting into tears.

"We heard about the library, and we thought…" She sobbed into Sinnan's shoulder. The other three embraced him as well, rustling his hair and patting his back.

"I'm sorry I worried you," Sinnan said. "Things took a bad turn."

Domitris walked up as inconspicuously as he could, not wanting to disturb the reunion. It ached inside him to witness the looks on their faces.

"Where have you been? Why did it take you so long to come back?" Amelia asked, her hand grasping his, Jenine still clinging to his neck.

"We only survived the fire because we got into the old mines beneath the city. It took us ages to get out again," Sinnan explained. It sounded even crazier said out loud than Domitris had expected.

Bardeia crossed her arms. "What?"

"I know. I'll tell you everything, but not yet. Domitris is taking me back to the palace to be patched up." He tried to point to his face with his free hand. Jenine let go and took a step back.

"What happened to you?" Bardeia asked, turning his face with her hand to get a look at the cut.

"It's a long story. I promise you'll hear every detail when I get back."

"You shouldn't go with him," Amelia said, a little more harshly than Domitris thought was necessary.

"I never meant to put Sinnan in danger."

"You stay out of this," Amelia snapped, pointing a finger to his face. Jenine took her other hand to hold her back.

"Stay away from us. Your incompetence is putting innocent lives at risk."

Sinnan stepped in front of her. "This wasn't his fault. It was an ambush. We didn't stand a chance, and there was no way Domitris could have known."

"Nothing good will come of this. I warned you," she said. That elicited a hasty reaction from Sinnan. He grabbed her by the wrist, and they rushed off to the side of the camp, hissing at each other. Amelia pointed her finger and Sinnan threw out his hands. Bardeia sidestepped slightly, blocking Domitris' line of vision.

"Are you unhurt?"

"Mostly, yes," he said, letting his attention be torn from Sinnan. "Have you all been safe?"

Jenine fiddled with something in her hands. "There have been guards all over the marketplace the whole night."

"And all over the city, from the sound of it," Bardeia added.

"Why?"

She shrugged. "They say they're sent from the palace to find the culprits, but they've mostly gone around and harassed people, searching tents and pockets, leaving a mess behind. They've searched our camp twice already."

"What were they looking for?"

"As I said, they claimed to look for evidence, but I don't know if there was anything else behind it."

They were interrupted by unintelligible shouting and then the words, "Let. It. Go!" It was Sinnan's voice. It was the first time Domitris had heard him sound genuinely angry. A second later, he came striding back towards them. He didn't look at Domitris, instead addressing the other three.

"I'll be back sometime later tonight, before dinner. Come, Domitris, let's get out of here." He didn't give any of them time to answer before he walked off. Domitris hastily said his goodbyes, then followed Sinnan's lead.

Sinnan kept clenching his jaw, gaze fixed on the ground.

"What was that about?"

"I don't want to talk about it," was all he said.

Domitris didn't mind letting it go. The night had been much too long already, and he had bigger problems to deal with.

Arriving at the palace gates, they met commotion. A mob of people filled the marble steps, shouting, waving objects and papers in their hands. The doors were flung open, and a few nobles and palace guards tried to handle the situation.

"–doing everything we can to put out the fire!" a noble at the door shouted. "We're still awaiting the riders. When we know the status, we will inform you!"

Domitris and Sinnan pushed through the crowd, getting squished by sweaty flanks and sharp elbows. When they emerged through the front, a palace guard with shoulders so large he barely fit into his uniform shouted, "Get back in line!"

Not even the palace guards recognized him. Domitris got the suspicion he looked as terrible as he felt. Trying to force himself past the guard wouldn't go well, but he had to get in somehow. He caught a glimpse of the black curls of Hephakles' head bobbing around somewhere inside. Domitris stepped as close as he could and joined the choir of shouting.

"Hephakles! Hephakles, it's me!"

"I said, get back in line!" The guard came forward with a hand on Domitris' chest.

Domitris shouted once more and, to his relief, Hephakles heard him. As he turned around, his bloodshot eyes grew to the size of apples, and he dropped the scrolls in his arms. He sprang forward, pushing the guard aside.

"Your Highness, you're alive!"

Those words changed everything. The guard fell a step backwards as though he had seen a ghost, and the crowd fell silent.

The same words rippled through the crowd. *The emperor.*

"Hephakles, get me inside."

The people around him didn't back up. Instead a small woman with ratty hair grabbed hard onto his forearm.

"Is my child alive?"

The question was repeated again and again around him, and he realized that no one knew what had happened at the library. From the upper city, only the column of red smoke was visible and there was no telling if it came from the library or the whole academy. He didn't know if it had spread.

He stood there, looking at the woman.

"I–I don't know."

She pulled back her hand from him, her face crumpling.

He wasn't able to bring them the solace that they craved.

"Get me inside," he said again to Hephakles, reaching for him with one hand and for Sinnan with the other. They were pulled through the crowd and into the entrance hall, out of sight.

Hephakles squealed when he looked at him. "Your Highness, your leg—you're bleeding."

"It's nothing. Tell me—is the council gathered?"

Hephakles wrung his hands, his shoulders shaking, the dark circles under his eyes standing out.

"Some of them, yes. They are in the council hall as we speak. Everyone thought... We thought you had died, Your Highness."

Domitris couldn't register what that meant.

"I want everyone to be present in the council hall within the hour. Is that clear?"

"Yes. Wait, I need to tell you something—"

"Not now. Find me later."

Hephakles' mouth opened and closed, but Domitris didn't have time for it. He turned on his heel and strode for his rooms, Sinnan following.

Inside his room, the sight that greeted him sent a twinge of pain through his heart. The morning sun lit up the white curtains where Lyra sat by the window in her night robes, her dark hair gathered in a single braid down her back. She stared absentmindedly out the window, clutching the golden circlet in her hands. The moment Domitris walked through the door, her head spun around, her eyes huge, her cheeks wet. She sat in stunned disbelief for a second before she scrambled to her feet so quickly the chair fell over. With long strides, she rushed over and flung her plump arms around him. She buried her face in his chest and sobbed with deep, ragged shakes. He laid his arms gently around her small shoulders and held her. Only when he heard the sound of Sinnan swallowing behind him did he let his arms come back down and tugged at her. She took a hesitant step back and looked up at him. Her eyebrows were bunched up, making her whole forehead wrinkle, and she bit her lip.

"You must have a million questions, and I promise we'll talk, but right now I need to show my presence to the council. I need your help to get me presentable."

When she remained silent and shaking, he took her face in his hands.

"I'm safe now," he said.

That made her wipe her eyes with the back of her hand and take a deep breath.

"I'm—" Her voice broke. She swallowed. "I'm so glad—" she tried again, but the words still didn't come. She gave a small laugh instead and threw out her hands. Domitris smiled at her and squeezed her arm.

"I know. Please, I need to be in the council hall as soon as possible."

She nodded and sniffled before rushing to the washroom. He turned to Sinnan, whose eyes were glossy.

"Not you too," Domitris said.

Behind them, Lyra disappeared into the dressing room.

Sinnan made himself comfortable in one of the chairs. He was covered in soot and chalk dust, his hair limp and greasy. The contrast of how dirty he was against the clean surfaces and the gauzy curtains was jarring. The wound on his cheek looked like it hurt. He leaned his head against the wall and closed his eyes. Domitris suspected he could fall asleep where he sat.

Lyra came back with an armful of white fabric. "The water should be ready. Go wash up while I get these in order."

"Thank you. I also need you to call for a physician. Have them ready for me after the meeting. And get them to take care of Sinnan while I'm in there."

"Wait," Sinnan interrupted, wide awake. "I want to come."

Domitris exchanged a glance with Lyra. She looked as though she was about to voice her objection, but she stopped herself.

"To the council? That's not a good idea." Domitris thought of the rumors that had been circulating all week. If he came in there with Sinnan at his side, the council would implode.

"It was a rough night. I want to know what's going on. I deserve more than a second-hand report," Sinnan said, his voice fragile. "Don't leave me here."

It only then occurred to Domitris that Sinnan didn't feel safe. The trauma of the day before hadn't yet taken hold of Domitris. He had to keep his focus on getting back and manifesting his presence before he could process it. He hadn't really considered that Sinnan's life had been in jeopardy as much as his own. A weird sense of guilt came over him.

"They'll tear me apart if I bring you."

Sinnan slumped back, the look on his face devastating.

"Fine," Domitris said. "But keep to the back. Be discreet."

Sinnan lit up. "You won't know I'm there."

"Go wash up, then. Be quick."

Sinnan disappeared into the washroom. Lyra raised her brow while unfolding the lengths of fabric.

"He'll be discreet," Domitris said, throwing out his hands. Lyra shook her head.

"I'll go find something for him as well, then."

Sinnan washed up surprisingly fast. He came in, drying the back of his neck. He had gotten the blood off his cheek, but the cut was still bright red and starting to swell.

"Your turn."

Domitris went in and found a cloth laid out. He dipped it in the dusty water. It was cold, but it did the trick. The water became a darker gray each time he dipped in the cloth and at last he had gotten most of the grime off. When he came out again, Lyra was making the finishing touches to Sinnan's clothes. He still had black smudges behind his ears. Lyra brought in a set of golden laurel pins meant for guests of the emperor and fastened them to Sinnan's clothes.

In what seemed like record time, Domitris was dressed and readied as well, and Lyra placed the circlet above his ears. His hair was a mess, but Lyra reached up and combed it back, fixing it as best she could.

"I'm so glad you're unharmed," she said, rubbing on a smudge at his hairline. "When he admitted to what he'd done, I was so sure–"

Domitris' heart skipped a beat. He grabbed her hand. "What are you talking about?"

Lyra clasped a hand to her mouth. "Wait—you don't know?"

Confusion churned inside him. "Know *what?*"

"What they did to that boy. The little, snarky one on the council. Gaius' nephew."

"Cassian?" Domitris' heart pounded in his ears.

She nodded. "He admitted to the whole thing late in the night. How he paid the archer, how he worked with a band of criminals who burned down the Panjusticia, how he planned for the destruction of the library when he learned you went there."

Realization hit Domitris as a punch to the gut. *He admitted to the whole thing.* The pit of his stomach sunk through the floor.

"He wept as he said it. Never have I seen something so disgustingly pitiful. He said he believed that the only way to save Marmaras was to take you down."

Domitris was frozen in shock. It couldn't be. He had suspected Cassian had been part of it, but for him to admit to it all? It reeked of scapegoat. There was no way Cassian had been acting alone. Domitris could believe Cassian had done those things, but if he had, it would have been by someone else's volition.

"Why would he do that? Admit it so openly?"

"Can you believe what he said? For glory. 'Glory for a thousand years, history will remember my name. Long live the empire.'"

He let it sink in. Those were Gaius' words. Cassian was just a boy; he had no ambitions of eternal glory. The only things he cared about were gold and status and what his vapid friends thought of him.

"And Gaius?"

"He seemed as shocked as anybody. He shut up like a clam and remained silent for the rest of the night, I've heard."

Domitris thought about it. A few weeks in a cell would do

Cassian good. Maybe then Domitris could get him to talk, and he could get to Gaius and finally get rid of him.

"Where are they holding him? Cassian, I mean. I want to talk to him, see if there are—"

She interrupted him with a hand on his arm.

"They slit his throat. They dragged him to the courtyard and put him down like a dog just hours ago."

"*What?*" Nausea swirled in his stomach and a ringing overtook his ears. Except for what happened in the Overthrow, nobles weren't usually executed. They were exiled or put under house arrest for life. Would Gaius really sacrifice his own family like that? Lyra kept talking, her words muffled and distant.

"It was gruesome. While he admitted to the whole thing, he still had that wrinkle of his nose, held his brow high, but when they forced him to his knees and bent his head, he begged and screamed for his uncle to do something. There was nothing dignified about it."

"That's awful," Sinnan said from his seat at the table. Domitris had almost forgotten he was there. He closed his eyes and took a deep breath. He had to draw on a strength inside him that wasn't there.

"At least now you know. You're not going in unprepared," Lyra said.

"I feel unprepared."

"I know. You should get going. You'll know what to do."

His breathing was still shallow, his stomach tying in knots. Lyra squeezed his hand.

"Promise me to get some rest when you come back."

"I will. And you should too."

XXIV

Even though it was mid-morning, most of the council seemed to have been rushed from their warm beds after too few hours of sleep. They sat in their seats with messy hair and disheveled clothing, leaning on their knees, yawning and scratching themselves as Domitris strode in. Out of the corner of his eye, he caught a glimpse of Sinnan slipping in and positioning himself behind one of the columns in the back. Hephakles sat neatly at his desk with a stylus held in a shaking hand to the scroll in front of him.

Murmurs broke out from every corner, echoing various versions of *'he's alive'*. Some frowned, some gaped in disbelief, Ignotus one of the latter in the front row. Domitris straightened his back and folded his hands behind him.

"There has been an attempt on my life this night," he began. "Someone tried to dispose of me like a coward, and what's worse, decided to sacrifice centuries of history and culture that we will never get back. On top of that, I claw my way back here only to find out that a judgment and an execution has been carried out in less than a day."

"Your—" someone started, but he didn't want to hear it. His nostrils flared involuntarily.

"Silence!" he yelled and sounded every bit as angry as he was.

The room fell quiet. He got up on the raised step behind the rostrum and examined the faces in front of him. He found Gaius in the back, who looked uncharacteristically gray and pasty. The seat next to him was empty.

"I understand this council thought it appropriate to administer an appalling form of punishment in my absence before my body had even been found."

He looked around slowly and let his words sink in.

"Tell me, Hephakles, on whose authority was this decision made?"

Hephakles fiddled with the parchment at his desk, not meeting his eyes. He bit his lip, his expression pained. Then it dawned on Domitris—was that what Hephakles had been trying to tell him? The silence went on for a beat longer than it should have, until a voice across the room broke it.

"Mine."

Domitris turned and faced Ignotus, who stood and met his gaze. His mind reeled. He had been so ready to rail against Gaius that he was thrown off guard. Anger simmered under his skin. How could Ignotus have done something so rash? His neck grew hot at the sense of disloyalty that snuck up on him.

"He put us all in danger. We thought he'd killed you! It was an affront to the crown and all of the empire, and he showed no remorse. What were we supposed to do? Send him to his room and wait for his plotting to continue?"

On the surface, Ignotus' voice seemed steady, but

Domitris could tell he was fighting to keep himself together. Domitris leaned his palms on the rostrum and drew in a breath, getting the anger inside him under control.

"That is a blatant overstep of the power of your office and the laws of justice. You do not have the authority to make that call. In fact, what you should be doing is overseeing the guard, but instead they're out all over the city, harassing people when you have apparently already placed judgment."

Ignotus shifted his stance and opened his mouth to answer.

"No! We will discuss this in private, Consul Ignotus. Spare your words."

It wouldn't look good for either of them to settle this in front of an audience. He could see Ignotus fuming all the way across the room, but that didn't matter right now. It hadn't just been him. The whole council was out of control and had been ever since Domitris had returned from the provinces. He had to rein them in. He had to assert himself and make sure there were no more obstructions before the signing of the treaty.

"This council has been divisive and uncooperative from the beginning. You are forgetting your place. You are *my* council. You are here to serve *me* and the people of Marmaras. The destruction our city has faced, not to mention the attempt on my life and the assault of the Dassosdan Minister, are all direct consequences of your petty power plays and shameless disregard for the new rule."

While he talked, Gaius rose from his seat. Domitris considered what to do. He could ignore him, dismiss him even, and be spared from his stupidity, but part of Domitris wanted to draw Gaius out now that he was at his most vulnerable, to see him falter and put him in his place once and for all. He needed to keep his head cool and not let himself be provoked. If he failed, the shreds of support he still clung to among the council might be truly lost.

Domitris paused for breath and left an opening. Gaius took the bait.

"You cannot blame the council for this," Gaius bellowed. "This is your doing by breaking with our traditions, culture, and history. The council is here to keep the emperor in check, to make sure the emperor does not lead us into ruin! Progress for progress' sake is a fools' errand and to insist on opening up to the north is to spit in the face of every Marmarasi soldier who has given their life for the greatness of the nation."

The sheer audacity of speaking out like that against him without acknowledging Cassian's confession had Domitris boiling. He examined Gaius' face. There was not a trace of grief or guilt to be found.

"And do you think we have succeeded in honoring those lives these past days? The city set ablaze, the legendary Library of Marmaras burned down, is that your idea of justice?"

Gaius' knuckles went white. His brows furrowed, the folds of his face twisting with hatred.

"The treaty is a naive and childish attempt at making a name for yourself. You are willing to sell out everything we stand for to gain a few lines in a history book. We got rid of one tyrant to gain another. The council is starting to wonder if the Emperor is fit for the task."

Someone had the gall to murmur, "He's right."

The knot in Domitris' chest tightened. He wanted to lunge at him, to pound the delusions of grandeur out of his head, to throw him in a cell and never see him again. But this was a critical moment. He had to come out of this looking composed.

"How dare you speak to me like this? The treaty is not my personal project. Bringing peace to our countries is the will of the people and what's best for this nation. Do not think for a second that I'm doing this for my own glory. This council has worked against me from the start. If you hadn't slowed us down and insisted on fighting this every step of the way, we wouldn't be in this situation now with our history and records lost in flames. Because of you, we are now without a past and with a future more uncertain than ever."

He made sure to keep eye contact with Gaius through every word. He wanted him to know that he saw right through him. All open accusations would only serve to bring the hall to a boil and allow anyone in on the conspiracy to either act or flee, none of which was what he wanted. Gaius wasn't stupid. He had managed to garner enough support with his lies that if Domitris locked him up, it would look irrational and untrustworthy and not much unlike the Supreme Emperor.

"You have no idea what you are talking about," Gaius spat. Red blotches spread across his face. "Your little dream of peace is an escapist utopia. I have seen what it takes to make the empire prosper. I was on this council long before you were born, and I suspect I'll be here long after you're gone."

The hall fell dead silent. It was an obvious misstep to everyone listening, losing his temper like that. A desperate attempt at a retort. Domitris let the comment hang until its echo died down.

"I think that's enough, Councilor Gaius. Sit. Down."

It worked. Gaius actually seemed to be flustered by his own blunder, dumbfounded for once in his life. He huffed and puffed but put his ass back in his seat. Domitris would have to find an appropriate way to deal with Gaius' insubordination and round up those loyal to him to uncover the heart of the conspiracy, but there would be time for that yet. In this moment, he had to use the opportunity to cement his authority. Most of the council were looking back at him, stunned and confused. He took the time to look around to examine every face in there. Right now, he had them. He took a deep breath.

"Two years ago, *I* was the first to be elected as the emperor of Marmaras. That means that both you, the nobles, and the people gave me a mandate to do what is best for our empire. I intend to see this peace through, and as long as I am here, that is exactly what will happen." He paused and looked around.

"If this country is to prosper while we open up to the north, we need to prepare for that and not keep fighting it. This is happening. The festival has showed clear as day that we are ready for it."

There were no objections this time. Now he needed to convince them to get behind him again. Ignotus had been right. He should have stayed within the palace, playing mighty and making small talk, nurturing his alliances.

He had to let the council think that he believed the conspiracy was over, that it died with Cassian. There was no way that was true, but it would take time to uncover, and he needed to win back the support of the council to stay on the throne.

"The traitor has been executed. Though this is not what

should be noted as justice under my rule, let us at least sleep knowing the conspiracy is over." The words came out hollow, but it was no use to let accusations fly and alienate anyone who could be won over with the right means.

"For the rest of the day and until the treaty has been signed tomorrow, the council will rest. Then we start a new era, one of peace, and we will get to work. You are all dismissed, and I will not hear arguments or suggestions before the treaty is signed."

Instead of the protests or disgruntled disagreement that usually followed the council meetings, there was a strange sort of quiet this time. If that was what it took to gain their respect, he would give it to them. He had his work cut out for him, getting the council back on track, but hard work had never scared him. To the relief of his tired bones, there were no more objections. He nodded in conclusion.

"Let's all get some rest."

Stepping down from the rostrum, he turned and exited the council hall with resolute steps. Sinnan slipped out from his cover and followed him.

Halfway down the hall, a call from behind stopped him.

"Domitris! Domitris, wait!"

Ignotus came running after him, and Domitris turned. He had no patience left.

"What do you want?"

"I wanted to see if you were all right. You seem beside yourself."

He couldn't keep it in. "Who gave you the authority to make that decision? Only the emperor can make the call for an execution."

Ignotus halted, his jaw set. "The emperor," he said through gritted teeth, "was presumed dead. Someone had to step in and make the decision. Don't think it was an easy one."

Something cracked inside Domitris, and anger came pouring out. He couldn't seal it away. It spilled out like molten lava.

"That's not the way of things! You shouldn't have done that."

Ignotus looked like he had been slapped across the face. "People wanted to see justice done. I did what I had to when there was no one else to do it. Isn't that why you made me consul?"

Domitris' shoulders had tensed up around his ears. He tried to relax them.

"What good are the reforms and the new laws of justice if we set them aside like they're nothing? People will have no faith in the new system."

"The circumstances were extraordinary. We needed to be decisive and show that plotting against the throne will have consequences."

"I think you've become too comfortable on my throne. You need to take a step back."

Ignotus narrowed his eyes. "Is that a threat?"

Domitris felt Sinnan's hand on his arm. "Come on, Domitris. You should get some rest."

Ignotus' gaze jerked to Sinnan. "Your whore," he said, looking Sinnan up and down. "I warned you about this one, Dom. Since when did you let whoever crawl into your bed and affect your decisions? You're not thinking clearly."

That was low, even for Ignotus. It took everything Domitris had not to punch him. "Worry about yourself, Ignotus. And get the guard under control!" He turned his back on Ignotus' hurt frown, and walked away.

XXV

When Domitris closed the door, he let his head fall back against it and rested his eyes. Sinnan went ahead and sat down at the table, where a tray of food waited for them.

"I hardly recognized you back there," Sinnan teased. "So firm... regal... angry."

Domitris smiled.

"Cut it out. I don't want to talk about it. Let's talk about something else. I feel like this is the first quiet moment we've had in days."

Sinnan looked longingly at the food. "I'm so hungry."

"Have at it."

Sinnan dug in with unparalleled gusto. Domitris joined him and picked up a piece of bread. Then he downed a glass of water and ripped the bread into chunks, which he devoured one by one.

Sinnan sat with his legs crossed, stuffing olives into his mouth by the handful. It was strange to see him in palace garments. The draping of white silk accentuated his collarbone and the delicate curves of his shoulders. The gold pins shone with the amber of his skin. His posture, his features, his movements—he was meant for fine clothing.

A firm knock rapped at the door, startling them both. Before he could get up, the door swung open and in strode a slim-lipped woman with gray hair in a swirly up-do so tight it was pulling up the sides of her face. Hossia glided in right behind her.

"Good morning, Your Highness," the medical scholar said with a mechanical bow and her eyes went instantly to Sinnan, who was most noticeably wounded. Her eyes grew a little wider and her fingers twitched.

"May I ask the first patient to sit over here?" She gestured to the edge of the bed while keeping her eyes on Sinnan.

Sinnan looked warily to Domitris as if to look for confirmation. He gave a small nod, though he had never seen the woman in his life. Sinnan brushed off his hands and went to sit on the bed.

Hossia put her wrinkly arms around Domitris. "Half the knowledge of the known world gone up in flames, but my boy made it out unscathed. Domitris, the Fireproof King of Marmaras. Doesn't sound too bad, does it?"

Domitris shook his head into her shoulder. "I hope you didn't come here just to flatter me."

"No." She sat down next to him, pulling the chair closer, until she was only a hand from his face. Behind her, the scholar pulled up her green sleeves and grabbed Sinnan's chin with a bony hand, angling it up in what looked like an uncomfortable position. She inspected the cut on his cheek, looking a little too eager.

"This requires stitching," she said, speaking through her nose.

Hossia snapped her fingers in front of Domitris' face and his attention returned to her.

"I know you said you didn't want to hear from anyone, but I hoped to be an exception," she said gruffly. The furrow between her gray brows was stark, the tension around her mouth uncharacteristic.

"What is it?"

"I'm concerned, my boy. There was something off about Cassian. It wasn't right what they did to him."

"No. Cassian was an arrogant fool who put himself where he landed, but I don't believe he was behind all of it."

"My suspicions exactly." She raised a bushy eyebrow. "You should have told me you had left for the library. You get yourself in danger when you keep me in the dark."

"I know."

Sinnan let out a yelp. When Domitris looked over, the physician had an alcohol-soaked cloth pressed to his face.

"Listen, I'm gathering my allies. I have people digging around, but you need to stay on guard. I won't be convinced until that treaty lies safely signed in the palace archives. The next day will be dangerous for you. I feel it in my bones." Her dark eyes were serious.

"What do you want me to do?"

"Nothing right now, but you need to be careful. Clear your schedule for the day. Don't draw attention to yourself. And don't let anyone know of your suspicions."

"I'm not staying in here all day like a sitting duck. I need to get out of the palace. I–I need to get away from it all for a little while."

She narrowed her eyes. "Where are you planning on going?"

"The baths, I thought."

Hossia put a hand to her chin. "I think that's a good idea. Not too public, not too private." She looked up at him, her eyebrows droopy, and placed a hand on his cheek. "You look like you need a good rest."

He smiled at her. He did feel safer knowing her agents would be out there, keeping an eye on him.

"The next patient can get ready now." The scholar put the last stitch in Sinnan's cheek. He was teary-eyed, his face scrunched up, and his hands were clamping down on the bedsheets. She clipped the thread and turned to Domitris. "Next patient, please."

Sinnan looked up at her like he was hoping for a reassuring word or a pat on the head, but none came. Instead, Domitris got up and Hossia did as well.

"We'll talk another time. Stay careful."

"I will, Matre, and you as well."

She brushed the air with her hand in a dismissive gesture, and then she was out the door, nodding to Sinnan on the way. Sinnan returned to his food, trying not to touch his cheek as Domitris sat down on the bed.

"Where's the damage?" the scholar asked, and Domitris stuck out his leg. She crouched down and held a hand on both sides of his shin, turning it from side to side, inspecting the wound.

"It needs to be disinfected; no stitching required." She rummaged around in her medic bag for the alcohol. "It'll leave a scar," she added.

If a scar was all he would take with him from the fire, he had no complaints. He gritted his teeth while she wiped hard at his leg with the cloth.

When the scholar finally left after severely instructing them both not to pick at their wounds, Domitris slumped back into his chair and looked at Sinnan. The cut on his face was red and swollen.

"Is it very bad?" Sinnan asked, seeing the look on Domitris' face.

He sat up and got his expression under control. "Not at all," he said unconvincingly, and Sinnan half-rolled his eyes.

"Does it hurt?" Domitris asked instead.

Sinnan had to stop his hand mid-air on the way to his cheek and caught it between his thighs instead.

"Like a bitch. Who was the old lady?" Sinnan then asked, taking a bite of a pear.

"My matre," Domitris said, but when Sinnan still looked questioning, he explained. "The title of older women in your family who are not your mother. Hossia is my mother's mother."

Sinnan nodded thoughtfully. "She seemed nice. It's good that you have her."

"I tell myself that every day."

Sinnan smiled, though there was sadness in his eyes. Sighing, he leaned back against the wall, his eyelids falling shut. "I don't want to be awake anymore."

Neither did Domitris. And he didn't want to be alone. "Stay. Get some rest."

Sinnan tilted his head and looked back at him with heavy-lidded eyes. "Really?"

"If you want."

He got up and stumbled onto the bed face-first. Then he

rolled over and got up on his elbows. Domitris sat beside him as Sinnan yawned.

"I don't think I've ever been this tired in my life. And that is honestly an achievement."

"I can imagine." Domitris lowered himself to the mattress. With a full stomach and finally lying down, he fought to keep his eyes open.

"It's ironic, isn't it?" Sinnan said and Domitris gave a start, realizing he had been skirting the edge of sleep.

"What is?"

"I've dreamed of seeing the Library of Marmaras most of my life and the first time I go there, it's burned to the ground."

Domitris huffed and Sinnan lay down beside him.

"I'm impressed you managed to make that about you."

"Well, I'm just saying," Sinnan said, lifting the sheets over them, "how fragile our dreams are."

That struck something within Domitris. He thought of their first night, when Sinnan had lain on the gallery floor and looked up at the stars in the ceiling. The man he had met that day was so different from the man who was lying beside him now.

"I'm glad I didn't have to go through it alone."

Sinnan adjusted his position and looked at him, his eyes shifting back and forward between Domitris' as if he wanted to say something. Sinnan stuck out his hand in the space between them under the covers. Tingles swirled in his chest, and he reached out his own hand to meet Sinnan's. Their fingers intertwined and they lay like that, silent and half-asleep, in the brightness that was barely dimmed by the curtains.

"I'm not going to stay," Sinnan said.

Domitris had felt it coming, but he had desperately hoped not to hear it. His stomach sank as he looked at Sinnan. The warmth of the moment disappeared, and reality tugged at him.

"I know," he said. "When?"

"When the festival ends, there'll be nothing more for us here."

Even though he knew what Sinnan meant, it still hurt. *Nothing more for us here.* Domitris held on a little firmer and caressed the scars on the back of Sinnan's hand with a thumb.

"Besides," Sinnan added, "you have an empire to rule, and it seems like you have enough trouble in your life already."

"Are you calling yourself trouble?"

"I think that's beside the point, but, oh Domitris, you have no idea."

"I think I like trouble," Domitris said.

Sinnan couldn't hold back the smile, and he turned his head into the pillow and sighed.

"I'm here for now. Let's hold on to that and deal with the rest later."

Domitris looked at him. He didn't say anything, just watched him in the fuzzy light. It didn't take long for Sinnan's breathing to become deep and steady. Domitris smiled to himself. It had been a lovely dream.

XXVI

When he opened his eyes, the room was bright. Dust particles danced in the ray of sunshine slashing the room in two. Domitris had slept terribly, his dreams filled with fire and smoke and panic. The flames still burned somewhere in his mind and his body ached all over. The room was strangely quiet, and he had a feeling he had slept through the midday bells. So had Sinnan. He slept beside him, lying on his stomach facing the other way. The sun fell onto his hair, making the strands translucent dark brown. Domitris wanted to touch it. A flash of the first night they had spent together crossed his mind. He had touched his hair, then. It hit him how little bodily contact they had had since the next night, when he had asked Sinnan to stop. He thought of Sinnan's ridiculously soft lips. Something stirred in him. He reached out a hand and brushed the skin of Sinnan's naked arm. He didn't want him to go. He couldn't bear the thought of how different these past days would have been if he hadn't met Sinnan. He had saved his life.

Everything that had happened in the night came back and

filled his mind. He shuddered. Withdrawing his hand, he lay on his back, staring up into the blue canopy, his hands folded behind his head. He could have been dead. Should have been, if the plan had succeeded. He thought of Cassian pleading for his life as they slit his throat. Cassian had been a conniving bastard, but hadn't he also just been a stupid little boy, a spoiled palace-kid, not so unlike himself? Sure, Cassian had always been nasty and arrogant, but the palace had a way of instilling false ideas of your own importance in your head.

Sinnan turned around slowly, his eyes blinking open.

"I didn't mean to wake you," Domitris said.

"You didn't." Sinnan slid closer, laying his head against Domitris' arm. Then he kissed him on the side of his armpit. They lay like that for a while, things unsaid between them. Domitris turned around and, with his free hand, brushed a lock of hair away from Sinnan's forehead.

"Domitris, I–"

Sinnan didn't finish the sentence because the door swung open, and Lyra walked in with a platter of food. The two of them jerked apart as if they had been doing something indecent and Domitris cleared his throat. Lyra looked over at them.

"Don't stop what you're doing on my behalf," she said, oddly chipper. "Good thing you're awake. I wanted to let you sleep as long as possible, but I also wanted to make sure you're all right. You must be hungry after a night like that."

"Thank you," Domitris said, then added, "I'm taking the rest of the day off. Will you make sure to clear my schedule?"

"Of course, you should rest before the big ceremony tomorrow. Don't worry, I'll leave you alone. I know when I've disturbed something. There's food on the table." She smiled briefly and disappeared from the room.

There was silence again. Sinnan put the palms of his hands to his face and groaned.

"I slept like hell," he said, rubbing his eyes.

"Me too." The charred smell lingered in Domitris' nostrils, the taste of smoke still stuck in his throat. He got up and absentmindedly sat down at the table, helping himself to a portion of cured duck and date paste. Sinnan joined him, starting with a spoonful of fresh sheep's milk cheese, and they ate in companionable silence. Domitris ached all over, and the exhaustion in his body seemed to stretch into his soul. Even if he had washed off most of the grime, he felt dirty—the kind of dirty that wasn't only on the outside but somehow tainted his insides as well. He saw it mirrored in Sinnan. His nails were black, the hollow of his collarbone sooty, and his shoulders slumped in a way that even a good night of rest wouldn't fix. The fire had left more than the scars on their skin. He hated that he had gotten Sinnan involved, and an inescapable sense of guilt twisted inside him. He wanted to remedy it, though he knew he couldn't.

Domitris cleared his throat. "Will they worry if you stay out a little late?"

Sinnan licked the back of the spoon. "Why?"

"I want to take you somewhere today."

"Where? Nowhere flammable, I hope."

Domitris smiled. He didn't want to be without this. "It's a surprise."

"So, where are you taking me?" Sinnan kept looking around,

searching for something that would give him a hint.

"You'll see."

Olive trees and pines flanked the tiled road leading south beyond the marketplace. Small, emerald parrots flew from tree to tree, squawking at one another as the two of them strolled past. Slowly, the road started winding. Behind a thicket of tall trees, the baths came into view, the domes and rooftops towering over them.

Sinnan looked at him, eyes wide. "What is that place? It's enormous."

It was only a fraction of the size of the palace, but here, where the landscape was flat and no other buildings competed with it, the baths looked like a whole estate emerging in front of them. Domitris hadn't truly missed the palace while he had been on tour, but he had missed this.

"The Baths of Galana. It's the most relaxing place I know. It's open to all citizens. Everyone mingles here, nobles and commoners. You'll love it."

Sinnan inspected the building with awe while they approached the entrance.

"Are you ready?"

Sinnan gave a small nod and Domitris pushed open the gates.

Instantly, the temperature increased, and moist air filled his lungs. The sound of water splashing and people chattering bounced off the walls. Ten, if not twenty, men could stand on each other's shoulders and hardly touch the paintings of the vaulted ceiling. Domitris cast a glance at Sinnan who, to his satisfaction, was craning his neck to absorb every detail, his lips slightly parted. They removed their sandals at the entrance and followed the path cutting across the main room. A myriad of smaller, open enclosures stretched out to the sides, each one more marvelously decorated than the one before. The floors were masterpieces made up of die-sized stones, forming swirling patterns of creeping vines, mythical creatures, and ancient symbols. In the larger of the long pools, athletes practiced their technique, swimming back and forth with straining muscles and hard breaths between the strokes. Other bathing guests sat relaxed in the cool water pouring into the shallow basins from openings in the walls. Except for the occasional fine jewelry, it was hardly possible to tell who were commoners and who were nobles because everyone was naked and wet. Most of the visitors were caught up in their own business, but here and there, people turned to gawk and whispers carrying his name floated through the air.

Along the sides of the pools, marble statues of previous emperors alongside heroes from old legends and tales watched over the room. The last Supreme Emperor had been one of them, though after the desecration of the statue just before the Overthrow, it had been removed, leaving a vacancy in one of the most prominent spots.

The newest addition was two identical statues on each side of the next pair of doors depicting—himself. He knew they had been ordered after the coronation, but he hadn't seen the finished result until now. The statues were a head taller than he actually was and they hadn't held back with the carvings of the muscles. It also looked like the sculptor had put more effort into carving out his feet than his face. No wonder people didn't recognize him when he was out. Sinnan's eyes were fixed to the statues as they strolled past and entered the emperor's private baths.

The staff had seemingly been notified of his arrival the instant they got there because, inside, several bath attendants scurried around setting out towels, incense, and plates of fruit, and a few servants stood unmoving, ready to meet their every demand. Domitris wanted to spend what precious time they had without any distractions.

"Leave us," he said, and the servants and attendants immediately put down the things they were holding and, with respectfully deep bows, disappeared out through an invisible door in the corner. As the door closed, the stillness of the room was absolute except for the water softly lapping against the tiles.

"I would appreciate an uneventful day," Domitris said.

Sinnan looked around, silently taking in the place. This room was much smaller than the one they had crossed, but the ceiling was even higher, and a starry night was painted on a dusk blue background. White and rose marble carvings decorated every edge, and the tiles on the floor depicted elaborate flowers in all stages of blooming.

"No statues of you in here?" Sinnan said, turning to Domitris with a grin.

"I hate those things, but there are few limits to what the nobles will do to make sure everyone knows exactly who's in power."

"And who's not," Sinnan added.

"It is what it is," Domitris said.

"Well, in any case, I quite like the statues. They were all naked," Sinnan said, playfully changing the subject. He leaned into Domitris and let his eyes wander downward.

"Though I can attest to the fact that they didn't get your proportions quite right. I noticed that on all the other naked statues in this country. Are you afraid of big dicks or what?"

"I'm not," Domitris answered, and he could hear the casual boldness in his own voice.

Sinnan laughed. "I like it here," he said. "It's beautiful." He locked his arms around Domitris' neck. The stitches on his face were still swollen and pink. The bruise on his jaw was a marble of blackish blue.

"I hoped you would." Domitris' hands encircled Sinnan's waist and pulled him closer. Sinnan's head bowed down and snuggled against his collarbone. The more he held him, the more Domitris couldn't escape the thought that echoed in his head. *I don't want you to go.* What right did he have to say that? He squeezed him tighter. Sinnan lifted his head. The look in his eyes made Domitris' heart sting; it seemed so full of hurt. There was a universe behind those green eyes and Domitris wanted to dive into it, head-first. Sinnan got on his toes and combed a hand through Domitris' hair. Domitris looked from his eyes to the curves of his lips. This time, it was Sinnan who leaned in for the kiss. It was soft at first, tentative. His mouth was sweet and warm and gentle. There was something so innocent about it, almost like a first kiss, even though that was already long behind them and neither of them were fumbling youths.

Sinnan got more eager and pressed against him. When Sinnan's tongue parted Domitris' lips and entered his mouth, his thoughts evaporated. Sinnan let out a moan through his nose and the sound of it sent sparks flying through every inch of Domitris' body. Domitris moved his hand up to caress the side of his face and melted into him. Now he was the one leading the kiss. He slid his fingers into the hair at the nape of Sinnan's neck and tilted his head for the access his mind and body were craving. He wanted to drink him, devour him, consume him, body and soul. Domitris grabbed a fistful of hair and broke the kiss. His eyes were half closed, and he was panting slightly.

"Fuck me," Sinnan whispered into the space between them.

Domitris' heart rate picked up and, for the first time in what felt like forever, not because he was afraid.

"You just get right to the point, don't you?"

Sinnan smiled. "Isn't that why you brought me here?"

Domitris didn't answer. He felt himself getting aroused and he was a little surprised it didn't take more than that. Sinnan wasn't slow to pick up on his reaction and he loosened the pin holding Domitris' clothes together. It was casual wear that unraveled easily. He bent down and kissed Sinnan again, then tugged at his clothes. Sinnan didn't stop him, so he ran his hands up Sinnan's sides, bunching up the fabric and pulling it over his head. They had to break the kiss to get it all the way off.

Instead of picking up where they left, Sinnan went to the edge of the pool, where he stepped down the tiled steps into the water. Domitris watched him, the fabric still in his hands. He hadn't seen him naked before. For some reason he thought he had, but then again, the garments Sinnan had worn the first days they had been together had left little to the imagination. Domitris admired the lines of his back and the dimples above his ass. He caught himself thinking that somebody should make a statue of Sinnan instead. He would make the perfect subject.

"What are you waiting for?" Sinnan asked and went further into the water.

Domitris walked down the steps until his ankles were immersed. He sat at the top of the stairs and reached out a hand. Sinnan, who was out navel-deep, came back and crawled onto his lap. Domitris sat there naked, half hard, with his feet in the clear water and this gorgeous man on top of him.

They were both still beaten up by the events of the night, and the wound on his leg stung when it came into contact with the water.

"This is nice," Sinnan whispered, then stuck out his tongue. Warm wetness slithered into his ear, and it felt like it was touching his brain. Domitris' hand flew up to cover the side of his head, but he couldn't help smiling.

"You're too much."

"I can tell you like it," Sinnan teased, and started grinding softly against Domitris' abs. Sinnan bent down and kissed him, first on the mouth again, then along the cheek and down his neck. Domitris shuddered. He was getting fully aroused and felt himself poking against Sinnan's ass.

Sinnan smiled and came face to face with him again to plant an open-mouthed, wet kiss on his lips. Domitris was beginning to crave friction. His fingers dug into the skin of Sinnan's hips, pulling him closer. Sinnan moaned theatrically and Domitris twitched at the sound. He noticed Sinnan had gotten hard as well.

"Are you sure about this?"

Sinnan rocked against him more quickly. "Yes," he said

breathlessly. "Take me."

Domitris' heart pounded against his ribs. He leaned forward to suck on Sinnan's nipples, which elicited a very positive reaction of more loud moaning. For some reason, he had expected the golden metal stick in his nipple to be cold, but it was warm and clacked against his teeth. Sinnan took hold of his hair and lifted up his face to kiss him again. His movements were getting less controlled and more desperate.

"Take me," he repeated, almost pleading.

Domitris leaned off to the side and lifted one of the tiles at the edge of the pool that hid a small compartment full of vials of scented oils. He picked up one of them that contained pink liquid and he knew before he opened it that it smelled heavily of roses. As he pulled off the stopper and let it run down his fingers, the scent reminded him of the sweets they had eaten together at the market. Sinnan still sat half on top of him, his legs spread, waiting patiently. Domitris trembled with anticipation at the sight. How could Sinnan be so calm? He ran his hand down Sinnan's lower back, down over his ass and with his other hand, pulled his cheeks apart. Sinnan's breath was steady, only slightly quickened by the action. He didn't seem to be nervous about what would follow. Domitris' fingers found their goal and with the tip of his oiled middle finger, he pushed gently inside. Sinnan shuddered, relaxing into it, his eyes closed. Sinnan was mind-numbingly tight and warm. He exhaled softly at the penetration. Domitris worked his finger in a steady motion, pushing against the side to stretch him open. Sinnan was obviously experienced because it didn't take long for him to get comfortable and become pliant and eager for more. Domitris let a second finger join and worked him until his hand became tired.

When Domitris' hand lost its rhythm, Sinnan put his weight on his knees and rose slightly, signaling for Domitris to pull out. He did as carefully as possible and washed off his fingers in the water. Sinnan leaned over to take the oil and let plenty flow into his hand. Small, sticky drops slipped out between his fingers and landed on Domitris' thighs. Sinnan leaned backwards so Domitris' erection came into full view between them. Sinnan looked like he was enjoying himself, like he was doing something he knew he was good at. He grabbed hold with a glistening hand and stroked slowly, covering him in the rosy oil. His hand was warm and soft, his movements easygoing but methodical. By the stars, he was good. It was the right amount of everything—pace, pressure, oil. Rarely had Domitris wanted something so much in his life. He could hardly imagine what it would feel like to have him. The anticipation was too much to bear. He took a deep breath to steady himself. Then, Sinnan made eye contact and Domitris feared for a second that it would be enough to undo him. He stopped Sinnan's hand and took a ragged breath. "Careful."

Sinnan huffed, looking immensely pleased.

Domitris smiled through his attempt to catch his breath. He leaned back on his hands and closed his eyes, focusing on the splashing of the water and the cool feel of the tiles beneath his palms. It helped. When he opened his eyes again, Sinnan regarded him carefully.

"Has it been a while?"

"Shut up."

Domitris reached out and ran his hands up Sinnan's thighs. His thumbs lingered at his hips and pulled him closer. Sinnan shot him a look, as if to make sure he was ready. Domitris nodded. He forced himself to be still to make sure Sinnan was in control of the entering. These things could not be rushed. He had tried that on his own body when he was young and stupid and let lust come before restraint. He still remembered the humiliation and pain he had felt back then and hadn't been much for receiving since. It had given him a certain amount of respect for the process, even though the wait could be almost unbearable. Luckily, Sinnan worked quickly and efficiently and got himself in position above him.

Sinnan reached down and adjusted the angle while slowly lowering himself onto him. The tip soon met soft resistance, but even though Domitris was more well-endowed than his statues made him out to be, he went in without a problem.

Domitris involuntarily closed his eyes as every part of him was overtaken by the sensation. He opened them to Sinnan's flushed face. Lust burned like fire in his eyes. There was no fumbling or awkwardness about it. Sinnan slowly started to rise and fall and worked up a steady pace. When was the last time he'd had something like this? Never, he thought. Never.

Sinnan rode him, hard, and found a rhythm that evoked the result he wished for.

Domitris couldn't help the moans coming in time with each fall of Sinnan's body and he thrust helplessly against him. It was obvious that Sinnan enjoyed having that kind of power over him. So far, Sinnan had been focused on Domitris, but there was a shift when Sinnan closed his eyes and rocked much harder against him, finding his own pleasure. Domitris could tell Sinnan was closing in on the climax. He didn't want it to be over already. Without thinking, he shifted and held firmly onto

Sinnan's body. Then he got up, lifting Sinnan, turned around while still inside him, and laid him down on the tiled floor. The motion made him slip out, which solicited a surprised groan from Sinnan. Sinnan's legs were bent up in the air and Domitris repositioned himself between them.

He leaned his shoulders against Sinnan's thighs, angling him up for better access. Sinnan's breaths were heavy as he looked up at the ceiling, arms casually resting above his head. His hard cock strutted against his lower stomach.

Domitris stopped for a second to take in the sight. He thought to himself that he had never seen anything so beautiful in his entire life. Sinnan's hips bucked and Domitris didn't wait. Easily, he slipped all the way inside again. He held onto Sinnan's thighs and drove deep with each thrust.

Sinnan moaned loudly and lewdly and grabbed Domitris' ass hard, forcing him deeper. There were no thoughts left in his mind, only burning desire. Instinct took over as he plunged into him again and again. Sinnan's moans became uncontrolled and desperate, his hands scrambling on the tiles to find something to hold on to as his back arched. With a high-pitched moan, his whole body convulsed, and he came onto his own abdomen.

He lay there, sweating and panting, his cheeks pink and eyes half-closed. He didn't try to hide. Many people would turn away or cover their face with their hands, but Sinnan just smiled. The sight was too much to bear, and Domitris hardly made it through another thrust. The building fire in his stomach crescendoed, and climax came crashing over him. He cramped as he came and collapsed onto his forearms. He pushed himself hard into Sinnan as wave after wave of satisfaction rolled over him, and he clenched his teeth to stifle the groan that was forced from his lips.

For a while, the only sound was their panting. Domitris pulled out slowly, the sensation still convulsing through his body. Sinnan trembled underneath him as he slid out. They both caught their breath for a moment before Domitris bent down and kissed Sinnan's soft mouth. Sinnan kissed him back sloppily, with a fist buried in his hair. Domitris pulled away to look down at him. A curl clung to his cheek, and Domitris brushed it aside.

"I liked that," Domitris said, still short of breath.

"I could tell." The teasing gleam was already back in Sinnan's eyes.

Domitris huffed. His arms were trembling from the exertion. Sinnan looked down his body and ran a hand over the mess on his stomach.

"How practical that we're already in the baths," he said, amused. Then he slid away from under Domitris and out into the water.

XXVII

They stayed there for hours. They went in and out of the water multiple times and enjoyed the fruit and bread brought by the servants. They had both put on the loose-fitting, thin robes laid out for them and sat at the edge of the water on soft silk cushions. Sinnan had grown quiet and looked as though he were thinking about something far away. Domitris watched him. He had spent the past four days with this amazing man and had already had sex with him twice, but the trip to the library had made it clear that he definitely wasn't who Domitris had assumed him to be from the start. He gathered up the courage to ask the question that wouldn't leave him alone.

"Sinnan?"

Sinnan's attention returned to the room. "Mm?"

"When will you tell me your story?"

He sat in silence for a moment, eyes fixed on the water.

"When will you tell me who Aelias is?"

Domitris froze at the question. He must have looked as dumbfounded as he felt because Sinnan added, "You came up with that name so easily. I figured there had to be a story behind it."

Hearing his name like that from Sinnan's lips tore open a wound he hadn't realized was still scabbing. Domitris closed his mouth and considered it. His own curiosity overpowered the surge of agony in his heart. "If I tell you, will you tell me about your past?"

"That seems fair," Sinnan said, leaning nonchalantly back on his palms.

Domitris ran a hand over his face. "I haven't talked about this in a long time."

Sinnan looked back at him with the poorly disguised interest of someone waiting to revel in scandal. Domitris didn't know where to start.

"He was my… We were…" He took a deep breath. By the look in Sinnan's eyes he knew exactly what Domitris was saying. "We met at the academy," Domitris continued. "I was… smitten with him. It took years of courting but I finally…" he trailed off. "We became lovers," he stated, meeting Sinnan's eyes.

"You're not anymore?"

"No."

"Why not?"

Domitris pinched the bridge of his nose. It was more painful to relive than he had expected. "He started seeing someone else. Someone older—the general who trained us in the military."

"Ouch."

"A lot of things were going on in his life at that point. We were supposed to become engaged later that year. In my mind he could do nothing wrong, I thought he was just acting out because he was under so much pressure. I wanted to give him time to figure it out." Each word was a needle in his heart. Domitris dug his nails into his palm, trying to relocate the pain. "But his family got involved. They… let's just say after what happened with my parents, they were eager for him to marry into a more… prestigious family."

A defiant line formed between Sinnan's eyebrows. "And he listened to them?"

"Their expectations lived in him in a way I will never understand."

Sinnan nodded solemnly. "So he…"

"He chose the other man," Domitris finished. "But…" The next words stuck in his throat.

"But?" Sinnan straightened.

Domitris took a deep breath and let it out slowly. He thought he had gotten over it a long time ago, but saying it out loud brought the emotions back like a fresh whiplash. "A week later, he was sent to the front lines… and he never came back."

Sinnan gaped at him. "Wh—but—wasn't—"

"You don't have to say anything." Domitris knew well that no words would make it easier.

Sinnan bit his lip. "I didn't think—"

"It's fine. It happened a long time ago. It's behind me." Domitris made himself meet Sinnan's eyes, but the forced confidence didn't seem to fool him. He decided to change the subject before Sinnan could cut his heart open with any more questions. "Now it's your turn. What's your story?"

Sinnan closed his mouth and Domitris could see the

thoughts still whirling behind his eyes. He waited patiently, letting Sinnan process and compose himself. Finally his expression hardened and he adjusted his posture. "Give me a more specific question."

Domitris thwarted the emotions that competed for his attention by focusing on finally prying Sinnan open instead. "You said you grew up in the Heathlands—Háfren, right? But if you're Háfrenian, why are you... Why don't you..." He trailed off, not knowing exactly how to phrase it.

"Why don't I look the part?"

Domitris nodded a little sheepishly.

Sinnan shifted in his seat and drew in a breath. "Well, it's a complicated story."

When Domitris gave no indication of being discouraged by the fact, Sinnan continued.

"My parents are Solisian, as you had probably guessed." He gestured to his hair. "But they moved to Háfren when they were both young. I was born and raised there and have never seen Solis."

There was something about the way he spoke, the way he chose his words, that made it seem as if he wasn't completely comfortable with the topic.

"I was quite an eye catcher back in Háfren. The black hair and brown skin—the guys went crazy for it," Sinnan said, picking at his bread.

Domitris knew by now that Sinnan was good at derailing a conversation he didn't want to have.

"Why did you come to Marmaras? It's a really long way from the Heathlands."

Sinnan looked up at him, a glint in his eye. "I couldn't help it. I heard the newly Elected Emperor of Marmaras was the most handsome emperor to ever take the throne, so I just had to come fuck him. They were right about him, though, so I stand by my mission," Sinnan said, winking.

"You don't have to tell me if you don't want to," Domitris said, not taking any of Sinnan's nonsense.

Sinnan brushed his hands against each other and sighed, looking Domitris in the eyes. "Are you sure you want to know? I'll lose my mysterious charm if I tell you."

"I want to know."

Sinnan drew in a breath and looked at the ceiling. "How much do you know about the Heathlands?"

Domitris thought about it. He knew the Heathlands were a cluster of countries in the far north but since Marmaras hadn't had any interactions beyond Dassosda for centuries, it wasn't something they learned about in school, and there weren't many visitors from the northern countries in Marmaras either.

"Not much. I know there are harsh winters and that it's surrounded by ocean. I know there is a strong royal family, but that society's very different from here in the south. People say the Far North is less civilized, but I'm not sure how much of that is true and how much is a lack of understanding."

Sinnan nodded. "I guess that depends on your point of view. The roads are well kept, even better than here, and a courier can get to even the most remote islands in a matter of days. There are more castles than you can count, and the agricultural system is very well developed, which all seems pretty civil in my opinion."

Domitris nodded, confused at the harshness of Sinnan's voice.

"Society is another story. You know the importance of power, so you know the things people will do to attain it. Keep that in mind when I tell you the next part."

There was a strange edge to his voice.

"As I said, my parents are from Solis and my mother is actually the sixth daughter of the Solisian prince."

Domitris' mouth fell open.

"The king's brother, not his son," Sinnan corrected, though it would have made little difference to Domitris.

"You're a prince?"

Sinnan gave a smile that was more mocking than amused.

"No, I'm not. Being that distantly related to the crown makes me pretty much no one in terms of the Solisian royal line."

"But you're a noble."

"They call it 'of royal blood' in Háfren."

Domitris frowned, not following how the two were connected.

"The Solisian royal family is large and the further you are from the crown, the less you have a say in, well, everything. Like anyone else, my parents wanted more power, more status, more money, so they decided to go somewhere they would have that opportunity."

"So, they went to Háfren?"

"Yes. Where Solis has one king, one palace, and reserves power for the immediate royal family, Háfren is made up of a few smaller kingdoms. Each of those has their own royals and an assload of lords beneath them. So, if you are of royal blood and come from abroad, you become immediately interesting to higher society in Háfren."

"Why?"

Sinnan sighed, taking a moment to gather his thoughts. "Well, in Háfren, anyone of decent social standing wants to rub elbows with the royals and get invited to their stupid dinners and balls and outings. The chance of getting into those circles grows significantly if you have royal blood in your family. So naturally, every single one of those less important lords wants that. It's basically a ticket to high society, and you can imagine how valuable that is to people like that. They will give anything to marry off their children to foreigners of royal blood."

Domitris tried to process the information as he got it.

"So, they arrange the marriages?"

Sinnan blew a little air out his nose. "We can call it that. The common practice if you have royal blood is to have a lot of children and marry them into rich and prestigious families when they turn 20 to gain money and land that way. So far, not that bad, right? Marrying your children off for connections isn't that uncommon."

Domitris chewed the inside of his lip.

"But here's the catch. To get the most attractive deal, your kids must be 'untouched', to show the suitors how well raised and controlled they are."

Sinnan had been looking down on the table the whole time, twirling a pear stalk between his fingers, but at the last sentence, he met Domitris' eyes. There was a pause, but Domitris didn't say anything.

Sinnan let out a small sigh and continued. "As you might imagine, that wasn't the future I dreamed of. In Háfren it is considered a great honor to be sold off like that, being able to bring fortune to your family, but I came to despise the idea while I watched it happen to my four older siblings. I started to resent my parents and the future they had chosen for me. They were always too busy with their connections and their money, so I don't know if they ever noticed my feelings on the matter until it was too late. If your parents decide a path for you in Háfren, there are no other options."

To say it seemed restrictive was an understatement. It was different from Marmarasi culture in so many ways that Domitris found it hard to fathom. He furrowed his brows and listened quietly, as Sinnan continued, a hesitation to his words.

"I didn't give a shit about what my parents wanted, and I started seeking all kinds of trouble. 'No' wasn't in my vocabulary. I went to every kind of party I could find and got engaged in every kind of company imaginable. My parents never noticed. People did start to talk, but they didn't believe one word of it, they were so deluded by the idea of their 'perfect' children. In the meantime, I got a taste of the real pleasures of life. In the end, I was definitely not worth the immense fortune my parents had counted on."

There was another pause.

"How did they find out?" Domitris asked.

Sinnan smiled and ran a hand up the back of his head, turning his face to the ceiling. "I don't remember much from those days anymore, but I think I just stopped caring about what would happen. I got more and more reckless about whom I bedded, and where we did it, so one day the household maid walked in on me cock-deep in a friend who had been over to 'study'," Sinnan explained as he clenched his eyes.

"In that moment, my whole life collapsed. I really don't want to relive those days, but the short version is that since I wasn't 'suitable for courtship' anymore and had dishonored my parents irreversibly, I was disowned, and my family name was taken from me. Oh, and it earned me these, of course," he said, holding his hands up to show off the pale scars on the back. "Then I was banished from home and told not to come back. And that's more or less it," Sinnan finished a little rashly and looked up to meet Domitris' gaze.

Domitris found it hard to take it all in. He lessened the frown on his face, trying not to let the horror show in his expression. He had no right to judge Sinnan. After rubbing his hands together for a bit, he said, "I don't know a lot about Háfrenian culture, so I'm not sure how to ask this, but why did you lose your status as untouched, if you were not... the receiver?"

Sinnan answered plainly, but averted his gaze. "It works differently in Háfren. Anything involving any kind of sexual act is seen as a loss of purity. But it honestly wouldn't have mattered anyway. I had been on the receiving end, too. A lot. In some parts of the country, even touching yourself is not permitted if you want to be considered untouched."

Domitris shuddered.

"I'm not sure I really understand it," Domitris said, "how being untouched makes you purer. I've heard about the concept, but it isn't well known in Marmaras. It's like sleeping or fighting or eating. I mean, everyone does it."

Sinnan turned his eyes to the serenity of the pool again, smiling to himself. "Well. That's your opinion and your culture."

Sinnan clearly wasn't looking for a discussion.

Domitris let it go. "What did you do when you lost your home at such a young age?"

Sinnan rose from his pillow and went to sit by the edge of the water again, and Domitris joined him.

"Well, I had nowhere to go, no skills, and no income, and staying in Háfren when you've got the scars can be difficult. No one wants to hire you because they know you can't be trusted."

Domitris' stomach sank.

"I was lucky, though. I pretty quickly got a job as a farmhand with a very nice family. That went well, for a while."

A shadow crossed Sinnan's face, and he went quiet. "In the end I couldn't stay there, so I decided to travel south to get away from it all and find a place where people didn't know what the scars meant. I lived on the road, earning money the only way I knew how, and eventually ran into Amelia and Jenine in Valderin." Sinnan stirred the surface with his fingertips. He had stretched one of his legs into the soothing water and had the other bent in front of him, his head resting sideways on his knee.

Domitris didn't know what he had expected. For Sinnan to be a noble by Marmarasi standards and to have lost it all like that hurt inside Domitris in a way he didn't understand. The shame that followed those scars must be unbearable. Domitris never got the opportunity to make his parents proud, but he wished to, every day. He couldn't imagine a scenario where they would have done something like that to him.

He didn't know what to do, so he just said, "I'm sorry all that happened to you."

Sinnan turned his head to lean his chin on his knee instead and closed his eyes.

"Mmmh," he hummed in an acknowledging tone. Then he opened them again, stretched out his other leg and jumped into the water.

"Want to go for another swim before we head back?" Sinnan grinned at Domitris as if the conversation hadn't happened.

XXVIII

"I should be going back," Domitris said, glancing to Sinnan beside him. The pillowy clouds above them grew orange while they strolled towards the city.

"I can't go with you."

"I know. Let me walk you back to the camp at least."

"No," Sinnan answered with too little hesitation for Domitris' liking. When he looked at him, Sinnan fumbled a little. "I just mean, it'll be easier to let you go if we separate when we get to the road. I hate goodbyes."

Sinnan must have had thousands of goodbyes along the way. Domitris didn't want to be another one.

"Will I see you tomorrow?" he asked.

"Do you want to?" Sinnan replied, as if he didn't know the answer.

"Do you doubt it?"

Sinnan looked down, but he was smiling.

"Tomorrow is the last day of the festival," Domitris said. "When the treaty is signed, the market closes. I know you said you're leaving, so come see me in the evening."

Sinnan still hesitated. A million thoughts seemed to battle in his mind. Eventually, he said, "I'd love to."

The main road lay ahead of them and Domitris slowed down his pace, holding his hand out towards Sinnan. He decided to take it.

"Thank you," Domitris said.

"What for?"

"It's been nice having you here. Some sort of constant in my life amid all the chaos. I've really enjoyed these days with you."

Sinnan didn't answer, he just looked up at Domitris with an expression that somehow looked both happy and sad.

"I wish you didn't have to leave. I want to get to know you."

Sinnan let go of his hand, and a small breath escaped him. He stopped and looked up, eyes darting between Domitris', his breathing shallow as if he wanted to say something.

"What?" Domitris asked, puzzled.

Sinnan looked away and took a deep breath. "We have to," Sinnan said. "Leave."

"But why? If it's because of something you did, I can–"

"Please stop, Domitris. You can't help us with this. We need to go. That was always the plan."

Sinnan started walking again.

"Can't you make a new plan?"

Sinnan looked to the sky in exasperation. "You don't get it."

"No, I *don't* get it. Why don't you explain it to me?"

They had arrived at the main road where going south would take Sinnan to the camp and going north would take

Domitris to the palace.

"We'll talk about it tomorrow. I promise I'll tell you, just not right now."

Sinnan came close and laid his hand on the back of Domitris' head, brown flecks in his green eyes shining with the sunset behind him.

"Thank you for today," Sinnan said, then got up on his toes and kissed him. Domitris let the anger flow out of him, put his arms around Sinnan's waist and hugged him tight.

Sinnan eventually broke it, put his hand through Domitris' hair and said, "See you tomorrow." Then he winked at him.

Domitris stood motionless while he watched Sinnan walk away, still feeling the softness of his lips on his own. When Sinnan turned the first corner and gave a wave of his hand as goodbye, Domitris headed for the palace.

The evening was warm and mild, birds still chirping, racing across the sky. The atmosphere of the festival was thick in the streets. Concordia had come to life during the week with music and laughter flowing from every corner. Domitris could easily imagine this as the new normality, and they were only hours away from making it a reality.

The palace towered in front of him, visible from almost everywhere in the capital. He looked at it, breathtakingly beautiful, while the orange light colored every western surface golden.

When he came into his rooms, the quiet was overwhelming. With only minutes of daylight left, darkness crept over the walls. He lit the lamp at the table by the window. Energy buzzed through him, his chest so light he was sure he could do anything. He had the council under control for now, the treaty would be signed, and real progress was ahead of them. He would be the one to cement Marmaras' new status as an example of diplomacy and peace in a new era. It would be his legacy as an emperor, and he would honor his family name and everything his parents stood for. Afterwards, he would improve the internal relations between the provinces of Marmaras and maybe even bring Auxillien back into the fold. Greatness was within his grasp.

Deciding to get to work, he picked up the stack of papers Lyra had laid out on his desk. Something golden shimmered in the candlelight—Sinnan's bracelet. Lyra must have found it. Domitris put down the papers and picked it up. He could wait until the next evening to return it. He should. But the prospect of seeing Sinnan again, and maybe spending the evening with the troupe instead of alone in his room, was too tempting. He put the bracelet in the folds of his clothes and headed back out. He left a note behind for Lyra, making sure she wouldn't worry that he hadn't returned considering the events of the past days.

He almost ran all the way back to the marketplace and couldn't help smiling. He tried to picture the look on Sinnan's face when he returned it. Sinnan had been so upset about losing it, though Domitris suspected it was less sentimental value and more the fact that it was made of pure gold.

The path through the market had become familiar and though most of the shops were closed, many places selling experiences were open instead. He made his way through the stalls and went around the back to their camp, hoping to surprise them.

AS WE FALL

Closing in, he stopped in his tracks. The yellow tent lay deflated on the ground as Jenine, Ennio, and Bardeia packed up the poles. Closer to Domitris, Amelia and Sinnan were bent over, bundling up canvas. None of them saw him coming.

"I can't stand being here a moment longer. I feel like shit," Sinnan said, folding a piece of tarp.

"I told you from the start it was a shit plan." Amelia tossed a tent peg in a pile.

"Well, we had to do *something*. At least I tried to get us somewhere."

"And look where that got us. You fucked him and got too attached, and we still don't have enough money." Amelia got up and stopped dead when she faced Domitris.

"Sinnan," she said. He turned around, then froze.

Domitris' arms hung motionless down at his sides.

The look on Sinnan's face said he knew Domitris had overheard their conversation.

He didn't try to hide it; instead he picked up where he left off folding the tarp and looked down.

"Why are you here?" Sinnan asked.

A knot tightened in Domitris' chest, and he didn't know how to get the words out. "You're leaving?"

Sinnan didn't answer. Instead, he cast off the tarp to the side and made a dismissive gesture. The others stopped what they were doing. It was strangely silent except for the sizzling of the fire. When Domitris only stood and looked at him for answers, Sinnan rubbed a hand to his face and his expression hardened.

"What do you want me to say, Domitris?"

"I want you to tell me what is going on."

"You heard it."

"I want to hear you say it to me."

Sinnan sighed, his shoulders slouching.

Bardeia stepped forward. "I think you should leave, Your Highness."

"No." Domitris took a step towards Sinnan. "Come on, talk to me!"

Sinnan turned and walked towards his tent.

"Sinnan, come on. Don't walk away; talk to me."

He turned around again. "And say what? That I'm sneaking away in the night? That I've done nothing but fool you?"

"I don't believe you," Domitris said breathlessly.

"It was nothing personal. We tried to find the richest idiot we could. I just hadn't counted on it being the emperor."

Domitris' mind reeled, no coherent thoughts forming. "What are you talking about?"

Bardeia stepped forward again. "Sinnan, don't do this. Calm down, come on."

Sinnan ignored her. "Why do you think I've been throwing myself at you for days? Did you think you were just that irresistible?"

That stung. "I don't understand."

"Of course you don't! I've never in my life met someone so naive. You've been following me like a dog on a leash for these past days; you were just too easy."

He had seen Sinnan angry, had seen him steal and lie and cheat, but not once had he been malicious. Domitris scrunched up his brows. "You don't mean that."

Sinnan's eyes turned hard, and he swung around,

rummaging through the cart. Out of a dirty cloth, came something shiny. A tall silver pitcher, several pieces of familiar jewelry Domitris rarely used anymore, a couple of trinkets, and a small sack of golden coins. Sinnan chucked it at the ground in front of him.

Domitris looked from the effects to Sinnan in disbelief. Everything played through his head. Their first night together. Sinnan's reaction the next morning. He had let himself be fooled, carelessly and willingly. But he refused to believe that was all there was to it.

"What about today?"

"A good fucking doesn't mean anything. How stupid are you? We both knew I was leaving; that's why it happened."

"I thought—"

"Thought what? That I would stay here forever? Live in your palace suite? Marry you? Honestly, what did you think, Domitris?"

Domitris closed his eyes. He didn't want to acknowledge his own stupidity. "I liked you."

Sinnan whipped around, his eyes dark. "Stop it! You stop that right now. Are you really that dense?"

Domitris didn't answer. He stood there, nailed to the ground, blood boiling, not daring to move. He didn't trust himself not to do something stupid.

"Leave. Go away," Sinnan said with a wave of his hand. "We've indulged your role play long enough. Now go back to your fine wine and your silk sheets. You don't belong here, and I don't belong there. I'm no one! I'm a common thief, a filthy prostitute here to take your money and nothing more."

Domitris took a rushed step forward. At once, Bardeia was

up in front of him, a hand against his chest to stop him.

"Look at me!" Domitris shouted, hearing the quiver in his own voice. "Look me in the eye and tell me there was nothing there."

Sinnan glared at him, eyes cold. "Go home, Domitris."

Domitris strained against the arm holding him, which made Bardeia hold on tighter.

"I wouldn't do that if I were you," she warned.

He tried to control his breathing, looking at Sinnan, who faced the other way.

"I think it's time for you to leave, Your Highness."

Domitris' eyes stung, contempt burning inside him, as he looked from Sinnan to the rest of the troupe. Tearing himself away, he turned to leave, but remembered the bracelet tucked away in the folds of his clothes.

"Oh, I almost forgot—I came to give you this."

He hurled it at Sinnan's feet. Bardeia, mistaking his movement for a lunge towards Sinnan, grabbed hold of his arm, twisted it, and used his own momentum to shove him out of the camp. He stumbled as she sent him flying and landed hard on the ground. He sat up and they all stared back at him with stern faces, except Sinnan, who stormed off in the opposite direction. Someone from a neighboring camp snickered and before he could stop himself, the words spilled through his teeth like venom.

"You earned those scars."

Several other camps had quieted down and were staring at the display. Sinnan disappeared out of sight and Domitris' hands balled into fists. He scrambled to his feet and brushed off his clothes. With a huff, he glared around at the onlookers, daring anyone to provoke him. When no one did, he stalked away towards the palace.

Domitris had no memory of how he got back. Only when he shut the doors to his rooms did he gain consciousness. His thumping heart sent blood rushing in his ears. His vision swam. Walking through the dark room, he put his hands on the smooth surface of the table. Sinnan had seemed so real to him, so genuine, unlike every other thing in his life. Cold embarrassment dripped from his heart to his stomach, and he wanted to scream. After what had happened with Aelias, he had sworn to himself never to be broken like that again. Still, he had let himself be fooled by the first pair of pretty eyes batting at him. His brain was screaming at him, his muscles trembling. He wanted to do something—anything—to make it go away. He swung out his arm and sent the slender metal bowl of fruits flying across the room. It clattered to the ground with a ruckus, figs and oranges scattering over the floor. When that didn't help, he kicked one of the oranges and it rolled to the wall with a soft thud. He slumped down on the end of the bed and put his forehead in his hands.

The door flew open and Lyra came in.

"Is everything all right?" she asked frantically, before her distress fell to concern. "Why are you in here in the dark?" She slowed down and knelt before him. "What's wrong?"

He looked back at her, feeling the exhaustion in his body and the betrayal in his heart.

"Sinnan..." he said, his voice catching in his throat.

She didn't say anything, just came to sit beside him, holding his hand. Domitris lay his head on her small shoulder.

"You even told me to be cautious."

Lyra patted him on the hand and after a short silence she said, "I liked him too."

XXIX

When he woke, his mouth was dry, his heart pounding. It took a minute before it all came back to him.

He lay still, breathing deeply to get his pulse under control, but the feeling of something shattered inside him wouldn't go away. Glancing at the space in the bed beside him, he hoped to discover it was all a dream. Sinnan wasn't there, of course, but Domitris could smell him on the sheets. His stomach turned and his teeth ground against each other. The hollow pit inside him threatened to eat him alive. He sat up and put his feet on the cool stone, leaning his elbows on his knees. The images came involuntarily as the argument replayed in his mind.

"You earned those scars."

He wished he hadn't said that.

"A good fucking doesn't mean anything."

He buried his face in his palms, pressing his hands into his eyes, trying to block out the too vivid scenes forming in his head. How could he have been so stupid? His eyes hurt as dots and lines danced across his vision. He raised his head, gasping for air, realizing he had been holding his breath. He took his pillow and threw it across the room. Getting up, he flung the sheets away as he searched for anything that could get his thoughts to latch on to something else.

A small rustle sent his eyes to the floor. The embroidered pouch had fallen from the bed. He picked it up, crushing it in his fist, and the scent of chamomile, lavender and fenugreek took him back to their tent. It made sense now why they had been acting so strange around him. Even their kindness had been false. As he had suspected, the charm had done nothing to alleviate his nightmares. It was all lies and deception.

The overwhelming need to get rid of it suffocated him. The curtains hadn't been drawn yet, but the rim of light running along the foot of the curtains told him it was mid-morning. He parted the draped fabric and hurled the pouch out over the balcony. The tightness in his chest only grew worse as he watched it disappear. Leaning against the doorway, he peered out over the gardens. Something was off. Seconds later, it dawned on him that for the first time in months, the sun wasn't shining. A thin cover of gray clouds darkened the sky and gave the landscape a dull hue. He considered going back to bed when the servant's door opened.

"Oh, you're already up," Lyra said and carefully put a tray of breakfast on the table beside him. "That's good. You should be preparing yourself. It's a big day," she continued, while pulling the curtains aside. He wished she would leave. "Make sure to eat something, at least."

Domitris felt something boiling under his skin. "I'm not hungry."

Lyra touched a reassuring hand to his elbow. "Love isn't easy," she said.

"No? What do you know about that?" he said, not looking at her. She retracted her hand. A cold ache ran through him. He shouldn't have said that. She stood still for a moment, looking up at him, but he kept his eyes on the gardens. She turned away.

"I'll leave you to it then," she said, and the door closed behind her.

His hands trembled. His feelings raced inside him like wasps in a bottle. He slammed down a hand on the table, making a fork jump off the plate and rattle to the floor. The feeling didn't go away and now his hand was sore. He wanted to step out of himself, to put distance between his mind and the unbearable buzzing in his chest. He wanted to get it out somehow. It shouldn't be in here and he shouldn't take it out on Lyra, either. He decided to go to the arena. He shrugged on something at least half decent without bothering to tie up the strings properly and headed out the door.

The ground floor exit at the center of the palace was closest to the barracks, but he didn't want to meet anyone. Instead of taking the most direct route there, he detoured through the west wing. Only a few nobles had quarters in this part of the palace, but the palace archives were here, which ensured scholars were always roaming around the halls. Passing an atrium stuffed in as a chaotic addition to the wing, something made him stop. This particular garden was too small and too remote to be a location for entertaining, yet someone was standing in the far corner, her pale hair familiar. His halting footsteps made Dia turn around, and he cursed himself for having stopped. He couldn't continue walking because she opened her hand in a welcoming gesture.

"Your Highness."

He accepted the invitation and trotted out to her. It was humid and the warmth of the stones under his feet came through the thin leather soles of his sandals. She raised a brow at his clothing but had the decency not to comment on it. When he didn't say anything, she took it upon herself to further the conversation.

"They say it will rain, finally. The flowers will be glad to see it, I think." She lifted a drooping canary-yellow rose. The grass was crisp, the flowers hanging, defeated by the sun and neglected by the gardeners.

"Are you all right?" she asked, and he realized he had made no answer to her observation. He corrected his posture and looked at her, the anger inside him gone and replaced by exhaustion.

"Didn't sleep well."

She made an acknowledging sound and returned her attention to the design of the atrium. "This palace truly is beautiful. I've heard it described many times and have read about it, but it doesn't compare to experiencing it yourself," she said. "I've enjoyed it here, seeing it all firsthand. Despite the obvious," she added and lifted the arm still in a sling.

His head really was up his ass for not asking about it sooner. "How is it healing?"

"It'll be sore for a while," she said, moving her fingers. "But never mind that. I heard you've been through quite the ordeal yourself. How is your leg?"

His garment was only knee-length, the bandages covering his shin visible. He'd almost forgotten already.

"It's nothing more than a scratch."

They both watched as a bee flew from flower to flower.

"I'm sorry about what happened. The Library of Marmaras is legendary, even in Dassosda. I had hoped to visit it one day."

Domitris sighed, his chest tightening. The dull pain of grief bore its claws deep into his bones. "I don't see how we'll ever recover."

"You'll rebuild. Like we did. Like every other nation before you who lost part of their history."

"When the wound is so deep, can it ever truly heal? Will we not face this same conflict time and time again?"

Dia gave a thin smile. "'A mended bone is stronger than an unbroken one.' Do you have that saying here?"

He faced her, letting the phrase turn over in his mind. "We don't."

"Well, it's true."

Domitris' eyes fell to the ground. He moved his foot to avoid stepping on a trail of ants snaking across the stones.

"Were we too ambitious in thinking this would go well?"

Dia turned her face to the sky as the first raindrops fell on them. "Great change requires great courage and a will to act on it. If anything, we were too brave and relied too much on the assumption that this would pass as smoothly as we imagined."

Sticking out his hand, Domitris watched as droplets wet his palm. "I feel stupid. Naive."

Dia shook her head. "Your Highness, why are we here?"

Domitris looked around. "Enjoying a moment of quiet?" He knew that wasn't what she asked.

"No, I mean, what are we doing right now? Why are we going through all this when it is proving so hard?"

He didn't know how to answer that question, so he said nothing.

"We're here to end a war. We're here to bring peace to two peoples who have been separated for almost a century. Look at us. Just five years ago, this right here—us standing together only hours from officially ending this war—would have been thought impossible, but look how far we've come. Sure, it hasn't gone smoothly and there have been losses, but sometimes, that is what happens when things change. We're so close now."

He met her eyes. "How do you manage to remain so optimistic when things are so bleak?"

She tucked a strand of hair behind her ear with her good hand. "Honestly, I would be surprised if things didn't appear bleak considering our history and what has happened in the past few days. But consider everything our countries have lost fighting, how many lives and resources, and tell me we aren't in a better place, even with everything that has happened. None of us will win if it comes to open war again. Not even the one who comes out on top. That is why I'm optimistic. Because we're still standing, fighting for what's right, and we're declaring peace. Today."

She was right. A few years ago, any Dassosdan crossing the border would have been publicly executed. But in the past week, stories, wine, and laughter had been shared in the streets and in the halls of his predecessors. Without the Overthrow, without his adamant work to declare peace and bring their people together, and without Dia's willingness to do the same, they would still be sending soldiers half his own age to the front lines to die.

"Wanting peace is a more dangerous business than I had thought," Domitris said.

Dia laughed bitterly. "Having to fight for justice is never right, but it is always worth it in the end."

"I really hope you're right."

She gave a nod and started walking around the yard, Domitris following by her side.

"What happens afterwards?" he asked.

"Life goes on. The signing is not the end; it's the beginning of many years of hard work to come. I seem to recall a young emperor, aching to reform life for his people. This is where you do just that. You've been too focused on the treaty; now you need to focus on your people."

"The weight of an entire nation on your shoulders can be quite daunting," he said.

"Of course, having to make all the decisions yourself must be hard, but it's also the privilege of your position as a sovereign leader. If you don't like where your country is headed, you get to change the course. As much as I detest the idea, it is quite practical," she said with a raised brow.

"That's true, but I need the council and the provinces to cooperate to move in the right direction."

"I think they'll come around. In time."

"What makes you say that?"

"Forgive me, Your Highness, but even though I have enjoyed your company, I haven't been idle while staying in the palace," she said, her eyes gleaming. "I've been out making friends of my own. I've met with several of the border province senators, and they have been surprisingly willing to listen. I think they'll vocalize their support next time, if you were to ask for it."

Domitris stopped and looked at her, astounded. "I've been at them for years about opening up to Dassosda. How did you do that in less than a week?"

"I have something you don't. Wealthy connections in Dassosda," she said with a triumphant smile. "Once your northern nobles saw the opportunity for streams of money coming their way, they were much more willing to listen. In the end, I just had to speak their language, and we got along swimmingly. I've already spoken to the weavers' guild as well as the craftsmen's guild and arranged possible buyers and sellers."

Domitris raised his brows. "You certainly are efficient."

"I aim to be," she said.

The drops fell more heavily around them and the dry ground darkened in tiny spots where they landed.

"I'm glad to have you as an ally," he said as they walked back inside.

"And I you. Take care, Your Highness," she said, and they parted ways.

Domitris turned around and walked back to where he had come from. The anger inside him was gone, and he knew what to do.

AS WE FALL

XXX

Back in his rooms, he turned his attention to what needed to be done. The first was giving Lyra a proper apology. The breakfast still stood on the table, the cheese sweating and a fly buzzing over the glass of juice beside it.

"Lyra?" he called.

No answer.

He went to her door and knocked on the polished wood. Still no answer. She wasn't there. The apology would have to wait, then. Instead, he went into his study and closed the door on the world. Dia was right. This was the opportunity they had been fighting for and the work had only just begun.

He sat down and, as he always did when he needed to chase unwelcome thoughts out of his mind, he got to work. He couldn't stop Sinnan from leaving or his own heart from breaking, but he could do right by his people and fix the wrongdoings of his predecessors. Too long had emperors been content, expanding the palace and catering solely to their own interests at the expense of the people.

Sifting through the stack of papers, he found all accounts

of palace spending and produced a fresh scroll from a drawer. With renewed spirits, he drafted up a plan for which resources could be allocated from the capital to the outer provinces, starting with the ones that were in the direst need of help. Whenever he needed a break, he rehearsed the few lines he needed to remember for the ceremony in the evening. His chest buzzed with the anticipation of finally signing the treaty and achieving what he had worked towards for years.

The rain outside his window shifted from drizzling to heavy to drizzling again while he worked. He lost track of time until his stomach curled and told him he had yet to eat. As he contemplated getting up and checking if Lyra had made it back, a door slammed, and a panicked voice called out to him. He couldn't make out the words, but it was undoubtedly Lyra's, and her tone sent chills down his spine.

"Your Highness!"

Her voice was closer and shriller this time. Domitris got up and flung open the door to his bedroom, Lyra startling on the other side as she had tried to open it at the same time. Fear was painted across her face, and she gasped for breath, as if she had been sprinting.

"Your Highness, something is wrong." She grabbed onto his arm. "They are locking people in their rooms. Servants are fleeing."

"What are you talking about? Who is?"

"I don't know, I don't know," she said, her eyes searching for answers around the room. "You have to get out of here. I think they're coming for you."

He took hold of her shoulders and bent down to level their eyes. "Tell me what you saw."

AS WE FALL

"There's no time! The guards are mobilizing. They—they killed people. You need to go." She took his face in her hands. Her trembling fingers and the look in her eyes told him what he didn't want to understand—once again, his life was in danger. He let the realization overwhelm him, let fear sting his heart, but only for an instant. He pulled himself together with a sharp nod and hastened towards the servants' entrance.

"Not that way! They're moving through the corridors; they'll find you."

He went for the main door instead, only to find it locked. He shook the handle as hard as he could, but it wouldn't open.

"You're not coming out," a stern voice said from the other side and Domitris took several steps backwards.

"Open the door right now." His stomach tightened.

"We are under strict orders to make you stay here," the voice said.

"Whose order?"

"The Supreme Emperor's. Now step back."

The color drained from Lyra's face, and she closed her eyes, a single rivulet escaping down her round cheek.

"What do I do?" he asked her.

She took a deep breath and looked back to the servants' entrance. "You need to get out of here, or you won't survive the day."

She hurried to the door at the back of the room. "I'll go first. I'll go and find you a free passage out of here. No!" she protested as he followed. "You have to wait for me here. They won't care about me; I'll be able to go unseen."

She was out the door and halfway down the stairs before he could come up with a better plan.

"Wait here!" she called back, and she was gone. Domitris paced up and down the floor, contemplating what he could take with him as a weapon, but nothing in the room suited the purpose. He didn't keep actual weapons anywhere near his room, not even the decorative kind.

When she wasn't back after several agonizing minutes had passed, Domitris lost his patience. He went to the balcony to evaluate its suitability as an escape route, but looking down on the wet stones more than a story below him, he knew his odds of survival were better without shattered ankles.

Lyra still hadn't come back. His heart hammered in his throat. He needed to find her. He headed for the back door, but commotion outside his rooms stopped him in his tracks. He froze as yelling and footsteps from several people intensified. When the first crunch of splintered wood tore through the room, he grabbed hold of a massive candelabra half as tall as himself to at least have a fighting chance against whoever was coming for him. The door whined as the hinges gave out, and the next blow slammed it to the floor. More than a handful of people spilled in through the opening. Domitris raised the candelabra and braced himself for the fight.

"Put that down, silly boy," Hossia said, as she trotted in through the group of people.

Domitris let it fall to the floor in surprise, wincing at the deafening clang of metal against tiles.

"Matre?"

Her hair was unbraided, and she was armed with a spear taller than herself.

He looked from her to the group of people around them, some known, some not. "What is going on?"

"Irony has not been kind to us, my boy. It would seem that we find ourselves in the midst of yet another overthrow."

"Who—"

"We can't stay idle. Come, hurry; we'll talk on the way."

Domitris stopped in his tracks. "I can't leave Lyra. She's in the servants' halls."

Hossia grabbed his arm, pulling him onward. "We cannot waste another second. Give her more credit. She knows what to do."

Reluctantly, he let himself be shepherded on. As they rushed down the empty corridors of the west wing, their footsteps disturbed the eerie silence that had fallen over the halls. Shouts and screams, and the occasional clash of weapons, sounded from the upper floors.

"Tell me what is going on," he grumbled.

"They are locking up our people. The ones loyal to you. And everyone neutral, it seems. The city guards are in on it. They've swarmed the palace."

So, this was what it had come to—he had pushed Gaius over the edge. Domitris wanted to smash his head against the wall. Gaius had deep pockets. Of course, he had been paying off the guards!

Could he have been cooperating with Alba?

That would explain how the archer got through at the Panjusticia. And why the guards stirred up trouble at the market. To think he could have been so stupid—Alba must have worked with Gaius all along, giving him access to the guard. Those snakes! How long had she been cultivating the guard for her own benefit? No wonder Ignotus hadn't been able to control them. A chill went down his spine.

"And Ignotus? Is he safe?"

"We haven't been through the east wing. We came here as fast as we could. But Ignotus can handle himself. We've tried to get the word out to everyone to get to the theater."

Why hadn't he seen it earlier? How could he have been so blind? It was suddenly all so obvious. Ignotus had been right all along. If only he had listened to him and spent his time seeking out the conspirators inside the palace instead of running after Sinnan and being derailed by his own recklessness, he would have pieced it all together before it had come to this.

Hossia moved surprisingly quickly for her old age, one hand holding up the hem of her garment, and the other using the spear as a walking stick.

"Where are they now?" Domitris asked.

Hossia made a raspy, contemplative sound. "Not sure. We got word from the kitchens, and they said upper north part of the palace when we moved."

That was several stories and halls away from where they were now. They turned a corner into a hall leading east, away from the tumult.

"Are we not staying to fight?"

"No. You are headed for the theater where the rest of our group is waiting. We are headed to the east wing to help whoever else they have cooped up. Fleeing is the best we can do right now if they control the whole guard."

"I have to stay and help."

"No, you don't." Hossia looked sternly up at him. "We need you alive. If we get out of this victorious, we need you. You are the strongest symbol we have. No one can take your place right now, so your only job is to stay safe. Get to the theater and get away from here."

Domitris didn't like the sound of that. Running away was wrong. He wanted to stay, to fight, to end Gaius once and for all. He had brought this upon himself, and he needed to make it right.

"I see that look in your eyes," Hossia said. "Get that thought out of your head right now. Are you not listening to me? You need to stay safe! Get it through your thick skull! It's the only useful thing you can do. What do you think happens if you die? Marmaras will be thrown into anarchy."

They came to an intersection that split the hallway. Hossia cast a glance in both directions. "This is where we part. Get to safety. Go to the theater through the council hall. There's no getting out of the main entrance."

Despite every fiber of his being telling him otherwise, he acquiesced. She didn't wait for him to voice it.

"Get moving, we'll meet you at the theater." She managed a squeeze of his upper arm before hurrying off, followed by the rest of the group.

Domitris had no weapon, no armor, no shield, but the council hall wasn't far away. He just had to get there unseen and avoid combat. Luckily, he was familiar with this part of the palace like the inside of his own pockets.

Rushing through the stretching halls, he knew which shortcuts to make and every possible nook he could hide in. It was obvious that the fight hadn't made it to this floor yet because there were few guards stationed at strategic intervals only to function as alarm if resistance occurred. He snuck past each one of them without trouble.

The first major obstacle came when he crossed the long, enclosed bridge connecting the west wing to the center of the palace. A rustle of metal and the slaps of soles against stone alerted him to a group of guards closing in around the corner. They wouldn't have heard him—his own bare footsteps were soundless on the smooth marble—but they were coming his way and the unadorned passage offered nowhere to hide. He wouldn't have time to turn back, and he was outnumbered. Without a weapon, he didn't stand a chance if it came to a fight.

Frantically, his eyes searched for a solution—the archways. There was no time to think. With a sharp exhale, he flung his legs over the balustrade, grabbed hold of one of the decorative columns, and clung to the outside of the bridge for his life. The palace stretched out to each side, and he did everything he could to keep his eyes off the steep fall beneath him. The drizzling rain coated his skin and minuscule droplets clung to his lashes like tears. There were no paths bordering this particular bridge, as there were with some of the larger ones, only a slim, chiseled ledge at the bottom of the arches. His grip on the rough stone was terrible, his foothold even worse, but at least he was covered. He hoped.

It wasn't a second too early. The group turned the corner, jabbering as they came down the bridge. There were at least three, maybe four, people from the sound of their voices. He held his breath, waiting for them to disappear.

Only, instead of crossing, they stopped.

When Domitris heard the muffled pop of bottle stoppers and cheering, he realized what was going on—he had intersected with a celebratory drinking break in the middle of

AS WE FALL

the chaos. Domitris' underarms were already cramping from holding on to the wet stone. He tried to move them for better grip, but to no avail. Concordia sloped out behind him, its terracotta roofs darkened by the rain. Wind rushed in his ears and tossed his hair into his eyes.

Before he could figure out what the guards were celebrating, something interrupted the group. He hadn't heard the person coming, and neither had they.

"What are you standing here for?" a voice boomed and, to Domitris' grievance, it was a familiar one.

There was no doubt it belonged to Gaius.

"Get back to it!"

A scramble of armor and weapons sent them on their way.

Domitris' fingers ached where they clung on to the column, but he didn't dare move. He closed his eyes, his ears straining for signs that Gaius had gone with them, but he could only hear the patter of rain. His hands were soaking wet, and he tried to wipe his palm off on his equally wet clothes. Still no sound of Gaius. Domitris leaned his head against the column, steadying his breathing before trying to crawl back inside.

A huff and a set of hands slamming against the railing beside him almost made him lose his balance. Out of the corner of his eye, he caught a glimpse of Gaius' hairy knuckles clutching the balustrade. The column was the only thing that shielded him from Gaius' view. He sucked in his abdomen and pressed his body against the stone.

Gaius exhaled deeply. Even his sighs sounded smug and triumphant. He was so close that Domitris could reach out and touch him. If Gaius were to lean out less than an arm's length, he would see him.

Should he stand there passively and wait for Gaius to find him, or should he lunge at him and take him down in a fistfight? If it were only the two of them and neither had weapons, Domitris would win. Gaius had more mass, but Domitris was in far better shape. Getting inside again, especially with enough force to get an advantage and without being seen, was difficult. No. Impossible. He got the impulse to grab onto Gaius and pull him out over the railing. If only he could get a proper grip, he could end it all right now. Domitris would go down with him, but the fall wasn't far enough to kill a man. He could do it. He just had to make sure Gaius would land underneath him. Domitris shifted his weight, preparing himself.

The western alarm bell rang, and two things happened at once: Domitris' foot slipped just as Gaius whipped around, hurrying towards the alarm. Domitris' heart leapt into his throat as he fell, scraping his knees, arms flailing. Narrowly, he caught hold of a stone eagle protruding from the bottom of the column, and he clenched his teeth to suppress a groan.

His muscles screamed as he pulled himself up. Holding onto the balustrade, he regained his footing. As he hoisted himself over, he watched Gaius disappear around the corner towards the west wing.

Domitris sat curled up on the floor while he regained his composure. His hands were cramped from tension, and he had to forcefully stretch his fingers to get them to cooperate. Drops slithered from his soaked hair down his temple and neck. Now they knew he had escaped. They would be looking for him everywhere. He had to hurry if he wanted to use this chance of getting out alive. He allowed himself a few seconds to catch his breath before he darted off, headed for the council hall.

The clouds covering the sky outside the windows darkened the hallways, creating an illusion of dusk as he snuck onward through minor corridors. Without its nobles, without the servants and scholars, the palace was just a hollow mess of architecture erected by unhinged minds, trying to leave their imprint on the world.

Two more turns, and the entrance to the council hall would come into view. He slowed down as he came to the final corner and positioned himself for optimal outlook. As he had thought, the entrance was guarded. Two very young guards had been spared for the task. They looked fresh out of their military education in their bright red uniforms, their weapons a little large for them, their helmets not quite fitting. They wouldn't have had a taste of actual battle yet except for what they might have encountered today. Domitris still had no weapon, but against opponents like these, it was hardly necessary. He swallowed at the thought of adding new faces to his nightmares. Would they stand down if he ordered them to? It was a gamble, but he decided to try—from his position, it was no use counting on the element of surprise. He stood, shook his shoulders, and marched towards them.

"I order you to stand down," he said loudly enough to intimidate them, but not loud enough to alert nearby guards. The two of them started visibly, their eyes darting from Domitris to each other as if debating what to do, not yet taking proper stance. One of them raised her weapon, the other one still deciding, knees shaking.

It wasn't working. He had to put his qualms to rest if he wanted to get through. He gave them no time to consider it further, and with a few determined strides, he was upon them. His heart trembled as he rammed his hand into the helmet of the smaller guard, using all the strength of his momentum. There was a sickening crunch as her head smacked into the wall. With a gurgled noise, she collapsed and didn't get back up. He had to push back the horror that welled up inside him.

"Stand down, I said." He had hoped it would be enough to scare the other one off, but the remaining guard instead raised his weapon a little more confidently. They were equipped with actual longswords from the armory and not the spears and shortswords that the palace guards usually held. Domitris was a head taller than his opponent and it took little effort to avoid the first hesitant strike. Catching his wrist, he wrung the weapon out of his hand. He turned over the sword and yanked off the guard's helmet. Recognition flared in the guard's eyes, and he inhaled as if to call for help. Domitris grabbed him by the collar and threw him to the floor, pinning him down with a foot to his chest. He tipped the blade to his neck.

"You don't want to do that. And I don't want to cut your throat, so either you walk away from here, pretending you never saw me, or you lose your head."

The young man gulped, eyes wide with terror.

Domitris poked the tip into the flesh of his throat. "Understood?"

He nodded. Domitris released him. "Now, you better go find somewhere to hide."

The young man scurried to his feet and raced down the corridor. Domitris didn't trust for a second that he would keep his mouth shut. He held on to the sword and darted into the council hall.

It looked like it had been left in a hurry. Scrolls lay scattered around the room and the blue banners had been ripped from their fastenings. A trail of blood blemished the floor. He forced away all instincts of considering who it belonged to. Not daring to linger, he dashed towards the passage to the theater.

Involuntarily, his feet halted at the entrance. This time, there were no torches along the sides, no torchbearer leading the way, only a dark mouth ready to swallow him whole.

Faint footsteps in the distance pushed him into the darkness. He hastened forward through the black pit, stumbling several times over irregularities in the floor and once because he banged his head against one of the collapsed wooden beams. Not having time to nurse his bruises, he staggered onward. The sounds in the passage were muffled and confined in contrast to the ringing echoes of the tunnels below the library, but the feeling of disappearing into nothingness was eerily familiar. Except this time, he was alone.

Or not.

Dull thumps sounded far behind him—he was being followed. He should have taken out the guard. Domitris tightened his grip on the sword, hoping with everything in him he wouldn't have to use it. Reaching the end of the tunnel, a stripe of light illuminated the ladder. He scrambled up the coarse wood, each step taking him closer to his goal. As he ascended, panicked yelling and clashing of metal sounded from the theater.

He had expected it to be quiet, secret, a group of people ready to flee, but what he found was turmoil. Rain poured down over guards attacking a flock of nobles, their ivory garments stained with mud. Some nobles fought back, defending themselves. A few had won over weapons from the guards and others had brought their own. The water flooding the stage carried swirls of crimson in over the sixteen-pointed star and bathed Domitris' feet in blood. He stopped in his tracks, the taste of bile turning in the back of his throat.

The unmistakable hiss of a knife being unsheathed made him spin around. Sword lifted, ready to face his pursuer, he let out a sigh of relief. The person behind him was Ignotus. He let his shoulders come down and slackened his grip on the sword. It was almost funny, having stumbled, panicked, through the passage when it had been Ignotus all along. A muscle in his cheek twitched.

"Thank the earth you are safe. Hurry, we have to help the others!" Domitris called out, but the look on Ignotus' face concerned him. Ignotus took long, determined steps towards him, making Domitris back up.

"What's wrong?"

Ignotus didn't answer and didn't stop, and before Domitris could react, stinging pain exploded in his abdomen. Domitris' breath halted, his hands frozen down his sides as he dropped the sword. He looked to where the slender knife was eating into the fabric of his clothes. He lifted his eyes to meet Ignotus'. His face was pale and sweaty, his hair hanging in tangles over his shoulders, and it was as if Domitris hadn't truly looked at him before. His dark eyes were full of anger and sorrow, his jaw clenched shut.

"It pains me to do this." With a firm grip around Domitris, he twisted the knife. Domitris cried out as searing pain shot

AS WE FALL

through his body and turned to agony in the space of a heartbeat. Only when blood started gushing out, making the whole world spin, did Domitris realize what was happening. His balance vanished and his knees crashed to the ground. Ignotus crouched, leaning against him. A dull throbbing spread through his stomach and his vision blurred, his hands shaking uncontrollably as Ignotus withdrew the knife. Domitris closed his eyes, thinking only that he needed to get up, but his body wouldn't cooperate. The rain bit into his skin like flies. The knife shook in Ignotus' hand, dripping scarlet beads onto Domitris' clothes. Ignotus' breathing was ragged as he clutched the knife, about to stab again.

Domitris lay in his arms as Ignotus bent down to let his lips meet Domitris' forehead in a parting gesture. Domitris blinked rapidly, trying to get his vision under control. As the stubbly kiss met his skin, Domitris did the only thing he could think of and let his head sink backwards, then gathered all the strength he could muster and flung his head up, impacting perfectly with Ignotus' mouth.

His stomach shot blinding pain up through his body as his muscles clenched. Ignotus dropped him, hands flying up to cover his mouth. Domitris fell to the ground like a sack of flour, slamming his elbow against the wet tiles. He grabbed after his sword, trying to crawl as far away as he could. Stumbling to his legs, his whole body protesting, he lifted the blade. Ignotus turned to him, mouth full of blood, his long hair clinging to his face.

Domitris knew his head should hurt, but he didn't feel it, only the throbbing pain in his stomach as his whole body shook. Ignotus spat, hard, a spray of blood flying from his mouth. He drew the sword fastened at his side. An angry roar erupted from him as he closed the distance between them, letting the first blow fall.

Domitris averted it with his own blade, staggering back, doing his best to stay upright. When he made no move to retaliate, Ignotus came forward again, dealing another hard blow, shouting with the impact. Exhausted, Domitris parried again, and countered only with a cursory strike that Ignotus hardly had to sidestep to avoid. He took another step towards Domitris and tore a backhanded slash through the air. Domitris recoiled to dodge it, stumbling over a stray helmet that sent him to the ground once more. His side twinged and throbbed with his labored breathing. As Ignotus came for him, Domitris' aching muscles cramped, and his best effort hardly manifested as an actual attempt to hit Ignotus. Using his sword to parry, Ignotus flung the blade from Domitris' hand.

Domitris couldn't get his eyes to focus. Harsh fingers dug into his scalp and clung onto a fistful of hair, his skin burning where Ignotus yanked on the strands. Then Ignotus' knee came forward and smashed into Domitris' face. His brow stung as the skin split open and warm liquid poured into his eye, his vision becoming a sticky blur. The hand disappeared from his hair and Domitris scrambled to get up and put distance between them. He tried to wipe away the blood with his shoulder to little avail. The sword lay at his feet, and he picked it up, knowing he didn't have much left to give.

They stood on opposite sides of the star, panting, looking at each other.

"Stop fighting it! You've lost!" Ignotus shouted, the strain in his voice carrying through the rain.

Domitris panted, clutching his side. "Was it you all along?

AS WE FALL

You did this?"

Ignotus took a step forward, unable to control his anger. "No, *you* did this, Domitris. You gave me no choice! I've sacrificed too much to see this country torn apart once more. Sacrificing our culture, letting Dassosda take over, that was never part of the plan."

Domitris' mind reeled, turning over every conversation since his coronation. They had their disagreements, but he had thought it natural, healthy even, to be challenged in his decisions. Never had he thought it would lead to this. The pain grew vicious and transformed into anger. "Why didn't you talk to me?"

"I tried! So many times! You wouldn't listen. I didn't want to do it this way, but you won't give up. It ends now." Ignotus charged again.

This time, Domitris took the blow head on and didn't hesitate with retaliating as adrenaline took over. Ignotus weathered his strikes, but Domitris could tell he was getting tired, his reflexes a little slow, while his own were fueled by newfound rage. Domitris started aiming for where it would hurt and Ignotus had to put his whole body into it to avoid the blows that rained upon him. Dealing a hard strike, his arm outstretched, Domitris flinched at the sharp pain cramping in his side. His arm retracted involuntarily without the strike landing. Ignotus was desperate enough to notice and raised his arm high to cut for the neck. This time, Domitris knew the trick, and he wasn't going to fall for it twice. Instead of concentrating on the attack and parrying, he readied himself for the movement. The second he felt the kick coming, Domitris planted his sword firmly in the ground in front of him. Ignotus had no way of stopping his momentum and his foot smashed into the sharp edge of the blade. He screamed out, stumbling backwards.

Domitris knew this was the time to give everything he had left if he wanted to leave the fight alive. Despite his blurry vision and aching stomach, it worked. Ignotus had no stance and barely managed to parry. With the third blow, Domitris forced the sword from Ignotus' hand, and it clanged to the ground. Domitris swung out his sword-arm and backhanded Ignotus across the face with the hilt. A gurgled yelp escaped him, his mouth full of blood. Ignotus was still standing, but barely.

Domitris kept his distance, the vision of his old friend a ragged mess halting him from action. For a while, they only stood, both bent over, heaving for air, looking at each other.

Domitris drew himself up and threw his sword to the ground. "You were my friend."

"This wasn't about you," Ignotus sneered.

"How long have you gone behind my back? Was it really you who tried to kill me?" Domitris' eye stung, and he tried to wipe the blood from it.

"I'm sorry," Ignotus said, exasperated. "I couldn't let you keep the crown. I was finally in a position to be a great leader and lift the empire back from ruins! It should have been me. It should always have been me, and you know it. You've always been too soft. You didn't even have the guts to kill the Supreme Emperor when the time came."

Domitris hated that there was truth to his words. He had always seen his own mercy as the reason why he had been elected, but without Ignotus, without his ruthlessness, they wouldn't have been here at all.

"This isn't the right way."

Ignotus gasped out a bitter laugh. "Look around you!" Ignotus yelled, and it seemed to take him everything he had. "This is where your path has led us."

"This is your doing, Ignotus. Do you not see that?"

Ignotus panted more and more rapidly. With a sudden convulsion, he pulled out something from the top of his boot and hurled it at Domitris. A small dagger flew through the air, grazing Domitris' shoulder as he sidestepped. He only recognized it as an evasion when Ignotus charged at him, screaming. He flung his whole weight against Domitris, crashing them both to the ground. Unbearable pain exploded from his stomach as Ignotus sat astride him. His hands curled around Domitris' neck, his thumbs grinding into his throat. Domitris gagged and rasped for air, the pain of Ignotus' thigh crushing into his side blinding him. A dull ringing overtook his senses as his surroundings dissolved. Bloody pearls dripped from Ignotus' mouth onto Domitris' face, and he couldn't breathe. His hands fought helplessly, clawing at Ignotus' arms, but his weight and position were too much for Domitris to make him budge. The world blurred, and he registered only glimpses of Ignotus above him. His face was dark like wine, a vein throbbing at his temple. His bloodshot eyes overflowed with tears as the grip around Domitris' throat tightened and he let out a guttural scream. Domitris' vision blackened and pain overtook him.

He hadn't been strong enough, not good enough to save his country or himself. This was how his legacy would die, at the humiliating hand of betrayal. A fitting end for a failure.

A metallic clang resounded, and the grip around his neck slackened. Air returned to him. He didn't know where he was. Thick, green smoke filled the theater and his insides convulsed as he gasped and retched, trying to catch his breath. Memories of being caught in the smoke deep underground overwhelmed him, but the green smoke didn't scratch his lungs and throat. It was sweet, almost. He was moving, but he didn't understand how, his legs not cooperating. His knees gave out, and he expected to land on the ground, but he didn't. The endless pain in his side made him throw up down the front of his clothes.

"Come on, hurry! I need you to cooperate!" someone hissed too close to his ear. Not someone—Sinnan. Just as the smoke thinned and the outline of struggling figures everywhere became visible, two bangs went off and more smoke billowed up around them in an opaque cloud.

"Sinnan?" he croaked out, trying to stabilize his feet on the ground.

"Yes, now come, I'm begging you!"

He couldn't see. Didn't understand what was going on. Was he still alive? The pain told him yes. He used all the energy left in him on getting up and taking steps in the direction Sinnan was hauling him off the stage, out of the theater. He let his eyelids slide half shut, not using energy on looking at what was happening around him, only focusing on following Sinnan. He stumbled multiple times where Sinnan had to haul him to his feet and push on before they finally halted. His orientation went from vertical to horizontal and they were moving no more. He couldn't wait to close his eyes and realized they were already closed. He stopped struggling and everything went dark and quiet.

He woke sometimes, when the ground bumped beneath him and made his body hurt. Gray clouds and tree branches rolled past above him. He heard screams and loud voices but didn't understand.

A voice talked somewhere, far away. Closer than the shouting. It kept saying the same thing, but he couldn't make it out. Not until a hand was shaking him at the same time.

"Domitris." It was Sinnan's voice again. He sounded distraught. Domitris tried to open his eyes, but they just rolled around in his head.

"Domitris! Stay with us! Try to stay awake," Sinnan said in a low but stern voice. He kept shaking him. Domitris tried lifting his arms to stop the shaking, but he couldn't control them properly.

"Domitris," Sinnan called again. "You have to stay conscious."

He managed to open his eyes, one crusted with dried blood. Clouds moved past him too quickly above. How could he be moving if he was lying down?

"Where am I?" he tried, but Sinnan just looked at him, a deep furrow between his brows.

"What are you saying? You have to speak up." The shaking stopped.

"Where am I?" Domitris asked again and this time he could hear the words form.

"You're in our cart. We're taking you out of the city. In a little while, we have to hide you, and you have to stay awake, all right?"

Domitris sighed and closed his eyes again and he felt Sinnan's hand on his cheek.

"I'm going to cover you up now. Do you hear me? Stay awake."

Domitris was tired. He didn't understand why it was so important. He just needed a little rest, and it would be fine.

"Are you listening? We're close to the gates now. Stay awake. Domitris!" Sinnan said once more and shook his arm.

"I will," Domitris said, and a coarse blanket was pulled over his head and tucked around him.

The bells rang in the distance and the world disappeared around him once more.

When We Rise

Book 2 of the As We Fall series

Coming soon

ACKNOWLEDGEMENTS

The idea of As We Fall came to me during a sleepless night on a trip to Rome when my mind was desperately searching for the Right Book to write. Since I started daring to tell people I was writing it, I've been immensely lucky to meet nothing but interest and encouragement and I would never have made it this far without all that love and support.

First and foremost, to the light of my life, Jackie, without whom this book wouldn't exist: I will work the rest of my life to make sure I deserve you. You encouraged me from day one, back when you had to drag any thoughts about this story out of me, and right until the end while you look over my shoulder as I write these final words. You've picked me up more times than I can count, fixed innumerable plot holes, believed in me when there wasn't much to believe in, and you've cared for me, provided for me, and fed me through it all. No words will ever be enough to describe my gratitude.

To Kinny, my darling, you made me a better author in a matter of months and took my writing to a level I could never have reached alone. Your excitement and love for this story was what made me finally believe it was worthy of being published. Thank you for letting me lean on you so heavily, for all the passion you've put into helping this book shine, and for all the encouragement along the way.

Thank you forever to my dear mom who has helped me in more ways than she will ever realize. You've encouraged my writing since I was a child, took me to Rome during a difficult time of my life because you knew I would love it, you instantly understood the appeal of this book, you've helped me brainstorm and rooted for me every step of the way, and you've been nothing but supportive when I said I wanted to do this for a living.

Thank you immensely to Anna and Christine, the very first readers of this book when it looked nothing like the finished product. I could not have made it here without your thoughtful input, ideas, and excitement.

To Ariellah, Amalie, Mia, Catrine, Rikke, and Marc who were always kind enough to ask about the book and encouraged me to follow my dreams, no matter what the journey looked like; I'm immensely grateful for your support.

A special thanks to everyone in real life and online who offered words of interest, encouragement, and kindness throughout the years. Especially to all of my instagram followers who subscribed to my newsletter and voiced their anticipation for the book all this time. Your support means the world to me and played a big part in the decision to put this book into the world. Know that your words and support helped make a dream come true.

Thank you also to my editor, Nick Hodgeson, who did an amazing job with polishing my writing and who asked all the right questions.

Additionally, there have been a few people who have helped me without even knowing, and I want to extend my thanks to them as well. To the host of the Creative Penn Podcast, Joanna Penn, and the hosts of the Unpublished Podcast, Amie McNee and James Winestock, you have all taught me so much about writing, publishing, and about myself, and your words have picked me up and encouraged me to keep writing every time I lost hope. For that you have my gratitude. Finally, thank you to C.S. Pacat for the Captive Prince series, which rekindled my love for reading and writing.

ABOUT THE AUTHOR

Lucky beyond measure, Anya lives with her magnificent wife in Copenhagen, Denmark. She writes novels with beautiful, atmospheric settings, queer-normative worlds, steamy romances, and flawed characters with questionable morals. She wants LGBTQIA+ readers to see themselves in stories where being queer isn't the plot, conflict, or point of intrigue.

When she's not writing, she sews, reads, goes for long walks, snuggles with their cat babies, takes pictures, and makes YouTube videos with her wife.

While she has a master's degree in agronomy and environmental science, she picked up creative writing again during her study years and realized this was where her true passion lies.

After graduating, she turned to writing full time, and now lives her dream writing life - most of the time from their tiny apartment in the city and the rest of the time in their cottage in the forest. She loves connecting with readers and can be found all over the internet.

Website: https://www.anyawildt.com
email: anya.wildt@gmail.com
Tumblr: tumblr.com/anyawildt
Instagram: instagram.com/anya.wildt
Youtube: youtube.com/@WivesVsWorld

Thank you for reading!

Please add a short review on Amazon and Goodreads to help more people discover the book. I would love to hear your honest opinion!

Subscribe to the newsletter to get behind the scenes insight and updates on coming books:

Link to sign-up form: http://eepurl.com/h3aDXz

QR code for sign-up form: